"I want you

Cammie couldn't quite believe her ears. Really? Marc was asking her to work for him again? After everything he'd said?

"Why do you need me? There are plenty of good P.I.s in Denver. Figured you'd have used some of them this past year." She worked hard to keep her tone light, to not let some of the anger seep in.

"Oh, I have," he said quickly, "but the person I need to find is in this area."

Wasn't this the boss who'd once said she was the best investigator he'd ever worked with? That he was so offhanded about using other P.I.s since she'd left felt, oh, bad. And that he was only here, talking to her, because he didn't know any other P.I.s in this area felt, oh, worse. She straightened her shoulders in a show of bravado.

And to her surprise his gaze followed the motion.

Was the sun playing tricks on her, or was that a flush coloring his cheekbones as he checked her out?

"A good P.I. can conduct research from anywhere," she said matter-of-factly, ignoring the thrill his gaze had caused.

"I know that, but...you're the best."

Dear Reader,

The Next Right Thing marks my return to Harlequin and to my writing full-time again, both of them welcome events in my life! Where have I been? Working as a private investigator. Yes, really.

I had started a private investigations agency in 2003 with my then-boyfriend. My idea was for *him* to be a private investigator because he had trained dozens over his eighteen years as a former trial attorney. At the time I figured I'd manage the office and handle the bookkeeping. But before I knew it, I was sitting on surveillance in the wee hours of the morning, on the lookout for signs of a woman on the run with a baby. Almost sounds like a Harlequin story, doesn't it? Especially the part where, later, I eloped with my P.I.-partner boyfriend.

Over the years I'd occasionally touch base with Wanda Ottewell, my Harlequin editor. Last year, during one of our catch-up chats, I mentioned that I was cutting back on conducting investigations, and how much I'd love to write for Harlequin again. She said, "Why don't you send a story proposal?"

I did. It became this book, a story about a heroine private investigator, Cammie Copello, and a hero lawyer, Marc Hamilton. Although I don't have a penchant for bending the law as Cammie does, I've conducted cases similar to hers in *The Next Right Thing.* Like Cammie, I've also relied on tools, such as my smartphone, to solve whodunits.

Happy reading!

Colleen Collins

P.S. I love to hear from readers! Please contact me through my website, www.colleencollins.net.

Recycling programs
for this product may
not exist in your area.

ISBN-13: 978-0-373-71840-5

THE NEXT RIGHT THING

Copyright © 2013 by Colleen Collins

Printed in U.S.A.

The Next Right Thing

COLLEEN COLLINS

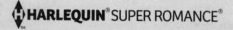

ABOUT THE AUTHOR

Colleen Collins is an award-winning author who's written twenty-two novels and two nonfiction books. She's also written articles for regional and national writing organizations, as well as for publications such as *USA TODAY, PI Magazine, Pursuit Magazine,* PINow.com and other periodicals. Like the P.I. heroine in *The Next Right Thing,* Colleen has also seen the underside of a pickup while placing a GPS and has stared down more than a few coldhearted felons.

Books by Colleen Collins

HARLEQUIN BLAZE

290—A SCENT OF SEDUCTION
333—WATCHING IT GO UP
354—SHOCK WAVES

Other titles by this author available in ebook format.

To my sister, Barbara Graham.

PROLOGUE

CAMMIE EASED HER 2006 silver Monte Carlo—named Phil after the fictional private eye Philip Marlowe—next to the dirt-crusted red pickup she'd been following for the past hour. The subject—Ray "Rebel" Nathan—had strolled his six-two, cowboy-booted self into the burger dive a few minutes ago. If he was picking up to-go food, he'd be out in ten minutes, maybe less.

Cammie had to move fast.

Earlier, she'd slipped the GPS device and its battery pack inside the pocket of her jean jacket. She double-checked the bulky parts with a quick feel, then slipped out the driver's side. Standing between Phil and the pickup, she blinked against the surging winds while quickly scanning the area. Across the parking lot, several teenagers squealed and laughed while chasing a plastic bag the wind had wrested from their hold. A late-model Dodge Charger droned by. Its driver, an older dude with a skinny gray ponytail, puffed on a cigar. Trails of blue smoke and the '70s Bee Gees hit "More than a Woman" wafted through the half-open driver's window.

More than a woman. Being female in the private eye business often felt like that, plus some. A woman had to be more resilient, sharper and often tougher to last in this male-dominated profession.

Dude turned right onto Boulder Highway, the Bee Gees' trilling vibratos merging with the drone of noon-day traffic.

Cammie quickly moved to the front of the pickup and plunked her butt down on the asphalt.

The device clattered out of her jacket pocket.

Cursing under her breath, she snatched the metal GPS unit and its egg-shaped antennae. After quickly verifying the connecting wire was intact, she shoved them into her jacket. Leaning back, she grabbed the grill with both hands and pulled herself underneath the pickup. Her legs stuck outside the front of the vehicle, but they were only visible from the Boulder Highway, a mash of speeding cars, honking horns and exhaust. It would take someone with a sharp eye to see her limbs—and if they did, who's to say those legs didn't belong to the owner of this truck?

Carefully, she inched the device from her pocket.

She'd always figured for most people life was a rush of events and faces, racing by like the Boulder Highway traffic outside. But whenever she was battling high emotions, time had a nasty habit of snagging her, pinning her like a fly. Caught, she would grow aware of every movement, sound, subtlety.

Like right now. Battling her anxiousness, time had slowed to a crawl. The stench of twenty different fluids from the engine stifled her breath. The heat from the asphalt seeped up like steam through her clothes. And that relentless Las Vegas wind swirled around her like a ghost, its chilly breath caressing and prodding her with things she didn't want to think about.... It'd happened so long ago, it no longer mattered.... *Go away, go away....*

A blustery gust of wind rattled past, chasing away the ghost. Particles of dirt spit at her face, stung her hands.

Time sped up, snapped to the present.

She pressed the GPS unit against the bumper, reassured by the clank of magnet against steel. Gotta love these older trucks and their metal parts. She lightly tugged the electrical wire connecting the unit and antennae until the wire was taut—didn't want it to drag, catch on anything in the road while the truck was moving. She positioned the antennae to the back of the grill, moving it back and forth until she hit a sweet spot where it would easily pick up satellite signals.

Done!

Her body tingled with that familiar rush of relief and satisfaction after successfully fastening one of these babies. Maybe her uncle thought she should have stayed in law school, but he didn't get that she dug the thrill of investigations. What lawyer got to crawl under cars, track missing people, find someone's long-lost sibling or high school sweetheart? A P.I.'s work was the most exciting game in town. Better than any eight-to-five.

After scooching from underneath the truck and carefully rising to her feet, she nonchalantly looked around as though absolutely nothing unusual had happened. She eyed a few parked cars, a woman in a blue jogging suit scurrying into a store, her cell phone glued to her ear. A burst of the teenagers' shrieks and laughter momentarily crested the wind, although they were no longer in sight.

No Rebel, either. Still inside buying his greasy burger.

Oh, so casually brushing dirt off her jeans, Cammie got back into Phil and drove off.

Across the Boulder Highway from the burger dive, she parked in the lot in front of the Firelight Lounge at Sam's Town. From here, she had an unencumbered view of Rebel's pickup. Time to relax, check the GPS tracking software on her smartphone, double-check everything was hooked up correctly and getting signals.

She knew Rebel Boy would likely next be heading down the highway to his paramour's apartment, and Cammie was in a primo spot to slide into traffic and follow. Her client, Rebel's wife, didn't know the girl's name, or her address, but had plenty of reason for suspicion. Lipstick on his tighty whities was the clincher. Then a friend who worked at Sam's Town had reported to the wife that Rebel's truck had been seen tooling east past here almost every day around lunchtime.

Cammie plucked the elastic rubber band that confined her curls in a thick knot. Ruffling her hair loose, she checked the time on her smartphone—12:20. Must be eating his lunch before his noontime tryst. Too cheap to buy the girlfriend a burger, too?

Distant sirens wailed. As their screams pulsed louder, she surveyed the highway for their approach. Two fire engines, horns blaring, careened down the highway. Cars pulled over to let pass.

More sirens joined the ruckus.

A police unit, lights sparkling, charged into the burger lot across the street. Another bolted into the Firelight Lounge lot, bouncing over a speed bump. Several white Crown Victorias—unmarked vehicles—trailed the police unit into the lot, all them bouncing over the same bump.

The first unit screeched to a halt.

Right. Behind. Her.

She froze, stared in her rearview mirror at the police vehicle with its blue, white and yellow lights swirling.

"This is a felony stop," a male voice barked over a loud speaker. "Keep your hands on the dashboard, continue facing forward, do not move. I repeat, *do not move.*"

Her body chilled to a temperature reserved for body trays in morgues. She didn't need to be told twice to not move—she wouldn't so much as twitch, shift, even flinch. A felony stop was serious business. One wrong move could mean getting shot.

"Raise your hands," bellowed the invisible voice.

She slowly raised them, one still clutching the smartphone, hoping the cop knew it was just a phone, trying not to think of that guy in Denver who got shot when the officer thought the soda can in his hand was a gun.

"Place your hands, palms down, on the dashboard."

She did as told. In the rearview mirror, an officer eased out of the driver's side, gun pointed right at Cammie. He approached and she remembered the three *C*s of felony stops: calm, comply and communicate. As he walked closer, he scanned the interior of her car. "Take your left hand," he called out, "and open the driver's door, slowly."

Bursts of wind didn't make it easy, but with some effort she pushed it open.

"Turn toward me and exit the vehicle."

She followed orders, ended up staring into the officer's face. Below thick eyebrows in need of some serious manscaping were eyes so black they could pass for bullet holes.

Fighting a shudder, she croaked, "It's a smartphone in my hand, officer."

"Drop it."

She watched it clatter to the ground, wishing she'd purchased a heartier case.

"Turn and face the rear passenger door. Place your hands on top of the vehicle."

The heated metal stung her palms.

As he frisked her, she asked in a forced-light voice, "I don't often ask men who have their hands on my thighs this, but is there a problem?"

Her answer came from the wild-eyed woman in a saggy blue jogging outfit who materialized in the background. Her curly hair writhed like snakes in the wind, giving her a Medusa-in-polyester look.

"That's her!" the woman screeched, pointing a shaking finger at Cammie. "That's the lady I saw planting a bomb under that truck! Same dirty jacket, oh, yeah, it's her all right!"

Planting a bomb? Oh, man, this was getting fugly, fast. Cammie glanced across the highway. Firefighters and dogs surrounded Rebel's pickup. Someone dressed in a space-age outfit—bomb squad, no doubt—was crawling underneath the truck.

Eyebrow Cop cuffed her hands behind her back, informing her of her Miranda rights before gruffly leading her to his vehicle.

Two more backup units arrived—five had now convened in the Firelight Lounge lot. People flooded out of the casino, many with drinks in their hands, to watch the real live cop show. Casino security guards were trying vainly to hustle them indoors.

"Watch your head." The cop cradled Cammie's skull like a basketball before nudging her into the backseat.

As he drove off, she looked through the rear window at Rebel's truck. Mr. Bomb Squad was holding up the GPS that had cost her five hundred dollars and seventy-five cents.

This monumentally effed-up excursion was going to cost her a lot more than that. A felony charge or three, a stint in jail, lawyer's fees.

This day was turning out to be more than even a woman who was more than a woman was ready to handle.

CHAPTER ONE

GREEN-AND-WHITE SPOTLIGHTS swirled. Trumpets blared.

"Ladies and gentlemen," boomed a male voice over the speakers, "our superstar show is beginning on the Shamrock a-Go-Go Stage! On this lovely April twentieth in glittering, glamorous Las Vegas—" the announcer's voice dropped to a tone reserved for funerals "—we're bringing back a star who is gone to the world, but here at the Shamrock Palace, he lives forever." The recording of trumpets replayed. "With no further ado," he said, all peppy again, "the one and only King of Pop, Michael Jackson!"

Cammie looked up at as Jeffrey, one of her fellow dealers, stepped onto the Shamrock a-Go-Go Stage, a platform not much larger than her uncle Frankie's dining room table, and four or so feet higher than the circle of green-felt-covered gambling tables. Jeffrey hailed from a town in Oklahoma—"So small, you'd miss it if you sneezed." After landing in Vegas two years ago with stardust in his eyes, and several failed stints as a backup singer, he'd eventually found employment as a dealer-performer at the Shamrock Palace.

A grind joint at the end of the strip, the casino advertised such luxuries as green beer, daily penny-slot tournaments and celebrity-impersonator shows every hour, on the hour. Jeffrey might have a Southern twang, stand six-four in his socks and be about as African-American as Blake Shelton…but he could do a mean moonwalk and never flubbed a lip sync. Slather on lots of makeup, a curly black wig, tight pants and voilà! A taller version of the King of Pop lived again.

While Jeffrey mimed and strutted his way through the song "Billie Jean," Cammie sipped her diet cola. Val, the Christina Aguilera celebrity-performer-dealer and Cammie's best pal at the job, sidled up to her. "Where y'at?"

Which Val had once explained was like saying "How you doin'?" in her hometown of *N'awlins*.

"Slow day at the Cave." Cammie nodded at her empty gambling table.

None of them ever called this part of the casino the Palace. Mostly because it was buried far back in the shadowy pits of the casino. To reach it, customers had to pass through several hundred slot machines, a belt of fast-food businesses employees called "Grease Gulch," and a Tiki Bar with a thatched roof and piped-in monkey sounds.

"Slow day, f'true," said Val. "I've made a whoppin' five bucks today in dealer tips."

Cammie glanced at Val's skimpy sailor outfit and sailor hat. "New song?"

"Lippin' 'Candyman' in an hour. Aguilera kicked some serious A in that video. I'm hoping to do the same, get some of these tightwads to open up their hearts 'n wallets and give me some tip love. Like Mama over there." Val gestured toward a fiftysomething woman in a low-cut leopard-print top stuffing bills into a silver bucket next to the stage. Jeffrey, as Michael, blew her a kiss with his white-gloved hand.

"Ya know," Val said, giving Cammie an appraising look, "with your long curly black hair and endless legs, you'd be an excellent Cher."

"Isn't she sixtysomething?"

"Girl, Cher could make eighty look hubba hubba. But I meant a younger, hotter Cher. You could lip 'If I Could Turn Back Time.'"

"Oh, yeah," Cammie murmured, "that'd be my song of choice."

Not.

Truth was, if Cammie could turn back time, she would probably do all her dumb mistakes again. She was a risk taker, had never believed in tiptoeing into a situation if rushing in head-first meant finding the clue, nailing the case.

But the problem with being the type of person to go full throttle and take chances was that sometimes she stepped into questionable legal areas.

Like that GPS debacle last month.

Oh, she'd had excellent reasons for doing it, all of them licit or at least with compelling legal potential. First, her client, Rebel's wife, had been worried about the welfare of their kids because she feared—and it turned out to be true—Rebel's paramour had a sideline business dealing drugs. Second, Rebel's wife was listed on the registration for the pickup, so technically Cammie had bugged it with the owner's permission.

The judge didn't buy either reason.

Regarding the girlfriend's side business, the judge claimed people distributing illegal substances fell under the jurisdiction of the police, not an overzealous licensed private investigator. And as to planting the GPS device, the judge ruled it wasn't enough that Cammie's client had her name on the registration because it was clear to the judge that the philandering husband had full-time possession and use of the truck.

He charged Cammie with wiretapping, which carried up to four years in the tank.

Fortunately, an attorney—a pal of her uncle Frankie's—stepped in and pleaded down the felony wiretapping charge to a misdemeanor trespass with a fine. Despite living in Vegas for only seven years, Uncle Frankie was well connected. To know him was to love him. Lucky for her. Instead of going to jail, the state regulatory agency suspended her P.I. license with the stipulation that after she fulfilled seventy-five hours' community service, paid a thousand-dollar donation to an inner-city youth scholarship fund *and* paid the P.I. licensure board for its prosecution costs, she could apply to have her license reinstated. Yeah, real lucky.

Unfortunately, with an economy as robust as a taco shell, finding a new job was next to impossible. Hearing Cammie's dilemma, Frankie's fiancée, Delilah, who owned the gift shop at the Shamrock Palace and got along well with the owner, helped Cammie obtain a dealer's license and interview. Because the Elvis and Marilyn performer-dealers were threatening to walk if they didn't get more stage time, the owner was downright gleeful that Cammie had no desire to be a lip-sync diva.

Although, she still had to wear a costume at work—corset, fishnet stockings and high heels. At least, Cammie kept reminding herself, this corset gig was short-term. Five or six months, tops.

The double glass entrance doors to the casino blew open and warm desert winds rushed inside. A drink toppled off a table. Several women giddily shrieked, holding up their hands as though that could ward off the gusty breezes. Jeffrey raised his arms to his sides, letting the currents blow his unbuttoned white shirt off his chest, never missing a lip-syncing beat, the ends of his black wig lifting with the gale. A classic wind-machine Michael Jackson moment.

"Jeffrey's killin' it," said Val, holding on to her sailor cap.

Several beefy security guards managed to shove the doors closed. The Shamrock Palace returned to its mix of jangling slot machines, buzzing conversations and "Billie Jean."

"Wonder why he switched the glove," Cammie mused. Normally, Jeffrey wore a white glove with gold sequins. Today it was white with tiny golden stars.

Val squinted, then smiled in surprise. "Dang, Snooper, you have superhero vision. Which is no doubt why you're such a talented private eye. Speaking of which, that lawyer you used to sleuth for still callin'?"

"Seems to have stopped." Cammie's heart shrank a little. It

hadn't been easy ignoring those calls. Of course, hadn't helped that she kept listening to his messages, which were friendly but devoid of any real content. "Hi, Cammie, how're you doing? Hey, give me a call." "Hey, Cammie, Marc again. Would really appreciate you returning this call, thanks." She wasn't sure what hurt more: what had happened that caused her to leave, or the fact that her departure meant nothing to him.

"Did I step in it?" asked Val.

Even through all that black eyeliner and mascara, Cammie caught the concern in her eyes. "I got that look on my face again?"

"Uh-huh."

"I'm not the glum type."

"Check it out," Val said, retrieving a hand mirror from her pocket and handing it to Cammie, "and tell me what you call it."

Cammie looked at her reflection. Glum all right. It'd been a year—technically a year and a month—since she'd left Denver, but damn if her heart still ached as though it were yesterday.

"Why does he still get to me?" she murmured.

"Some boys we never get over. I call 'em the Undo's—you know, after that Carrie Underwood song. But look on the bright side, Snooper. There's boys out there in that big bad world who've never gotten over us, too."

Cammie handed back the mirror, thinking of Joey Kozmarski, who'd nursed a roaring crush on her from sixth grade through high school. She only knew because he wrote her notes about it all the time, otherwise she would have been clueless.

It had been like that with Marc. Except she'd had the roaring crush, he'd been clueless. But at least she'd kept her mouth shut about her feelings. Had never breathed a word of it to anyone, except Val. And then only after she'd put hundreds of miles and many days between her and Denver.

Val put her arm around Cammie's shoulders, gave her a squeeze. "Girl, you and me, we're survivors. We might get slabbed and jabbed, but we still got our health, our spectac-

ularly good looks, our fantabulous jobs at the Cave—" She
arched a shapely eyebrow while scrutinizing the flocked gold
ceiling, circle of gambling tables and dealers who looked like
Night of the Living Celebs. "Okay, kidding about the job part,
but I'm jumbo serious when I tell you that we got the most important thing in life. *Family*."

At eighteen, Val had lost everything in Hurricane Katrina.
Had gotten *slabbed,* a reference to the cement slab founda-
tions left after people lost their homes and everything in them.
Worse, she'd lost her beloved grandmother—Nanny—who'd
raised her. After relocating to Houston, then to Phoenix, Val
learned her second cousin's family had reunited and were living in Vegas, so she moved here.

Cammie's story wasn't as tough luck, fortunately, but she
knew how it felt to lose the one person who made up your
home. And, like Val, she'd relocated to Las Vegas to be with
the only family she had left.

"Even poor Trazy don't have family," Val added.

Trazy was the stray cat that had been hanging around behind the casino this past week. They'd started giving it scraps
of food on their breaks.

"Anyways, I had a brainstorm last night," Val continued.
"When you open up your detective agency, how about me being
your apprentice? We could be like those Charlie's Angels."

"I'd rather be Cher."

"C'mon, Snooper, those gals were tight."

"They were fluff and a guy ordered them around."

"Okay then, let's be the girl equivalent of Sherlock and
Watson."

The small crowd around the stage a-Go-Go erupted into
applause as the strains of "Billie Jean" faded. After one last
Michael Jackson crotch-grab, which triggered a chorus of
squeals, Jeffrey stepped off the stage, waving to his middle-
aged groupies.

"First things first," Cammie said in response to Val's proposal. "I need to get relicensed then we'll talk apprentice-ship—"

"Ladies, cut th'chat," growled a male voice, "an' get back t'yur tables." R.J., the chain-smoking, coffee-guzzling, fifty-something pit boss, made the word *crusty* look soft. His pecu-liar dialect of slamming words together increased whenever he was stressed or upset, which Cammie had learned was most of the time.

"Yes, sir," Val murmured, adjusting her sailor cap.

Angry voices from another table drew R.J.'s attention. Mut-tering a curse, he stubbed out his cigarette in one of the green glass ashtrays dotting the tables and left.

When he was out of earshot, Val murmured, "R.J. could do a kick-ass Keith Richards."

"With that bad black dye job, he'd be a shoo-in, but can he sync?"

Val laughed. "You're okay, girl. Sometimes I worry you're getting too serious, then you mix it up with some humor." Val started heading to her table. "Know how I'm always callin' you Snooper?"

"Yes."

"You, my friend," Val said over her shoulder, "can start cal-lin' me Watson."

"YOU'RE CHECKING YOUR cell again." Emily took a sip of her strawberry-fields shake, one of the pesticide-free, gluten-free, low-fat-content concoctions at Free Cream, an organic ice cream parlor in Denver. After swallowing, she continued, "You need to let it go. Be easy. Dependency makes people slaves."

Marc met his fifteen-year-old daughter's gaze. "More Tol-stoy?"

"No. Fritz Perls said that."

"Was he a spiritual anarchist, too?"

She barely suppressed a sigh. "Famous therapist, hello?

Worked at Esalen, where a lot of really together people, like Joan Baez and Ray Bradbury, hung out."

"Wow, you know who they are?"

Emily gave him a look he'd grown familiar with since she'd arrived from Maryland two days ago. Part know-it-all, part curious, a lot confused.

He related to all three.

It wasn't easy for either of them picking up the threads of a father-daughter relationship months later. Last time he'd seen her, she'd still been his little girl, hanging on his every word. In her place was this opinioned quasi woman who had made it clear from the get-go she wished she were spending her spring break with her cool pals rather than her bourgeois-attorney dad.

Nothing like being a part-time dad.

But he had to rise above it, try to be a good parent, even if it sometimes felt as though he were fighting a losing battle. "Sorry about that you-know-who-they-are crack."

She shrugged. "I was surprised you knew about Miz D and the Political Refugees."

"I checked out the playlist on your iPod."

"You *checked out* my iPod?"

He nodded.

"Like, you powered it on, searched the tunes?"

"Sure. I was curious what you listened to."

"What about my expectation of privacy?"

"You left it on the kitchen table, honey."

"Fourth Amendment protects electronic devices. From fathers."

"Not if they are left on the kitchen table, dear. You left it there for the world." When she started to speak, he made a let-me-finish gesture. "Although, come to think of it, technically I'm not just any third party because I bought that *electronic device* for your last birthday." When she turned fifteen going on thirty-four. "Therefore, *I'm* the registered owner."

"Oh." She blinked her blue eyes, probably the only feature

they had in common. Her strawberry-blond hair and pixie face were definitely her mother's. "But considering possession is nine-tenths of the law..."

He couldn't hold back a smile. "For a person who thinks lawyers epitomize decadent capitalism, you sure sound like one in the making."

They stared at each other for a long, drawn-out moment. In the background, a flute solo played airily over the speakers. The tropical-print wallpaper and hanging plants made this place seem more like a rain forest than an ice cream parlor, which he supposed was part of the intention.

But what did he know? He still bought food from the supermarket he'd shopped at for years, enjoyed an occasional cigar, still read books made from trees. He thought he was doing the proper green thing by recycling glass and paper, but Emily had started a compost pile in the backyard within hours of her arrival.

"I probably sound like a lawyer because I've been raised by two of 'em," Emily muttered. "Although Granddad was a pretty cool lawyer." She was thoughtful for a moment. "We used to eat licorice while he taught me to play chess. Well, he *tried* to teach me—it wasn't really my thing. But we had some great talks while we played." She blinked a few times. "I miss him."

"I miss him, too, honey."

She straightened, cleared her throat. "Mommy says after she gets married, she won't have to work anymore."

"She's thinking of marrying *again*? Isn't three times enough?"

Emily pursed her lips, obviously not wanting to get involved in discussions about her mother. Hell, he didn't want to discuss his ex, either, hadn't wanted to since their divorce nine years ago. But getting remarried and divorced two more times? He didn't like that Emily had been dragged through all that. After Bethann, his first and only wife, went through her last messy divorce, he'd filed a motion to be Emily's custodial parent, but the ensuing court hearing had turned into a freak show rampant with ugly accusations and character attacks. Emily, who had just turned thirteen, started losing weight, had difficulty sleeping and her grades dropped. Seeing how his and Bethann's battling was negatively affecting their daughter, he'd halted the proceedings, swearing he'd never put Emily through that again.

Which meant he'd bite his tongue about Bethann taking on husband number four. Poor sucker. He was about to lose most of his net worth in a very short time.

"Let's change the subject." He took a sip of his certified-fair-trade coffee.

"Okay." She gave him a funny look. "Every since I've gotten here, you've seemed…zonked."

"Zonked?"

"You know, tired."

"Got stuff on my mind." He forced a smile. "Not to worry."

"I could always go home—"

He hated that she called where she lived with her mother *home,* yet hadn't once used that word for his house.

"We've already discussed this," he said, fighting the urge to add *at least a dozen times.* "I know you miss your friends, miss your habits and hangouts, but this is my week, my *only* week, to be with you. To be…your father."

Another foreign word. *Father.* To think the courts of law actually thought they were courts of justice.

"Let's pick another subject to change to," said Emily. "Such as how often you're checking your cell. If it's, like, a new lady friend…well, it'd be smart, you know, to take a break after Gwen."

This wasn't his choice for a changed-to subject, but he didn't want to shut down every topic. At least he and Emily were communicating.

"Lady friend? No, I'm calling a business acquaintance who moved away from Denver a year or so ago. She's the best person for a certain, uh, investigative task."

"But she's not returning your calls, right?" She slowly stirred her straw—made of organic paper, no doubt—in her milkshake.

"Right."

"What's her name?"

He paused. "Cammie."

Those blue eyes widened. "Wasn't she the detective who sat in that weird little office next to the supply room at your firm?"

"She was my lead private investigator, yes. And her desk was in the alcove next to the supply room. She was gone a lot conducting investigations in the field and pulling court files, so she didn't need a full-blown office per se."

"You sound defensive."

"Probably because you sound like a prosecutor."

She made a huffing noise. "There you go again. No way in this lifetime or the next I'll ever be a lawyer. Back to your voice-messaging skills. Tell Cammie what you want. All you ever say is, 'This is Marc again. Please call me at…' and you leave your number."

He wondered if she was this dictatorial with her mother, but knew better than to ask. "Can't."

Emily, fishing a strawberry out of the glass, flashed him a why-not? look.

"Because…I once put her on probation for investigating the person I'm asking her to investigate again."

Emily frowned. "Is this about your former fiancée Gwen?"

"Yes."

"I was never clear what came down between you two."

He'd never been clear, either. Anything Gwen wanted, she got. She'd asked to be his bookkeeper so she could earn her own money. At the time it had surprised him that she wanted to work an eight-to-five job. But later, after learning she'd siphoned thirty grand from his law firm, he wasn't so surprised. She'd used him, stolen from his clients.

He wrote her a letter, officially terminating the engagement and her employment, and emailed it to her…but it bounced back. Email address unknown. She'd disconnected her cellphone service, as well. The way she disappeared, leaving no trace, led him to believe she'd planned this all along.

The same day he'd sent her the email the Colorado Attorney Disciplinary Agency initiated an investigation into Marc's clients' missing funds, focusing on him as the culprit of the fraud. As soon as he'd discovered the missing funds, he'd made restitution from his own pocket. But the damage had already been done. The missing money wasn't as important as the principle involved. A client's funds are inviolate. Although Marc had no knowledge of Gwen's theft, he was responsible. Because his father—the other Hamilton in Hamilton & Hamilton—was in prison for stealing clients' funds years ago, *The Denver Post* ran the story titled Like Father, Like Son.

Great advertising.

Marc had hired several local P.I.'s to find Gwen, but they kept hitting dead ends. She'd once made a reference to Southern California, and after combing the investigators' reports, he learned she possibly had relatives in Las Vegas, Nevada. Because the latter was where he'd heard that Cammie had moved to live with her uncle, he wanted to hire her to conduct surveillances, knock on doors, do whatever it took to find Gwen. Also, Southern California wasn't far from Vegas, so Cammie could easily travel there, too. She was a pro, the best P.I. he'd ever worked with, and now his best, if not only, chance to help him find Gwen and make her accountable for her theft.

"I mean, I'm not clear about the details," Emily continued, "but I know the major stuff. Mom told me you could lose your law license over something Gwen did."

He took a moment to gather his thoughts and suppress his anger. He'd specifically asked Bethann to not discuss this situation with their daughter.

"Not lose it," he finally said, keeping his voice even, "just have it suspended."

"And Cammie could help you keep your license."

He nodded. "But let's skip the specifics, all right?"

Emily shrugged. "Okay to ask how long she worked for you?"

"A few years."

"How many?"

"Five."

"That's more than a few." She looked at him for a moment. "You and Cammie...were you ever, you know..."

"What? Involved romantically?"

She nodded.

Pairing him with Cammie made about as much sense as pairing Hamlet with Stephanie Plum. Although Plum was a bounty hunter, if he recalled, and a bit silly. *Silly* was the last word to ever describe Cammie.

"No," he said, "we were strictly business associates."

His cell phone vibrated, clattering lightly against the Formica table top. He glanced at the caller ID.

"Maybe Cammie's finally calling back." Emily craned her neck to read the screen.

"Don't recognize it," he muttered.

"Maybe she's calling from another number."

"Maybe you're right." He snapped up the phone. "Marc Hamilton," he answered.

"Hi, Marc? It's Kathy Blegen. We met last year at the Historical Denver fund-raiser. Gwen and I were volunteers."

He'd met a squadron of people at that fund-raiser. "Wish I could remember everyone I met that night."

"Everybody calls me Half Pint. That's my nickname."

"Sure, I remember." Short, bobbed red hair, irritating laugh.

"I've been meaning to call you. Heard about what happened...you know, Gwen and *all that the loot*...thousands, right?"

He didn't respond.

"Shocked me and the other volunteers, I'll tell you. But on the other hand…well, she had a way with people."

"Did you want to discuss something?" He didn't have time for calls like this. People who had nothing better to do than dig for dirt and gossip.

"Yes. It's important. To you, although maybe you don't really care anymore about other news Gwen is hiding…"

"Hold on a minute," he said, getting up from the table. He pulled out a twenty, set it in front of Emily. "Pay the bill when you're done," he said quietly. "I'll be outside."

"Okay."

He stepped outside Free Cream. He caught the scent of lavender as he walked down the sidewalk, his phone to his ear.

"What else was Gwen hiding?" He tried to sound casual, although his body felt tense, wary. After everything else he'd learned, what more could there be?

"Well, um, you know Gwen and I had a few lunches after that fund-raiser…girl talk, drinks…"

He halted, turned his face up to the sun, but the fat golden ball in the sky was a fake. In late April, Colorado held on to its cold spells, even dumped the occasional snowstorm, as though winter refused to leave without having the last word.

"…a week or so before she disappeared…she told me…she was pregnant."

It took a moment for the words to sink in. If he'd felt chilly before, he felt downright frigid now. "Gwen was pregnant?"

"That's what she said."

An empty ache coursed through him. She'd disappeared in December, so she had to be… "Five, six months along?"

"Um, don't know. Seemed like she'd just found out."

"Was she…happy about it?" Damn it. Did he really want to know this much?

"I guess…she seemed more…surprised, you know?"

"Do you have any idea where she might have gone? Who would hide her whereabouts?"

"I didn't know her that well. I was, um, surprised she even shared that with me, you know?"

Emily stepped outside the ice cream shop, looked around for him.

"I have to go," he said and ended the call. Couldn't say more, had to wrap his head about this new piece of news.

He waved, got Emily's attention. As she walked toward him, the sunlight caught streaks of gold in her long, straight hair. Maybe she was a fledging socialist intent on changing the world, but in her jeans, peasant blouse and sandals, she looked like any other teenager. She was a good kid.

He sucked in a deep breath, blew it out.

Gwen's carrying my child.

The urgency to locate her ratcheted up several notches. This was about more than making her accountable for her theft, for saving his reputation, for enabling him to defend his father in the upcoming parole hearing...

This was also about claiming his unborn child.

Emily stopped in front of him, tilted her head as though to see him better. "You've got that zonked look again."

"You've been bored staying with me."

She bobbed her head. "Yeah."

"I've taken this week off to be with you, and I hate to see you bored, so..."

The thought had been percolating, and now it formed fully in his mind. He knew exactly what he and Emily were going to do. He had no choice, really. Either he kept asking and reaching out, or he made it happen in person.

"Emily," he said, "we're taking a trip."

CHAPTER TWO

O<small>VERHEAD</small>, <small>GREEN-AND-WHITE</small> spotlights whirled. The recording of trumpets blared, crackling with static.

"Ladies and gentlemen," announced a male voice over the speakers, "it's time for our hourly superstar show on the Shamrock a-Go-Go Stage! On this lovely April twenty-first in bedazzling, beautiful Las Vegas, I introduce—" the trumpet recording blasted again "—the one and only Christina Aguilera!"

The boogie-woogie melody of "Candyman" boomed as Val, dressed in her scanty sailor outfit, stepped onto the cramped stage. She smiled sassily at the audience and tipped her cap. Somebody wolf whistled.

It was a bustling day at the Cave. There was some kind of college volleyball competition in town, which meant a gazillion young adults were flooding Vegas, loving the 24/7 party life. This time of year also attracted a fair number of senior citizens. As one of them had confided to Cammie, May in Vegas could be miserable because of the heat, but April was lovely "despite those damn winds."

Several young men wearing Beer Pong T-shirts stood in the crowd at the foot of the stage. The guys clapped and whooped as Val pranced and lip-synced. Cammie marveled at her friend's talent to mime and dance and rake in the bucks. Those Beer Pong dudes were flicking bills into the tip bucket so quickly, they were candidates for carpal tunnel.

Cammie lightly tugged the stiff-laced edge of the corset where it chafed her hip. Hated these outfits.

"Wazzup, baby, hit me," said a glassy-eyed guy, nearly falling off the stool as he sat. He wore a black T-shirt, ripped at the arm holes. A fiery skull tattoo decorated one flabby bicep, a black panther with laser-green eyes the other. A multitude of eyebrow and ear piercings accessorized the I'm-so-bad look.

"This is a poker table," she said tightly, "not blackjack. Can I see your ID?"

"Wha—" He smiled sloppily, nearly toppling off the stool again to retrieve his wallet. "I'm legal, baby!"

His buddy, bearing even more tattoos and piercings, staggered up to the table, checked out Cammie's outfit. "Yo, let's poker!" he crowed, as though that was the funniest joke ever told.

Which apparently it was to them. The two of them laughed, slapped high fives.

Shamrock Palace was like a magnet to these types. Something about green beer, bad food and cheap slots attracted guys whose personalities had been shaped by too much reality TV and not enough real-world socialization.

For selfish reasons, she didn't want to call over R.J. Being the newbie dealer, she didn't want to look weak, incapable of handling a situation. She needed this job.

That didn't mean, however, she wasn't above issuing a threat.

"I'm happy to deal cards to you two fellas," she said tightly, "but if one of you makes a crack like that again, I'm calling security and you'll be escorted outside so fast, your nose rings will rattle and your—"

A "Candyman" horn crescendo prevented anyone nearby hearing the rest of her colorful warning.

The first guy blinked at her, then slid his ID to Cammie. As she checked it, he made a great show of lighting a cigarette. Twenty-two. She asked to see the second dude's ID. Twenty-one. She dealt the cards, reminding herself that coping with casino jerks and drunks was a temporary speed bump on the road to regaining her P.I. license.

"Hello, Cammie."

She froze, at first unsure she'd actually heard her name. But that voice...*his* voice.

Low-throttled with a sophisticated edge. The voice that used to fill her days, sometimes still filled her nights in dreams. The sound reverberated through her, thundering, pummeling her pathetically beating heart.

Somehow she forced herself to turn and look at him.

Marc.

Tall, as ever. At six-three, he usually towered over others in a room. The same stylishly cut chestnut hair, worn slightly longer than she remembered. A tangerine-colored polo shirt that would have set off his tan if he had one. He loved skiing during winter, golfing and jogging the rest of the year. Not like him to be indoors a lot, except for office tasks and court appearances, and...

Why the hell should she care?

But as soon as her anger tried to take a stand, something in his expression made it retreat. She looked into his strikingly blue eyes, saw the trouble within them.

From the shadow on his usually clean-shaven chin, and the wrinkles in his polo shirt, he'd arrived in a rush. Straight from the airport, she guessed. She hadn't returned his calls, but if he'd wanted to talk to her that badly, he could have explained why in a voice message or sent an email.

What was so important that he'd travel all the way here?

"Cammie," he repeated, his voice softer.

The way he looked at her gave her heart a squeeze.

"Babe, gimme two more cards!" The first pierced dude, sucking on his cig, shoved two cards in her direction.

"And make that one for Heltah-Skeltah, babe," said his pal.

"She's not a *babe*," growled Marc, pinning them with a look.

This was not like Marc, who she'd seen mediate dozens of angry, confrontational clients and more than a few opposing counsel, as well. That's how he'd earned the name Mr. Cool in the courtrooms.

"It's okay," she said, "I have this under control—"

"Back off, Polo Boy," said the guy, smoke escaping around his words. "Me and him was here before you. *And* she carded us."

As if that had anything to do with something. "Look, fellas," she said in her let's-all-be-friendly voice, "we don't need to—"

"What'd you call me, *Panther* Boy?" Narrowing his eyes, Marc leaned closer to the dude.

Who flexed his bicep. The panther wriggled.

"Oh, yeah, we're getting downright scary now," Cammie muttered, glancing over her shoulder to ensure R.J. wasn't alerted to the testosterone smackdown at her table.

Polo Boy's and Panther Boy's faces were so close, they could probably count each other's nose hairs.

"Want to take it outside?" Marc growled, looking dangerously bad for Mr. Cool. Bad and tired. She noticed the shadows under his eyes, the edge of exhaustion in his voice.

Panther Boy growled back, "I ain't never wanted to do nothin' so bad in my life."

"Yeah," Heltah-Skeltah added, shuffling the order of his cards.

Oh, good grief. As if any of them were all that interested, rested or—to look at the potbelly on Panther Boy—in good-enough shape to carry out these he-man threats.

"Dudes, chill," Cammie said calmly. "If you want to play cards, you can stay. But if you're more interested in playing Who's the Biggest Badass, you'll have to leave." She gave a knowing look to Panther Boy and his sidekick. "Don't make me threaten to call security again because this time it'll be more than a threat."

She slid them their cards.

"I'm not here to *play,* Cammie," said Marc, his voice oozing sincerity. "I want… I *need* to talk to you."

"Can't chat while playing." Cammie rolled her shoulders. "You in or out?"

He raised a cynical eyebrow. "In," he muttered. Marc bought twenty of the blue five-dollar chips with a one-hundred-dollar bill and placed his ante on the green felt.

She counted out five cards, slid them facedown to Marc.

He frowned at his cards, darting a look at her before setting them all facedown on the green felt. "I'll take five. An entire hand."

As she reached out to take his cards, he laid his hand on top of hers. His large, warm hand. She stared at it, dumbfounded, caught up in a stupid flashback to that night so long ago....

"Because that's what I need, Cammie, for you to give me a helping hand." He gave hers a squeeze. "If you'd answered my calls, I could've talked to you about it, but you refused, so here I am—"

"There a problem'ere?" R.J., a cup of coffee in one hand, a cigarette in the other, hovered next to Cammie. He stared at Marc's hand on Cammie's.

She withdrew hers. "We're all fine."

R.J. shifted a scowling gaze at the three men, who offered their answers.

"Him and me, we're cool."

"Yeah."

"There are no issues at this table."

For what seemed an excruciatingly small eternity, R.J. eye-locked each man as though he could probe their every depraved thought. Man, she thought she was good when it came to staring down people during interviews—R.J. raised it to an art form.

He looked at Cammie. "Take fifteen. Dee Dee'll cover f'ya."

Relieved for the chance to escape, she murmured her thanks and speed walked toward the exit a few feet away. Or tried to speed walk. Navigating in these nosebleed heels, it was more of a determined totter. For work, she'd wear sneakers to the table then slip on her heels there. Rule was, she had to keep the heels on for her shift, so she only had to deal with walking in these stupid things on breaks. How women functioned in high heels was beyond her.

Before hitting the door, she snagged a few cheese strips from Eddie, who ran the pizza stall. Outside, she sighed heavily and collapsed against a wall, munching on a strip.

"That was fugly," she murmured.

Above, fronds of palm trees rustled and swayed. Sunlight sparkled off cars in the parking lot. Staring up at the sky, clear and blue, she took in a deep breath...which she immediately regretted. The Green Palace liked to pump scents from its fast-food vendors—a mash of pizza and burgers—into the air as though a place with an Irish name that served greasy American food was some kind of customer magnet.

If you make them smell it, they will come.

"Mrowww..."

Something soft curled around her leg. She looked down into Trazy's uplifted furry face. Its green-gold eyes darted between hers and the cheese strips she held.

She offered a piece. Trazy scarfed it up, her fluffy tail curling in the air.

"I'm having a bad day," Cammie confided, breaking off another piece. "That guy I've been telling you about showed up at work. Total surprise. Of all the times I dreamed of seeing him again, I'd always imagined I'd be at the top of my game, making the bucks, and, of course, I'd look drop-dead amazing...."

Meow.

Trazy snagged the cheese Cammie offered and ate it. "Instead he surprises me at the Cave, where I'm dealing others' games, dressed as though any moment I might start belting 'Let's Do the Time Warp Again.'"

A shadow fell over Trazy.

"You look better than that, Cammie."

She squeezed shut her eyes. Oh, man, this whole effing

situation was too pitiful. Why couldn't the world open up and swallow her whole right now?

"How much did you hear?" she asked, not looking up.

"Of your conversation with the cat?"

She straightened, tossed the paper napkin into a nearby trash can. "Yes, with the cat." She met Marc's gaze, wondered what was burdening him so, even while wishing she didn't give a damn. "She and I are like this." She crossed her fingers for emphasis. "Right, Traze?"

Meow.

A hint of a smile played on Marc's lips. "I only heard the part about the *Rocky Horror Picture Show.* That's some name, Traze."

Considering she hadn't seen his shadow before then, she was willing to buy that's all he heard. She slumped against the wall and crossed her arms. "My friend Val wanted to call her Crazy, I wanted to name her Tracy, we compromised on Trazy." She gave him an assessing look. "How'd you know I worked here?"

"Called your uncle." Seeing the look on her face, he made a hold-on gesture. "Hey, it was easy to look up his number. Told him I was flying out to Vegas, wanted to see you when I was here—"

"I can't believe you flew *all the way out here* because I didn't answer your calls." *Whatever it is, it's eating you up.*

He paused. "It's important."

"I guessed that."

"Make that critical. For me. For the law practice. For my employees. For—"

"World peace?" She meant to say it lightly, but it came out harsh and she left it that way. Because what he'd done had been harsh. And wrong.

"Cammie, you left Denver so quickly…we never had a chance to come to terms—"

"You only offered me *your* terms."

"Please…don't be… I need you."

How many times had she wanted to hear him say those words? But not like this. She had no idea what *for me* was about, or even why he was concerned about his law practice. When she left, it'd been thriving. Several years running he'd been voted one of Denver's top one hundred attorneys by *5280* magazine. Thriving business, several über-talented paralegals, lots of referrals…what went south?

Oh, great, here she was caught up in his problems.

I don't want to care about you.

Warm breezes gusted past. Trazy scurried to the side of a metal trash can and hunkered down, tufts of her fur rising.

"I want you to be my investigator again."

"My uncle didn't explain?"

"Explain what?"

"About my…investigations business?"

An empty soda can clattered across the parking lot. That can was kinda like her P.I. career—empty, rattling along, going nowhere.

He looked confused. "No. He told me you worked here, and I assumed I'd find you working security, or maybe loss prevention, although those were never your specializations."

"I'd rather poke a stick in my eye." Although she took the occasional cheating-spouse or missing-person case, her specialization was assisting attorneys by doing legal investigations.

That almost-there smile again. "Yeah, I couldn't imagine you playing store cop, either. Anyway, I got here and saw Phil parked in the lot, so figured you were on shift. Went inside and asked around…then I found you.…" He gestured to her outfit, his eyes darting down, then back up more slowly, lingering on her breasts.

Was the sun playing tricks on her, or was that a flush coloring his cheekbones as he checked her out? Although it wasn't any tricks of sunlight that shot sparks of white-hot sensation through her as she did her own checking out. He'd always been a muscled but trim kinda guy, but add that black stubble, mussed hair and sullen look, and he could be Mr. April in the Bad Boy Lawyers calendar.

"Found me working as a dealer," she finally finished for him, her voice barely a whisper.

"Well, I was surprised," he said, dragging his gaze back to hers. "I mean, are you…one of the, uh, performers?"

She laughed. "You really think— Oh, *no*. Not Cher, not that, not ever. I'd rather poke a stick in *both* eyes."

"Cher?"

"You said you needed me," she said quickly, "for an investigative assignment. It's just that right now I'm—"

"Moonlighting," he said, nodding knowingly.

One thing about trial lawyers, they always spoke as though they knew the answer. Even when bluffing in court, which was much of the time, they acted as though their words were the absolute, undeniable, undisputed truth.

She'd roll with it. Then she wouldn't have to explain the mess she'd gotten into with her Nevada license.

"You're right," she said forced-brightly. "I'm moonlighting. But as to your investigation needs, there's a lot of good P.I.'s in Denver. Figured you'd have used some of them this past year."

"I have," he said quickly, "but the person I need to find is in this area."

Wasn't this the boss who'd once said she was the best investigator he'd ever worked with? That he was so offhanded about using other P.I.'s since she'd left felt, oh, bad. And that he was only here, talking to her, because he didn't know any other P.I.'s in this area felt, oh, worse.

She rolled her shoulders as much as the sadistically tight straps on the corset allowed. "A good P.I. can conduct research from anywhere," she said matter-of-factly. "If they need to do some footwork in a remote area, they contact other qualified P.I.'s located there. If they don't know anyone, they can ask around for references."

"I know that, but…you're the best."

Okay, she felt better.

But how ironic that the very skills he'd once chided her for, threatened termination over, were the very same ones he apparently traveled all this way to ask for again. The guy had no idea what that threat had cost her. How she'd left behind her life, her friends, everything she'd ever known, even her mother's grave to relocate to a strange town. Her uncle had insisted she stay with him, save money while she earned her Nevada license and built her P.I. business. Things had been going well until the GPS disaster crashed everything.

Now here she was, stuck in the Cave, dealing with losers who wanted to be winners, yet again paying her dues, biding her time, waiting to regain the very thing she'd once had, and lost.

The bottled pain, hurt and losses rolled hot and angry from deep inside and out her mouth before her better, wiser self could intervene.

"Screw you, Marc. You've never cared about the people who're on your side. It's all about you. What *you* want, what *you* need, how *your* world is hurting. You're clueless, damn it, *clueless*."

She turned and walked away.

CHAPTER THREE

STUNNED, MARC WATCHED CAMMIE totter away at a glacial pace on those sky-high heels.

What the hell had that outburst been about?

He thought back, trying to nail whatever he'd said that had triggered that meltdown. Yes, they had some unresolved history, but hadn't he admitted as much? And that clueless crack— clueless about what? If he correctly recalled, he'd actually said she was the best investigator he'd ever had right before she snapped.

Women.

If he understood them better, he wouldn't have an ex-wife who despised him, a daughter who confounded him and an ex-fiancée who'd stolen from him.

He took a step toward her. "Cammie, please stop. Let's talk."

"I need to get back to work."

At her snail pace, it was a cinch to keep up.

"You're angry."

"What makes you think that, Einstein?"

"Tell you the truth, I have no idea, but it doesn't take a ge-nius to interpret that fit of yours to be a whole lot of repressed Cammie unleashed. You know, if you'd let your feelings out *gradually,* like when events actually occurred, you wouldn't have to erupt like Mount Vesuvius—"

She half turned, teetering before catching herself. "Not only a lawyer, but also a shrink?"

"C'mon, I'm not—"

"And for the record," she said, angling up her chin, "I understand the reference to Mount Vesuvius. Did a report on it in eighth grade." She continued toward the casino.

"I didn't say you didn't know… I didn't mean… I—"

"I, I, I," she said. "Thinking of only yourself again."

He stopped, bit off a terse response and counted to three. Heated emotions wouldn't get him anywhere. The past twenty-four hours had been intense, rushed and, to be totally honest with himself, frightening. He'd never believed in spontaneously handling issues, especially if the end result was highly questionable. But he certainly hadn't taken his own counsel. No, he'd packed up his daughter, even though he knew Emily would hate Vegas, and hopped on a plane to see a woman who had made it perfectly clear that she didn't want to talk to him.

He'd never felt this out of control. Even when his father had been indicted, found guilty and put into prison, Marc had felt strong enough to move forward and rebuild the law firm. But this situation left him feeling rattled, off center.

Nevertheless, he was here. He had to try to get through to Cammie, appeal to her sense of justice. It was his only option.

"Cammie," he said, enunciating slowly, calmly, "I *do* think of others. All those years we worked together, I *knew* you were on my side. Hell, you weren't only the best investigator, I made sure to compensate you well. In fact, you were one of the top-paid investigators in Denver, remember?"

He paused, dragging a hand through his hair. Underneath Cammie's tough act, he knew she had a wicked sense of humor, even about herself.

"So let me guess," he said. "You're performing 'Let's Do the Time Warp Again'? Does…" He thought back to the flick, which he'd probably seen a hundred times the summer he turned fourteen. "Is Dr. Frank-N-Furter making an appearance? Do the gamblers all do the dance? Even that scary-looking pit boss?"

She'd stopped, her shoulders shaking. Either she was laughing or crying, but unless his dumb jokes totally sucked, he'd go with laughter.

"Considering the strange-oids this casino attracts," she finally said, "I probably *should* lip that song." She expelled an audible sigh. "I'm sorry. That tantrum…you're right. I'm a poster girl for *repressed.* That Mount Vesuvius crack was a bit over the top, though."

"Sorry. Want to…talk about it?"

"Old history, Marc," she said softly. "Let's drop it." She continued her plodding expedition. He'd had clients who'd been charged while driving with double-digit blood alcohol do a better job putting one foot in front of the other. Obviously she managed to keep her balance while dealing cards, but the way she moved now reminded him of a documentary he and Emily had watched on the flight of baby penguins. He only hoped Cammie didn't take a dive and start sliding on her tummy.

Thinking about it, Cammie and baby penguins weren't so dissimilar. Living in harsh environments—he'd known Cammie to work some tough neighborhoods while investigating cases. Dealing with predators—nobody put one over on Cammie, not even those jerks at the gambling table.

They differed, though, in that baby penguins were protected for a long time by their parents. From the few things Cammie had mentioned about her upbringing, there had never been a father, and her mother had been more a child than a parent.

"Whoa-a-a!"

She stumbled over a streak of gray fur that bolted across the sidewalk and disappeared under a hedge. As Cammie leaned forward to catch her balance, the corset crept up, exposing a glimpse of two round, firm half-moons.

He tried not to stare at that flash of behind, but he was, after all, a man with a pulse. He couldn't think of a time he hadn't seen Cammie in jeans, a variety of T-shirts and sneakers, although he had a vague recollection of a holiday party a year or so ago where she wore a dress. A pink, maybe purple, number. She'd looked pretty, soft…

She began to topple, emitting a shrill choice epithet as her arms windmilled frantically.

He closed the space between them in two bounding steps, surging forward as she keeled over.

With one arm, he caught her around her waist, hauled her to him with a yank. She slammed against his body, her breath escaping in a loud wheeze.

They stood in an awkward embrace, their breaths mingling. Or what breaths she could get. She was still gasping from their body collision, sucking air in fast, hot pants. Hell, so was he. Although suddenly, he wasn't feeling quite as tired.

As their gazes met, he wondered if he'd ever realized she had green eyes.

Which widened as she started to fall backward again.

He lurched forward with her, tightening his grip. They held the position, she damn near parallel to the ground, he looming over her, his face pressed into her neck.

"My…foot…slipped," she whispered shakily.

"I got you," he mumbled, his lips brushing moist, soft skin.

She smelled of soap and something unbearably sweet and familiar, like flowers and almonds. He recalled her wearing that scent at work, its fragrance lingering wherever she went. Hadn't realized until this moment how much he'd missed it.

With some effort, he straightened, hoisted her to a standing position. "You all right?"

She nodded. "You?"

"Fine. Not sure I have the energy to do that again, though."

She smiled, more genuine this time. "Thanks."

"My pleasure."

Red spots appeared on Cammie's cheeks. "Your hands…"

He looked down, saw he was gripping her hips. The corset was cut so high, his fingers splayed across fishnet and bare skin. Warm, butter-soft skin.

He dropped his hold, his palms tingling. "Sorry."

Her lips puckered into a funny smile. "S'okay."

Clearing his throat, he glanced at her heels. Or meant to glance at her heels. It took a few seconds to get there with those ridiculously long and well-toned legs in the way.

"Can't you wear more functional shoes? You used to have at least a dozen pairs of Keds."

"Some were Reebok. Casino wants us to look…sexy." She rolled her eyes.

"Well, you do. Look…"

Desert air rushed past. Cammie grimaced slightly, blinking against the currents. "I need to get back inside."

"One more minute? Please? After all, I just saved your life."

"Just like a trial lawyer to try and seal the deal, even when it's down to the wire. Okay, Mr. Cool, who's the skip?"

He paused. "Gwen."

He'd known their discussion, if it got this far, would inevitably come to this bad crossroads in their past.

"I investigated her once before, Marc," she said coolly. "Remember?"

"I remember. And I'm sorry I didn't believe you."

She did a dramatic double take. "Not believing me is one thing. Threatening to *fire* me another."

"I didn't fire you. I put you on probation."

"You threatened termination. That's darn close to firing someone."

"I'm sorry, Cammie!" *Stay cool, don't blow it.* "Looking back, I get it. I shouldn't have put you on probation. You're right, I was *clueless.* But that's the beauty of hindsight—it gives one twenty-twenty vision. Back then, I couldn't see the whole picture, was furious you'd willfully stepped into a legally gray area yet again. But if you can find it in your heart to fast-forward, tell me what I can do *now,* what I can say to make this better."

Cammie shook her head. "I can't work for you, Marc. I'm…

taking another investigative position here—prestigious law firm...starts soon."

As she turned to leave, he grabbed her arm, forced her to look at him. "Hear me out, damn it. Gwen...stole from the firm. Thirty thousand dollars. The Attorney Disciplinary Agency is investigating *me* for the theft. This could take me down, Cammie. Me, the firm, my dad... I need to get her served, to get her to a hearing in Denver, to show them she stole, and that I did not get careless with my clients' money."

As suddenly as it had started, the wind died down.

He knew her too well. She was fighting to keep her face impassive, stoic, but that wasn't how she felt inside. She and his dad had connected during those interviews at the prison. His dad once mentioned that Cammie had opened up, talked about things he promised he'd keep confidential. In turn, his father had let his guard down, let her see that he wasn't the formidable, coldhearted bastard the press had painted him as for years. That he was an old man at the end of his days who wanted to make amends.

Even if she hated Marc's guts, she had a soft spot for his father.

"Are the vultures onto this?" she asked quietly.

He nodded. "*The Denver Post* ran a headline—Like Father, Like Son. News stations are sniffing around. I need to find Gwen, make her accountable, safeguard my license, because if I lose it, my father might never..."

It was like a cold fist closing on his heart. This was tougher than he'd thought.

"If my license is suspended, I won't be able to represent him at his parole release hearing," he continued. "Cammie, I *need* to be there for him."

She dropped her head into her hands, stayed that way for a moment. When she finally raised her head, she looked around, avoiding his gaze.

"I've met some P.I.'s in Vegas who are experienced at finding people. I still have your cell number…I'll text you a few contact numbers, okay?"

She turned, started heading back to the casino.

"Cammie, please…"

She didn't stop.

This time, he didn't try to make her.

Back in the rental car, he took out his cell and dialed the hotel room. When Emily answered, he said he'd be back in a few minutes.

"That's all?"

"How's the ice cream?" As luck would have it, there was an organic ice cream parlor—named Herb's, which he guessed was somebody's name or the ingredients—near their hotel.

"Awesome. So I take it she said no."

"That she did." He blew out an exasperated breath.

"'The two most powerful warriors are patience and time.'"

"Tolstoy?"

"Yep."

"So if I have patience and give this time, Cammie will see the light and work for me?"

"Exactly."

"I love you, Em, but unfortunately, I'm running out of both."

In the background he heard people yelling, guns shooting. For all of her lofty proletariat chatter, Emily was still a kid who dug music and ice cream and true-crime TV shows that contained more drama and villainy than he'd seen after years in courtrooms.

"So, like, we flew all the way to Las Vegas for nothing?"

"Something like that," he mumbled. Enough of this toil and trouble. He'd put it aside, spend some time with his daughter, deal with the Cammie issue later. "Hey, let's grab lunch, do some shopping."

"Oh, what a capitalist idea. Let's spend money."

"Em, cut me some slack. Marx is dead, we're alive. Las Vegas is a restaurant mecca. If we can find an organic ice cream parlor here, I know we can find some awesome eco-vegetarian-gluten-free-green restaurants, too."

After ending the call, he stared out the windshield at the Shamrock Palace. Damn it all anyway. Flying hundreds of miles with a sullen teen who viewed their destination as the epitome of bourgeois depravity was bad enough without also being rejected by a corset-clad, wobbly heeled, unforgiving private eye.

He glanced over at a billboard with pictures of showgirls, men in tuxes throwing dice, a curvaceous bikini-clad redhead lounging by a pool. Underneath were the words *What happens in Las Vegas stays in Las Vegas.*

"Got that motto wrong," he muttered. "Should be *It ain't gonna happen in Vegas, buddy, so why'd you travel all the way here?*"

CHAPTER FOUR

A LITTLE AFTER SEVEN that night, Cammie walked into her uncle Frankie's ranch-style house, ablaze with lights because he never wanted her to come home to a dark house. When she'd first moved in, she'd told him he didn't need to crank up his electrical bill on her behalf, but he was adamant that a little extra for electricity was a small price for her well-being.

"Besides," he'd said, "you never knew what you were coming home to as a kid. With me, lights on, no surprises."

He rarely minced words.

After leaving the casino several hours ago, she'd headed to her community-service gig at Dignity House, a residential treatment center for troubled teenage girls on the outskirts of southeast Las Vegas. Located in a former boardinghouse, the center accommodated a dozen or so girls, ages thirteen to seventeen, most of whom were court ordered to be there. All of the girls attended counseling and in-house lifestyle courses as well as going on field trips to Hoover Dam and Red Rock Canyon. Some of the girls took academic courses within the facility while others attended the local public school.

On her community-service days, Cammie changed into jeans, T-shirt and sneakers before leaving the casino. Because Mojave Desert winds could turn chilly this time of year, today she'd also worn her powder-blue hoodie with *Denver Nuggets* in big yellow letters across the front. She dug the Nuggets, but they were on such a losing streak, she felt like less of a sports fan and more of a cheerleader for the underdog. She was starting to think her team was a bunch of brawny bridesmaids who'd never make it to the altar of the NBA finals.

After toeing off her sneakers in the living room, she headed into the kitchen with its lingering scents of bread, tomato sauce and garlic, and tossed her purse onto the dining room table next to a handwritten note.

Food's in fridge. Eat!

He'd signed it with a big *XO.*

Some things never changed. Uncle Frankie had been there for her when she was growing up in Denver, and he was here for her now in Vegas. At six foot, her uncle had that swarthy-brawny-Italian thing going for him, although his love of food was evident in his paunch. As he liked to say, he'd never met a pasta he didn't like.

He'd also never met a glass of Chianti he didn't like. Bottles from his favorite vineyard filled the wine rack underneath framed photos on the wall of the pope and Frank Sinatra. Cammie was an occasional drinker. Sometimes she joined him with a glass or two at dinner, and sometimes, like now, she needed a couple of belts all by herself. Not that Chianti could erase her memory. It wouldn't be that easy.

She selected a bottle, half read its label, her mind elsewhere. After Mr. Cool's surprise visit today, she'd managed to get through the rest of the afternoon at the Cave, had even made some okay tips. She'd managed her duties at Dignity House, too, which mostly involved ensuring the teens finished their chores and did their homework. Cammie, still reeling from her encounter with Marc, had thought she was keeping it together until a fourteen-year-old named Takira commented that she looked "tink." When Cammie had asked what that meant, another girl had translated that it meant *awful*—as in feeling bad kind of awful.

Everybody seemed to have a line on her emotions today. First Val with the *glum.* Then Takira with the *tink.* They were right. Cammie could add a few more, like *rejected, angry* and, as much as she didn't want to admit it to anyone else, *contrite*.

And *smitten*.

Oh, yeah, still head-over-heels gaga over a guy who had no idea. Totally oblivious. *Clueless.* She snorted a laugh. Even when she used that term today, he'd thought *clueless* referred to something else. If there was a superclueless, that was Marc.

And to think she had the brilliant idea that running away to another state would fix that. Hell, she coulda stayed in Colorado and not put herself through all these changes!

But she had. Turned her life inside out only to be starting over from scratch, same throbbing heart on her sleeve.

She slipped the bottle into the rack, wanting something stronger than a glass of vino.

A few minutes later, she poured some vodka into a blender jar filled with ice cubes, a drizzle of limencello and a hearty squeeze of a lime. A few whirring, grinding moments later, *voilà,* a pitcher of… She took a sip, wincing as she puckered her lips.

"Too much lime," she rasped, heading for a cabinet. She retrieved a bag of granulated sugar, added three hefty spoonfuls to the concoction and punched the pulse button again. She took another sip and smiled.

"When life hands you limes, make spiked limeade, baby."

Picking up the blender jar, she crossed through the living room, opened the sliding glass doors and stepped onto the covered backyard patio. Quiet. Except for the distant barking of a neighbor's dog.

Hard to believe the flashy, boisterous strip was only a few miles away.

Looking over the brick wall at the settling dusk, she drank directly from the blender jar. The burn felt good, centering, as it glided down her throat. The first star twinkled to life in the northwest sky. Farther in that direction lay the mysterious Area 51 and a long, lonely stretch of road called the Extraterrestrial Highway. Her uncle said people were always calling into local radio stations, claiming strange aircraft were spotted in the skies over that highway, but he thought it was more likely people, after a few too many drinks, were imagining stars and clouds to be spacecraft.

She took another sip, wondering if she could ever get that tipsy. Nah. Even in a dead sleep, she'd never dreamed of things like aliens and space travel. Growing up, her mom had loved watching *Star Trek,* which Cammie had thought was ludicrous. She'd once watched the movie *ET* with a friend, who cried at the ending. Cammie thought it was a cute flick, but totally unbelievable.

More stars twinkled on the horizon over the outlying Extraterrestrial Highway. Huh. Okay, what if those stars morphed into some kind of cool-looking space-travel vessel that zapped over here, right in Uncle Frankie's backyard, and alien beings, who miraculously spoke English, convinced her to travel to some distant galaxy...?

Marc would probably show up there, too, wondering why she hadn't answered her phone.

Clouds drifted in front of the moon, shading the twilight a deeper blue.

She took another sip—less burn, more buzz—and contemplated the hazy, silver-edged clouds. Wherever she was in this world, even if she were magically whisked away to another star system, Marc could convince her to return for one person.

His dad.

Harlan Hamilton, whom *The Denver Post* had tagged "the roar of the Rockies" for his booming voice and gutsy legal maneuvers, was a Colorado legend infamous for defending some of the state's most notorious, high-profile criminal cases.

His personality was as big as, if not bigger than, his courtroom antics. Part bulldog, part raconteur, he had a reputation for intimidating people one second, charming them the next. Wife number three, furious upon learning he had a girlfriend on the side—later to become wife number four—had called him "beyond a reasonable lout"—a moniker that became yet another news headline.

Who knew what demons drove the elder Hamilton to cross the line and steal money from clients? Some guessed past debts, others claimed his tyrannical ego, while others pitied him, surmising his downfall was an act of self-destruction because even he didn't believe he was as great as the legend.

Cammie hadn't known what to believe when Marc first asked her to visit his father in prison and start compiling a witness list for the next parole hearing. She'd been nervous, curious and intrigued. Harlan had once thrown a chair at opposing counsel, sued a reporter who had dared to ask the wrong question and called a judge he deemed backward-thinking a "troglodyte." People either detested him or loved him. And loved him plenty of women had, although with his shiny egg-shaped head and bulbous nose, he hardly looked like a chick magnet.

But the blustery luminary had been nothing like the man she'd met. Frail, circumspect and soft-spoken, Harlan had been like a smoky trace of his former fiery personality.

As she took another long sip, breezes ruffled her hair, and she thought how she'd grown to like and respect him. At their prison meetings, they'd started out discussing potential witnesses in detail. After a few visits, they'd wrap up their meetings with some quiet conversation about their lives. He'd told her how his parents, Scottish immigrants, had come to America to find a better life. She told him about her Italian grandparents who had done the same. He'd confided that although his father had loved this country and made a success of his life, he was often absent, which made his mother very unhappy. Cammie shared that her father split before she was born, and that her mother had never recovered from that abandonment. Or maybe she was fundamentally an insecure person. Whatever the reason, her mom had teetered through life like a lost soul.

Harlan had listened carefully, then surmised that Cammie's

mother must have also been a person capable of great love and compassion. When Cammie asked how he knew, he responded that he saw those same qualities in her daughter.

She'd never said goodbye to Harlan. Maybe some people lived their lives with no regrets, but Cammie had a bunch of them. Not saying goodbye to that gentle man was one. Although she still had time to see him again and tell him how much he meant to her, she couldn't deal with his son. *Wouldn't* deal with him. Refused to let him stomp all over her heart.

Clouds scurried past the face of the moon.

As the shadows lifted, she heard several phantomlike warbles, each ending on a rising note. The never-ending questions of burrowing owls, or what her uncle like to call "billy owls," that inhabited this region.

She sauntered over to a chaise, liking the warm, oozy effects of her drink, and sat. Cradling the cool jar between her hands, her thoughts shifted from the elder Hamilton to his son. Should she have told Marc the truth about why she couldn't work for him?

An owl's ghostly chirrup sounded like *Any why not?*

"How would I have said it?" she asked softly, thinking it over. *Sorry, dude, but my Nevada license was suspended last month.* No, a casual, it's-not-a-big-deal admission wasn't her style, not over an issue this important to her career, her life.

As she drank, another trilling question.

The query nagged her into admitting that maybe she should have simply come clean with Marc, had the guts to explain her license was suspended. Of course, that lovely little confession couldn't have been left at that. He would have wanted to know the reason behind the suspension, which would have opened up a can of worms about her role in the messy tagged-truck incident.

More chatter from the owls.

She held up her hand, as though that would stop the night critters from bombarding her with questions.

But she hadn't had enough to drink to believe her imaginary furry friends were actually asking the hard questions.

Truth was, she felt ruffled and anxious over Marc learning the truth about the suspension. *He would've assumed I'd once again boldly gone where no P.I. should tread, that I'd trespassed into the effing gray area, and I'd get a lecture about how my concepts of the law aren't necessarily the law itself and blah, blah, blah and so forth and so on....*

The irony was that if Marc had paid attention to the information she'd gathered, he wouldn't be in this mess. Okay, he hadn't exactly *asked* her to investigate Gwen, who was acting as his bookkeeper, but it was as obvious as Johnny Depp's Van Dyke beard that the woman was up to no good, as in fooling around with somebody other than Marc. Problem was, Cammie had gone a teensy bit overboard into what Marc referred to as "the gray area." With the help of a P.I. pal back East, she'd gotten her hands on Gwen's cell-phone records. Illegal? Yes. But very useful. From the number of phone calls to a certain private number, it was obvious that Gwen had a lover and was cheating on Marc.

Unfortunately, Marc didn't want to hear that evidence. When she'd tried to tell him what she'd found, he'd interrupted her to ask how she'd found out. As soon as she mentioned the phone records, he'd gone ballistic. Instead of being angry at Gwen, he'd jumped on Cammie.

She still remembered the anger in his eyes when he'd told her that he wouldn't tolerate illegal procedures. And she might have said something about not being able to tolerate an idiot as a boss. The rest of their argument escalated. He put her on probation. She snapped back with a variation of *You can't put me on probation because I quit.* And so forth and so on...

She made a rolling motion with her hand as she took another sip. Hearing the low-pitched grind of the garage door opening, she got up with some effort and walked toward the sliding glass door.

Stepping into the living room, she heard another ghostly warble behind her back.

She shut the door a little too hard, cutting off the rest of the question.

"Where's my li'l *figlia?*"

Frankie's voice boomed through the house. Didn't matter if her uncle was on a football field or in a church, his volume control was permanently stuck on High.

"Here, Uncle Frankie," she said, sauntering into the kitchen.

He gestured to the pitcher. "What's this?"

She set it on the counter. "Spiked limeade."

"Drinking straight from the jar?"

"It's called *cowboying it.*" A term she typically used for hours-long surveillances when you're cutting the niceties and making do with whatever you have on hand. At the moment, swigging spiked limeade straight from the blender jar fit that category perfectly.

"Cowboying it, huh?" He picked it up, took a swig. Lowering it, he nodded approvingly. "Not bad. Special occasion?"

She opened her mouth to say something, anything, but it stayed open with no words coming out as she stared into her uncle's brown eyes, which looked even larger behind his horn-rimmed glasses.

"Camilla?" he prodded.

Maybe she'd gained some false courage thanks to the green slush, but it was dissolving, fast. She scratched her chin in an attempt to cover its quivering. No way she'd let waterworks happen. She was a grown woman, not some angst-ridden, heartbroken teenager.

"My baby girl Camilla," he said in a surprisingly modulated voice. He set down the container and walked to her, his arms open wide. "C'mere."

So much for being a grown-up. She more or less fell into his arms, her face pressed against his turquoise-and-black-front Hawaiian shirt. He smelled like steak, cigarette smoke and his signature musky-lemony aftershave. He kept patting her back, saying things like "Let it out," and "It's okay, kid," but she refused to cry. A whimper or two, fine. And that sniffling was simply to clear the sinuses.

Finally she pulled back and looked into his face.

"Sorry," she croaked.

"For what?"

"Acting like a baby."

"Because you needed a hug? Everybody needs to know they're loved and cared about. That's what hugging is for. Crying isn't such a bad thing, either."

"I never cry."

"What? Is that a badge of honor? That first year of your life, that's all you did was cry. And when you weren't crying, you were eating or pooping. Since then, not so much. The crying part, I mean. The other two, though—"

"Uncle…"

"So? I tell it like it is. You get that from me, y'know. I was there changing your diapers, feeding you strained peas, burping you, too. You should really call me Dad, not Uncle, but I'll forgive you. By the way, *never's* a big word." He steered her toward the dining room table. "You need to eat."

"You always say that."

"That's because you never eat."

"I eat all the time!"

"Never enough." He pulled out a chair.

She slumped into it. "I thought you said *never's* a big word. You've used it twice."

"Okay, I'll never use it again."

She laughed despite herself.

"Good. I like that. Laugh. Eat. Life's short, my li'l *figlia*, trust me on that one. Today you're sad about a job or what somebody did or said or how they crossed their eyes, then one day you look back and don't remember the bad stuff all that well. But you do remember a tree swing at a friend's house that was torn down long ago or how sweet someone's perfume always smelled, and you yearn for what used to be— Where'd I put that bowl? Ah, there it is."

As he banged about in the kitchen, she stared at the picture of Pope John Paul II, who her uncle considered to be a man of the people even if he wasn't born in Italy. She vaguely recalled how that picture had hung in the dining room at her grandmother's house in Philly. Those walls had been covered in grayish wallpaper dotted with clusters of white-and-blue flowers. When she was four, she'd gotten in trouble for coloring some of the white flowers bright red. She'd imagined her grandmother walking into the room and gasping with delight at the bright addition.

Instead Cammie learned that some surprises aren't good things. Her grandmother had wanted to spank her, but Cammie's mother intervened. Those were the good days. When her mother still had the wherewithal to deal with life's ups and downs. The small ones, anyway.

She shifted her gaze to the Sinatra photo that hung next to the pope's. The singer leaned against a wall, his fedora pushed back, tie loosened, a burning cigarette dangling between his fingertips. He smiled languidly at the camera as though staring into the eyes of his lover.

Ol' Blue Eyes had been the perfect nickname for the famous singer. In color photographs, his eyes had been shockingly blue. Like Marc's.

She imagined Marc in that photo, leaning against a wall, looking into her eyes. She thought to that night so long ago, dancing on the lawn outside the party, their lips touching…

"*Buon* appetite!" Her uncle set a steaming plate of spaghetti heaped with marinara sauce before her. He sprinkled cheese on the food. "I grilled steak at Delilah's, so I'm not joining you. Will grab a glass of your *fabuloso* spiked limeade, however, and sit with you." He kept sprinkling. "Say when."

He knew her downfall was cheese. If she could live on bread

and cheese alone, she would. She waited until the shaved Parmesan began to resemble a snowdrift before making a stop motion.

As he headed to the kitchen, she dug in, realizing she was famished. A moment later, Frankie returned with a wineglass filled with frothy green liquid and sat opposite her.

"Good?" he asked.

She nodded, her mouth full.

"You look better already. Got color in your cheeks." He took a sip of the limeade as she spooned another bite. "So, yeah, Delilah and I, we grilled New Yorks. I made bruschetta. She whipped up a barley salad with those little baby corns. Corn on the cob for mice! She said they're harvested mostly in Thailand. Who knew?"

Delilah cooked, tatted lace, decorated entire rooms with hand-printed wallpaper, carved intricate designs in pumpkins at Halloween…you name it. She and Martha Stewart were like twins separated at birth, except they looked nothing alike. Delilah, at sixty, looked more like the actress Lainie Kazan, who played the mother in the movie *My Big Fat Greek Wedding*. Except Delilah wore enough gold jewelry to fund a small revolution, dyed her hair champagne-blond—"the best blond for my coloring, dear"—and wore clothes that never let the world forget she had cleavage.

Delilah's and Frankie's only arguments had been in the kitchen. That's what happened when two food divas fell in love.

As Cammie finished her meal, her uncle asked, "So…you gonna tell me what happened? 'Cause if anybody gave you a bad time at that job, you tell your uncle Frankie about it and I'll make sure the problem goes away."

"Like you're a wise guy."

"Don't need to be no wise guy to protect the ones you love. Or the ones you do business with."

"This is how you treated problems when you owned your taxi businesses?"

"Sometimes people need a strong talking-to, that's all. Then, after they *understand* the situation, the world is a beautiful place full of lollipops and rainbows."

"You like to act tough, but I got your number. Deep down, you're a softy."

"Keep it to yourself or you'll ruin my rep. Through with that?" He nudged his chin toward her plate.

"Yes."

"There's still a few bites left."

She huffed a sigh. "I've gained seven pounds since I moved here."

"And so you should! Don't know what they were feeding you in Denver, but when you got here, you were skin and bones! A scrawny little string of vermicelli." He wiggled his pinkie finger. "Now you look stronger, healthier…just not…" He got up, took her plate to the kitchen.

After he returned and sat, she asked, "Just not what?"

"Just not what, *what?*"

"You said I look healthier, just not…"

"Oh." He took another sip, shrugged. "Just not so happy. Not only today, but in general. Except today more so."

"I could blame you for that, you know."

"Me?"

She decided Italian men were the only ones who could look grossly affronted and incredibly innocent at the same time. "You told Marc where I work."

"Marc…the nice gentleman who called the house today asking for you?"

"The *only* gentleman who's ever called the house asking for me, yes."

"First of all, *figlia,* I knew who he was, even though he was polite enough to introduce himself—full name, very mannerly like—and explain he'd been your employer back in Denver. You'd just gotten that job when I left Denver, 'member? I'd call there off and on to talk to you when I couldn't reach you on your cell. Even if I'd never heard of him, you talked about him when you first got here…."

Yes, she'd talked a lot about Marc when she'd first arrived, but had never, ever admitted that she'd had a thing for the guy. If her uncle had thought somebody had broken her heart, even if that someone had never known how she'd felt, he probably would have hopped the next flight to Denver to have a man-to-man talk about his *figlia* and how to treat her right. Make sure Marc *understood* the situation, although she doubted that would have resulted in her world being showered with lolli-pops and rainbows.

Funny how she suddenly had men in her life ready to hop flights between Denver and Vegas to have one-on-ones.

"So, of course, I figured you were friends," Frankie said.

"Right," she murmured.

His features softened. "You like this man." It wasn't a question.

"It's not what you think."

"I asked if you liked him, not what am I thinking."

She fought the urge to roll her eyes. "It's just not…you know."

"Consummated?"

"Uncle Frankie, please! We're not talking sex."

"It tends to go hand in hand with love, y'know." He clapped his hands together and gave them a shake.

Oh, this conversation was going so very well.

"I understand what you're saying. I wasn't born yesterday." Oh, hell, this was a losing battle. She might as well talk about it…parts of it.

She straightened, looked her uncle square in the face. "Look, Marc's a friend. And my former boss. He wasn't very happy with how I conducted some research, something you and I have discussed in the past so no need to rehash it, and I ended up moving to Vegas, and you know the rest of my story after that. Can we consider this conversation over?"

"No." He brushed at his shirt. "I want some explanation for your sniffling on my favorite Hawaiian shirt, then after that, there's something else I'd like to discuss with you." The last two words sounded like *wi-choo*.

"What's that?"

"No misdirecting the conversation. But first, I need some more liquid refreshment." After setting the drink down, he leaned his forearms on the table and clasped his hands. "So... you like him, just not enough to have him visit you at work."

"I wasn't ready to...talk to him...especially at that dive—" She caught herself. "*Dive* doesn't include Delilah's gift store, of course."

"From your mouth to God's ears," he said, gesturing to the heavens. "Tourists love that stuff—today she sold two of those little knitted Las Vegas rat-on-string sweaters. Seventy a pop."

She let that sink in for a moment. "Seventy dollars for a hand-knitted sweater for a Yorkie or Chihuahua?"

"Yeah, and other small-like dogs. Maybe cats, too. Hey, how's that stray?"

"Trazy's still there. Thought she'd go home after a day or two."

"Sorry you can't bring her here."

"You're allergic to cats. No way. I'm going to make an appointment at a vet's, see if Trazy has one of those chips. Have to at least try and find out who her owners are." She thought of those little doggie sweaters. "Seventy bucks. That's more than I've ever spent on a sweater for *me*."

"But they're hand-knitted. Sparkly thread the color of her hair...you know..."

"Champagne."

"Yeah, champagne. She knits little pictures in them, too. Tiny dice. Martini glasses with olives. Girl dog sweaters have little faces of Marie knitted in them, too. Boy dog sweaters get her brother, what's his name?"

"Donny."

"Yeah."

"She knits the faces of *Donny* and *Marie* in them?"

"Tiny faces, but they're good, y'know. Big toothy smiles an' everything. That Delilah, she's talented. Has lots of plans…" He flashed Cammie an expectant look.

"Like what?"

"You're misdirecting the subject."

"I think you did."

"Then I'm going back to the other one. Okay, where was I…? Ah, right… Sounds like you're bothered he saw you in that outfit, right?"

A rush of heat crawled up her chest as she thought of Marc this afternoon, seeing her in that cover-nothing getup. "Right," she said quietly.

"Men who like women tend to really like them in outfits like that."

"Uncle Frankie, he likes women, just not *this* woman in *that* way." She flashed on Marc's former fiancée Gwen, who liked to call herself "Swagtastic"—gag—and had that hot-bod, bad-girl Cameron Diaz thing going for her. Sometimes her spray-on skirts had been so high and tight, Cammie wondered if she'd accidentally worn her Spanx to work. Especially annoying was the baby talk and the way Gwen's eyes would get all big and her fake lashes would flutter, and Marc would melt. How could he be so dumb to fall for such a cliché?

A thieving cliché, come to find out. Maybe that sexy act had been just that. An act to gain access to the firm's money. If only Marc had allowed Cammie to finish her investigation…

"But he liked you, right? In that hotsy-totsy number."

Took her a moment to realize her uncle was still talking about Marc seeing her at work. "I doubt it. You see, we had a disagreement."

"In the casino?"

"Outside. On my break. Work stuff."

"He flew out here to talk about work stuff? You left there over a year ago!"

She closed her eyes for a moment, then slowly reopened them. "I love you, but I don't think I can talk about this anymore. It's just—" She swallowed, hard.

He paused, seemingly weighing the scenario. "I'm sorry, sweetheart. Didn't know it'd be that uncomfortable, his showing up at the casino and all—"

"No need to apologize."

"So, wanna ask him over for dinner now that he's in Vegas?"

"You're incorrigible. No!"

"He could come over, see you in regular clothes."

"The answer is still no—"

"I'll make my famous marinara sauce. Delilah can make a salad with those baby corn on the cobs. You can make your electric limeade. I mean, this stuff alone could make a guy fall in love."

"He's not falling—"

"That's how I met Regina, you know." He got a faraway look in his eyes. "My buddy invited her over for dinner. My bachelor days ended the moment our eyes locked, God rest her soul." He made the cross, touched his hand to his lips. "Twenty-six wonderful years."

"You gave her a good life, Uncle Frankie. She had everything she wanted."

"Except a baby." He swiped at the air as though erasing the thought. "Enough looking back. Time to think about the present." The expression on his face shifted, and she caught a funny, almost secretive smile. "I got a favor to ask."

"As long as it has nothing to do with Marc and electric limeade, sure, anything."

He paused. "You know Delilah and I are betrothed now. Took me a long time after losing Regina to lose my heart again. But now that I've lost it—" he slapped a hand over his chest "—it ain't going anywhere, ever again. Anyway, I'm turning sixty-three next month, and Father Time is breathing down my back...."

"You're a spring chicken, Uncle Frankie."

He shrugged. "You're a sweetheart, but I see what's staring at me in the mirror every morning. And Delilah, she ain't getting younger, either, although she's one helluva good-looking woman for her age. Hell, for a woman half her age! So, what I'm trying to say is...it's time for me to start living under the same roof with my lady. Delilah and I as man and wife proper. The way we see it, the sooner the better."

"You're eloping?"

"Sorta. We have a chapel in mind." He glanced at the Sinatra picture.

Las Vegas was full of funky wedding chapels. At least a dozen that featured Sinatra impersonators. Some who were also ministers.

Oh, no.

"Don't tell me you're getting married by a minister dressed as Sinatra."

"No, we're not."

"Good."

"But you're close."

She could think of one infamous chapel that featured equally infamous impersonators, the kind that cropped up in all kinds of cheesy Vegas lounge acts.

"Please say it's not the Elvis Chapel," she whispered.

"Okay, I won't say it."

She scrunched her face. "No, not the Elvis Chapel." Anybody who spent more than a day in Vegas was destined to see a billboard or TV ad for the place. "Where that skinny Elvis impersonator in a shiny gold jacket is the minister? Where people can get the dueling Elvis wedding package—" She caught a look on his face. "Uncle Frankie, you're not getting married by dueling Elvises, right?"

"Actually, we're thinking of the Burning Love package.

Complimentary limousine, DVD of the ceremony, plus a live web cam for her relatives who can't make it."

This wedding was starting to sound uncomfortably like her job at the Cave. "Does the Elvis actually sing? Or is it lip-synced?"

"He sings. Several songs of our choice."

She clamped shut her mouth before she said something she regretted.

It was so quiet in the room, she could hear the tick-tick of the kitchen clock. It took her a moment to adjust her attitude and see her uncle for what he was: a man in love. She remembered how sad and tired he'd looked during Regina's long illness, and how disconsolate he'd been for months after she died. After meeting Delilah, he'd found happiness again. Some people spent a lifetime looking for that and never found it.

"Did you take a tour of the inside?" she asked, sincere this time.

"It's nice. Green plants. White columns like the Greeks had outside their homes, but these are inside, of course. We liked the chapel idea because it's going to be a small wedding. She's inviting some relatives from San Bernardino."

"Sounds nice."

"And…she'd like you to be her maid of honor."

Cammie felt as though someone had dumped a bucket of cold water over her head. Her brain froze. Followed by her face, then her chest…all the way to her toes. After a few moments, her voice thawed enough to speak.

"Isn't there somebody from San Bernardino…a sister, a niece?"

He shook his head. "There's a niece, but Delilah isn't very close to her. She wants you."

Cammie blew out a puff of air. "I'm… This is…"

"Look, I know you hate these kind of formal affairs, but this would mean a lot to me, Camilla. I also know Delilah shoulda asked, but…I told her I'd like to do it, the pre-invitation. Because, deep down, this is really *me* asking you to stand up there on this important day…the most important in the last chapter of my life."

She glanced toward the kitchen, wondering how much of that electric limeade was left.

Forget it. This was the time to think clearly.

Okay, her uncle had always been there for her. Those years when it had been so tough at home with her mom, he'd always been a phone call away. And when she died, he insisted Cammie move into his place, and he helped her get on her feet. Tried to talk her into being a lawyer, but she'd refused. When she'd decided to become a private investigator, he'd made one request. That she specialize in legal investigations. She'd never regretted that career path.

And then when everything had blown up in Denver with her job at Hamilton & Hamilton, he'd encouraged her to relocate to Vegas and move in with him until, again, she got back on her feet. He was right. Uncle Frankie was more a father than the one she'd never met.

The thought of walking down an aisle in the Elvis Chapel— oh, Lord, would "Burning Love" be playing over some boom box?—pained her. The primary thought shrieking through her brain was *I'd rather have a root canal than wear one of those butt-ugly dresses with bows the size of Kansas,* but what came out of her mouth was balanced, sane-sounding.

"Yes, Uncle Frankie. It's my privilege to be your maid of honor."

CHAPTER FIVE

THE NEXT DAY was a relatively uneventful day at the Cave except for "Marilyn's" wardrobe malfunction in the middle of her lip-syncing "Diamonds Are a Girl's Best Friend." When she pulled up after a give-it-all-you-got shimmy, the top half of her dress truly gave it up.

Later, Val swore there was no malfunction. "I saw Felicia insertin' Velcro strips in her top before the performance. That girl was ready to open the cupboard and show the goods before she even *stepped* on that stage. She'll do anything to get these tourists to open up their wallets."

"Maybe," Cammie agreed. "'Cause she certainly got the best tips of the day."

"Snooper," Val said, fisting her hand on her hip, "if I were to accidentally wardrobe misfunction, I'd have the best tips of the *year*."

"Please don't go there."

"Not to worry. I like to keep my pride *and* my clothes intact. Hey, hear from lawyer boy again?"

Before work, Cammie had given Val the lowdown about Marc's surprise visit.

"No."

"He wants to hire you as a P.I. Here's your chance to get back in that biz."

"Like I told you, he has no sway with my Nevada license."

"F'true? The way I see it, lawyers are like dogs. You take a poodle halfway around the world and it might not understand what people are sayin' or where it's supposed to lie down and

sniff, eat and all that dog stuff, but you hook it up with another poodle and those curly-haired mutts get *down*. Know
what I'm sayin'?"

"If you want to view poodles as lawyers, keep in mind that
each state has its own dog-attorney rules."

"There you go again."

"What?"

"Got that wall up."

"We're talking about legalities."

"You're glum again, too."

"Because I said there's different dog-lawyer rules?"

"No, because you're not talking about your real feelings.
You're talking the brain side of things."

"The factual side?"

"Uh-huh."

Cammie tried to give her best you're-so-wrong look, which
crumbled under Val's I-am-so-right-again one.

"Maybe," Val said, "those walls give you an excuse to not
go where you want to go."

"Marc's not going to help me get relicensed."

"There's that brain side again. You're talkin' about your
license. I'm talking about a place inside that you're trying to
ignore."

"This is getting too deep for me."

"Hmm." Val gave her friend an assessing look. "Like my
nanny used to say, joy is the sign we're fulfillin' our dreams."

"And I'm not joyful because I'm not fulfilling my dreams.
And that joy is deep inside. But brain side, the wall, keeps getting in the way."

She snapped her fingers. "Nobody can ever say you aren't
quick, Snooper. Let me give you a tip."

"A tip...to help me get to the joy?"

"Uh-huh. It's a technique my nanny used to practice. Sometimes I practice it, too, when something's difficult, sad or it
just plain hurts to think about it. Replace the bad thought with

a beautiful image. It's called distractin' your thoughts. Like, you realize you're fixating on your P.I. license being gone. Poof! You replace that thought with an image that makes you happy. Like that car of yours."

"Think of Phil?"

"Why not? He might be oversize and a bit cranky, but he never lets you down."

One thing about Val, she spoke her mind. Which was one reason that Cammie liked her, although she wasn't so sure about this whole distracting-oneself-with-happy-thoughts trick. That was a bit too la-la-out-there for her taste.

On the other hand, she wasn't wild about being called glum. Cammie had always prided herself on being coolheaded and together, not sulky and petulant, which sounded a lot like glum.

Maybe it was time to tap on that wall Val kept harping about.

"I like Phil, but I'd rather think about the Nuggets."

Val grinned, held up her hand for a high five. "Whatever cranks your joy, girlfriend."

At five o'clock, Cammie's shift ended at the Cave. In the employees' locker room, she changed into her casual clothes for her scheduled stint at Dignity House. Tonight she was the girls' study monitor from six to seven, which meant she babysat them as they did their homework—no cell phones, no iPods, no TV and, unless it had something to do with their homework, no internet. And if any of them had a creative excuse for not doing homework—and Cammie had heard plenty of those—she brought some of her detective novels for them to read, including a well-worn copy of Raymond Chandler's *The Long Good-bye,* which touched on political, social, racial, sexual, even environmental issues. Phil Marlowe was, after all, a gumshoe before his time.

On her way out the back door of the casino, she found Trazy lying on the cement walkway, fat and furry, lolling in the sun without a care.

Cammie leaned over to pet the cat. "Enjoying the warmer weather?"

Lazy Trazy managed a raspy meow.

"I see that Val replenished your water on her last break. Looks as though you're set up for the night." This morning, Cammie had brought some cans of cat food and two bowls—one for food, one for water.

The cat flopped over, sluggishly half pawed the air as though, if it really had a mind to, it could run or pounce or do something equally amazing.

"It's time I take you to the vet," Cammie whispered, stroking the cat under her chin. "See if you have one of those embedded chips that identifies your owners. If you don't, I'll hang up some flyers, see if somebody claims you. Time to get you off the streets."

Trazy reached out a paw and touched Cammie's hand.

"Am I interrupting?"

That familiar male voice.

She stood, met Marc's eyes. Her heart picked up its beat, drumming like a wanton tom-tom.

He'd obviously spent some time in the sun. The burnished glow of his skin made his blue eyes more vivid, startling. His short-sleeve shirt, its yellow color reminding her of aspen leaves, had obviously been recently purchased as it still had crease marks.

"Marc, I—" Hell, she didn't know what to say. Even if she did, she wasn't sure she could speak around the pounding pulse in her throat.

"Let me talk first, please."

She nodded.

"I'm sorry."

She did a double take. Not that the man didn't know how to smooth over rough edges in a discussion—he was, after all, Mr. Cool in the courtroom—but she hadn't expected him to apologize before he'd even said hello.

"I shouldn't have come to your work yesterday," he said. "That wasn't considerate."

"I was embarrassed that you—" she cleared her throat "—saw me in that outfit."

"Don't," he whispered, touching her arm. "You looked very attractive."

Was it her imagination or had the temperature shot up several degrees?

"And I shouldn't have bugged you with my problems like that." Marc nodded as though agreeing with himself. "First I surprised you, then I heaped my issues on you."

He was still touching her arm. That and the intense, unsettling look in his gaze made her feel more than a little unhinged. This was the moment to get back to center, tell him she was working on getting a few names of local P.I.'s, pull away from his touch, get on with her life.

Instead she stood and stared into his eyes.

And he stared back.

And, damn, if the moment didn't morph into something deliciously perfect. His fingers on her skin, the warmth of the sun, mysterious scents in the breezes, those extraordinary blue eyes melting into hers...

If this wasn't joy, baby, she didn't know what was.

Marc wrinkled his nose. "What's that smell?"

"Huh?" She blinked a few times, ripped from the dream.

He looked around, dropped his hand. "Smells like burgers and...tacos."

She pulled herself erect, released a breath she hadn't realized she'd been holding. "The Shamrock Palace likes to push those scents outside from some of its fast-food vendors. They think it lures people inside. I've only been here a little over a month, but I've never seen someone walk in wide-eyed, their arms outstretched, under the spell of the smells." *I'm running my mouth about burger-and-taco scents. I need to get out of here, pretend to have a life.*

"They actually force those smells outside?"

"Yep. Push 'em out into air." She made a pushing motion with her hands as though that helped explain the physics of it all. "Well, I need to be go—"

"Snooze!" He pointed at the logo on her T-shirt. "Now, there's a great Denver restaurant. Didn't know you liked it."

"Best pineapple pancakes and glazed doughnuts in the world. Haven't found anything like them in Vegas. We also had a few office lunches at Snooze...remember Megan's birthday party?"

He thought for a minute. "No."

"She turned forty, and we brought black balloons with dumb sayings on them, like Aged Like Fine Wine—Fruity and Complex, and I'm Forty, What's Your Excuse?"

"Memorable sayings, certainly."

"But you don't remember them."

He looked perplexed. "My life is a blur of business meetings, client luncheons and court appearances. But I do vaguely recall a lunch at Snooze where there were black balloons."

Wonder if you vaguely recall we sat next to each other. "Yeah, Megan and I used to go there a lot. She gave me this T when I left."

An awkward silence. Trazy wove around her legs, meowing.

"That cat likes you," he commented.

"She needs a home. Hanging outside a casino isn't good."

"Maybe you should give her a home."

"Oh, no. My caretaking days are over. Anyway, my uncle's allergic to cats." She plastered on a fake smile, started edging toward the parking lot. "Hey, about yesterday. I'm sorry, too. Got my boy shorts in a knot, said some things—"

"Didn't know I was clueless."

"Uh-huh." *Damn it. He's following me.* "Things like that. Look, I gotta go—"

"How about dinner?"

She stopped. So did he.

A fat blackbird landed on the branch of a palm tree and emitted a rapid-fire ki-ki-ki.

"No." She headed to her car.

"Couldn't you pretend to at least think it over? My daughter, Emily's, with me, but she has big plans tonight and I'm free. Was hoping you were, too."

"Sorry," Cammie called out, "I have things to go, places to do." Damn it. "I mean…never mind."

"Where?"

"None of your business."

"Jeez, Cammie, you don't have to— Look, how about a quick drink instead?"

Ki-ki-ki.

What was going on with the birds? Last night, the billy owls asked questions. Now this blackbird was following her. "Can't. It's a business appointment."

"Dressed like that?"

She stopped, pivoted to face him. "Nice," she said, elongating the single syllable so its that-was-a-very-unpleasant-thing-to-say-buddy meaning rang clear.

He swiped his forehead. "I meant, you're dressed casually, that's all."

"Because it's a casual business appointment."

"What time is this appointment?"

"Soon."

He blew out an exasperated breath. "Does *soon* mean you have a few minutes now?" He looked over her shoulder. "There's Phil. Maybe we can sit inside where it's more comfortable, chat for a few minutes."

"Phil's dirty. Cleaning lady didn't come this week."

"Cammie." He took a step forward, placed his hands on her arms. "I know you're still hurt. And angry. But if you'd give me five minutes of your time, just *five minutes,* I'd be forever indebted to you."

Her gaze dropped to the firm line of his mouth, then lifted

to the forceful look in his eyes. When had he ever needed her like this?

Oh, there had been the cases they'd worked on together. He'd needed her investigative expertise for those, certainly. Sometimes deadlines were intense, caseloads mushroomed and the work became challenging, if not overwhelming, and they'd snap at each other, his needing this or that ASAP.

But in all that time, he'd never told her he needed *her*.

Ki-ki-ki.

She glanced at the blackbird. This had to be an omen. Was it a warning or was it encouraging her?

She'd go with the latter. "Sure," she croaked. "Five minutes."

A few moments later, they sat in the front seat of Phil, their windows open. It was comfortably warm, almost balmy.

"Neat," he said, looking around.

"Obviously you mean *neat* as in *cool,* because this is hardly spotless. Still get your car detailed every few weeks?"

He was picking up something from the floor. "Yes."

"If I took Phil in to be detailed, they'd find stuff dating back to the Bush administration. The last Bush, not the one before."

"I know the reference. Wrote a report on the first one in eighth grade."

They laughed. Reminded her of the old days in the office when they'd give each other a bad time over silly stuff.

He held up a fake plastic rock. "What's this?"

"A stone with a motion-sensor camera inside."

He turned it this way and that. "Is it taking a picture of me now?"

"No, I need to get batteries for it."

"Did you use it when you worked for me?" Setting it down, he quickly added, "No, don't tell me."

"Okay, I won't."

He looked around at black tinted windows, a wadded-up bag of Cheetos and several empty diet-cola cans in the backseat, a photo of a guy in a fedora, smoking a cigarette, stuck to the dashboard.

"Who's that?"

"Phil's namesake."

"Philip Marlowe."

"The same."

"Is Phil treating you well?"

"Always there at my beck and call. Smokes a little, but not too much. Drinks a lot, though."

"Doing a lot of driving?"

"Commuting to Dignity House eats up a lot of gas."

"What's Dignity House?"

Shit. "A brunch place."

He looked confused. "Odd name for a brunch place. Now Snooze…" He looked at her shirt. "That's a great name for brunch."

He focused on her chest for a moment with drowsy concentration.

She couldn't allow herself to be lulled into letting her guard down. Slipping up with the name of Dignity House reminded her of the other things she was hiding from him. Marc wasn't an idiot. He'd figure out what was going on with her Nevada P.I. license sooner or later. And when he did, it was going to hurt.

But she couldn't look away. She lowered her head and stared at him through her lashes. He'd shaved today, which made the sensual curve of his full bottom lip all the more apparent. Maybe it was being in a smaller space, but she could smell his scent. Soap from his morning shower. Sunscreen. And if she wasn't mistaken, there was a hint of…

"Apple cider?" she said almost before she'd realized it.

"What?"

"I swear I'm smelling apple cider."

"Oh." He touched his neck. "Must be the herbal cologne Emily insisted I buy today."

"Herbal colognes. Wonder if they have tomato sauce. My uncle would love that. Speaking of Emily, how old is she now?"

"Fifteen."

"Last I saw her, she was eleven, maybe twelve. Wore braces and loved hamburgers."

"Braces, gone. So's the meat, as she's become a vegetarian. She's talking about adopting a vegan diet, but I've asked her to reconsider because I'm worried she might not get adequate nutrients." He gave his head a shake. "But who am I to tell her what's good and bad?"

"You're her father. That's what dads do."

He smiled, or that's what it seemed he was trying to do. "Forgot to mention she's a fledgling socialist proletariat who loves to quote Tolstoy, but today she was willing to put aside the revolution to do some serious shopping."

"Did that have something to do with her serious Las Vegas plans tonight?"

"Only the part where we bought organic popcorn and soda. She and her friends are watching a chick flick tonight. Emily from our hotel room, her pals from their homes back east. A virtual party, if you will. They'll be texting or tweeting or something throughout the movie."

She eyed a crease in his shirt. "Besides apple-cider cologne, looks as though you bought a new shirt today."

He fingered the material. "Made of hemp."

"I had a hemp purse once," she said. "When it got wet in the rain, it smelled like pot."

He gave her a look. "Seriously, I had no idea the fabric would be so soft."

"Sounds like another Emily suggestion."

He nodded. "It's grown without pesticides or synthetic fertilizers."

"Admirable. My idea of recycling is to wear the same shirt twice."

"I thought I was being sufficiently eco by recycling glass and paper, but I've been told that I need a compost heap, too."

They said the same word at the same time.

"Emily."

"Emily." His eyes crinkled with a smile. "She's an enigma wrapped in an organic mystery, but she's a great kid. You should see her, Cammie. She's growing up to be a beautiful young woman."

This time when their eyes met, she felt her breath go away. Turning away, she pretended to check the time on the analog clock she'd stuck on her dashboard—handy for surveillances because it didn't emit light like digital clocks—and did her best to look impassive, all business, unaffected.

"We've used up half of those five minutes," she said. "What did you want to tell me?"

He looked surprised. "Yes. You have an appointment, so let me lay it out." He spread his hands wide, as though setting the playing field. "As I told you yesterday, Gwen stole thousands of dollars from the firm, and the Attorney Disciplinary Agency is initiating an investigation into my practice, or more specifically investigating *me,* for the theft."

What happiness she'd seen in his face dissolved. He looked pensive, worried.

"As I also told you, this could backfire horribly. The board could suspend my license. If they do, I can't represent my father at his parole hearing in June."

"When might they suspend your license?"

"If I'm lucky, it won't happen before the parole hearing."

"And if you're unlucky?"

"Any day."

She blew out a soft whistle. "That sucks."

"But if I can find Gwen, subpoena her to a deposition with the Attorney Disciplinary Agency present, where I can confront her with her theft and show them how she hid that theft, then the agency may not suspend my license."

"Because they'll see the extent to which Gwen hid her crime."

"Correct. This could persuade the agency to drop any action against my license altogether before this case goes to trial, and it may even persuade the police to go after her for theft. At the very least, having her deposed should delay actions against me so that I can represent Dad at his parole hearing, at which I'll need you to testify. You're my best witness to testify about his rehabilitation."

"Of course. You mentioned before it's in June—what's the exact date?"

"The sixth. You're also a critical part of that deposition, Cammie, because of your background with forensic accounting, proving civil cases like this, and your testimony about your investigative efforts to find her."

"That's *if* I take the case."

"Which I hope you do."

Cammie folded her hands together and stared at them for a moment. "She could lie in that deposition."

"She could, but that'd be a dumb thing to do. And she knows it. Besides helping me track her, I figured down the road you'd conduct other investigations…research her assets, track her spending habits these last few months, find any places she might have hidden money…that sort of thing."

She picked at a speck on her jeans to keep from meeting his gaze. Everything he'd said sounded reasonable. But she couldn't get involved without admitting what she'd done. "Marc, as I told you before, I've accepted a job from that law firm. I'm sorry, but I can't be working for you now or later." And here she'd accused Gwen of possibly lying. Cammie was doing the very same thing, right to Marc's face. Didn't feel right to deceive him and fabricate a silly excuse. Better to tell him the truth.

"There's something else," he said. "It's important."

"Okay. Shoot."

"Gwen... I just found out... I didn't know..." He dragged a hand through his hair. "Sometimes I'm not sure if I should believe it or not—haven't told anyone else—"

"What else did she do?"

"Do? No. It's that...she's pregnant."

For a surreal moment, the world shut down. The breezes stilled. Scents of apple cider disappeared. Through the dirt-specked windshield, Cammie watched a couple holding hands as they walked through the parking lot. The girl's face was turned to the sun, mouth open, lips curled up at the corners. Laughing, Cammie guessed, but she didn't hear the sound.

Gwen was carrying Marc's child.

At least, *he* believed she was pregnant with his baby. If he'd allowed Cammie to tell him what she'd learned with her "gray area" records of Gwen's cell phone, he would have known that Gwen had another lover. There was a chance the baby wasn't his.

"That's some newsflash," Cammie murmured.

"You're telling me."

"How far along?"

He gave his head a shake. "Maybe five months? Not sure."

"You could have mentioned this earlier."

"You sound...perturbed."

"Maybe I am."

He made an incredulous sound. "Because I didn't tell you before now? Oh, let me figure out when that golden opportunity would have presented itself. Maybe when you acted so happy that I showed up at your work? Or how about when you said you couldn't help me but you'd forward me the names of other P.I.'s, which I never received?"

She glared at him. "You're not my boss anymore. I don't owe you squat."

Working his jaw, he stared out his window. "Says the woman hiding her own impressive newsflash."

"What?"

It was comfortably warm outside, but the look he gave made her shiver.

"I've been trying to be nice, Cammie. Trying to understand why you keep avoiding me, but it's really tough when I feel as though I'm doing all the work bridging the gap between us. You agree to talk to me, I open up, and you're pissed off again. Because I'm telling you something you didn't know. A *newsflash,* as you called it."

She eyed him levelly. "Maybe I don't like surprises."

"Well, you obviously don't like someone groveling at your feet, either." A muscle ticked in his jaw. "I read an interesting newsflash, too."

"Thought you didn't like that word—"

"Knock it off, Cammie."

She pursed her lips. Now was probably the time to think something distracting, put her thoughts into some far-off happy place, but it took every ounce of her energy to sit still and not say something she'd regret.

Like how his newsflash stirred all those old feelings she'd tried so hard to bury.

Damn. She never wanted to fall in love again.

AFTER A FEW MOMENTS of silence, Marc asked, "Want to hear about my newsflash?"

She nodded, her eyes so big and glossy, it made him wonder if she was…sad?

Cammie, sad? No way. She'd been caught, that's all. He was done playing games with her. No more lies or half-truths. He knew what she'd done.

"This newsflash was about a restaurant and school that were evacuated a month or so ago because of an alleged bomb. Turns out the bomb was actually a GPS device illegally planted by a private investigator. Is that why you moved to Sin City, Cammie? To more freely wade into those gray areas?"

"You don't know the whole story—"

"After all, Vegas is one of the most dangerous cities in the U.S. Much easier to wade into those felonious waters if you're working in a crime-ridden city, right?"

"Now you're assuming—"

"I mean, who's going to notice one pretty P.I. with long legs who slaps a GPS on an unknowing citizen's vehicle? Lucky the judge didn't hand over your electronic transmission violation to the feds—federal wiretapping convictions are minimum four years *mandatory* prison sentence—"

"Stop!" She cupped her ears. When he didn't say anything more, she lowered her hands. "I know I screwed up, okay?" she said quietly. Her green eyes darkened, the color of the sea under cloudy skies.

"I'm sorry every single day for what happened. I'm paying for what I did, Marc. It will take me months wearing a humiliating outfit to a job I hate, where drunks make passes at me as though I'm a piece of meat, but I'll pay my dues."

He felt like a dog. Even in ugly court battles when opposing counsel played low and dirty, Marc had always prided himself on being a gentleman. Maybe an incisive, calculating gentleman, but he had a reputation for playing the game with class.

But in this car with Cammie, he'd lobbed a low blow.

He waited for her to say more, but she just looked at him with those storm-green eyes. Finally she broke their stare to glance at the clock on the dashboard.

"I need to leave. Despite certain snarky things we've said to each other, I'm still going to contact some P.I.'s here in town, see if any of them have the time to help out on a time-critical case. If it's okay with you, I'll leave them your cell-phone number."

"Sure."

She started to speak again, but stopped, her lips quivering. Seeing the emotional toll he'd exacted made him feel even worse. He never expected this independent, self-sufficient woman to break down. Tears from Cammie? He couldn't believe it.

"Cammie, look, I'm—"

"Please go."

Her face was flushed, her eyes glistening. He knew it was smart to leave, not try to smooth things over with apologies and further explanations.

He exited the car.

As she accelerated into traffic, Phil burped a trace of white cloud. Like a stream of smoke from a dangling cigarette. Tough-guy Phil, having the last say. Marc could almost imagine the words.

Don't like your manners, Marc. Talked to her like she was some kind of trained seal. Ever hear the saying "You catch more flies with honey"?

That was either a very smart car or Marc was finally coming to his senses.

It was time to talk to somebody who understood Cammie better than anyone else.

And to bring on the sweet.

CHAPTER SIX

A LITTLE AFTER SEVEN that night, Cammie drove Phil to her uncle's. It had been a tough day at work, a tougher late-afternoon weird-talk with Marc, and a regular night playing study monitor at Dignity House, which was, by nature, always tough. The latter was weighing on her mind as she drove.

Fundamentally, she empathized with the girls at the center. At their young ages, most had already seen and done things that few people experienced in a lifetime. Some of the girls had parents who were drug addicts or dealers, others had been abandoned by their families, several already had rap sheets. The nonprofit Dignity House residential treatment center provided a healing living space where teenage girls could develop personal life skills and learn to make appropriate choices. For the older ones, this might be their last chance to take steps toward more positive, productive lives. According to statistics, only 35 percent actually hit that goal.

On the way to learning better choices, some of the girls continued to practice the same old bad ones. Like fabricating whoppers to get out of responsibilities. Takira, the resident drama queen, had barely cracked her algebra book before falling facedown on it with anguished groans. Seemed her cramps were "killing" her and she needed to "go to my room and lie down, Miss Copello, please." Health concerns were legit, but when Cammie later caught Takira teaching another girl the Dinki Mini, a dance slightly less inhibited than Madonna in her "Girl Gone Wild" video, she marched the two of them back into the study room.

In the minutes Cammie had been tracking down Takira, the study room had become part hair-styling clinic, part who-has-the-baddest-'tude. Cammie won that last one when she threatened everyone with a three-hour, mandatory study time—and yes, she'd sit there for every single minute of it, thank you—if they didn't get their acts in gear. As they settled down, she picked up a tube of styling gel and a big sticky glop squirted on her T.

The only one who'd continued studying throughout the fracas was Amber, a gloomy fifteen-year-old who insisted everyone call her Daearen, the ancient Celtic word for *earth*. She believed the world would end in 2016, the inevitable result of the thinning ozone layer, diminishing natural resources and overpopulation. The other girls made jokes behind Amber's back, and basically steered clear of her dark-cloud prophesies. Amber was one of the girls who was house-bound, tutored at Dignity House instead of attending public school.

Although keeping her 24/7 seemed severe, Cammie had been told that Amber was disruptive in the public school setting with her depression and her oppositional behavior. Seeing how isolated Amber-Daearen was, Cammie always tried to spend a few minutes with the girl each visit, although try as she might with jokes and funny stories, Cammie couldn't roust Amber from her funk.

The girls eventually settled down and completed their study hour, but the battle to get to that point, plus the emotional upheavals of the past few days, had left Cammie bushed. By the time she parked in front of her uncle's house, all she wanted to do was crawl into bed, watch some TV and get some *z*'s.

As she opened the front door, she heard her uncle laughing.

"Winters! That's another thing I don't miss about Denver!" Her uncle stopped short when he saw Cammie. "Well, look what the Mojave blew in."

Her uncle sat on the couch, facing a visitor who sat in a

high-back chair, blocking Cammie's view. Swiveling in his seat, he looked at her.

Marc.

Her heart pounded so hard and fast, for a crazy moment she wondered if it would explode. Easing in a slow, calming breath, she gripped her trembling fingers around the handle of her purse.

Black lashes narrowed over his blue eyes as his gaze darted to her T-shirt.

"Styling gel," she explained.

When his eyes met hers again, they were twinkling. Smart man, he didn't say anything. Obviously they'd both said plenty to each other recently. And she'd had a couple of hours since their last meet-up to think about her prickly reaction to learning Gwen was pregnant. It was none of her business, of course, which was why she now felt embarrassed at her "newsflash" swipe. Obviously he and Gwen had been engaged, so of course they were doing the horizontal mamba, and, therefore, it wasn't exactly *unlikely* a baby might be the end result.

The hard part was realizing, and accepting, that the baby... the unborn child...was a concrete reminder of everything Cammie and Marc weren't. A reminder that, within weeks of the passionate kiss she and Marc had once shared, he found something better in another woman's arms.

Out of a day filled with tough events, that epiphany had been the toughest.

"I invited him over," her uncle said quickly, his voice so loud it was a miracle the glass bowl on the coffee table didn't shatter.

She nodded, not really wanting to know who called whom or how this impromptu get-together happened, although she smelled a setup by her uncle. At least her heart was stuttering back to its regular beat and her fingers were trembling less. The best way to handle this strange interlude was simply to walk right past it. Go to her room, get into her jammies, read a little Chandler, go to sleep.

"It's been a long day," she said. "I'm going to hit the sack."

"But, Camilla," her uncle said, his voice booming, "it's not even eight o'clock!"

"Oh, good," she said quietly, "I'm sure the rest of the neighborhood was wondering what time it was, too."

"Cammie," Marc said, standing, "I shouldn't have surprised you like this—"

"Camilla, sweetheart," Frankie said, "he called and, like I said, I *invited* him over for a beer. When I learned his little girl had plans tonight, I thought it'd be nice if we all got together for dinner."

After a beat, she asked, "We?"

"You, Marc, me and Delilah."

"We're cooking spaghetti and making miniature corn-cob salad?"

"No. We're going to make a night of it, celebrate Del's and my impending wedding. Made reservations at Piero's. Delilah's on her way. Hey, come with me a minute…need to ask you something."

Cammie dutifully followed her uncle into the dining room, where Marc couldn't see them. Miraculously, Frankie lowered his voice to an almost-whisper range.

"Hey." He put his arm around her shoulders. "I know this was a surprise."

"You got that right."

He patted his heart. "But your old uncle meant well. Delilah, y'know, wanted to ask you in person to be her maid of honor. I did the pre-invitation, but she wanted to ask you in person. Has a gift for you, too, but act surprised. Tell you the truth, I'd already made the reservations for three, then Marc called, and I figured, hey, let's make it a foursome. Didn't want to bother you at Dignity House, figured I'd explain after you got home."

"You could've left a message on my cell."

"Coulda, yeah. Didn't think of it."

"Uncle…"

"Yeah, okay, I thought of it, but was afraid you'd hear the message and not come home."

"Because I would've felt set up. Which I feel anyway."

"With a man you care about."

"Who doesn't return my feelings."

"Maybe he needs the chance to develop those feelings!"

"Shh." She glanced toward the living room, then to her uncle. "Forcing him to eat Italian food with me won't develop them." She pointed at her eye, an Italian gesture her uncle used to indicate someone had been a slick operator.

"Madonna," he pleaded, pressing his palms together as he stared at the ceiling, "help me to help this child."

Man, he could pull out all the stops. Her uncle had missed his calling as a soap-opera actor.

"You two all right?" Marc called out.

She and her uncle yelled back at the same time.

"No."

"Yes."

In the ensuing silence, she and Frankie locked stares. Looking at those big brown eyes, brimming with apology, twice their size behind those horn-rim glasses, she couldn't keep up the attitude. He was besotted with Delilah and ridiculously, hopelessly in love. He was a man "under the influence" and shouldn't be censured for his lack of social graces.

This time, anyway.

"Okay, let's all go to dinner." She gave him a warning glare. "Just don't play matchmaker anymore. This is a friendly dinner, not a double date."

He raised his hand as though taking an oath. "Never!"

"I thought you promised to never say never, like Justin Bieber."

"Who?"

"Keep your voice down. And so you know, Marc read that article on the internet and knows all about my license being suspended. But that doesn't mean we need to dredge it up, discuss the particulars."

"Deal."

The doorbell chimed.

"Delilah's here." Frankie grinned. "Let's go make introductions."

Moments later, Delilah waltzed into the room, her gold bracelets clinking, the scent of Chanel No. 5—"the best perfume a woman of a certain age should wear"—wafting behind her. She wore an animal-print top cut so low that her popping cleavage looked like a baby bottom. Below her beige stretchy pants, red-tipped toenails peeked out of a pair of gold strappy sandals.

"Darling," Delilah cooed. She planted a kiss on Frankie's lips, then turned and looked expectantly at Marc.

Who stood as Frankie made introductions.

"I've heard so much about you," she said, placing her hand in his. Marc bowed slightly and kissed the back of her hand.

"Such a gentleman." She cast an approving look at Frankie.

Delilah lifted a bright pink bag embellished with the words *Maid of Honor* in cursive silver and handed it to Cammie.

"My dear, I know your uncle, my husband-to-be, asked you to be my maid of honor last night. I hope you understand his asking you before I did. You two are so close, after all."

Cammie nodded, wondering what the hell was in that bag.

"Now that we're all together, I'd like to ask you in person. Will you, dear, be my maid of honor?" Delilah blinked back emotion.

Cammie put on her best game face. "Of course, Delilah, I'd be honored."

Delilah hugged her, smothering her in a fog of Chanel. "Oh, my dear, thank you! I'm so happy. My darling husband-to-be is happy." She pulled back and looked at Marc.

"And…I'm happy, too!" he added.

Delilah laughed, her nose twitching like a bunny's. Turning serious, she gestured to the gift. "To honor this occasion, a special gift to my maid of honor."

Cammie flashed on the various tacky "Maid of Honor" tops she'd seen every week, if not daily, at the casino. Ever since that movie *Bridesmaids,* it seemed every bride-to-be wanted to host her bridal party in Sin City. She'd actually seen tops that read *Maid of Honor aka the Bride's Bitch,* and *As the maid of honor, your main responsibility is to help me pee without getting my massive dress in the toilet.*

Of course, Delilah had too much class for that.

Cammie glanced at the older woman's backpack-size gold purse, decorated with large silver buckles, rhinestones and what appeared to be a cheetah's face peeking through some jungle foliage.

"I would have brought a gift for the bride-to-be," she said, "but I didn't even know we were celebrating tonight."

"Pshaw," Delilah said, making a dismissive gesture. "This is a spur-of-the-moment event, just the way our wedding date was picked spur of the moment, wasn't it, my little boo-bear?"

"Yes, my little kitty doll," said Frankie.

"Open it, dear," Delilah said, waggling her red nails at the bag. "I can't wait to see how you look in it."

Look in it? *Maid of Honor aka the Bride's...*

Cammie extracted a bundle of soft apple-green material. The front of the top was covered with a bunch of sparkly beads, but no sayings. Life was good.

"It's lovely," she murmured.

"Frankie said it's your favorite color," Delilah said.

"It is." She looked more closely at the gold, silver and yellow beading on the green mesh overlay. "Is that...Humphrey Bogart?"

"When Frankie explained your car was named for that private eye Bogie played in the movies," Delilah said proudly, "I made a pattern of his face from an old movie poster to create this bead design."

"The Big Sleep?" Cammie asked.

"Yes! You recognized it."

"Delilah can make anything," Frankie said to Marc. "That Martha Stewart could take lessons from her!"

"Stop it, Frankie, you're embarrassing me." Delilah beamed at Cammie. "I'd be honored if you wore it to dinner tonight."

Cammie blinked, mentally backpedaling. She'd gone from agreeing to going out to dinner to dressing in a beaded number that, based on the light from the coffee-table lamp, seeping through the fabric, was also see-through in parts.

"I, uh—"

"Of course she will!" Frankie patted Cammie on the back a little too hard.

"It'll look fabulous on you," Delilah said, picking up her backpack-purse. "Oh, I'm having another wonderful idea! Let's be girls and play dress-up. I happen to have my makeup bag with me!"

Breathe, Cammie counseled herself as she headed toward her bedroom, the tap-tap-tap of Delilah's heels behind her. *Everything's going to be all right. You're going to look fine.*

She looked like hell.

As the four of them walked into Piero's for dinner an hour later, Cammie jumped when she caught her reflection in a mirror. It wasn't that she didn't like to wear makeup, it's that she liked to wear a *little*. Delilah believed the more, the better. Plus the older woman had insisted on giving Cammie an "upswept hairstyle"—hair piled high, curls cascading down the sides of her face, little flower clips pinned here and there. Cammie was waiting for someone to offer to buy the hanging flower basket on her head.

Below the neck had its pros and cons.

She actually liked how Bogie's—aka Philip Marlowe's—face sparkled under the lights. And lime-green was her favorite color. It was the view of her not really there cleavage through the sheer chiffon-mesh stuff that made her feel, well, lacking. The corset contraption she wore at work at least made her boobs look as though something could roll off them. But as she didn't own any push-up bras, and refused to accept Delilah's offer to "work some magic" with duct tape, the peek-through top didn't offer much to peek at. At least she'd gotten her way with the rest of her attire. Her favorite black skinny-leg jeans with black patent-leather flats.

As the maître d' escorted them to their table, Uncle Frankie explained to Marc that the restaurant was once a favorite dining spot for Tony "The Ant" Spilotro, a mobster who later met his "unfortunate demise," which Cammie took to mean a shallow unmarked grave somewhere beyond the Extraterrestrial Highway. Half the room turned to look at Frankie as he broadcast the tale. Which was probably why the maître d' led them to an isolated corner in the far room.

Fortunately, the lighting was set low at Piero's. Unfortunately, it created the kind of moody ambiance that encouraged whispered conversations and amorous looks. Which Delilah and Frankie would be doing, of course. Cammie supposed she and Marc might ask each other to pass the salt in low, meaningful tones.

Of course, if that office luncheon at Snooze was any indication, she'd remember this dinner forever, and he wouldn't even remember she'd been here. Which didn't bode well for her ego, considering she was wearing a frightful hairdo *and* a see-through top. Hell, she could probably strip naked, grab a candle from one of these tables and sing Springsteen's "I'm on Fire," and Marc *still* wouldn't remember she'd been here.

Maybe it was time to practice that mental imagery technique Val talked about. Except thinking of Phil wasn't going to cut it. She mentally gave herself some instructions. *When you start thinking of how electrifyingly blue Marc's eyes are, imagine...* She wasn't sure what that would be, but there had to be something. The blue skies over Sky Pond, a favorite hiking spot in the Rockies. The soft blue in the Nuggets logo. One of those should work.

Their table was lovely. White linen, shiny silverware, flickering candles. An old Dean Martin hit, "You're Nobody 'Til Somebody Loves You," played over the speakers, a song her mother liked to play when she was feeling particularly maudlin. Her mother would retell stories about Cammie's father—how they met at a dance, their first date at the movies, how he had black, curly hair like Dean Martin. *That's where you got your black curls, baby.* The same stories over and over as the song played again and again.

Frankie pulled out a chair for Delilah, who cooed and blew a kiss at him as she sat down.

Cammie reached for her chair.

"Let me do that," said Marc, pulling it out for her.

"Such a gentleman," murmured Delilah.

A waiter appeared, handed out menus with a flourish. Minutes later they ordered. Frankie ordered the house specialty, osso buco, for him and Delilah. Cammie ordered *fettuccine a modo mio,* and Marc, *linguine portofino.* Frankie ordered a bottle of their best Chianti, and a martini for Delilah.

"Marc, tell us all about your law practice," said Delilah.

While they sipped their drinks and ate their salads, Marc told them about working his way through law school as a hospital orderly, where he did everything from prepping patients for surgery to scrubbing floors. Although his father already had a thriving law practice and was paying Marc's steep law school tuition, his dad was also paying alimony to three ex-wives, and child support for Marc's two half siblings. Marc had thought it only fair that he pay for his day-to-day living expenses while in school.

"I've since thought," Marc said, "that more lawyers should have worked such jobs because they encourage compassion for others less fortunate."

"Noble," murmured Delilah.

"I know what you mean," Frankie agreed. "Back when I was still driving taxis, I met people from all walks of life. Taught me compassion for some, except when I got stuck driving some ignoramus yahoo. Pass the salt, kitty love?"

"And after law school," Delilah said, handing the shaker to Frankie, "how difficult was the bar exam?"

"Happy to say I passed on the first try."

"Took John Kennedy, Junior—God bless his soul—three times, I heard," Frankie said.

"In his favor, the New York bar exam is one of three most difficult exams to pass. The other two being California and Florida, although Massachusetts is no slouch."

"After passing the exam, you went to work for your father?" Delilah asked.

"I could have, I suppose, but at the time we weren't very close." He took a sip of his wine. "Instead, I cut my legal teeth at the state public defenders' office."

"You probably met a lot of poor, desperate people," Frankie commented.

"Poor, desperate, addicted," Marc said. "Outcasts. People who'd fallen through the world's cracks."

"Few are willing to help those less fortunate. World needs more people like you." Delilah nibbled an olive off a swizzle stick. "Caring and smart and so very handsome."

Cammie quietly munched on her salad. She was playing nice, but having to listen to the Let's Put Marc on a Pedestal show was wearing a little thin. She felt like saying, *Enough already, I know the man possesses charm and brains and looks in abundance! That's not the problem. He doesn't think I rank all that high in those categories.*

No, she took that back. He gave her credit for brains. And she liked to think she occasionally exercised charm. But until she got this bird's nest off her head, forget the looks department. Although…he had made that comment earlier today about her being a pretty P.I. with long legs.

She studied his face as he spoke. Even in this subdued lighting, she caught flecks of hidden light in those blue eyes. And had she ever before noticed how thick and long his eyelashes were? He still wore the hemp shirt and pants, which told her he'd come straight to her uncle's after the invitation. The stronger scent of apple cider also told her he'd taken the time to splash on more cologne.

For a pretty P.I. with long legs?

Reel it in, Cam. She poked a fork into her half-eaten salad. *That kind of wishful thinking made you miserable back in Denver, remember? He's here in Vegas because he wants you to work for him, nothing more. That's what you were, what you always will be—a business associate.*

"Tell us about one of your big cases," prodded Delilah. "Did you ever have one like those on *Law and Order?*"

"Want to share one of the cases we worked on?" Marc asked Cammie.

"Nope." She reached for another slice of garlic bread.

Marc stared at her for a moment, then turned his attention to Delilah. "One time I defended a dog owner who'd been charged with possessing a dangerous animal because it had bitten a cable-TV repairman who'd crawled, unannounced, over the owner's fence. The D.A. sought to have the owner fined and the dog destroyed."

"Oh, that poor animal!" Delilah exclaimed, clutching Frankie's hand. "What kind of dog was it?"

"Golden retriever," Marc answered.

"Oh, how sad!" She took a fortifying sip of her martini.

"Those are good dogs," added Frankie. "Lived next door to one years ago. Dog barked up a storm, but didn't have a mean bone in its body. Name was *Santo.*" He brushed a knuckle lightly across Delilah's chin. "That means *saint,* baby."

After they briefly kissed, Delilah looked at Marc. "Please tell us you saved that dog's life."

"After refusing to accept the D.A.'s deal, the case went to

trial. In my closing argument to the jury, I showed pictures of the dog as a puppy, and told how the dog had once pulled an infant child from the shallow waters of a backyard pool. Even the judge was brought to tears. Jury deliberated all of five minutes. Verdict—not guilty." He paused. "To this day, I still get a Christmas card from that owner with a picture of the dog and the child on Santa's lap."

"You're a *santo,* too." Delilah dabbed at the corner of her eye.

Cammie downed the rest of her glass of wine, wondering what else Saint Marc would share.

"That dog taught me a lot about life, Delilah," Marc said.

Obviously, she wasn't going to have to wait long.

"Loyalty, integrity, commitment," he continued. "After that case, I decided to give back to animals in need. I now provide pro bono services to Max Fund, a no-kill shelter in Denver."

This was getting deep, fast. Cammie reached for the bottle of wine.

"No," Marc said gently, "let me get that for you."

As Delilah and Frankie canoodled some more, Marc filled Cammie's glass. "Shame you left when you did," he said quietly, "because I could have used a top-notch investigator such as yourself on a case with Max Fund."

"That's me, top-notch investigator." She took a sip.

"Speaking of animal stories," Frankie said, a fresh lipstick smudge on his chin, "how's that cat you're helping?"

"Cat?" Delilah daubed at the smudge with her napkin. "But dear, you're allergic to kitty cats."

"Nah, it's been hanging around the back of the casino, right, Camilla?"

Cammie brushed a wayward curl out of her face. "Val and I have been bringing her scraps, and today I brought some cans of food. But it's time to find out if she has owners in the area. Figured I'd take her to the vet clinic tomorrow, see if she had one of those chips in her head."

A determined look crossed Delilah's face. "Dear, if you can't find an owner for the cat, I'll take it in. My little Maltipoo and kitty will be fine. I can keep her in the back room." She stroked Frankie's hand. "We're never near that room, sweetheart, so your allergies won't act up."

While the lovebirds whispered some more conspiratorial sweet nothings, Marc leaned closer to Cammie.

"Is something wrong?" he whispered.

"No."

"I don't believe you."

"Okay, yes."

After a beat, he asked, "Is it what I said in the car earlier today?"

She imagined a Nuggets jersey in her mind. A softer, muted blue unlike the explosive blue of Marc's eyes, which were actually filled with confusion and regret at the moment. No, probably just confusion. The regret was more wishful thinking.

"Let me take you to the vet appointment tomorrow," he whispered. "After all, you can't hold a cat and drive at the same time."

"You'd be surprised what I can do while driving. Remember the Housewright case? I took *exceptional* video footage while driving eighty-five miles an hour."

"Of course I remember. Your documentation broke the case—"

"That's me, all right. Private eye extraordinaire. I break cases, but never hearts."

"What's that supposed—"

"Wonderful! Dinner's here," cooed Delilah, pulling away from kissy-face with Frankie.

A few minutes into eating the main dish, Marc said, "I have an announcement."

In the moment of silence as everyone stopped eating, Frank Sinatra crooned over the speakers.

Marc turned slightly to Cammie. "I know you're currently…

unable to work as a private investigator in Nevada until your license is reinstated."

"But we're not discussing particulars," Frankie said.

Marc nodded politely. "However, Cammie, the case I mentioned to you? The one where I'd like you to conduct a locate, which might include some field work?"

The pasta in Cammie's tummy felt like a heavy rock. She nodded tightly.

"Did you also know that you can legally work for me, even as an unlicensed investigator in Nevada, because your work will be on behalf of my Denver law firm? As you're aware, Colorado currently doesn't require licensure for P.I.'s, so there's no issue with my retaining your investigative services."

"Cammie, dear, what a wonderful offer!" When Delilah clapped her hands together, the gold bracelets jingled softly.

"That's not all," Marc added. "I'd like to double your hourly rate, Cammie. First of all, you're worth it. Second, I'd like you to be able to pay off those fines as soon as possible because I know how much you dislike working at the casino." His voice lowered to a solemn tone. "And how much it means to you to be a licensed private investigator again."

"He's a champ," Frankie murmured.

As Sinatra's voice swelled with "Fly Me to the Moon," Cammie wished she could fly away, too. See what spring was like on Jupiter, Mars, anywhere but here. She'd had enough wine that she almost had enough false bravado to say the truth and screw the consequences. *Marc, I can't look for Gwen because she's everything I'd always hoped to be. The woman you loved, and the mother of your...our...*

Our?

Whoa!

Where did that come from? Unrequited crush was one thing, but Cammie wanting to be a mother with a child? No way. She had an analog clock in Phil, not a biological clock in herself. After all the years she'd spent being a parent to her own mother, the last thing she'd ever wanted, ever dreamed about, was having to take care of another human being. She'd spent long, painful years being responsible for her mother and cleaning up her messes. Sure, babies were cute. But they grew up and turned into hostile, smart-mouthed teenagers like the girls at Dignity House.

Fortunately, she didn't have to explain her silence because Marc's cell phone started chirping.

"Sorry," he said, retrieving it. "I usually turn off the ringer, but…" He checked the caller ID. "It's my daughter. I told her to call if she needed anything." He lifted the phone to his ear. "Hello, Emily?" He frowned. "What is it, honey?"

He stood abruptly and walked away from the table, his shoulders hunched.

When he was out of earshot, Delilah leaned forward. "Dear, that job offer sounds wonderful."

"You'd get a chance to do the kind of work you love again," added Frankie, "at double your usual."

"Uncle Frankie, you know I can't—"

"Can't what?" asked Delilah, looking from Cammie to Frankie.

He put his hand on Delilah's. "Speaking of good offers, I have one, too, which is another reason why I brought all of us here tonight. What d'ya think of our having the wedding reception here?"

"Here?" Delilah heaved a sigh. "Oh, Frankie, this place is perfect!"

"I mentioned it to the maître d' when I called. He said he'd drop by the table to discuss it, and this would be a perfect time with Marc away on a phone call. Camilla, would you mind asking him to drop by our table? I'd like for Delilah and me to ask him a few questions."

Cammie welcomed the opportunity to escape. She needed to breathe, regroup, imagine the Nuggets jersey.

But when she brought the maître d' over, Marc sat alone at the table.

"The other couple had to leave unexpectedly," Marc explained to the maître d', "but Delilah left her card, asked if you'd please call her tomorrow." Marc handed it to him.

"Certainly." The maître d' accepted it with a small bow. "Shall I have your dishes wrapped up to take home?"

"Please." Marc looked at Cammie. "You can take theirs home with you."

"Okay." She watched the maître d' walk away. "Why did they leave?"

"Delilah left her wallet at the chapel the other day, wanted to pick it up before the place closed."

"I thought Vegas chapels stayed open 24/7."

He shrugged. "Never been in one, have no idea. Told them I'd be happy to give you a ride home. Just need to drop by the hotel first and check on Emily. She said she heard noises in the hallway and that she's afraid. The room door's locked and bolted—no way someone can get in—but I called hotel security and insisted they get up there ASAP. They'll stay with her until I arrive." He punched a number into the cell. "Told her I'd call back, see how she's doing."

"Okay."

Cammie looked at the empty seats across from her. She didn't believe a word of that lost-wallet story.

CHAPTER SEVEN

A LITTLE AFTER NINE O'CLOCK, Marc and Cammie walked into his hotel room on the twentieth floor at the Aria, a luxury glass-and-steel high-rise on the strip. After passing through a foyer, they entered a spacious, modernistic living room with a wall-to-wall view of the twinkling lights of the strip. Trying not to look agog at the plush digs, Cammie set her purse and the doggie bag filled with garlic bread and Marc's pasta dish on the granite counter of a mini-kitchenette.

In Denver, she'd been inside Marc's house once, a high-end Tudor in Denver's fashionable Belcaro neighborhood, and it had the same kind of pricey charm as this room, although his home was much larger, of course. She remembered at the time thinking how empty the house felt, despite its expensive furniture and stylish decor.

In spite of the spacious design, hostility sucked all the air out of this living room. Emily and a female security guard sat at opposite ends of the long sofa. Both of them looked puffed up and pissed off.

"Mr. Hamilton?" the guard asked, standing. She adjusted the walkie-talkie on her belt.

"Yes." He looked at Emily. "You all right, honey?"

"I'm fine." Her face was freshly scrubbed and a scrunchie held back her mane of reddish-blond hair. She wore a nightshirt decorated with the words *Heal Our Planet*.

She cast a look at the guard. "I told her she could leave, but she insisted on staying."

Dressed in a black Acme Security uniform, the security

guard was physically fit with shiny black hair knotted at the base of her neck. She fixed her obsidian eyes on Marc. "You asked me to stay, sir, so I did." Her voice was cool, professional, but Cammie detected an underlying thanks-for-making-me-babysit-your-spoiled-brat tone.

"Thank you for complying with my request." He checked her name tag. "Iona, did you happen to see anyone suspicious in the hallway?"

"No, sir. Your daughter said somebody kept knocking and trying to use their room key, which, unfortunately, happens at least a dozen times a day. Usually, it's drunks who've forgotten their room number, or somebody gets off the elevator on the wrong floor and goes to a room they think is theirs. However, I asked security to check any surveillances tapes of this floor."

"They witnessed a person trying to get into the room?"

"Cameras didn't show the area directly outside your room, sir, but there was an elderly lady trying to use her room key on several other doors. We believe that is the person who was at your door, as well."

Emily gave her an incredulous look. "You could've told *me* that."

"When I tried," Iona said tightly, her gaze never leaving Marc's face, "you asked me to not interrupt your call with your father."

Cammie swore a look of pride flickered across Marc's face. "My fault," he said, serious again, "as I'm the one who insisted my daughter stay on the phone with me."

Which they had. The entire drive from the restaurant to the hotel. Cammie hadn't minded because it meant she and Marc weren't discussing whether or not she'd accept his job offer. She still didn't know what to do. Although she'd always prided herself on being a quick decision maker, lately her thoughts felt muddled and burdened, as though a fog had settled in on her life. She hoped that somewhere on the other side of that gray mass lay the answers to a lot of questions.

Marc pulled out his wallet, extracted two bills and handed them to the guard. "Thank you, Iona."

The guard rolled her shoulders. "You don't need to—"

"Please." He smiled. "You helped above and beyond your duties. Do you have children?"

"A little girl."

Cammie glanced at Iona's hand. No ring. Single mom, working night shift as a security job. Had to be difficult.

"Then do something nice for her," Marc said.

After a pause, she accepted the money. "Enjoy the rest of your stay at the Aria, Mr. Hamilton." She nodded to Cammie. "Mrs. Hamilton."

"Oh, I'm not—"

But Security Guard Iona was already striding toward the door, ready to tackle her next assignment.

"Did you get to see any of your movie with your friends?" Marc asked gently, sitting next to Emily.

"Some, not all." She shifted her gaze to Cammie. "You're the private investigator who worked for my dad. I remember you." She glanced at Cammie's hair.

"But not the weird hairstyle, right?" Cammie laughed. "That's okay. I hate it, too."

"Didn't say I hated it."

"Then you must need glasses."

Emily sputtered a laugh.

"My stepaunt-to-be insisted on giving me this hairstyle before dinner." Cammie did a dramatic eye roll. "I look like Little Richard on a bad-hair day."

Emily frowned. "Who's Little Richard?"

"Well, if you don't know who he is, you probably have no idea whose face this is." Cammie gestured to the sparkling design on her top.

"It's a guy in a hat."

"Philip Marlowe, private eye, in a fedora."

Emily stared at the design. "That's totally intense. I love

true-crime shows and detectives, but I don't know who Philip Marlowe is."

"He's one of the fictional variety. People mistakenly refer to him as hard-boiled, but they're wrong. It's the world that's hard-boiled, not Marlowe."

"I...hope I didn't offend you," Emily said softly, "saying it's intense."

"No offense taken." Cammie looked at her top. "I find it totally intense myself, in a good way."

"Speaking of offending people," Marc said gently, "I'm afraid you were a little chilly to Iona, who was only doing her job. If you're going to talk power to the proletariat, you also have to walk it."

"What does that mean?" Emily asked.

"It's not enough to talk about the need to respect a worker's democracy," he answered, "you also need to show people, especially hard-working people, respect."

"So you're saying I should've been more respectful to Iona."

"Yes."

"I didn't like my privacy being violated without my permission. She wouldn't leave."

"As long as you are in my custodial care, I define *privacy*. I think we've had this talk before."

After heaving a weighty sigh, Emily stared out the window.

"Hungry?" Marc asked. "We brought leftovers. Garlic bread and a killer pasta."

"Probably loaded with pesticides," she mumbled.

Marc's face seemed drawn and sad as he looked at his daughter, who continued to stare at the glittering lights of the strip. To some people, the display of neon and extravagant architecture was beautiful. To others, a garish display of commercialism. What you saw depended on your perspective, which was something Emily was still defining for herself.

Cammie decided to lighten the mood. "I read once that garlic is a natural antibiotic. Considering how much they put on that bread, it's probably killed off any pesticides."

She caught Emily's reflection in the glass. The girl wasn't staring at the lights, but watching Cammie.

"Are you going to find Gwen?" Emily asked.

Cammie did a double take. "I'm not sure what that has to do with garlic, but the answer is…I don't know."

"Why not?" Emily turned around.

"Yes, why not?" echoed Marc.

"We haven't really had a chance to discuss it." With both of them staring at her, she saw they shared the same vivid blue eyes. "Like the terms of the work, deadlines, expectations. I don't want to commit to anything without weighing the pros and cons."

"As Tolstoy said, 'Man discovers truth by reason only,'" Emily said solemnly, "'not by faith.'"

"I agree." Cammie crossed to where she'd left the doggie bag. "All that talk about garlic bread got me hungry. Mind if I nuke some?"

Emily made a face. "Yuck."

"I'll take that to be a no. Marc?"

"Sure."

As she fished in the bag, Cammie asked, "What else are you doing while in Vegas, Emily?" She extracted a cardboard box and set it in the microwave.

"Eating. I don't believe in shopping for the sake of spending money, but it was cool today finding a store that sells organic and hemp clothing. I like this room, but whenever we go down to the lobby, there's all these people drinking and putting money into machines." She feigned a shudder. "They look like zombies or something."

"If you think it's gross here, you should visit the dive where I work." Cammie punched a button on the microwave.

"Where's that?"

"Shamrock Palace. Trust me, it sucks. I also volunteer at a

center for teenage girls, which has its challenges, but it's also more rewarding."

"A center for teenager girls?" Emily asked.

"Actually, it's more like a home for girls who are struggling with life issues."

"Are they criminals?"

"Some have had run-ins with the law," Cammie admitted. "They've made poor choices, often the result of no support systems or families who haven't encouraged them to do their best. These girls end up with bad attitudes about themselves and life. Not like you, Emily. You know better because people have taught you the difference between right and wrong. Or smart and foolish. Or polluting and living green."

She paused, gave the young girl a thoughtful look. "I just had a thought. How about visiting Dignity House with me sometime? Your ideas would be a positive influence."

Emily looked at her feet for a long moment. "I'm not really… all that good with people."

Cammie exchanged a look with Marc, who gave a subtle shrug.

"Know what?" Cammie finally said. "Neither was I at your age. But restoring the earth is kinda like restoring people, don't you think? Just hanging with these girls means your ideas might rub off on them and as Tolstoy said, 'Plant an idea and it will grow.'"

The timer dinged.

"I've never read that one," Emily murmured.

"He was green before his time, what can I say." Cammie took the bread out of the microwave, set it on the coffee table and opened the cardboard flaps. Scents of butter and garlic infused the room. She crossed to the minifridge and opened it. "They stock diet colas in this place?"

"For like a million dollars each," Emily answered. She looked shyly at Marc. "Okay with you if I go to Dignity House with Cammie?"

"Fine by me. I'll even drop you off, save her the gas money." He raised his voice. "Help yourself to any of those drinks, Cammie. You're worth at least a million."

Those last words, said so low and earnestly, vibrated up her spine. Leaned over the still-open fridge door, Cammie glanced at his face, glad to see his mood had lifted. Was he affected by her reaching out to his daughter? Their relationship seemed strained, but maybe that was the nature of parents and teenagers. Or the by-product of not seeing each other often. He probably welcomed a woman stepping in, helping bridge the gap.

"Thanks for your offer, but I'll have tap water instead."

Emily rose from the couch. "It's been a long day. I'm going to bed." On her way to the bedroom, she paused, fiddled with the sleeve of her nightshirt. "Cammie?"

"Yes?"

"Maybe before I leave Vegas, you'd like to watch a true-crime show with me?"

"Like *48 Hours?*"

"Sure, or one where real-life P.I.'s, like you, solve crimes. I saw a show last week where this older Florida P.I. guy found a family's heirloom Bible. He must have been in his forties, but he rode a kick-ass Harley."

"Sounds cool," Cammie said. "So where'd this older kick-ass P.I. find the family Bible?"

Emily ambled to the bedroom. "In the—" she yawned "—remains of an alligator. G'night, everybody."

"Good night, honey," Marc said. "I love you."

The bedroom door closed with a soft click.

MARC LOOKED AT the closed door, wishing he understood what made his daughter tick. Sure, he got why she touted capitalistic exploitation and the organic movement—she was young, trying on her beliefs for size. Some might stay with her for the rest of her life, some might not fit in a year. When he was her age, he'd been passionate about Frank Zappa for president, which irritated his father no end. And although Marc wasn't all that comfortable with Emily's fondness for true-crime TV shows, obviously she got something out of them...including an introduction to the U.S. justice system.

But beyond her TV habits and her T-shirt slogans, he didn't really know what mattered in his daughter's world.

Didn't know why she couldn't say she loved him.

"In the remains of an alligator?" Cammie said in a stage whisper. "Whoa. I'm all into digging for clues, but I'd never go *that* deep."

His mind caught up with Cammie's comment. "Oh, you would," he said gently. "When you're hot on the trail of a case, Cammie, you're unstoppable."

"I draw the line at carcasses, though. Wouldn't want to chip my manicure." She caught him looking at her hands. "That was a joke."

He sort of smiled. "It's just that the rest of you looks...so put together...I figured you'd had your nails done, too."

"You call *this* put together?" She gestured dramatically to herself as though he'd missed something obvious.

"I do," he said quietly. "Obviously you don't see yourself the way the rest of the world does."

She eyed her reflection in the window. "Oh, I think I do." She blew out a low whistle. "Jeez, I'm wearing so much makeup, I look prepped for a viewing at the mortuary. And this hair! Add two white zigzags, and I could pass for the Bride of Frankenstein—"

"That's enough!" But he couldn't suppress a laugh. "Your wicked sense of humor is intact, but let me give you a different perspective." He looked at her hair. "Those beehive styles are back in vogue, you know. JLo wears them. Beyoncé. It's a dramatic style, which probably makes you uncomfortable because you like to blend in."

She looked surprised. "How do you know JLo and Beyoncé wear beehives?"

"The magazines in the waiting room at my office."

"And how do you know I like to blend in?"

"Any good investigator has that talent. But you're also uncomfortable being the center of attention."

She made a scoffing noise he didn't believe for an instant.

"As to the makeup," he continued, "you're right. Delilah slathered it on like a Gauguin Tahiti painting. I'd never let a client take the stand wearing that much makeup unless I had a point to make."

"A garish one."

"I prefer the word *bold*. Or *alluring*. After all, there's a reason why colorful stones and kohl residues have been found in archaeological digs. Makeup draws the attention of men."

A look of uncertainty clouded her face. "But I'm no Shopping Mall Queen. I'm…"

After a beat, he asked gently, "What are you, Cammie?"

"Tougher."

"Than a Shopping Mall Queen?"

"Than what it represents."

"Shallow, perfect?"

"And weak and unpredictable."

"Shopping Mall Queens are more complex than I realized. All right, I'll buy that you're tougher than a Mall Queen, but even Minnie Mouse is more rugged than one of those."

"But not as tough," she said in a mock gangster voice, "as Cammie Copello, Hard-Boiled Private Eye."

"Hard-boiled, eh?"

"Dat's right. Following scents right into da remains of alligators." She jutted out her hip and stuck out her index finger and thumb like a gun.

It was supposed to be play, but at that moment she looked like a fantasy pulp cover come to life. The overhead light gilded her piled-on hair, touched fire to her lips and fingered its heat through that gauzy material, down to the pale bare skin of her chest. And that look in her eyes... Was it his imagination or did those smoky eyes look hot enough to spark a fire?

Wait a minute. This was Cammie. They didn't exchange looks like that.

Did they?

But that look.

He dared to peer deeply into her eyes, which had lightened to a color he hadn't noticed before. A sparkling green like sunlight on water. He wondered what it would be like to fall into those eyes, learn what secrets lay deep below the surface.

"This is silly." With an awkward smile, she dropped her hands to her sides. "I've never even been to Florida, much less seen an alligator."

"Right," he whispered, his gaze dropping to the beaded, sparkling face, then sliding down farther to those form-fitting pants that sheathed her long, tight legs. "So silly," he murmured as his gaze traveled up the sultry, puzzling creature who'd taken over his former private investigator's boyish, businesslike self.

"I should go," she said. "I'll grab a taxi downstairs."

"Stay." He picked up the box. "There's garlic bread. And million-dollar sodas."

She gave him a funny look. "This is about the job, right? You want to talk about it."

"Right." He took a slow, calming breath. In these past few minutes, he'd forgotten all about that job, but yes, it was a topic that needed to be addressed.

He patted a spot on the couch next to him. "We'll take a few minutes and discuss the pros and cons, nosh on the best garlic bread this side of Denver's Little Italy, and I'll convince you that drinking expensive cola is better than no cola at all."

Either he was convincing or she was still hungry—more likely the latter—because she walked over, sat, slipped off her flats and plopped her bare feet onto the glass-and-chrome coffee table. Catching his stare, she quickly set them on the floor. "My bad."

"Relax," he said, "prop up your feet. I do it all the time at home."

"But there's nobody there to correct you."

"Just Emily once a year if I'm lucky."

"Once a year?" She put her feet up again and he did his best not to stare at her distracting legs.

"Kids her age—" he handed the box to Cammie "—are busy with friends and activities. It's not always fun to hop a plane and be stuck visiting a dad whose lifestyle and values are a throwback to another era. Plus she doesn't have any pals in Denver, no places to hang."

"Wherever you go, there you are," Cammie murmured before taking a bite of garlic bread.

He thought that phrase sounded familiar, like the title of a book he'd heard about. He didn't ponder it long and let them eat in silence for a while.

"About this afternoon..." Through the overpowering smell of garlic, he caught a hint of her sweet almond scent, which didn't help him remember whatever the hell he'd started to say.

"We didn't end on such great terms while sitting in Phil," she finished for him.

"Right. And I'm sorry for the inconsiderate things I said."

She cocked her head and looked at him. "Do you really think I moved to Vegas to be a felon?"

"I don't believe those are the words I used."

"To engage in felonious activities?"

Those were them. "Those were indefensible, rude words." They were sitting so close, their thighs pressed together. Although her jeans barely grazed his trousers, it felt as though he were being branded with her heat. "I, uh, can't remember exactly how you dissed me, but whatever you said, I forgive you, too."

"I said you weren't my boss anymore and that I don't owe you squat." She took another bite.

"Thank you, Miss Total Recall. Leading question, but I assume you're sorry for your words, too."

She nodded, chewing.

"While we're on the topic of me boss, you P.I., what's holding you back from taking the job? Because even if I say so myself, it's a wonderful offer."

A drizzle of butter edged down her chin. He reached over and swiped it, rubbed the drop of warm liquid between his fingers.

"Didn't want it getting on that beautiful top," he said, his gaze drifting to Phil's face. "Delilah did a great job."

He was trying to look at Phil's face. But he'd have to be blind to miss the soft mounds of her breasts underneath that filmy material.

Cammie nodded, swallowed. "I typically view her as being extreme Martha Stewart, but I love this beaded design of Philip Marlowe. You know, your dad borrowed *Farewell, My Lovely* from the prison library. That's what really broke the ice for us. We'd talk about Raymond Chandler's life and how we related to it."

"How?"

"The three of us had had fathers who abandoned their families. I'm not divulging a confidence because I know your dad talked about his family history to the press."

"I never heard you refer to your father."

She pursed her lips. "He left before I was born, so I never knew him. But in a way, it's as though he never left. His ghost, I mean. My mother must have really loved him, or maybe didn't love herself enough…whatever, she never got over his abandoning us." She thought for a moment. "In a way, she was like a Shopping Mall Queen."

"Weak and unpredictable?"

She nodded. "And I was her mother."

"The strong, stable one."

"I didn't always feel that way, but I tried. I'd put her to bed, get her clothes ready for the morning, cook for her. Well, not cook as in turn on the oven. Let's just say I can make any kind of sandwich imaginable."

"All while going to school."

"And not much else." She released a heavy sigh. "I hated to leave her alone. Every day at school, I'd worry what I'd find when I got home. To be honest, after years of being a parent to my mother, I've never wanted to have a child of my own."

It had never dawned on him to not have children, although these days he often wondered if having half a child was better or worse than having had none. He couldn't help feeling a spark of excitement at the prospect of another baby. Even if lying, thieving Gwen was the mother, he would be a good father.

Cammie gave a funny smile. "Remember when I was delivering those restitution checks to the victims on behalf of your father?"

The victims of his father's fraud. He nodded.

"At one house, a woman answered and stared at me as I explained I was there to deliver a restitution check on behalf of Harlan Hamilton. Without a word, she disappeared, then returned with a little girl, probably eight or nine, who explained that her mother was deaf and she would interpret for me. So I again explained why I was there and the little girl used sign language. The woman watched the little girl intently. After I'd finished talking, the woman looked confused. The little girl made a gesture…"

Cammie made a sign with open hands closing into fists that reminded him of catching someone who was falling.

"Later I learned this means *trust*." She gave her head a slow shake. "That really affected me because as a child, trust was never that simple."

She became preoccupied with her hands. "My fingers are all buttery from that garlic bread. Did they toss any napkins into that doggie bag?"

"There's a towel in the kitchenette. I'll get it."

Sitting back down, he took her hands in his and began wiping them with the towel, which he'd dampened with water from the tap.

"I can do that," she said.

But when she tugged, he held on.

"Let me," he whispered.

He stroked the damp cloth across her slim fingers, over the ridges of her blunt nails.

"My father sometimes told stories how his father, my grandfather, spent most of the day, seven days a week, managing a small textile plant. This resulted in my father's mother becoming a very lonely, unhappy woman. You'd think my father would have wanted to be different, but no. He also stayed away from home a lot, but unlike his father, he didn't pretend the marriage was working. Not for the first marriage…or the second or third ones, either."

He turned her hand over and lightly stroked the napkin along the inside of her palm. She took in a sharp breath.

"I thought I was smarter than my father and grandfather." He set down her hand, gently picked up the other one. He dabbed the cloth over her fingers. "But I've unwittingly continued the legacy. My grandfather was an absentee dad, as was my father, as am I."

"You're a good father to Emily."

"I try. But it's not about my intentions, it's that I see her so rarely. This visit is the first in ten months. Do you know how much a child can grow in ten months?" He squeezed Cammie's hand. "I loved seeing how she let her guard down with you tonight. She's like that with her granddad, too. Maybe he and I weren't close, but the two of them are."

"Harlan used to talk a lot about her."

"Emily likes you, too. For someone who doesn't want kids, you're awfully good with them."

"I guess being a caretaker is second nature. Besides, she's more like an adult than a teenager."

He nodded, growing somber. The corner of his mouth twitched, but he said nothing.

OVER THE NEXT FEW MOMENTS, as Cammie looked at Marc, it was as though she were seeing him for the first time—observing him with her eyes, and not her heart. He wasn't Santo Marc, the lawyer who saved abused puppies. And he wasn't the man who had destroyed her with a single kiss. He was just a guy with problems like everybody else.

His blue eyes were darker, the color of the sky at twilight. A lock of his hair curled like a question mark over his forehead. He looked more rested today, but that was surface only. She sensed how, inside, he was tired of what life had handed him. One child who'd become a reluctant visitor, another a secret within a woman who'd betrayed him. That treachery could mean the loss of his career, which, in turn, would likely seal a permanent loss of his father.

Impulsively, she swept the curl off his forehead. "You should move into a different house," she whispered. "One that's smaller, less lonely."

"But it's where we lived when Emily was born…"

His words trailed off, but the rest of the sentence was as clear as if he'd spoken it out loud. The big house contained all the memories, all the dreams, all his history. If he left, where would they go? Perhaps more daunting, who would he be?

"It's getting late, and I have work in the morning," Cammie said quietly. "About the job…I need to sleep on it, think some things over."

"What things?"

She'd shared parts of her life tonight with Marc that she hadn't discussed with anyone in years, if ever. And he'd shared his concerns about his life, his daughter. The fence was down. But they'd done more than simply share secrets—they'd bonded in a quiet, intangible way.

If there was ever a time to ask what had been heavy on her

heart for the past two years, now was it. She wanted to know. Needed to know.

"At a Christmas office party a few years ago…" She paused. "Do you remember our…dancing together?"

He quirked an eyebrow. "If it was at the party at Red Lion Inn, I'm afraid I was celebrating too much that night. We'd won that big case."

"Maxwell versus Richards," she murmured. "Yes, it was that party."

"Why, did I step on your toes?"

More like my heart. "Obviously you don't remember that night all that well, but there's something I want to ask." She took a deep breath. "Have you ever…had feelings for me?"

A perplexed look flickered in his eyes. "Feelings?"

Men, even the smart variety, could be so damn dense sometimes.

"Romantic feelings." There. She'd said it.

"You mean, have I ever been attracted to you?"

Really, really dense. "Yes."

"No."

No hesitation. Just a simple, direct no. She felt like an idiot for asking.

"Why?" he asked.

He hadn't had feelings for her then or ever.

She sat next to him, immobile, as the seconds stretched into minutes. During that span of time, she was vaguely aware of the distant whir of a helicopter outside, the trace of apple cider in the air, the strangely intent expression in his eyes.

Most of all, she felt the dull, aching thud of her heart as it absorbed the truth.

He'd never, not even once, viewed her as more than Cammie Copello, his private investigator. If only she could be as hard-boiled as they'd joked about earlier, his answer might have hurt less.

The painful spell vaporized and time slogged back to normal. She looked around the room. Nothing had changed. Down on the strip, neon marquees sparkled. Marc still had that puzzled look as he stared at her.

But she'd changed. It wasn't so much that the truth hurt as growing wiser did. She'd always thought the term *growing pains* referred to physically growing, but it was as agonizing, maybe more so, to grow emotionally.

With great effort she stood, crossed to her purse and picked it up. Her back was to him, but she didn't turn around. She'd seen, heard, felt enough. Call it pride, but she didn't want him to see the injury stamped on her face. Even a ton of makeup couldn't hide that.

As she walked toward the door, he said something but she didn't pay attention. Had to go, get away as fast as she could. Stepping into the hallway, she shut the room door behind her and blew out a long-held breath.

As she headed down the hallway to the elevators, she swiped a tear off her cheek.

CHAPTER EIGHT

A LITTLE AFTER ONE the following afternoon, Cammie was back at the Cave, strapped into her corset and dealing cards to a sixtysomething woman whose platinum pageboy matched the color of her pearls. She had been sitting at the gambling table for several hours playing poker while smoking gold-tipped cigarettes and nursing a gin and tonic. None of the activities seemed to entertain her, as though gambling was more of a duty than fun.

R.J. materialized next to Cammie, a cup of coffee in his hand. "Yer doc appointment," he growled. "Time f'you t'go."

Cammie nodded in agreement. When she got into work this morning, she'd told him she had a doctor's appointment at two o'clock and needed to leave work early. The appointment was actually for Trazy with a vet.

A shimmer of movement caught her attention. Across the casino, near a bank of slot machines, Delilah waved at Cammie. The older woman wore a shiny metallic outfit that made her look like a life-size bullet. A bullet with cleavage, of course.

Delilah mouthed something while pointing to her feet.

Cammie frowned. "What?" she mouthed back.

A ridiculous exchange because it was impossible to hear with all the jingling slot machines and buzzing conversations, and she doubted either of them could lip-read at twenty feet.

Delilah leaned over and straightened, holding high some kind of box that sparkled under the overhead lights. She mouthed something again.

"Wha's Del holding?" R.J. flicked his lighter and fired up a cigarette.

"Something from her gift shop, I guess." Cammie slid a new hand of cards to the woman at the table.

"Why's she pointing at th'exit?"

Delilah, the glittery contraption in one hand, pointed the other at the door. Her red-slicked lips dramatically shaped more words.

"S'mthin about taking it outside," R.J. interpreted.

"Impressive," Cammie muttered. But then, after several decades being a pit boss and keeping an eagle eye on everyone and everything, R.J. could probably read lips in the next county.

"Therz th'guy again," he groused.

Next to Delilah stood a tall man wearing a pair of jeans and a blue T-shirt. He was pointing at the exit, too.

Marc.

Cammie's heart stuttered as her mind attempted to rein in her swirling thoughts.

He still wants an answer.

He never had feelings for me.

Damn, he looks hot.

"I've got to get off ground zero," Cammie mumbled. "Make up my mind, face the facts, get on him."

Over the top of her cards, the woman's gray eyes peered curiously at her.

"I meant *over* him," Cammie corrected.

R.J. exhaled a stream of smoke as he continued staring at Delilah. "Why sh'keep holding tha'disco ball?"

A stressed-looking dealer dressed like Alice Cooper approached R.J. The two of them stepped away, discussing something in low tones.

"Life's a little like poker," the woman said in a gravelly voice. "You either accept the hand you're dealt, or you shake it up and make it different. If I were you, ducky, I'd stick with *on*." She slid several cards toward Cammie. "Three, please."

A bit taken aback, Cammie was dealing the cards when Val sidled up next to her.

"Where y'at?" Val wore a new curly blond wig and a scantier version of her already scanty sailor outfit.

"I'm okay."

"Uh-huh." Val smiled at the woman, who nodded before taking a sip of her drink.

"You got yourself a humdinger cat carrier for Trazy," Val said.

Across the room, a smiling Delilah held up the sparkling kitty carrier.

"Saw it earlier when I was in the gift shop getting gum," Val continued. "Has a little mirror inside and some mice made out of pink felt. Supercute." Her heavily mascaraed eyes opened wide. "Hold me down, mama. Is that guy next to Del your lawyer boy?"

R.J., like a vampire, materialized again in a cloud of cigarette smoke. "Val, back t'yur table. Cammie, Jeffrey's taking over. On yur way out, tell Del and th'boyfriend of yours to stop distracting my dealers."

"He's not my—"

But R.J. was making a beeline to another table where a drunk was arguing with the dealer.

Cammie turned to the woman who calmly laid out her cards. "Full house," she said.

"You're telling me," Cammie murmured.

Minutes later, Cammie was changing her clothes in the employees' locker room when Val entered.

"Delilah said to tell you she's put the kitty carrier outside the exit door, the one we leave by on breaks. Ya know, where we first found Trazy."

"Is Marc out there, too?"

"Oh, Lord, I hope so. That boy's so hot, you could fry an egg on 'im." Seeing the look on Cammie's face, Val turned serious. "Aw rite, 'fess up, Snooper. What you done gone and done?"

"We had a heavy talk last night."

"How heavy?"

"I asked him if he'd ever had feelings for me."

"Extra heavy. What'd he say?"

"No."

Val winced. "Ouch."

"Yeah."

"What about his job offer?"

Cammie shot her a glare. "He made that offer last night over dinner. How do you know about it?"

"You're not the only one who knows how to snoop."

"Delilah said something," Cammie guessed.

"And it sounds like a sweet deal. So where y'at?"

"He still wants me to take it. I think."

"You don't know?"

"I left right after he said he'd never had feelings for me."

"No talk? You just up and left?"

Cammie nodded.

"Where were you?"

"His hotel room."

Val arched a shapely eyebrow. "You leavin' out the good parts of this story?"

Cammie rolled her eyes. "We weren't in his bed, if that's what you're referring to."

"Shame. But walking out without saying goodbye? That's cold, girl."

"Didn't mean to be. I was afraid if I spoke I'd—"

"Show your feelings," Val finished. "Okay, rewind to the job-offer part. Who said what last?"

"I said I'd think about it."

She considered this for a moment. "Okay," she finally said, "it's time to stop thinkin' and take it." She held up her hand to halt Cammie from butting in. "You told me once that being a P.I. meant you worked alone a lot. Finding this Gwen person means the most contact you'll have with lawyer boy is an occasional phone call, right?"

"We may need to meet in person. Sometimes there's paperwork to go over, that sort of thing."

Outside the lounge, there was a loud electronic screech followed by thumping noises on a microphone.

"Ladies and gentlemen," announced a male voice, "it's time for our hourly superstar show on the Shamrock a-Go-Go Stage!"

Another screech and a muted curse. "Sorry, ladies and gentlemen, but we're experiencing a minor technical difficulty. Just a few moments and we'll be ready."

Val checked herself in the mirror. "I keep tellin' you to get past your brain side, Snooper, but maybe I'm wrong. That brain side can protect your heart, make it possible for you to work together again."

"But I'm tired of being Miss Unrequited! It makes me feel so…pathetic."

Val leveled her a look. "Lots of things in life are worse than bein' around somebody you're hung up on. So you're sweet on him. His deal's sweet, too. What you got here is a real candy man ready to give you some goodies, like being a private eye again, and you're worried about your heart? Get over it. You and me got a business in our future, and you stagnating in heart troubles ain't gonna get us there. Got it, Sherlock?"

Cammie stared into her friend's eyes, reminding herself that one of the things she most liked about her friend was her straightforward style, but ordering her to work again with Marc? That crossed the line, damn it.

But, hell, Val had a point.

A good one.

Marc was opening a door and Cammie would be a fool to not walk in.

"Got it, Watson," she quietly answered.

A FEW MINUTES LATER, Cammie stepped outside. Breezes whipped the air. A blackbird swept through the air with a piercing ki-ki-ki. In the shaded area underneath a bottlebrush tree sat the sparkling kitty crate like a hidden treasure. On the top of the crate, the word *Trazy* shimmered in pink.

"Hi, Cammie," said a familiar voice.

With her long hair pulled back in a braid, wearing a pink-and-orange tie-dye dress and sandals, Emily looked like a throwback to the 1960s. Except the shadows in her face didn't reflect peace and love.

"What's wrong?" Cammie asked.

Emily shrugged. "Nothing."

As if Cammie believed that. She looked around. "Marc here?"

"In the car." She gestured toward the sea of cars in the lot. "We're parked next to that tall palm tree. The green Prius. Runs on gas and electricity."

Cammie had a good idea who picked that out. She hadn't paid much attention to the eco-car last night when she rode with Marc to the hotel. "You're a good influence on your father."

"I try."

"Are you coming with us to the vet?"

"I've got a cat allergy." She rubbed at her nose in a very unconvincing way. "I volunteered to stay here with Trazy until you came out. Somebody named Delilah's picking me up—I'm going to hang in her gift shop."

Before Cammie could ask how that came about, the girl continued talking.

"That cat looks so doo-doo-mama in her glitter crate. Did you know there's even a cat-size mirror in there?"

"I heard. Doo-doo-mama?"

Emily shrugged. "You know, so out of fashion."

"Like a smashed disco ball."

The corners of the girl's mouth quirked. "Yeah, like that. I mean, who puts glitter on a cat crate?"

As though on cue, the back door to the casino opened. Delilah stepped outside.

Cammie didn't think she'd ever seen someone's mouth literally drop open, but at the moment Emily's did.

"Darling, you're as adorable as Marc said. I'm here to escort you to the gift shop. We'll have to walk past the fun stuff because you're underage, but when you're twenty-one, Aunt Delilah will show you how to play backgammon and order the perfect martini."

"What's going on?" asked Cammie, filling the gap for the stunned Emily.

"I'm giving Emily a lesson in retail management," Delilah said, "and if there's time, I'll teach her to knit, as well."

"I meant," Cammie said, "what's with the vet appointment intervention?"

Delilah pursed her shiny red lips. "We're…helping you, dear. By the way, Frankie mentioned that tomorrow is your day off, and I've had a wonderful idea! Let's try on bridal dresses at Bergstrom's Bridals in the morning. They have the cutest line of gowns called Princess Fantasies, which are utterly enchanting. They come in all kinds of yummy pastels—I think you'd look fabulous in a peach or apricot."

Two words flashed through Cammie's mind. *Oh, crap.*

"Delilah," Emily said softly, "would you mind giving me a moment alone with Cammie? I have something to say to her."

"Of course, dear! I'll wait for you just inside this door."

Emily smiled awkwardly. "I don't want to lie to you. I don't have an allergy. And I don't really want to do this gift shop thing—"

"At least you're not stuck in a Princess Fantasy. A fruit one at that."

"Yeah, that sucks. If it helps, you don't look anything like the princess type."

"Thanks. I guess." Cammie gave her head a shake. "Anything else, or did you want to hang out here and commiserate about being stuck in Delilah's retro-glitter world?"

The girl hung her head for a moment. When she lifted it, her eyes were filled with confusion and pain. "I never liked Gwen. I don't know exactly what happened, only that he might lose his law license over something she did. He's so…zonked over this." Emily worked her mouth as though she wanted to continue talking, but no words came out.

"I, uh, never liked Gwen, either, but we don't need to say more than that on the subject."

Emily started pacing. "Ever since we got to Vegas, he's been happy. Not crazy happy or anything like that, but happier. But then I haven't seen him in so long, I don't know what's happy for him anymore." She halted, kneaded the air with her hands as though shaping an idea. "I think he's happier because he believes you're going to help him. I mean, who else can?" She started pacing again. "My mother should, you'd think, but she's too busy nonproductively consuming time. Anyway, my parents are like Tolstoy and Shakespeare, you know?"

Cammie was mentally jogging to keep up with the girl's random thoughts. "No, I don't."

"Tolstoy was repulsed by Shakespeare. Called him stupid, tedious, worn-out. That's kinda how my mom talks about my dad. I have to listen to that stuff all the time and I hate it. I tell her I don't want to be in the middle, but she doesn't listen to me, doesn't respect how I feel, just goes on and on how he didn't watch over his own dad well enough. That my grandfather is no better than a common criminal, and his imprisonment tainted their law practice and its earning capacity." She swiped at her flushed face. "Did you know I haven't seen my granddad in person since he went to prison? I'm too young, they say, to be allowed visitation rights because he is my grandfather, and juveniles are only allowed to visit natural or stepparents."

"I'm sorry, Emily."

"My mom… It's always about money. I guess whatever happened with Gwen is about money, too, but nobody tells me. I'm not stupid, though. A lawsuit's brewing."

The girl abruptly stopped pacing, clutched her arms around herself and drew in a shaky breath.

"My mom's getting ready to marry her fourth husband. Some guy named Barry or Bernard. All I know about him is he has *earning capacity.* That's all she cares about! Not if I'm doing well in school or if I have any *real* friends or if—" She clamped shut her quivering lips.

Cammie waited, but Emily didn't say more. The palm fronds swished in the breezes and Trazy meowed.

"You're upset," Cammie said gently. "Are you sure you don't want to come with us to the vet's?"

"No," Emily whispered. Brushing at the corner of her eye, she continued, "I know how much he wants to hire you. I wanted you two to be alone and talk more about it."

Cammie glanced at the Prius. Marc sat in the front seat, watching them. Seemed another talk was inevitable.

Looking at the girl, Cammie pondered her comment about not having any real friends. Wasn't last night's movie-and-tweeting supposed to be with her friends? Maybe there'd been a recent falling-out with one of them. Or maybe Emily was tired of hanging out with grown-ups all the time.

Cammie remembered the idea she'd had last night.

"We talked about your visiting Dignity House—how about we do that later today? I'm supposed to be study monitor, meaning I sit with them while they pretend to do their home-work. After that, I'm overseeing dinner preparation for the first time. My idea of cooking is to make a sandwich, so I'm going to need help."

Emily perked up. "I could bring some organic fruits we picked up yesterday and make a salad."

"Excellent. Tell your dad to drop you off anytime after five. I'll text him directions." She headed toward the kitty carrier. "I should be going—"

"If he loses his law license," Emily said, following her, "what will become of him?"

Cammie thought about Marc in that big house by himself, alone, no career, living with too many ghosts. A sad picture but not her problem. He'd already said that he didn't care about her. Didn't share her unrequited feelings. "He'll figure it out."

"Please, Cammie. You're his last hope."

A dramatic plea from an impassioned teenager, but it resurrected memories of her own life at Emily's age. "You understand, don't you, that it's not your job to take care of your dad."

"That's why I'm asking you to help."

And that was the difference between Emily and herself. Cammie had often resented being a caretaker, but she'd kept her frustration and her pain bottled up, had been afraid to reach out. There had been her uncle, of course, but Cammie hadn't fully opened up to him, or anybody else. Maybe if she had, somebody would have stepped in and changed hers and her mother's lives for the better.

Emily had been brave to admit her fears.

In a rush of understanding, Cammie realized that life wasn't always about weighing the pros and cons until finding the perfect balance, because there were no foolproof answers. Sometimes making a decision was simply about doing the next right thing.

"I'll find her."

A hesitant smile replaced Emily's frown. "You promise?"

"I promise."

As she headed with the carrier to the parking lot, Cammie prayed to God that she didn't break that promise.

CHAPTER NINE

SITTING IN HIS CAR, Marc watched Cammie approach. The sun sparked off the glittering carrier in her arms. When they'd worked together in Denver, she'd walked like she did today with a jaunty confidence.

But now he saw so much more. In his mind's eye, he could still see the Cammie who looked meltdown sexy in a corset, fishnet stockings and heels. Alongside that image was Cammie from last night in that wild beehive, vibrant makeup and a top that shimmered and teased like a bon-ton burlesquer.

He'd always known the purposeful, pragmatic woman striding toward him. But now he'd had glimpses of the other layers beneath that surface—an alluring Cammie, a dramatic Cammie and, maybe the most surprising, a hesitant, secretive Cammie.

He got out of the car and headed toward her. As they neared each other, he caught the glint of uncertainty in her eyes.

She stopped, her long dark curls lifting with the breezes.

"I'll take that," he said, reaching for the carrier.

"It's not that heavy."

"Humor me."

She acquiesced and he carried it to the Prius, placing it on the backseat.

"I suppose I have no say about you going to the vet appointment with me."

"I suppose you're right. Frankie said the appointment's at two, and it's not very far from here, which leaves me a few minutes to—" he reached in the open passenger window and retrieved a small pink cardboard box off the seat "—give you this gift."

"What is it?"

"Open it and see for yourself."

She peeked inside. "Doughnuts!"

"From Ronald's Doughnuts. Em found it—place is run by Buddhists, and 80 percent of their doughnuts are vegan. She insisted we buy you a few of those, but the honey glazed are the real deal. Hope these make you forget the ones you miss at Snooze." He returned her appreciative smile. "*Some* things I remember."

"Can't believe you did this."

"I'm trying to be sweet. How am I doing?"

"Quite well." She lifted out a doughnut. "I skipped lunch and I'm famished."

"Go for it."

She flicked her tongue on the icing and emitted a small groan. "Tastes like honey."

"That's one of the honey glazed." He cleared his throat. "I was going to get their apple fritters, but I wasn't sure…"

Of what he had no idea. Hell, watching her take a slow, nibbling bite, he wasn't even sure of his own name. With her eyes closed, she pursed and puckered her lips, then chewed slowly, methodically, while a low-throttled sound of pleasure emanated from somewhere deep within her.

Blowing out a puff of pent-up air, he shoved his hands into his pockets and watched her run the tip of her pink tongue around her lips before taking another smacking bite. She didn't look at him, didn't comment on how tasty it was, she just *ate,* caught up in a glazed world where nothing existed but her and that doughnut.

It was almost indecent to watch.

His gaze dropped to her T-shirt and the rosy tips that pressed through the thin material.

She's not wearing a bra.

Best to not look at her at all. With affected nonchalance, he glanced around, forced himself to think about the Broncos and whether they would ever win the Super Bowl again. Was Elway out of his mind to ditch Tebow for Manning?

Was *Marc* out of his mind to not have realized before now that Cammie was an exciting, attractive woman? And to think last night when she'd asked him if he'd ever had feelings for her, he'd answered no.

"Yes," she murmured.

Taken aback, he looked at her. She was licking her fingers. Her sugary, honey-glazed fingers.

"Yes?" he repeated.

"Yes, I accept your job offer, but I was ready to say that before being bribed with doughnuts."

"Then give me back that box," he teased, reaching for it.

"No!" With a laugh, she fell against the side of the car, clutching the box to her chest.

"I said give it to me," he growled, stepping closer.

Grinning, she thrust the box over her head. "And I said no!"

He caught a whiff of her almond lotion. "You know I could take them from you."

Winds feathered her hair. Her eyes sparkled with mischief. "You and what army?"

He stretched out his arms and, in a flash of movement, circled both wrists with one hand while snatching the box with the other, then set the box on top of the car.

Standing there, the two of them sharing ragged breaths, he pressed even closer, shackling her taut body with the mass of his own. Her long legs intertwined with his. Her soft breasts yielded against his chest.

"Cammie," he whispered, sliding his hands down her back and drawing her to him.

Her arms dropped around his neck. Her hot face brushed his cheek. Red-hot urges blasted through him at the feel of her body pressed against his, the scents of honey and almonds, the puffs of her warm breaths on his ear.

If he hadn't been attracted before, he hadn't been paying attention.

Hanging on to his last shred of lucidity, he pulled back his head and looked at the sky. Was vaguely aware of the splintered sunlight through the swaying fronds, the hum of traffic, the unintelligible chatter of people walking through the lot.

He was acting like a fool, an adolescent instead of a man. Clumsy and greedy. He was Mr. Cool, who always strategized the game plan, stayed in control. Pinning Cammie against his car in broad daylight was sheer juvenile madness.

He looked at her.

She appeared dazed, a little bewildered. The sunlight pierced her wide-open green eyes, sparking hidden flecks of gold.

Stepping back, his words rumbled up from his chest. "I'm sorry."

Her arms dropped limply to her sides. She nodded once, slowly.

"We need to get to the vet appointment," he muttered, smoothing his palms along the sides of his jeans.

She stood there, looking confused. Her lips parted.

"What?" he prodded.

"Those are some doughnuts," she murmured.

ON THE DRIVE TO THE VET'S, Marc and Cammie didn't talk about what had happened in the parking lot. Instead they sat quietly, listening to a local jazz station on the radio, punctuated with mewls and cries from Trazy. Cammie was feigning cool on the outside, but inside she was one with that cat. The near meltdown in the parking lot had her internally mewling for more.

But as she listened to Billie Holiday croon "All or Nothing At All," she was also glad nothing more had happened. She'd already been through a similarly hot interlude with Marc two years ago. Hot stuff happened, and then he acted as though it never had. Except this time he could never claim he didn't remember.

It crossed her mind that maybe he behaved this way with random women and thought nothing of it. But it was too cliché, too convenient, to slap a label of Neanderthal on a guy like Marc.

Whatever had happened, obviously he didn't want to talk about it, and truth be told, neither did she. Especially as she'd accepted the job, it was wise to get down to business and not mix pleasure into it. Wading into gray zones—legal or romantic—could only cause problems.

At the vet's, they learned Trazy didn't have a chip, so the cat was officially ownerless. On the drive to the Shamrock Palace, Cammie called Delilah, who was delighted to take Trazy into her home. Cammie said she'd drop off the cat at the gift shop.

After that, she told Marc how she'd invited Emily to visit Dignity House that night. "That's okay with you, right?"

"I think so, but tell me a little more about the place."

"It's a nonprofit residential facility, mostly privately funded, but there are some state grants to offset the costs, similar to foster care. There are always at least two adults to supervise twelve to fourteen girls."

"You mentioned that it was mostly court-ordered kids," he said. "Any dangerous offenders?"

"Dignity House isn't juvenile detention. These girls are troubled. Or they're troublemakers. But they aren't hard-core. This facility is a chance for them to get their act together."

He seemed pleased, agreed to drop her off around six. "It'll be good for Emily to be around other teenagers who aren't pampered and spoiled."

His words struck her as a harsh assessment of Emily's friends. Did he also view Emily as being that way? Cammie had gotten to know a different girl, one whose feelings—especially the hurt over her fractured family—ran deep.

She debated whether or not to share some of the things Emily had said—her angst about her mother, the impending fourth marriage, her worries over Marc—but decided it wasn't her place to be in the middle. When the opportunity presented itself, she'd encourage Emily to open up to her dad.

When Marc parked in the Shamrock Palace lot, he turned off the ignition and turned to Cammie.

"I'm only in Vegas for a few days," he said, all businesslike. "We need to move fast on this case. I'd like to meet as soon as possible to go over leads to Gwen's whereabouts."

"Okay."

"Tomorrow morning?"

"Promised Delilah I'd meet her to try on bridal gear."

"Afterward?"

"That works. I'll give you a call when we're wrapping up."

As she exited the passenger side, Marc got out of the car, too. He walked around to meet her.

"I'll bring the carrier inside." He retrieved the pink box and handed it to her. "Don't forget these."

How could she?

They walked through the casino, surrounded by jangling slot machines and people whooping and groaning, depending on whether they were winning or losing, at the gaming tables. As they entered Winning Gifts, Delilah's gift shop, they found Emily sitting behind the counter, wrestling with a pair of knitting needles and a wad of yarn. Next to her, Delilah sat with her own needles and yarn, a pair of reading glasses perched on her nose.

"Tighten slightly, dear," Delilah instructed. "That's right. Now— Oh, hello!"

Marc set the carrier on the end of the counter. "Here's your new family member."

"Wonderful!" Delilah stood and peered inside the crate door. "Welcome to the family, Miss Trazy. I'll be escorting you to your new home shortly."

Emily held up a needle with a row of uneven stitches. "My first knitting project! Aunt Del gave me this organic yarn, which is veggie-dyed. Isn't that cool? It's called Pakucho, and it's from Peru."

Aunt Del? Even Cammie didn't call her that, although technically Delilah would be her aunt in a matter of weeks. Obviously the older woman and Emily had bonded quickly.

"That's great, Em," Marc said quietly.

Cammie couldn't interpret the look on Marc's face, which seemed downcast yet tender.

Emily looked at the pink box Cammie was holding. "How'd you like the doughnuts?"

"Good," Cammie snapped.

"Fine," Marc said at the same time.

Emily, oblivious to their curt responses, continued chattering. "I found Ronald's Doughnuts on the internet when I looked up *vegan doughnuts.* Did you know they've been voted best doughnuts in Las Vegas several times and that people travel from other states, even other countries, just to buy their stuff? I got a Boston cream vegan when we picked up your gift, and it was delish!" Emily opened the box. "Oh, the vegan ones are still here. Cammie, want to try one?"

"No." Her gaze swept past Marc, Delilah and Emily, and back to the box. "I mean, maybe later," she mumbled, "when I'm alone."

After giving Cammie a questioning look, Delilah turned to Marc. "I invited Emily to join Cammie and me tomorrow morning while she and I try on dresses for the wedding. Is that all right with you?"

"Certainly."

"Only problem is, as much as I'd love to pick up your lovely daughter at your hotel, I live at the other end of town. Would it be too much trouble for you to drop her off?"

"No problem."

"Wonderful!" Delilah smiled so broadly, Cammie swore she could count every tooth.

Marc looked at Cammie. "I could find a coffee shop nearby, wait there until you're through."

Delilah perked up. "Oh! You two are getting together tomorrow?"

"Just for a meeting," Cammie said abruptly.

"Meeting," Marc echoed, nodding his head.

"Wonderful! You know, Bergstrom's Bridals is in a renovated Victorian home. Very quaint, with an elegant sitting area where everyone sips champagne and eats French pastries. Much better to wait there than at some stuffy old coffee shop."

Cammie picked up on where this was going. "He wants to drink coffee, not champagne—"

"Oh, there's coffee, too, dear. Plus, there'll be plenty of time for you two to meet, both while I'm conferring with Mr. Bergstrom and in between your dress fittings."

You're not my mother.

The words bubbled up so quickly inside Cammie, it took her a moment to mentally catch up. Of course Delilah wasn't her mother. In fact, Cammie couldn't think of once that she'd ever compared Delilah to her mom.

But this wasn't about her mother—it was about not sharing this event, the kind mothers and daughters should share together. Until this moment, Cammie hadn't realized that some secret part of her wished her mother had lived to participate in such life passages. Wished that tomorrow morning she'd be meeting her mom at that bridal salon, the two of them giggling over silly princess dresses, when instead she'd be meeting Delilah and acting serious. Or trying to.

It wasn't fair or rational to resent Delilah for that, but Cammie did.

On the other hand, it was absolutely fair to resent the older woman for creating yet another trumped-up reason for her and Marc to meet in a romantic place. Cammie could try to put a halt to this, but that would be about as useful as yelling *stop* at a locomotive barreling downhill with no brakes. Easier to simply accept that there would be ridiculous matchmaking activities over the next few days and to ignore them.

"I need to go," Cammie said, picking up the box of doughnuts. "I'm submitting my resignation today at the Shamrock."

"Oh?" Delilah looked very interested.

"Yes, I've accepted Marc's job offer."

Before Delilah could emit another "Wonderful!" Cammie quickly continued, "Emily, your dad will be dropping you off at Dignity House around six."

The girl clapped her hands. "Wonderful!"

THAT NIGHT AT DIGNITY HOUSE, Takira kept trying to lead the girls in another Dinki Mini dance, claiming she needed to practice it for the school talent show. Cammie countered that unless the public school system was now staging burlesque shows, Takira wasn't performing the Dinki Mini there *or* here, and if the girls didn't start opening their books, study hour would end at eight instead of six.

After some grumbling and looks, the girls settled into their studying. Except for Amber aka Daearen, whose nose had been in her social studies book the entire time. Cammie had asked her a few questions to get the girl to open up, but Amber only offered monosyllabic answers, if that.

At six o'clock, one of the resident counselors, a prematurely gray thirtysomething with earnest eyes, joined them and herded the girls to the kitchen. Volunteers like Cammie often worked study hour by themselves; otherwise there were always two adults on the premises. Posted in every room was also the phone number for an on-call nurse.

While waiting for Marc and Emily's arrival, Cammie sat on the porch in a white plastic chair, watching the winds torment a couple of trees across the street. Dignity House sat on a couple of acres with no other houses in the immediate vicinity. The isolation was a good thing. Most neighborhoods aren't thrilled to have a facility like this next door.

From the porch, Cammie looked to the west, across a wide, flat, dull-colored landscape of scrub and juniper, to the jagged outline of rocky foothills. In the distance, she could see the snow-covered peak of Mount Potosi. She hadn't done a lot of exploring outside Las Vegas, but Frankie had told her that the town of Pahrump was in this direction. She'd like to go there. Mainly because saying "Pahrump" made her grin. And the town was the site of the famous Chicken Ranch, a legendary brothel. Pahrump might have some interesting stories to tell.

The strong gusts of warm air made her skin itchy. Or maybe it was being a P.I. again.

Each investigation was like taking a road trip. You knew the destination, but nobody handed you a map for how to get there. Sometimes you bounced over a clue before realizing its importance, other times you ran smack into a dead end. Good news or bad, you kept moving forward—or what you hoped was forward—to find the answer.

When she'd worked at Hamilton & Hamilton, she knew Gwen well enough to say "Good morning," "Have a good night" and "Are the checks ready?" Otherwise, they didn't talk. Cammie dredged her memories for any recollections of photos or mementos on Gwen's desk. She'd often seen a lipstick-stained coffee cup with a logo of a chicken on a skateboard, which had always struck Cammie as odd because Gwen didn't have much of a sense of humor. There were no pictures of family, not even of Marc. A large mirror. Of course.

Otherwise the desk had always been neat. Immaculate, even. Like somebody who hadn't planned on staying long?

The Prius parked at the curb. Marc and Emily exited, the breezes fussing with Marc's hair. Emily, smart girl, wore hers in a long braid.

He wore the same blue T-shirt and jeans that he'd worn that afternoon. She swore she could still smell his apple-cider scent, feel the hard contours of his body pressed against hers, see that look of need in his eyes.

Damn those doughnuts anyway.

"Hi." Marc stepped onto the porch, dragging his hand through his mussed hair. "Winds are picking up."

"Locals say it's only windy in the fall and spring, and after that, the rest of the year." She mentally congratulated herself on sounding upbeat and pretty darn near close to normal.

"That's why the Indians named this place Las Vegas," he said. "It means 'hold on to your hats.'"

"I didn't know that," she said.

"Made it up." He winked.

"Huh." She'd never seen him wink before. Seemed they were both trying to be their best light-and-bright selves.

"Good to see you, Emily." Cammie peeked in the fabric bag the girl carried. "Wow, look at all that food!"

"We picked up some extra things at the organic market," she said proudly.

"Cool. Everybody's in the kitchen. Follow me."

The kitchen was at the rear of the house. It was a large room, the result of combining the original much smaller kitchen and a glassed-in patio. In its former life, the tri-level house had been a men's room-and-board residence, and the proprietress and her family had cooked meals back here. As Dignity House, the girls and staff together cooked all meals, a task meant to foster the mission statement posted on various walls—community, responsibility and leadership.

Some of the girls were arranging dishes. Others were preparing drinks and setting out food. Through the windows that looked out on a strip of grass and some lawn chairs, Emily saw two of the girls talking earnestly to the counselor.

"Everyone," Cammie said loudly, "this is my friend Emily, who's joining us for dinner. She knows a lot about organic food and cooking healthily, and we can learn a lot from her."

Emily, smiling nervously, set the bag on a small side table.

She wore a Make Love, Not Trash T-shirt with a long skirt and a pair of sandals. Her pulled-back hair emphasized her pink, freshly washed face.

The girls stared at her in silence.

"Look who's coming to dinner," Takira muttered. "Taylor Swift."

"Takira," Cammie warned quietly.

"Well, she ain't no hoodrat," added another girl.

A smattering of giggles.

"Hey," said another, "be easy on the bougie."

Marc looked around and smiled, although you could see his patience was thinning. "My name's Marc and I'm Emily's father." He put a supportive hand on her back. "She's here because she wanted to meet you. In fact, she brought organic food to share with you. But if you can't speak respectfully to her, she's leaving."

Cammie had never seen so many eyes grow wide, but Marc was right. The girls had behaved badly, probably out of jealousy, and Cammie should have stepped in first to put a stop to it. She was, after all, the one in charge here.

"Girls," she said, "let's—"

"Anybody else have something to say?" Marc said.

She started to override his churlishness, but stopped when she saw the fiercely protective look in his face. This wasn't about him being rude or defensive, this was him being a father defending his daughter.

"Because I invite you to step forward and speak your mind," he continued. "But one *caveat*—I challenge you to share something meaningful and important, because it doesn't take much intelligence to deride others." He looked around the room, making eye contact with each and every girl. "On the other hand, it takes character, a person destined to be a leader, one who chooses to educate and uplift her fellow humans, to take the floor. Who would like to speak now?"

Amber drifted forward, her large dark eyes staring intently at Marc as though to ensure he was properly listening.

"The world's going to end in 2016," she said quietly.

A crash shattered the silence.

"Shit, it's ending now!" one girl yelled as she dove for cover. Several girls ran squealing into the dining room, others fell to the floor. Air rushed through a hinged window that had been blown open by a fierce blast of desert wind, the force propelling the window against the wall and shattering its panes. Dust swirled, papers fluttered, glasses smashed onto the floor. Instinctually, Cammie gathered Emily and a few other girls and made them crouch low to the ground, their hands over their heads as if they were in a plane that was about to go down.

Air rushed through the room. A steel bowl rattled across the floor.

Then, silence.

Cautiously, Cammie looked up.

Marc stood at the broken window over the sink, pressing the top of the side table over the gaping hole to block the wind. His shirt had ripped at the armhole, exposing a tanned, muscled deltoid. He looked over his shoulder at Cammie and grinned.

"When I lifted the table, caught the leg in my sleeve. Tore the shirt getting it loose or I'd have gotten to the window sooner."

The way his hair fell over his forehead, that isn't-this-just-the-damnedest-thing grin and that flash of muscle, he looked like a rugged, save-the-day hero on a romance book cover.

There was a time she would have found such an image to be silly or superficial, but at this moment it hit her completely differently. He'd been quick thinking, strong, protective. No paperback hero, but the real deal.

She straightened, trying to ignore the small, hot thrill in the pit of her stomach. "Everybody okay?" she asked, helping the other girls up.

"Fine."

"Yes, Miss Copello."

"Got a toolbox around here?" Marc asked.

"There's one downstairs," Takira offered. "I'll go get it."

As she jogged out of the room, Cammie said, "Let's get things cleaned up." Everybody pitched in without a single gripe.

The counselor and the two girls entered through the back door, their hair tousled, looks of surprise on their faces. Cammie assured the counselor that the girls were okay, explained how Marc had closed the broken window.

"Could one of the other windows blow?" one of the girls asked.

The counselor shook her head. "We've all known that window needed fixing. Should've secured it weeks ago."

"Is there a piece of plywood around?" Marc asked. "Something large enough to nail across here?"

Cammie thought for a moment. "Got a piece of wood that might work in my car. I use it to stabilize the camera on surveillances."

Marc laughed. "You're like Felix the Cat. Always got something in your bag of tricks."

"I'll take that as a compliment." As she left, she noticed Amber and Emily working together to sweep up the broken glass. Funny how those two girls, who seemingly had little in common, had gravitated to each other and were working so well together.

Reminded Cammie of her and Marc. When they met, they were near opposites, yet they'd ended up working well together.

But would they work well together again?

Only time would tell.

Twenty minutes later, Emily was at the kitchen counter, showing Amber and another girl how to make hummus. Other girls were cutting slices of the gluten-free, organic bread, while others were setting up plates of avocado and cheese slices, bean sprouts and other items for make-your-own sandwiches.

On the opposite counter, Marc and Cammie were chopping lettuce and tomatoes for a salad.

He'd hesitated to stay, because this evening was about Emily, but the counselor Carolyn had insisted. Out of earshot of the girls, she'd said, "We like the girls to experience a positive family environment when it presents itself."

So here he was, the symbolic father figure in a family of a dozen or so girls, some of whom had that look of ghetto hardness he recognized from criminal cases he'd handled. Children who had learned, some before they could even talk, that only the strong survived and only fools trusted. These kids never seemed to relax, their bodies tense, their eyes constantly darting about, their brains always juggling life's stacked odds.

He'd challenged Emily to show people respect, especially hardworking people, which these girls were, because they were trying to change for the better. It made him proud that Emily was meeting the challenge.

He glanced over at his daughter explaining to several girls that, although she didn't eat meat, she supported organically fed livestock because they weren't fed antibiotics or genetically modified foods.

"Why's that so good?" asked a girl.

"Means you're eating healthier food," Emily said, "plus the animals are raised humanely."

"What's *humanely* mean?" another girl asked.

"Like how we're being raised here," Amber said, who had positioned herself next to Emily, "and not like what we experienced before."

After a moment of silence, Takira said, "For sheezy!" which got a laugh.

Lowering his voice, Marc asked Cammie, "What's *for sheezy?*"

"For sure," Cammie said.

"I'm never going to have children," Amber announced. "It's irresponsible to add to a world that is already overpopulated."

"Fewer people," Emily added, "less ozone depletion."

"Exactly," agreed Amber. "You have a mother?"

"Yes," Emily answered.

"Does she work?"

"Not if she can help it."

"What does she do?"

"Marries men who have money."

Marc moved his head closer to Cammie. "For sheezy," he muttered.

Cammie shot him a smile, which he returned, but as they resumed their chopping, he mulled over Emily's response. As much as his ex-wife irritated the hell out of him, it hadn't felt good hearing Emily's toss-off remark. If that's how she viewed her mother's "career"—as marrying for financial gain—how would that affect Em's future relationships with men? If only he could have more time with Emily, help her nurture more positive views of men and women.

If only.

"What about your mother?" Emily asked.

"She's dead," Amber said matter-of-factly.

Marc darted a look at Cammie, who gave a slight shrug.

"I didn't know," Emily said. "I'm sorry."

"No big deal," Amber said. "She died when I was little. I barely remember her. I've lived in a lot of foster homes. Nobody wanted to adopt me but I don't care. I didn't want to be adopted by any of them, either. Nobody cared about changing the world, just consuming it."

Takira and some of the other girls started singing a rap song, "Hate It or Love It," and the mood in the room lifted as they danced and sang. Cammie silently congratulated Takira for keeping her moves G-rated.

"Em and Amber are connecting," Marc said. With all the commotion in the room, they could safely talk without being overheard.

"Amber's found a kindred spirit." She paused. "And Emily, too. Maybe Amber is somebody she can genuinely relate to."

He nodded, appreciating Cammie's insight into Em.

He'd always known Cammie to be independent and driven, but here at Dignity House he was seeing her sensitive side, too. She was good with these girls. He supposed that could be due to her being a caretaker for her mother, but this felt different. More nurturing, intuitive. Shame that someone who had such natural mothering instincts was adamant that she never wanted to have her own children.

"I overheard them talking earlier about an Eco-Glitter rally," he mentioned, switching gears. "What's that?"

"You're asking me? I still eat meat and sugar, and wonder if vegans are distant cousins of Vulcans."

"Sounded as though Amber wants Em to go with her."

"Ain't gonna happen. Amber is a house resident, meaning she never leaves the facility except for supervised group activities."

"Sorry to hear about her mother."

Cammie looked around, then said quietly, "Actually she's not dead. But Amber tells everyone she is."

"Did her mother abandon her?"

"Yes. In a Dumpster. Amber was only a month old, so she doesn't remember the incident, of course, but she knows the truth and it hurts to know she wasn't wanted."

He chopped in silence for several moments.

"Unlike us," Marc said quietly. Both of them had had their parental issues, but at least he and Cammie had both known they were wanted and loved.

"Yes," Cammie said softly.

Their eyes caught, and in that singular moment, he realized they shared a secret.

They yearned for family.

Maybe because they'd both come from broken homes, they were still searching to fix that as adults. Or maybe they'd been

orbiting in their own worlds for so long, they wanted to return
to a home base, to make the circle whole. He wondered if her
volunteering at Dignity House—even though it was court-
ordered—partially fulfilled that need within her. Without a
doubt, his proposing to Gwen had been a badly thought-out
plan to fulfill his. He'd been looking for someone who needed
him, and Gwen did an excellent impression of helplessness.

He observed Cammie's profile as she focused on her dicing
and chopping. No one would ever call her helpless. He noticed
the feathery texture of her eyelashes, the strong line of her nose.
He lingered on the lips that he'd almost kissed earlier today.

At the time he told himself he'd pulled back because he was
out of control, acting juvenile. Now he realized he'd gotten too
close to something that felt too real.

Just because he yearned to complete the circle, didn't mean
he was ready for it.

In fact, he was terrified of it.

CHAPTER TEN

WHEN CAMMIE ROLLED PHIL into Bergstrom's Bridals' parking lot at 9:30 the next morning, Delilah's red Fiat 500 was already there. No Prius. Good. She wanted a few minutes alone with the older woman before Emily and Marc arrived.

The front door was large and white with the words *Bergstrom's Bridals* scrawled across it in shiny gold letters. Cammie turned the knob. Locked. After punching the bell, she heard distant bells playing "Here Comes the Bride." Moments later, a middle-aged gentleman wearing a buttoned-up suit with a matching bow tie opened the door.

"You must be Miss Copello," he said, enunciating each word. "I'm Mr. Bergstrom."

They shook hands.

"We keep the door locked during appointments so I can give my undivided attention to the bride. Please come in and make yourself comfortable. Would you like a cup of coffee?"

"Yes. Thank you."

"Cream? Sugar?"

"Cream."

With a twitch of his manicured moustache, Mr. Bergstrom exited quickly.

Walking into the bridal salon was like going snow-blind. Except for the polished hardwood floors and a crystal chandelier that looked like an upside-down Vegas showgirl's headdress, everything was a shade of white. Over the speakers, violins trilled in a classical piece.

A high-back white couch faced a small white stage surrounded by floor-to-ceiling mirrors. On the glass coffee table was an arrangement of off-white roses.

From behind the mirrors, Delilah sashayed out wearing a cream-colored caftan that blended into the decor, giving her the eerie impression of being a floating head and cleavage.

"Darling," she cooed, carrying two cups of steaming coffee, "Frankie told me you're feeling a tad uncomfortable trying on these dresses. So I put a little comfort in your coffee." She set down the cups on the table, then settled on the couch. "Come, sit." She patted the seat next to her.

"What kind of comfort?" Cammie asked, sitting.

"Frangelico. Just a drop." ·

She took a sip and coughed. "More like six or ten."

"Enough to take the edge off."

Delilah had a valid point. After taking another sip, she set the cup down. "Delilah, I need to ask a favor. I know you're thinking of me, but please…no more matchmaking."

The older woman gave a who-me look.

"You know what I'm talking about," Cammie continued. "Promise me you won't say anything this morning that even hints at Marc and me getting together."

"Getting together," she repeated slowly, as though she'd never before heard those words in the English language.

"I know you know what I mean," Cammie said, speaking through her teeth. "The other night you left me in the restaurant, alone with Marc, who would have had to drive me home if—" She didn't need to go into what happened in his hotel room. How he'd rejected her. How she'd walked out and grabbed a cab.

"I know my uncle has told you I had a crush on Marc for a long time, but not anymore. Well, soon it'll be not anymore. I'm working on it. For the record, he had a chance to kiss me yesterday and he didn't want to." She waved off Delilah's interruption. "What matters is that he and I are *business* associates. I need to keep that line firmly drawn in the sand—" she drew the line in the air with her index finger "—because he's the boss, I'm the employee, and that's that."

Delilah picked up Cammie's coffee cup and handed it to her. "Have another sip, dear."

Cammie did. It seemed the right thing to do.

They shared a companionable silence, occasionally nodding with the music or staring off into space. It was actually quite pleasant. Surprisingly so. Cammie didn't know if she'd ever been this comfortable around Delilah. Maybe there was something to this Frangelico.

Finally, the older woman stood and adjusted her caftan. "I won't say anything to him, dear. I promise. Although I've already told Emily that I'll need her help in the dressing room, so please know my whisking her away isn't part of some wicked matchmaking scheme."

Cammie nodded. "Thank you. He and I will sit out here going over the case. When you need me to try on something, give a holler."

"Wonderful."

Electronic bells played "Here Comes the Bride."

Mr. Bergstrom appeared from behind the mirrors, walking purposefully toward the front door.

"That's my bridal assistant and her adorable father," Delilah said in a singsong voice as the gentleman passed. "Please bring my lovely assistant to the dressing room. The father will stay out here with his business associate."

And with that, Delilah floated away, merging with the white.

MINUTES LATER, Marc and Cammie sat by themselves on the couch. They hadn't talked one-on-one since preparing the salad last night. During dinner, the girls had bombarded Marc with questions about the law and his legal practice. Some girls had questions about their pending criminal cases. Such as sixteen-year-old Deniqua, who'd been charged with creating a public nuisance, or fourteen-year-old Wanda, who was facing two counts of shoplifting.

"I enjoyed last night," Marc said, opening a manila folder filled with papers. "Nice how some of the girls walked us out to our car afterward."

"You and Emily were big hits."

"Before we drove off, Takira leaned in and bumped fists with Emily."

"Good sign," Cammie acknowledged.

"It's funny—she didn't talk about missing her friends today. Which is a good thing because it was tough feeling like the bad guy for taking her away from them." He pulled out a sheet of paper. "Ready to be my investigator again?"

"It's like coming home."

He studied her face for a moment before looking at the paper in his hand and passing it to her.

"This report run by a Denver investigator a few months ago shows Gwen had relatives here in Las Vegas."

Cammie scanned the document. "One's dead." She pointed to a symbol next to the name.

"I wondered what that meant."

"I've run reports using this database before," she explained, reading the report. "Appears the second relative left Las Vegas seven years ago, and there's no current address for him."

"I'd noticed that."

"Awfully convenient."

"How?"

"Those are the only two relatives listed in this report. With both of them unavailable…well, that's convenient for Gwen because it makes it difficult to find family members who might know where she is."

Marc took a sip of his coffee, which he'd requested black. Delilah hadn't seen the need to add any comfort to his cup.

"Did she ever mention having relatives in Las Vegas?" Cammie asked.

"Never. It was a surprise to me that it came up in a report."

She tapped her finger on her bottom lip. "You mentioned she had ties to Southern California, but this report doesn't list any such addresses. In fact, her address history abruptly ended five years ago."

"I thought she'd lived in Southern California because she'd once told me that she and her girlfriends loved to bodysurf. I asked which beach, but I got interrupted by a business call and the subject never came up again."

"She could've bodysurfed in Florida."

"You ever been there?"

Cammie shook her head no.

"Waves are puny. Too many sharks. Which is why I thought she meant Southern Cal." He glanced at the report. "Why do you think her address history ended five years ago?"

"Information on a person can dry up when they stop applying for credit or start dealing in cash only or somebody else starts paying for everything…lots of reasons." Cammie frowned. "Didn't you find it odd that she never talked about the town she grew up in, or that you never met her parents?"

He shook his head emphatically. "No, because she said her dad was in the military and they moved around a lot. Seemed a painful topic, so I didn't probe. Anyway, figured we had lots of time to get to know each other better. As to her parents, Gwen would say they were traveling overseas, or that they were back east visiting an ailing relative. There was always a reason. She showed me photos of them once."

"Was she in any of them?"

"No."

Cammie thought back to how quickly Gwen came on board at Hamilton & Hamilton. If only Cammie had conducted a cursory computer check, like this P.I., she would have seen warning signs. But Cammie hadn't been content with subtle. She'd immediately gone for the jugular with her illegal phone record retrieval.

If Marc had listened to her first suspicions instead of booting her out the door, he could have saved himself a lot of trouble. Coolly, she said, "I'm going to guess you hired her without conducting any sort of background check."

"Correct."

"Started dating and within weeks, you offered her a job as your bookkeeper."

"We got serious, fast."

"Or you did." Cammie tried to keep the bite out of her voice, but it wasn't easy. "I think your fiancée was using either a stolen ID or an ID for someone who is deceased."

As though on cue, a dramatic organ riff played over the speakers. Marc cracked a droll smile. "Bach's 'Toccata and Fugue in D minor.' I feel as though I'm starring in a bad remake of *Phantom of the Opera*."

"Where the mysterious Gwen is the phantom."

"So to speak."

"For Gwen, the mask would be an improvement." It was fun to be lighthearted for a moment, but Cammie saw the worry return to Marc's eyes. "What is it?"

He rubbed his neck. "I've heard from a friend that the Attorney Disciplinary Agency is taking steps to suspend my license."

His apprehension was almost tangible. She could feel it like a force field around him. "Does your dad know?"

"No. I haven't felt comfortable discussing it over the phone. Supposedly all our calls are protected by attorney-client privilege, but I've known the feds and the state to tap in anyway. Plus he's had health issues."

"Anything serious?" She remembered how Harlan's hands shook slightly. Sometimes he'd abruptly stop talking and, with a surprised look on his face, ask to be reminded what he'd been talking about.

"Some kidney troubles. High blood pressure. Although these are not uncommon health problems for the elderly, I'm still concerned because—let's be honest—prisoners don't get the best medical care even if they are Harlan Hamilton. He needs to be paroled so he can get proper, ongoing healthcare."

"And be with his family."

"Which is me. And Em when she visits."

She'd thought Marc was sitting alone in that big house with nothing but memories for company. It was more than that. He wanted to bring home his father and take care of him.

"You're the best lawyer to represent Harlan at his parole hearing. Nobody else has the balls or the intelligence."

He cocked an eyebrow. "That's a resounding recommendation."

"The only way to stop the Disciplinary Agency from taking away your license is to find Gwen, which means we have to act fast. When are you returning to Denver?"

"Thursday, 8:00 p.m."

She blew out a low whistle. "Gives us three days. Of course, there's a lot I can do on my own after you leave, but while you're here I need you to prepare the subpoena *duces tecum,* which includes of course the date and time for her deposition. You've already scheduled that, right?"

"Yes."

"Could you have that paperwork ready this afternoon?"

He nodded.

"Good. I'll keep the papers with me so the instant I find her, I can serve her."

He straightened. "Ideally, I'd like to be there, too. It's my shot to try to reach a settlement, to tell her I won't sue her civilly if she admits to the theft and returns the money. Or as much as she has left."

In general, she preferred working alone to having a partner, especially not a partner with intoxicating blue eyes, who had the power to crush her willpower with a single doughnut. Still, she had to admit, this conversation had been thoroughly businesslike. No heartthrobs. No inappropriate thoughts. Maybe he wouldn't be a huge distraction, after all.

"Not much time. You're leaving Thursday."

"As you said, we have to act fast."

"Darlings?" Delilah called out.

They looked over at the stage, where the older woman posed in a long, satiny dress the color of peaches. Emily hovered behind her, adjusting the short lace train.

"What do you two think?" Delilah asked.

"There's no cleavage," Cammie blurted. She barely recognized Delilah with her breasts covered up.

The older woman sighed dramatically. "I know, it's the first thing I noticed, too. How do you like the dress, Marc?"

"You're a vision," he said. "A bride above all brides."

Mr. Bergstrom strolled onto the stage with a wide-brimmed peach-colored hat. "This is an exact replica of what the Crown Princess Victoria of Sweden wore to the royal wedding. It will look divine with your dress."

As he and Delilah fussed with the hat, Cammie whispered to Marc, "'A bride above all brides'?"

"Can't claim the best track record with marriages," he said quietly, "but I'm enough of a sensitive male to know a woman deserves the best memories surrounding her wedding day. After all, life is all about memories, isn't it?"

"Cammie, darling," Delilah interrupted, "there's a Princess Fantasy apricot dress just begging for you to try it on. Ready, dear?"

Cammie inhaled a deep breath. "Yes?"

Marc hummed a few bars of the old song "Memories."

Cammie stood, holding up two fingers in the rock-on gesture. "Your maid of honor is ready to rock that dress!"

A FEW MINUTES LATER, Marc was typing into his smartphone when Emily plopped onto the couch next to him.

He looked at her. "That's some dress."

Emily ran her fingers over the tulle skirt. "Isn't this color yummy? Mr. Bergstrom says the dress can be worn to a prom or a wedding. Aunt Dell says the color is champagne. Did you notice the beads on the bodice?"

He supposed if she'd call him Dad, it wouldn't matter if she made familial references to anybody else. Hell, she could call Alice Cooper Uncle Al for all he cared. But to be excluded was like a punch to his heart.

He cleared his throat. "They look like sequins."

"No, they're beads. She says their use in clothing goes back thousands of years and that some civilizations used beads as health amulets. Isn't that cool?" She ran her fingers over the netting. "I need to ask for something."

"You want me to buy you this dress?"

She took in a fortifying breath, then released it in a stream of words. "There's an Eco-Glitter rally day after tomorrow here in Las Vegas and I really, really want to go."

"Whoa, slow down." He set aside his smartphone. "Eco-Glitter rally. Is that what you and Amber were discussing?"

"Her name's *Daearen*." She shot him a skeptical look. "Were you listening in on our conversation? I thought eavesdropping was illegal."

"Em, one of you said *Eco-Glitter* rather loudly in a crowded room. No expectation of privacy under those circumstances, honey." As she started to talk, he raised his hand. "Let's save the Fourth Amendment for later. Right now, tell me about this Eco-Glitter rally and why you want to go."

"It's an ethical jewelry protest. Many people don't know that mining the earth for precious jewels and metals creates environmental problems, dangerous work conditions, and if there's no fair-trade agreement, businesses often take advantage of workers by paying them ridiculously low wages. Like, poverty wages. This is more than just a rally. This is my social responsibility."

He blinked. "And to think I thought diamonds were a girl's best friend."

"I'm serious!"

"I know." He placed his hand on hers. "Tell me more."

She explained how there would be displays of recycled and earth-friendly jewelry, plus an awesome rock band would be performing.

"You asked me to walk the talk," she said, "and by attending this rally, I'll be putting my beliefs into action. Plus I want to represent those who can't be there, like Daearen."

"Did I ever tell you that I once gathered signatures for Frank Zappa for President?"

"Who's Frank Zappa?"

"Let's just say I applaud what you're doing, and yes, you can go to the Eco-Glitter rally with a chaperone."

"But I'm fifteen! Chaperones are, like, for people dating in Sicily."

He bit his tongue not to smile. "We're in Las Vegas, honey. If this rally were in Omaha, fine, go alone. Las Vegas? Two chaperones."

"But you just said *one*." She slumped into the couch, looking like a dejected princess.

"Okay, one. Me."

She rolled her eyes. "Going to my first rally with my parent? I'll look so lame."

"I'm sure there'll be so many people there, nobody will notice your father, Em—"

"Wow!" She bolted upright, distracted.

He followed her line of vision.

For a moment he forgot to breathe.

Cammie, swathed in a cloud of apricot, was a vision of beauty. Her long black curls had been pinned up, which emphasized the curve of her slim neck. Pink dotted her cheeks, which at first he thought was makeup until he realized she was likely embarrassed. Around her bare shoulders lay a mantle of spun gold, or that's what it looked like. Had to be some kind of gold-threaded shawl. And lower, pushed above the tight satin bodice, the creamy mounds of her breasts.

"Huh." He meant to say something more intelligent, but his mouth and brain were having trouble connecting.

Delilah stepped onto the stage behind Cammie. "Doesn't she look divine?"

His head bobbed.

"Awesome!" Cammie said as she made the rock-on gesture with both hands.

"We have one more dress we'd like your perspective on," Delilah said, taking Cammie's hand and ushering her off the stage.

"I want to help!" Emily said, jumping up. She looked at Marc. "So you agree? I can go to the rally?"

He had to mentally shake himself back to reality. "Yes," he said, finding his voice. "With me."

"Thank you!" She leaned over and gave him a peck on the cheek, then ran back to wherever people went behind the mirrors.

So what if she didn't call him Dad. She treated him like one, right?

As Vivaldi's *Four Seasons* began playing, he again picked up the report, refocusing his thoughts to the next steps of this case. He could easily prepare the subpoena this afternoon, but could they find Gwen by Thursday? He nearly laughed at that thought. He'd worked with enough investigators to know how difficult it was, even if one was top-notch like Cammie, to find a person who didn't want to be found. Sure, people, even those on the run, often returned to where they once lived, but even surmising that Gwen once lived in Southern California, where in those several thousand acres of land and dozens of cities might she be? Hell, they didn't even know her real name.

"What do you think of this one?" Delilah asked.

He looked up at the stage.

His mouth went dry. He vaguely wondered when jungle drums had been added to Vivaldi's chamber music piece, then realized it was his thundering, pounding pulse.

"Marc?" Delilah prodded.

If he'd thought he'd had trouble connecting his mouth and brain before, it was damn near impossible now.

CHAPTER ELEVEN

LOOKING AT CAMMIE on the stage, Marc recalled a favorite piece of candy he'd liked as a kid. It was called the Firecracker—a hard crimson confection that tasted like a burning, sweet fire, and he couldn't get enough of it.

Right now, he couldn't get enough of Cammie poured into a red dress that hugged, squeezed and clung to every inch of her body. Looking at her was like walking into fire.

The overhead lights showcased her, making the parts of her body not wrapped in red to look luminous, as though she glowed from within. With the wide cut of plunging neckline, no way she wore a bra. In fact, considering its insanely tight fit, no way she wore anything underneath that dress.

She's naked under the red.

As if he needed that news alert sizzling along his already singed synapses that were sputtering and popping with libido-fueled power surges.

A voice from somewhere off in the milky ether of the bridal salon penetrated his consciousness.

"Marc?" Delilah asked. "How do you like it?"

"That's a...bridesmaid's dress?" he rasped.

"Maid of honor," Delilah corrected.

No maid ever wore a dress like that and kept her honor. Not for long, anyway.

"In Las Vegas," Delilah added, "anything goes, you know."

With great effort, Marc shifted his vision to Delilah, still dressed in the peach number, standing next to Mr. Bergstrom, who held one hand airily at his side as he scrutinized Cammie.

"Red is stunning on you," he said, walking in a half circle around her. "Definitely your color."

From somewhere beyond the mirrors, Emily called out, "Help, I'm caught up in tulle!"

"Could you assist that lovely young girl in taking off the prom dress?" Mr. Bergstrom asked Delilah. "I'll stay here and check any necessary fittings."

After Delilah left, Mr. Bergstrom made some adjustments to the dress. A tug here, a pluck there. Cammie looked bored. Or perturbed. Marc tried to act as though thousands of years had passed since ridge-browed Neanderthals trundled about foraging, hunting and mating. Especially mating.

He reminded himself that the last thing he needed to be doing was entertaining hot thoughts about another coworker... and yet he'd be kidding himself to think she was only that. A coworker wouldn't care about his family the way Cammie did—in fact, she probably had more of an inside track on what made his dad tick than Marc did. She'd known he was desperate to hire her, enough so that he flew all the way to Vegas to talk to her, but unlike other employees he'd known, she didn't take advantage of his need to hire her by demanding more money or perks. No, Cammie had kept turning down the job until her conscience told her otherwise.

And she wasn't just a coworker because what he felt for her went beyond an employee-boss relationship. He had feelings for her. Feelings that rattled, confused, sometimes even infuriated him.

He'd had these feelings before. Back in Denver, working late at night with Cammie on an impending trial, he'd sometimes felt unnerved, thrown off by something she did or said. Back then he'd chalked it up to litigation jitters, but now he realized it was sometimes more than that—he simply hadn't wanted to acknowledge those desires.

Of course not. If he had, he would have been stepping into his own gray area about her. A place he stood now. Not a boss, not a lover, but somewhere in between. He didn't like it. Made him feel out of control—the last thing he should be feeling with so much at stake right now.

Fortunately, he'd be leaving in a few days and didn't need to figure all this out. Until then, he would try to put his feelings on ice and stay focused on why he was here—to find Gwen.

"Walk around, see how it feels," Mr. Bergstrom instructed Cammie. "I'll be in the back selecting another dress for Delilah."

Alone with Marc, Cammie said, "Can you believe Delilah wants me to wear this? I look like Little Red Riding Hood gone bad."

He picked up the sheet of paper, pretended to scan it. "Very bad," he murmured.

"Look at this slit!" Cammie turned to the side and stuck out her leg, her foot in a sneaker. "Do you know it goes all the way up to here?" She pointed at her hip as though he might not see exactly where the slit ended.

He glanced up then back down to the paper. "Disgraceful."

"And red!" Cammie gestured at her tightly wrapped self as though Marc might have missed the flaming color. "She'll be in ivory or peach and I'll be in *red?* What happened to the sugarplum-fairy dress or whatever it's called that she wanted me to wear? Red is for harlots and roosters."

"Well, you hardly look like a roost—"

Cammie cut him off with a loud gasp, her hands held high in a stop-the-presses gesture.

"Rooster! That's it!" Waggling her fingers in front of her, she stepped off the stage and toward him. "Need my smartphone."

With every move, the material shimmied and the plunging neckline teased. When she sat next to him, a long, toned leg escaped the slit.

He reminded himself, again, he needed to put his feelings on ice. Big buckets of it.

Her fingers flew over the keypad of her phone. "That rooster was riding a surfboard."

"What rooster?"

"The one on the coffee cup that was always on Gwen's desk. Remember?" She glanced at the paper in his hands. "How can you read that?"

"What?"

"The report. It's upside down." As he turned it around, she went back to typing. "Anyway, you said she and her girlfriends like to bodysurf. I recalled the rooster on some type of board, and I'll bet my favorite autographed Nuggets baseball cap that it's a surfboard."

"It was fairly new. Didn't have any chips or cracks."

"Which tells us she got it recently—" She stilled. "Well, lookie lookie."

He glanced at the screen, saw a picture of a rooster on a surfboard. "It's a brand."

"For a restaurant in San Clemente, California. The Surfing Rooster. Established 2011, which corroborates the cup looking fairly new. She either lived in or visited San Clemente right before she moved to Denver."

"Could be a gift."

"Could be, which still says to me that the location is significant." Beaming, she held up her hand. "Give me five, baby! I nailed the city."

He slapped his palm against hers.

"I have an idea how to find out her real name. Remember how Gwen liked to refer to herself as Swagtastic?"

"I've tried to forget."

"I'm going to pretext The Surfing Rooster—"

"I know private investigators rely on pretexting, or fabrications, Cammie, but I'm not wild about it."

She leveled him a look. "Marc, please, this is legit. If I were to pretext for financial information, or pretend to be a lawyer or cop, *that'd* be illegal. All I'm doing is fishing for a name, and if it makes you uncomfortable, go stand across the room."

"I'd rather stay here," he murmured.

"This will take me a minute. Need to punch in a spoof number so it appears I'm calling from that area code." Cammie punched in a series of numbers, then waited.

"Oh, hello!" she said, in a kinda-dumb, California beach-babe voice. "Is this The Surfing Rooster? Far out. I've done, like, the silliest thing. Told Swagtastic I'd meet her there, but I'm, like, running late and her cell's broken. She there? *S-w-a-g-t-a-s-t-i-c.* Uh-huh. Nuh-huh. Okay. Peace out, man."

She ended the call.

"Peace out, man?"

Cammie slanted him a look. "That was me going undercover with my voice. Figured it'd work well for a Southern Cal chick."

"Word."

She broke into a grin. "You got it, dude." Turning serious, she continued, "He had no idea who Swagtastic is, but he's only been working there a few weeks. Said there were a couple of customers in the place, but they were guys." Cammie typed on the keypad. "Let's do a reverse on Swagtastic on the internet, see what pops up." She scrolled through several screens. "Seems dozens, if not hundreds, of people like referring to themselves as Swagtastic. It'd take me forever to follow up on all these references." She looked at Marc. "The convertible she drove—what kind was it?"

"Mustang GT."

"Year?"

"Two thousand six."

"I doubt she'd still be driving it. Better to sell the car and buy a new one than risk being tracked." She tippy-tapped on the keypad. "Let's run a reverse on that make of car, see if an ad pops up." After a few moments, she gave him a look. "Bingo. There's a Craigslist ad for the exact same car three months ago. Seller was based…drum roll, please…in San Clemente."

He grinned back. "You're good."

"Word. Good ol' Craigslist provided a cell-phone number in this ad. I'll submit it to a telecom database, see what name it's registered to." Within seconds, Cammie said, "Ta-da. Laura McDonald, San Clemente, California."

"Laura McDonald," he repeated. "Sounds so…normal."

"Yeah, I had fantasies of her name being Natasha or Cruella. Now let's run her real name in the county assessor database for San Clemente." After another short wait, Cammie put down her smartphone and flashed a Cheshire-cat smile. "Laura McDonald has owned a home in San Clemente since 2009. According to tax assessor data, she didn't live there throughout 2011—which we know is the year she lived in Denver—but is now receiving mail in San Clemente again."

He shuddered as a chill passed through him. The truth felt as good as it felt bad. They'd found her, and now he had the key to proving his innocence and salvaging his father's freedom. But it disgusted him to realize that he'd loved a woman who was a shadow, and that this stranger carried his child.

"San Clemente is a four- to five-hour drive from here," Cammie continued. "If we leave soon, we can be there and back by midnight."

"That's if she's home."

"It's Tuesday. Most people take off on weekends."

"I only have one thing to add to that."

"What?"

"Who's driving first?"

It took Marc five minutes to write the subpoena, another five to print the papers on Mr. Bergstrom's printer. After making arrangements for Emily to stay with Delilah, Cammie and Marc were on Interstate 15, heading west to California by 11:00 a.m.

By two that afternoon, they'd driven past Buffalo Bill's Resort and Casino, which advertised the world's only buffalo-shaped swimming pool, and Peggy Sue's 50's Diner in Yermo,

California, which advertised the Buddy Holly Bacon Cheeseburger and the Mickey Mouse Club Sandwich. Along the way, Cammie ran several criminal checks on Laura McDonald, and learned the Spanx-wearing Cameron Diaz lookalike had an impressive rap sheet—theft, third-degree assault, several DUIs, time in the county jail and violation of a restraining order.

"Theft is no surprise," Cammie said. "Wonder what she did to pick up that third-degree-assault charge. Did she ever drink and try to pick a fight?"

"The opposite. She had me convinced that she was sweet as honey and delicate as a violet. Obviously, she was on good behavior when she was with me. After all, my law firm was a theft in progress. But that assault charge accounts for the stint in county jail."

After a pause, Cammie said quietly, "Sorry."

"For what?"

"For what you've been through."

He tapped the wheel with his forefinger, a look of intense speculation on his face. "I can chalk up my life's mistakes to lessons I needed to learn, but…" He slowly shook his head. "There's an innocent baby mixed up in all this. I'm going to fight for custody of that child—and I'm going to win."

For a while after that, they drove in silence with Cammie biting her tongue to keep from telling Marc that the baby might not be his. His completely mistaken impression of Gwen as an adorable blonde innocent was enough for him to deal with at the moment. He didn't need to be clobbered with the additional news that she'd cheated on him.

Of course, it hadn't worked out so well the last time she withheld information from him—hiding the fact that her license had been suspended—but that issue had been a fact, something between she and Marc. The news about Gwen's philandering, and the baby, was wrought with painful questions and betrayal—at the moment, she wanted to spare Marc that emotional minefield.

But she wasn't so naive to think she could avoid the issue for much longer.

Around 3:40, they drove through Riverside, California, and its famous Mission Inn, which boasted such visitors as Humphrey Bogart, John F. Kennedy and Harry Houdini. Around five o'clock, they rolled into San Clemente, with its breezy ocean air, wisps of fog and Spanish Colonial architecture.

On the drive, she'd looked up directions to The Surfing Rooster, and gave instructions to Marc. Rather than show up at the place and possibly run into Laura McDonald, they parked across the street at the drive-through restaurant Mr. Taco's, where they noshed on chips and salsa while watching the comings and goings at The Surfing Rooster, a food stand with a giant surfing rooster on its roof. Seating consisted of several outdoor picnic tables.

"According to MapQuest," Cammie said, "Laura McDonald's home is up in the hills above Interstate 5. Shouldn't take us more than ten minutes to get there."

Nodding, Marc rubbed his neck.

"Keep the motor running so we can take off as soon as I get back to the car."

"I'm going to the door with you."

"You're the plaintiff. You can't serve the lawsuit."

"I know that, Cammie. I just don't want you going to her door alone."

She heaved a sigh. "Look, I'm going to pull my hair back in a bun and wear my sunglasses. She won't recognize me. And we rarely spoke at the law firm, so I seriously doubt she'll remember my voice, especially as I'll be saying these four words—*Laura McDonald, you're served*. But if you're standing there, she'll put two and two together and know she's being hit with a lawsuit. That'd be the moment she'd go for another third-degree-assault charge."

He examined her face with amused tolerance. "Point taken."

"But I also know you wanted an opportunity to negotiate a

possible settlement with her. So here's our plan. If she seems relatively calm, I'll cue you to join me at the door."

"What's the cue?"

She thought about this for a moment. "We'll call each other on our cell phones before I get out of the car. My phone will be in here—" She pointed to the pocket on her T-shirt. "This material is thin enough that you'll be able to hear anything I say. Cue will be the word...*rooster.*"

"I hear the word *rooster,* I head to the door."

"Right."

A shadow darkened his features. "Let's do it."

TEN MINUTES LATER, Marc parked across the street from a fifties-style, flat-roof house perched on the hillside with a view of the Pacific Ocean. An arched wooden gate led to a courtyard, the only entrance to the home. To the right of the gate was a driveway leading to a two-car garage.

"Someone's been home recently," Cammie said, securing her long hair into a knot with a rubber band.

"How can you tell?"

"In the driveway, see the tire tracks in the dirt?"

He squinted. "Barely."

"With the garage door closed, it indicates someone probably recently backed out a car. Not necessarily Laura, though."

He nodded, his blue eyes turning frosty. "Boyfriend. Or husband."

She hadn't wanted to bring up that possibility.

"I know we agreed you'd walk to the front door by yourself," he said, "but I don't like that I can't see you in that courtyard."

She punched in his cell number. "Remember I'll have my phone in my pocket, turned on, so you can hear everything that's said."

His phone rang. He punched the talk button. "We need a cue word for trouble."

"Okay, how about...*Tolstoy?*"

He smiled. "Emily can never know."

After dropping her cell in her pocket, she put on her sun-glasses and stuck the folded papers into a pants pocket. "I'm heading up there now."

"I'll be listening. And, Cammie..."

She had her hand on the door handle. "Yes?"

"No wading into gray areas."

"Marc?"

"Yes?"

"You're getting on my nerves."

After exiting the car, she walked briskly toward the gate. Over the years, she'd learned it was smart to work fast when conducting process services, and to keep the papers out of view until the last moment so as to not alert the person what was coming.

The wooden gate creaked as she opened it. She tried to leave it slightly ajar so she could quickly exit, but the heavy gate shut with a solid thud. She walked past a pond with fat golden koi fish surrounded by manicured bonsai trees. Cyprus trees scented the air with a sage-woodsy scent. Laura McDonald lived in a nice place. Cammie had to wonder why Laura would invest the time and effort to romance Marc and pull off such a risky scam for a mere thirty thousand dollars.

She punched the doorbell once, twice.

No answer.

She knocked loudly.

No answer.

Cammie stood, listening carefully. Didn't hear voices, no sounds of TV or music. Not even a dog barking.

She stepped off the porch and onto a rock-strewn path that curled around expansive plate-glass windows. Stepping off the path and over a small hedge, she cupped her hands around her eyes and looked inside the house. Teak furniture, oriental rugs, a painting of a beach scene over a fireplace. The woman who called herself Swagtastic had expensive taste. On a coffee table were two coffee cups—one with lipstick marks—and several dirty plates.

Laura McDonald lived with someone.

Cammie retraced her steps to the car and climbed inside.

"Nobody home," Marc said.

"That's right." She retrieved her phone and turned it off.

"See any signs of people being recently there?"

"Yes."

"And?"

She didn't want to lie, but she also didn't want to hurt him by describing the two coffee cups. Sure, Marc had already mentioned there might be a boyfriend or husband in the picture, but intellectually understanding something didn't mean a person was emotionally ready for it.

And, after all, he'd been engaged to Laura-Gwen. He'd loved her. He might still love her.

"There were…some dirty dishes," she said casually, "so someone is around."

She hadn't lied. In fact, it was technically the truth. But leaving out significant details—that there were two cups, two sets of plates—felt bad because, in an attempt to spare his heart, she'd waded into its gray area. At least she hadn't promised not to go there.

OVER THE NEXT HOUR AND A HALF, they returned twice more to the house. Both times, nobody was home.

"It's almost seven," Cammie said. "I'm thinking that she's out for the evening."

"I was thinking the same thing."

"Rather than driving back and forth, which can be a problem if neighbors start noticing, I activated a motion detector program on my smartphone and left it on a corner of the window ledge."

He blinked. "You sound like that sleuth and her electronic gadgets in that old TV show *The Avengers*."

"You're a fan of that show, too?"

"Yes, Mrs. Peel."

"Excellent, Mr. Steed. Let's take off. I'm starved."

He frowned. "Shouldn't you have left the phone near the front door?"

"There might be an entrance to the home from inside the garage. I figure she'll pick up those dirty dishes after she gets in, which are close enough to the window to trigger the motion sensor. The phone will take fifteen seconds of video and send it as an attachment to your email."

"But won't she notice your smartphone when the camera light goes on?"

"Turned it off. Figured there'd be enough light inside to see her." As they drove off, she asked, "Did Gwen like to stay out late?"

"Always. She'd complain if we got home before ten."

"We shouldn't serve her papers that late. People tend to get squirrely when their doorbell rings after nine or ten at night."

He puffed out a breath. "This is becoming a long day. If—and that's a big *if*—we serve her by ten, we wouldn't get back to Vegas until 3:00 a.m. I vote for our finding a few rooms at a motel."

"Good idea. If the motion detector alerts us that she's home at midnight, we'll show up on her doorstep around seven tomorrow morning."

"Is that a little early?"

Cammie shrugged. "If she's working, she might be leaving the house at that time."

"Working." He snorted under his breath. "More like plotting to steal from some employer who probably thinks she loves him."

Cammie pondered his comment as they wove their way down the hill. All the time Marc believed that someone, Gwen-Laura, who loved him actually didn't, he never knew that someone else, Cammie, did.

But did she still?

The past few days with Marc had been confusing, at best. She'd like to blame that near-kiss interlude on aphrodisiac-laced doughnuts, but the truth was there had been an over-load of chemistry. In hindsight, she wondered if *she'd* been overloaded and Marc had been, well, slightly loaded. That the passionate burst, like a voltage surge, had been nothing more than a system malfunction.

To be totally honest with herself, her part in that malfunc-tion could have simply been a result of her long-buried, pent-up feelings. Kinda like what scientists called a *false positive*—a given condition appears to be present, but it's really not. Maybe she'd carried her overloaded feelings for Marc for so long, she mistakenly believed them to be true, but they no longer were.

She released a small sigh. At least her smartphone still worked properly.

CHAPTER TWELVE

OVER THE NEXT HOUR, Cammie and Marc picked up some incidentals from a convenience store and found a couple of available rooms at The Beachcomber, a family-run lodge with private yards that led to the beach. From there, it was a short walk to the San Clemente pier and its Fisherman's Restaurant, which advertised itself as being the best seafood in town.

After checking in, they headed to the restaurant, where they purchased two T-shirts from its gift shop so they would have something clean to wear the next day. Cammie got a pink T-shirt with the words *Live, Love, Surf in San Clemente*. They had only one left in Marc's size. It was black with the words, in big white letters, *Chicks Dig Me, Fish Fear Me*.

"Maybe I'll wear it to court sometime," Marc joked.

"Right," Cammie agreed. "It screams 'like me' to a jury."

A young man, his sun-bleached hair flopping into his eyes, led them to their table on the pier. Heat lamps and a Plexiglas wall protected them from chilly breezes and spray from the crashing waves below. As he lit a candle at the table, Marc ordered a bottle of wine.

"Where's your phone?" Cammie asked.

He patted his shirt pocket. "On vibrate *and* ringer. I'll feel and hear it when that motion detector sends the message."

"Good." Cammie looked out at the white-capped waves as they rolled toward the shore. "My mom and I used to fantasize about visiting the ocean, but we never did."

"This is your first visit?"

"Second. Uncle Frankie and Regina invited me to join them

on vacation to San Diego. We stayed in Little Italy and visited the zoo, went to the beach, even visited Tijuana."

"Regina?"

"His first wife. They were besotted with each other. After she died, I didn't think he'd ever love like that again. Then years later he and Delilah found each other."

"Why didn't you and your mom—"

The waiter appeared, opened the wine and poured two glasses. Marc ordered the swordfish, Cammie the white salmon.

After taking a sip, she answered his question. "When Mom was feeling good, she loved to talk about 'Racy Tracy' traveling and visiting places. But the truth was she rarely left the house."

"Racy Tracy?"

"Oh, that's what she liked to call herself. She wasn't racy— that term refers to her love of horse racing. Her name was Tracy."

A question flickered across his face. "Isn't that—"

"My contribution to Trazy's name, yes."

His eyes searched hers. "When did she die?"

An old ache gripped her heart. "When I was sixteen."

He waited. "Is it all right to ask…?"

"I came home from school and found her lying on the floor," she said, keeping her voice level. "Aneurysm, they said. Supposedly she went quickly."

"You'd always been there for her," he said gently.

Cammie nodded.

"Her caretaker."

"Not a very good one, obviously," she scoffed.

"You couldn't help that she—"

"Died when I wasn't there?" She took another sip, set down the glass. "That was my greatest fear. Didn't matter how many times I called in sick to school so I could stay home with her, or came home early to check on her, or the evenings and week-ends I didn't go out because I didn't want her to be alone."

Cammie looked at the setting sun, its orange-and-yellow light sliding down the horizon. "She checked out all by herself. Didn't wait for me."

Their food arrived. As the waiter fussed over the table, she shook off her painful thoughts. Did no good to talk about what happened. Much better to keep a lid on it, let the past be the past.

As they ate, she said in a chipper tone, "Did I mention that Val and I want to open a detective agency?"

"Val?"

"Christina Aguilera at the Shamrock Palace."

"Well, she's obviously good at disguises." He swiped his mouth with a napkin. "I've often thought that women make better investigators because, generally speaking, they're more intuitive about people. Compassionate, too. I know you're fond of Philip Marlowe, but that style of tough-guy shamus is better in movies and books. In reality, it can be off-putting to people."

"You view me as intuitive and compassionate?"

He gave her a serious look. "Absolutely."

When it came to his opinion of her work as an investigator, he was full of compliments, which was more than a little ironic. He thought she was intuitive, compassionate and as clever as Mrs. Peel. He'd chased her a thousand miles from Denver to Vegas to hire her. If she was so great at her job, why had he put her on probation? What would he have done if he'd thought she was incompetent? Shoot her?

She realized that she might have taken offense too quickly. Marc might have been willing to forgive and forget her slip into the gray area if she'd stuck around and negotiated with him. But she'd been hurt for reasons that had nothing to do with her job.

She'd been desperate for his approval.

It felt more than a little embarrassing to admit that to herself—after all, she'd always prided herself on her independent ways—but back in Denver, she probably would have done backflips for a smile, a congratulatory nod.

Now, it seemed, she had that approval back on a professional level. He couldn't stop applauding. It was time to give him some approval, too. Time to cut him some slack and stop obsessing about the probation. Like her uncle had said, life was short, and she didn't want to waste any more of it on old recriminations.

A young man strumming a guitar walked below them on the shoreline, the notes floating through the air as the last golden drop of sun disappeared off the edge of the world.

AFTER DINNER THEY WALKED along the beach to the motel. Deep in the west, the sky burned orange. Overhead, seagulls squawked as they circled, flashes of white against the approaching night. The lights from the pier cast a hazy glow on the beach.

Cammie, swinging her sneakers by their shoestrings, walked barefoot at the edge of the receding waves.

"This wet sand and cold water feels better than a foot massage," she said, teetering a little.

They'd shared a bottle of wine, less than two glasses each, so he chalked up her imbalance to the slanting shore.

"Your pants are getting soaked." Marc wove his arm through hers and gently pulled her onto drier sand.

In the distance, breezes blew toward the shore ripples of dark water, which built in intensity until they crashed in white frothy waves.

She halted and smiled up at him, the lights from the pier burnishing the ends of her dark curls. "You're such a gentleman."

"I try."

"Wish you wouldn't be."

He wasn't sure how to respond to that. "Come on, it's a short walk back to our rooms."

But she refused to budge. "What'd you think I meant...when I said you shouldn't be a gentleman?"

"Cammie—"

"I *meant*," she said, leaning forward, "that you should roll up your pant legs, too, and feel the water. But you thought I meant sex."

Maybe her nearly two glasses had had more of an effect because she'd eaten so little prior to dinner. "Cammie—"

"But while we're on the subject, I think it's time we talked about sex."

"How'd we get from walking barefoot to sex?" When she started to speak, he made a cut-off gesture. "Don't answer that. Let's bench this discussion for later—"

"No. I want to talk about it now."

He knew that tone in her voice. Had heard it plenty of times over the years when they'd worked together. She wasn't budging from this subject for one millisecond, so he might as well listen.

"All right." He sucked in a big breath of fortifying air. "Go for it."

She stepped right up to him, so close he could smell that familiar scent of flowers and almonds. The hazy light played across the swell of creamy flesh over the neckline of her top. She stared up at him, a look on her face he couldn't decipher.

She let go of her sneakers. They dropped to the sand with a soft whump. She lifted her hands and cupped them around his face, her touch soft and warm.

"I love you," she whispered.

The words hit him with an invisible force, as shocking as a splash of cold water. Reminded him of the times as a kid when he'd cannonball into a pool, the onslaught of chill ripping the very breath from him.

That's how he felt right now.

Stunned.

Speechless.

Still cupping his face, she tilted her head toward the first stars as though they'd encouraged her boldness. Hell, it couldn't have been *only* that measly glass and three-fourths' wine.

Ocean breezes scurried past, lifting her hair. The long dark strands seemed to float about her face.

The moment felt surreal, yet magical. His senses felt sharpened, raw. He was acutely aware of the waves pounding the shore, her pale oval face framed with a wild afterglow of sunset, her excruciatingly silken touch on his skin. She was breathtakingly beautiful. Like a nymph risen from the dark depths of the sea.

With a secret risen from the depths of her heart.

Just like when he'd been a kid barreling into the pool, after the initial shocking splash and some flailing about, the waters turned warm and welcoming and became the only place he wanted to be.

Cammie heaved an audible sigh and dropped her hands. "I take that back. I loved you when I worked for you, and I loved you after I moved here, but I'm not sure I love you anymore."

"Uh…" It was the most intelligent thing he could think to say.

She leaned over and picked up her shoes. "I feel so much better getting that off my chest. Let's get to our rooms. Tomorrow's going to be a busy day."

"Uh." He trudged behind her, glad one of them felt better.

A SHORT WHILE LATER, Marc wandered around his room. Pressed his hand against the bed mattress. Firm. Good. He checked out the kitchenette. Old stove, but clean. In the cabinet were an assortment of pots and pans, dishes, a red plastic colander. On the linoleum counter sat a coffeemaker that looked as if it had logged several thousand cups of java. He'd bought a toothbrush and toothpaste earlier in the day. Had a clean, funky T-shirt to put on in the morning.

Home sweet motel-home.

He pulled off his shirt, hung it on one of the wire hangers in a cramped closet next to the bed. Tugged off his loafers. Caught his image in a mottled mirror hanging on the wall.

His hair was disheveled.

He needed a shave.

That hungry look in his eyes had nothing to do with food.

"Damn it," he growled, raking his fingers through his hair. Outside, the turbulent surf hissed and pounded. Felt too damn warm in here. He stomped to the window and shoved it open. The curtains danced and fluttered as ocean breezes surged into the room. He licked his lips, almost tasting the salty wetness in the air.

He walked in a half circle, turned and paced back. Images of Cammie seared through his brain. Cammie in a corset, Cammie with her hair piled high and eyes thick with liner, Cammie in a body-clinging red dress.

Cammie on the beach, holding his face, whispering that she loved him.

He halted, blew out a pent-up breath.

So that's what she'd meant by his being clueless. Damn, she was right.

But then she'd wiped the slate clean. Taken the words away. Something about loving him years ago, even recently, but not now.

What the hell was that supposed to mean?

To think he'd wanted to hear a term of endearment, just one, from his daughter, then Cammie lays it on him in one humdinger of a confession that she then rescinds. Just like that.

Not fair.

Shaking his head emphatically, he stormed to the door. Just because *she* decided the conversation was over didn't make it so. Even Cammie knew that in a courtroom, both sides had the right to present their case.

CAMMIE WAS CHECKING OUT the cramped bathroom, wondering if the kitschy yellow-and-pink wallpaper was new retro or leftover from the nineties, when a pounding on the door made her jump.

She felt her pocket, belatedly remembering she'd left her smartphone at Laura's. Shit. What if she needed to call 9-1-1?

More pounding. "Cammie, open up!"

Marc?

She crossed to the door and opened it.

He stood there, shirtless, out of breath, one arm pressed against the doorjamb. He was insanely masculine, from his wild mass of chestnut hair to the determined, simmering look in his eyes, to his hairy, muscled chest.

Which she couldn't stop staring at.

It wasn't that she hadn't seen a man's chest before, it's just that she hadn't seen Marc's, and it had a helluvalot more hair and muscle than she'd given him credit for. Dark hair feathered his forearms, building to a carpet of the stuff from his clavicle to his pecs. It spilled over the latter, converging into a line that meandered over a tight stack of ridges before ending at a juncture between his flat, brown stomach and the button of his pants.

She sucked in a breath of air as her insides turned liquid. Nobody said anything, so she figured she should…say…something. That or start climbing the man.

"Hot." That pretty much summed it up.

Maybe he stepped inside, or maybe she fell against him. Whatever, they closed the space between them faster than the Big Bang.

The next thing she knew, their lips met and she was lost in a kiss that tasted like wine and the sea. Ocean currents barreled through the open door, carrying the sounds of the angry, pounding surf that merged with their hammering hearts, creating a swirling vortex within which only the two of them existed.

She had no pride, no sense of decorum, was only aware of her unleashed desire and need. She ravaged his mouth with hers while exploring his naked chest with her hands, stroking his muscles and fingering slick strands of chest hair. He returned her ardor with a carnal fury, kissing and nibbling and licking like a man who had been denied food and drink for too long, and she was his banquet.

Without warning, he ripped his mouth from hers and lifted her off the floor into a crushing embrace. She buried her face in the thick strands of his hair, inhaling scents of shampoo and the salty night air.

Panting, holding each other, they stayed immobile for a long, stretched-out moment. Then Marc eased her down until her feet again touched the cool floor. Leaning over, he gently kissed her, once, before pulling away. He closed the door, which shut with a resounding click.

It was as though a blanket fell over the room.

The breezes hushed.

The thrashing surf quieted.

Running a hand through her hair, he looked at her through heavy-lidded eyes. "I've waited days for that kiss."

"For me," she murmured, "longer."

He studied her face, his blue eyes glistening like the vast Colorado skies. Then he pulled her to him, grazing her cheek with his stubbled chin. "I was a fool to not realize—"

"Let's not." She didn't want to dissect and analyze her confession. She only wanted these moments, this now with him. Sweet bits of time that she'd hold forever in her heart.

He pressed his lips to the sensitive hollow behind her ear. "Then let me say," he whispered, "we both waited too long for our first kiss."

"Second," she whispered back.

"Second?" he murmured, nuzzling her lobe.

"That was our second kiss. At the Christmas party, year before last—" her breath caught as he nibbled on her neck "—you'd drunk a bit—"

"And?" he growled, his fingers sinking into the flesh of her behind as he tugged her even closer.

"You—" she fought to keep control of her voice "—asked me for a dance…"

He dragged his mouth to hers again, his lips lightly brushing against hers as he spoke. "And you said…"

"Yes." The word escaped on a sigh as his hand crept under her top, the pads of his fingers burning a path along her skin as he stroked and caressed her back. "You took me outside… we danced on the lawn…under the shadows of a pine tree…"

"Like this?" He pulled her against his hard body and pressed her head against his bare chest. As they swayed in rhythm— one, two, one, two—he slow-danced her to the light switch and flipped it off. The room submerged in shadows.

"Yes." She rubbed her cheek against his chest, liking the feel of his strength against her skin.

"Was there moonlight?" he asked.

"A little."

He steered them another few steps to the window and pulled back the curtain. Hazy moonlight filled the room.

They danced in silence for a minute or two, keeping time with the distant waves that crashed far, far away in another world.

"Did I tell you how beautiful you were?" he murmured.

"You compared me to a painting by Chagall. *La Mariée.*"

"One of my favorites," he murmured.

"I had to look it up after that. The woman is in a red dress with a white veil." She'd also learned the translation of the title was *The Bride,* but skipped that part.

"She had long, dark hair…" He tangled his fingers in her hair. "And she's quite beautiful, the focus of the painting."

"There's also a goat playing a violin."

He chuckled under his breath. "Actually, I believe it's a cello. Behind him is a man playing a clarinet and a fish jumping over a table. It's about joy, and yearning for what is lost."

He dipped his head and played his mouth along her throat. "Speaking of which, I yearn to remember kiss number three…"

Closing her eyes, she parted her lips.

But he didn't kiss them.

Instead he planted gentle kisses on one eyelid, then the other. "For your green eyes," he whispered. "Sometimes they sparkle like emeralds, other times they turn turbulent and gray, like a storm at sea."

She opened one eye and peered at him. "I hope you see emeralds more than storms."

He smiled. "I do. Are your eyes still closed?"

She closed them. "Yes."

A light, soft kiss on the tip of her nose. "That's for being a great private investigator who's always sniffing out clues and following the trail until you solve the case."

"What's next," she muttered, "a kiss on my cheek for being cheeky?"

She felt a peck on her cheek. "Anything else, Miss Smarty Pants?"

"Yes. Are we still on kiss three?"

"Merely opening arguments… Now for the evidence."

But it wasn't just a kiss.

He made love to her mouth.

His tongue lightly flicked across the sensitive inside of her top lip, then her bottom lip, asking permission. When she opened wider, he emitted a low-throttled groan as his tongue slid slowly inside, exploring the wet warmth. His mouth was knowledgeable, his tongue gentle yet demanding, causing her senses to spin higher and hotter until she couldn't think, only act.

She returned his passion, entwining her tongue with his, their kisses growing searing in their intensity. White heat sparked and caught fire in her as their tongues darted and plunged with building compulsion. He tugged off her top, finally breaking the kiss to pull it over her head and toss it aside.

They stood there, breaths heaving.

He made a sound somewhere between a curse and a prayer.

"I like it when you don't wear a bra," he murmured huskily.

She didn't want to say they'd been in such a rush to get to California that she hadn't bothered to put one on. Instead, she soaked in the compliment, her hands hanging at her sides, letting him see her, wanting—no, needing—to know he liked what he saw.

"Lovely," he murmured in a low, throaty voice. Stepping closer, he slowly circled one nipple, then the other, with his index finger. Under his laser-hot touch, her nipples pebbled as electrical currents shot straight to her groin. She stifled the urge to whimper, but it came out anyway in a lengthy, reverberating moan from someplace deep inside that she hadn't even known existed.

He dropped to one knee and undid the button on her jeans. "I want to see all of you," he murmured, plucking the zipper. He pulled down her pants, and she stepped out of them, grateful she'd worn her pink briefs. Then realizing in this light, who knew the exact color or style?

And who cared? They were off in seconds anyway.

Now she stood fully naked in front of him.

"Cammie," he murmured, "you're a beautiful woman."

That was the kind of compliment she'd been waiting for. But she didn't waste time savoring his words. She wanted his body. She wrapped her hands around the nape of his neck, threading her fingers through his hair. Boldly, hungrily, she pulled him forward, felt as he placed a single kiss on her stomach before he stroked his cheek against her soft skin, brushing slowly back and forth, the sensation prickling but surprisingly pleasurable.

She looked down at him just as he looked up at her. In the muted light, his eyes were dark pools, his hair a wild black mass. Moonlight rippled over his back and arms, skimming muscles with silver and delving into shadowed ridges. In between the worlds of light and shadow, real world and fantasy, he looked mythical and powerful, a savage knight who knelt before her, ready to do her bidding.

"Take me," she whispered.

CHAPTER THIRTEEN

HEAT SHOT THROUGH MARC like a gamma ray blast. Lunging to his feet, he scooped her into his arms and carried her—his prize, his woman—across the room. When he reached the bed, he gently lowered her onto the mattress.

Perhaps it was the moon rays sifting through the window, or the play of shadows and light in the room, but her skin had a soft, almost luminescent glow. Her hair fell in ebony curls around her pale face. He couldn't see her features clearly, just the impressions of her eyes, mouth and, below, the dusky circles of her nipples and triangle of her sex.

She looked like the shadowy essence of the woman in *La Mariée,* the real maiden underneath the colorful dress and whimsical caricatures in the painting.

Maybe what lay in the shadows was what was most real.

Maybe what he'd thought he'd lost, he'd found.

"Cammie…" His throat felt tight, parched.

The moment was more powerful than he'd anticipated.

Leaning over, he lifted her hand and gently kissed the inside of her palm, then pressed it against his cheek.

"Your hands are so soft," he whispered.

Taking her other hand in his, he gently pulled her to a sitting position. She glided her hands up the sculpted ridges of his chest, burrowed her fingers into his chest hair, then let her fingertips trail slowly down to his waistband.

She popped the button and pulled down the zipper, followed by his pants and shorts. Even in the shadowy room, his erection had a rock-solid silhouette.

"Wow," she whispered, staring at it.

Her eyes looked like large, dark orbs. Or maybe his male ego wanting her to be that impressed.

"It's *huge*," she murmured.

"I assure you," he said, fighting a smile, "it's average. Maybe you've lost your sense of perspective." Another thought surfaced. Maybe she hadn't been with that many guys.

Or *any* other guys.

No, impossible. She was thirty-one, maybe thirty-two—he forgot exactly—which seemed one hell of a wait to lose one's virginity, but he'd never heard of her romantically linked to anyone in the entire time he'd known her. And she'd never shown up at any company parties with a date. And she'd made that comment about loving him for years....

"Cammie," he murmured, "is this...your first time?"

After an instant of silence, she stifled a laugh. "You're kidding, right?"

"No, I— It's just...you'd said...and I thought—"

"It's been a while," she admitted, probably to save him further embarrassment. "Okay, four years, to be exact, and before that there'd been a few...involvements. I'm not exactly what you'd call a fast-track kinda gal, but I know enough to judge size, thank you."

Well, that wrapped up that conversation. And nearly wrapped up his hard-on, which had started flagging with the conversational right turn.

She ran a fingernail slowly from the end of his shaft to almost the tip, then back.

"Plus," she said in a throaty whisper, "as you probably recall, I have a killer memory when it comes to numbers." She circled his penis with her hand and gently squeezed. He hissed a breath between his teeth. "And this bad boy is *big*."

He started to laugh but his mind rocketed to another dimension when she flicked her tongue slowly around the ridge. With a strangled moan, he took her hands into his and squeezed them tight as he caught his breath.

"Let's take this a bit slower," he rasped. "I might have forgotten our first kiss, but I don't want to forget our first time."

As he lay next to her, the words he'd spoken resonated through his mind. *Our first time* connoted more times, as in months, maybe even years or a lifetime. A twinge of uncertainty rose within him, but he shoved the question down. He'd spent enough time lately worrying about the future.

Tonight was about living in the present.

Cradling her head in his hands, he reveled in the feel of their naked bodies pressed together. He loved how her long legs intertwined with his, how her curves fit snugly against his angles, how her round, pert breasts flattened against his chest.

This time when he kissed her, he took his time, letting his lips discover her warm, soft, pliable mouth. Tasting the faint buttery chardonnay from dinner, he flashed on their talk, how close he'd felt to her.

"Don't close off from me," he whispered huskily. "Let me know you."

He nuzzled her ear, his senses taking in the flowery scent of her perfume. He kissed then suckled her earlobe before seizing it lightly with his teeth, liking how his warming breaths triggered goose pimples to flare lightly over her skin.

Returning to her mouth, he resettled his lips on hers and whispered the things he wanted to do, encouraged by her responding soft whimpers.

Cradling her face with one hand, he slid the other down her body, sculpting her rib cage, her waist, then back up, pausing just beneath her plump breasts. Slowly, he caressed and cupped one mound, letting his fingers draw up until they lightly pinched the pebbled tip. He rolled it gently, teasingly. Her breathing grew rapid, choked.

He dropped his head to the other breast and laved it with his tongue while stroking and plucking the other. Continuing those ministrations with his hand, he wrapped his lips around the other morsel and flicked his tongue on the hardening nub.

Hearing his name escape her throat in a groan, he opened his mouth wide and sucked, nipped and licked until she writhed, pushing her cleft restlessly against his erection.

He released the breast and dragged his fingers slowly down her middle, over her stomach, and lower. Reaching between her legs, he slipped his middle finger through the slick crevice, straight to her wet core.

Her body shuddered. "Marc, I want you…"

Starting slow and building, he circled her crux with his fingertip while simultaneously clasping his lips around her nipple again, sucking it firmly into his mouth. As his fingers glided and plunged, she convulsively drove herself against his hand.

"I want you," she cried softly, tilting her hips, "now…oh, please, *now.*"

"Let me get…protection," he said between pants. He fumbled in the dark, mentally congratulating himself on finding his wallet. "I'm like a prepared Boy Scout," he said lightly. "Always carry one, just in case."

He slipped it on, then, with a growl of need, rolled on top of her and spread her legs. As he inched his shaft inside her, she mewled into his mouth, shifting and grinding to more deeply accommodate his entry. Finding their rhythm, she wrapped her legs around his waist, her fingernails digging into his back.

Propped on his elbows, he pushed harder, deeper, their bodies slick with sweat and heat and need. He thrust again and again, riding her cries of pleasure, gritting his teeth as her insides convulsed in paroxysms of contractions until, unable to hold back any longer, his breath ripped loose in a hoarse cry as he reached a mind-rattling climax.

Afterward, he rolled onto his back, pulling Cammie into an embrace. They lay there, breaths heaving, their bodies wet with exertion.

"That…was…spectacular," Cammie whispered.

"Unbelievable," he murmured.

He stared out the window at the moon, Cammie close in his arms. After a few moments, her head sank heavily against his body and she started snoring lightly.

He scanned the shadows in the room, lingered on spots lighted by stray beams from the moon, until eventually he stared at the pale form of the woman slumbering in his arms, her dark hair lying splayed across his chest.

"La Mariée," he murmured softly, stroking her hair.

CAMMIE AWOKE TO THE SCENT of coffee and something sugary and fragrant. She forced open one eye and saw a dark blurry figure hovering next to the bed. After several blinks, the image sharpened into focus.

Marc, dressed in slacks and his Chicks Dig Me, Fish Fear Me T-shirt, stood next to the bed, holding a mug of coffee.

He smiled, his eyes twinkling. "Good morning, Sleeping Beauty."

"Thank you." Her voice sounded like something that had been dragged along a dusty interstate. She cleared it, tried again. "Thanks, charming prince." She accepted the mug with a grunt of pleasure.

After swallowing a sip of coffee, she smiled. "You remembered I like cream in my coffee."

A glazed doughnut magically appeared in his hand. "And that you like these."

"It's not vegan, is it?"

"No, flour, lard and sugar."

She waggled the fingers of her free hand. "Come to mama."

Munching on the gooey concoction, she looked out the window at the dull gray-blue skies. She looked around the room for a clock.

"It's a little after 6:00 a.m.," Marc said.

"Where'd you find doughnuts at this hour?"

"Across the street. Place opens at five. Several surfers were already there."

"I like swimming, too, but not at predawn hours." She took another bite.

"I have good news and bad news," he said solemnly. "Good news is Laura got home around two this morning. There's video of her stumbling about her living room, cleaning up plates and cups."

"Had she been drinking?" Whether or not the baby was Marc's, Laura shouldn't be boozing it up.

"I sure as hell hope not. She was wearing a robe, so I couldn't see the baby bump." He paused. "A man was with her."

She nodded, wondering how that had affected Marc when he saw it. After taking another sip, she set down the cup and tossed back the blanket. "I'll get on my clothes. We need to serve her."

"If you serve her around eight, that'd be good. Considering the late hour she got in, I doubt she holds down a regular job."

She picked up what was being said between the lines. "You're leaving soon."

"That's the bad news. Not that it's negative news, just that Emily texted me about the Eco-Glitter rally today that I'm accompanying her to. She begged me to please pick her up at Delilah's by one at the latest. Seems there's an eco-radical band called Flames of Dissent performing at the rally and she has her heart set on seeing them. I'll need to leave fairly soon to get to Vegas in time."

"I understand."

"I started a fire in the pit outside. Thought you might enjoy the warmth, as it's chilly out there."

"Great idea." She stood, naked, and looked around. "I seem to remember being dressed when I entered this place."

With a low chuckle, Marc retrieved a folded blanket from a shelf in the closet. Shaking it open, he wrapped it around Cammie's shoulders, pulling her closer.

"You're beautiful in the morning."

She hiccuped a laugh. "Now I'm wondering about *your* perspective."

He grinned, his eyes shining. "Making love with you last night…I'll never forget it." He gave her a soft pat on the behind. "The fire pit is just outside the door. You can snuggle up in this and enjoy your coffee and doughnut."

She stepped outside in their private court, a small grassy yard with palm trees, a rock-lined fire pit and two white Adirondack chairs that Marc had positioned next to the pit. The yard was rimmed by a privacy hedge, over which Cammie had an unobstructed view of the Pacific Ocean and the distant San Clemente pier. In the sparkling ocean, half a dozen surfers bobbed on surfboards.

Cammie sat, adjusting the blanket, warming herself next to the fire. Marc brought out her doughnut on a plate, and her mug.

"I've already reserved a rental car for you," he said, sitting in the chair next to her. He picked up his coffee cup and took a sip.

"This early in the morning?"

"Don't forget we're in the sprawling L.A. metropolis, not some small town in the Midwest. I called a lawyer I know in the area, and he connected me with a car rental agency that offers twenty-four-hour service. Car will be delivered by seven-thirty."

She recognized his lawyer persona—in control, officious. A necessary defense to the upheaval in his life, but she sensed the pain roiling beneath that together surface. Had to hurt like hell to be wrestling with the repercussions of "Gwen's" deceit, to know this was his best, and maybe only, chance to make her accountable. And then there was the baby, a child he so desperately wanted. He hadn't said it in those words, but Cammie knew.

She couldn't fail him. Wouldn't fail him.

"May I see the video?" she asked.

"Sure." He retrieved his phone from his pants pocket and handed it to her.

She set the doughnut aside and checked out the video. It'd been dark outside, with lights blazing inside the house, so the recorded image was startlingly clear. And different. Gwen-Laura's long blond hair was now dark brown and cropped close to her head in a pixie cut. She wore a low-cut caftan that would have made Delilah jealous, and bloodred lipstick that would have driven Philip Marlowe crazy.

In the video, she staggered around the room while picking up the dirty plates and cups. A slim man with graying hair, wearing a white T-shirt that emphasized his tan, sat on the couch smoking.

"Ever meet him?" Cammie asked.

"Yes."

She looked up. "And?"

"I saw him outside her apartment twice, figured he was visiting somebody in the building or that maybe he lived there. Once we commented about the Rockies' new pitcher. A passing conversation, nothing special."

"Did you ever see men's clothes—or other personal items—around her apartment?"

"Never." His voice was hard enough to ward off any hint that Laura's boyfriend had lived with her in Denver. "But I wasn't at her apartment all that much. We usually met at my place."

She handed back the phone. "I'm sorry."

He shrugged. "I was played. But we've found her, and I'm going to bring her to justice if I have to drag her there, kicking and screaming." His voice dropped. "Because if I don't—"

"You will, Marc. I promise you."

Holding the blanket around her, she crossed to him. Standing before him, she asked softly, "May I?"

He set his mug on the ground and opened his arms.

She settled on his lap and nestled into his embrace.

"Thank you, Cammie."

She felt the shift in their energy, like the ebb and flow of the tide. A fierce ardor for what was right, and just, surged within her.

"I'll serve her if I have to live in that rental car night and day surveiling her place."

"But no—"

"Oh, please, are we really going there again?" She huffed a sigh. "I won't do anything illegal." She held up two fingers. "Girl Scout promise."

He frowned. "I thought they saluted with three fingers."

She added one. "Better?"

"Cammie, I know it irritates you to be reminded, but you are my *key* witness at not only Laura's trial down the road, but also at my father's impending parole hearing. If you look dirty, my case looks dirty, and dirty legal cases end up in big, ugly garbage dumps."

"Thank you, Mr. Positive."

"Okay, I got a little heavy."

"Ya think?"

He held up one hand in apology. "One last point, and it's constructive. Do you know if there's another exit to Gwen's— I mean, Laura's—place? Don't want her slipping out the back while you're out front."

"I already checked the former real estate agent's data. No back door. She either leaves through the front, that garage or the chimney. Whichever way, I'll be waiting."

"Chimney." He chuckled under his breath, then turned earnest. "I hate to leave you here alone. I'd hoped to get that chance to negotiate a deal with her."

"You might've gotten her to agree to certain terms, but, Marc, let's be real. You would've walked away with empty promises."

She stared into his solemn eyes. The fire crackled and sputtered. Breezes carried scents of the salty ocean and sweet honeysuckle.

"C'mere," Marc said, tugging her closer. "I don't have much time...."

Snuggling into his warmth, she looked into his face. Morning light caressed the firm line of his jaw, gleamed on the reddish-brown of his hair. She gazed longingly at his mouth, then slowly, her eyes rose to meet his hard gaze.

He took an agonized breath. "I should've been with you," he murmured, "not her."

Her fingers tightened on his shoulders as he lowered his lips to hers.

Their kiss was intense, hungry. Underneath her, she felt his thighs tighten as he reached for her beneath the blanket. His large, warm hand stroked and caressed her naked body, stoking her internal fires.

She sucked in a sharp breath as he touched her *there*.

"So good," she groaned, moving her hips in time with his hand.

She felt his erection press hard underneath her.

"Take off," she whispered mindlessly, half turning and fumbling for his pants.

He clamped a hand over hers. "I want you so bad, it hurts," he said in a thick voice, "but we used my only condom last night.... Today it's just for you...."

He wet his finger with his mouth, then zeroed in on the center between her legs. His eyes holding hers, he rubbed her nub in tight, slick movements.

"Is that good for you, baby?"

She bit her lip, a whimper escaping her throat. Locked on his eyes, she stared into those glistening blue depths as her body rocked to his movements, driving her closer and closer to the edge.

She stilled, her entire body suspended on a precipice. Then her insides exploded in wave after wave of release.... She cried out, the sound lost in a kiss as Marc held her.

Afterward, she lay in his arms, vaguely aware of the distant pounding surf, the smell of the fire, the warmth of the sun on her face.

"I have to go, Cammie," Marc whispered.

"I know." She paused. "I'm sorry you didn't get to..."

He pulled her close, holding her so tightly against himself she swore she could feel his heart hammering through his shirt.

Stroking her hair, he whispered into her ear, "I'll wait for you, Cammie, as your man, your lover, your friend. I'll always wait for you."

She pressed her head against his shoulder, fighting a well of emotion. For a hard moment, she regretted ever telling him about her mother's death, how it had felt to come home and see the single most important person in her world had left her forever. She hadn't realized it until this moment, but she'd never wanted anybody to be that important to her again.

"Did you hear me?" he asked.

She nodded, her face pressed against his soft T-shirt.

"I mean it, Cammie."

"I know you do."

"Always," he repeated.

AT 7:35, CAMMIE DROVE the rental—a blue Kia Rondo—to Laura's house. She'd checked out of the motel and tossed her few possessions into the passenger seat.

In her investigations, she often rented different cars when conducting multiday surveillances, to avoid detection. Even better that the Rondo had a California plate, a different state than the rental from yesterday.

After hitting some local traffic, she arrived at the house at ten to eight. She parked across the street, one house down, and checked out the place. The garage door was closed. The standing mailbox door, which yesterday had been closed, hung open. They'd either checked for mail when they'd gotten home in the wee hours or within the past hour or so.

If somebody was up, Cammie wanted to make this fast.

After sticking the papers into her pocket, she quickly exited the car, headed to the gate and peered over it. Nobody in the yard, no motion in the window. She quickly entered, letting the gate swing quietly shut behind her, and headed to the corner of the window where she'd left her smartphone.

It was gone.

She scanned the ground underneath the ledge. Nothing. Looked around a hedge near the window. Nothing. Surveyed the immediate area. Nothing.

A grinding metallic sound diverted her attention. The garage door was opening. From inside came the splintered rumble of a cold engine.

Cammie bolted across the yard and shoved open the gate as a red Dodge Viper hurtled backward down the driveway, spun a ninety-degree turn in the street and halted, facing forward.

The gate slapping shut behind her, Cammie ran into the middle of the street while fumbling to get the papers out of her pocket. Stumbling to a stop fifteen or so feet in front of the car, she held them up for the driver to see. Bright morning sunshine glinting off the windshield, obliterating the face behind the wheel.

What the hell. She had fifty-fifty odds.

"Laura McDonald," she yelled, "you are served!"

The car lurched forward, smoke spewing from its spinning tires as it bore down on her. Cammie jumped out of the way, gripping the papers.

"Crap!"

She jogged to the Kia, hopped inside and started the car. Seeing it was clear both ways, she spun a one-eighty and sped down the street, keeping her eye on the flash of red.

It swerved left several blocks ahead.

She followed suit and slammed on her brakes.

In front of her, kids were boarding a yellow school bus, its red lights flashing. A few mothers hovered nearby, looking tired or relieved. One wagged her finger at a grumpy-looking kid strapped into a superhero backpack. She flashed on a long-ago memory with her mother, who'd felt well enough that day to walk Cammie to the bus stop. They'd held hands and laughed, making up silly stories about a cat named Crusader. Her mom could have such a wonderful sense of fun and creativity about life—Cammie liked to think she got some of that from her.

But today was about creativity, not fun.

She glanced around for any police units. Seeing none, she pulled out and drove past the school bus, waving at the matron bus driver who looked about as happy as a prison guard.

Cammie scoured the road ahead, peered down side streets, checked if the red car had tried to hide by parking behind a Dumpster or truck.

Nothing.

The road curved around to a stoplight at the main drag, El Camino Real. For a heart-stopping moment, she thought she saw the Viper zipping past before realizing it was an Audi.

She'd never been one for theatrical outbursts, but at that moment she could have out-acted Meryl Streep in the melodrama department. Cammie wanted to cry, curse, pound her hands against the steering wheel. She hadn't come this far to *fail*.

She flashed on Philip Marlowe's line in *Murder, My Sweet*. "I felt pretty good—like an amputated leg."

"That feels about right," she muttered, debating if she should turn north or south. Eenie, meenie, minie…north. She turned the steering wheel and eased into northbound traffic.

Spying the big rooster on a surfboard ahead, she had an idea. Maybe it would work, maybe not, but it was her best hope.

Her only hope.

CHAPTER FOURTEEN

CAMMIE TURNED INTO The Surfing Rooster. A gangly girl in a string bikini and a red-haired boy in flowered swim trunks sat at one of the picnic tables making out, oblivious to the world around them.

A swell of feeling, like a wave, rolled over her. She missed Marc.

After parking in one of the three parking spaces behind the restaurant, she walked around to its order window. A guy stood with his back to her, his brown hair tied in a scraggly ponytail. He was chopping onions in time to a reggae number, heavy on the reverb, that played over an iPod-speaker setup on the shelf next to a jar of pickles.

"Hello?" Cammie called out.

"Hey," he said, setting down his knife. Wiping his hands on a cloth, he turned and smiled at her, his eyes pinker than a Mary Kay Cadillac.

"Dude," she said, "I'm, like, in a major jam."

"Yeah?"

When he leaned closer, she caught a telltale whiff of ganja. "Yeah. Lost my cell phone."

"Bummer."

"Yeah, and I'm lost and I need to call my sister to get directions to this major family reunion thing. You got a phone?"

"Huh? Oh, yeah." He looked around, lifted a towel, pushed aside a bowl. "There it is." He handed it to her.

"Far out." Sometimes the goodness of people gave her hope. Especially people who'd upgraded to smartphones. She tapped on the keypad, checked the GPS results. If Laura had her smart-phone—which likely she did—this would give the location.

"Biggee's Burgers—is that nearby?"

He looked confused for a moment, then pointed at El Camino Real. "Take a left. It's about a mile or so. Can't miss it. Says Biggee's Burgers on the outside."

No kidding. "Thanks." She handed it back to him.

"Wow," he said, "your family reunion's at Biggee's Burgers?"

"Uh, yeah," Cammie said, walking away. A reunion of sorts, anyway. One she was primed to attend.

"Have a groovy one," he called out after her.

"Oh, I will," she murmured, picking up her stride.

Back in the car, she retrieved a rubber band from her purse and secured her hair into a bun, put on her big sunglasses and swapped her fresh T-shirt with the one she'd worn yesterday. Then she started the car and headed to Biggee's.

A few minutes later, she parked in the lot adjacent to the restaurant, out of view of Biggee's customers and its parking lot, and stuck the papers in the waistband of her pants, covered by her T-shirt. Then she got out and walked into the restaurant.

"How many in your party?" asked a girl with curly brown hair and braces on her teeth.

Cammie looked at her name tag. "Can I look at a menu first, Alison?"

Alison, flashing a silver smile, handed one to Cammie. Holding it up, Cammie peered over it at the room. No Laura. As Alison escorted a middle-aged couple to a booth, Cammie walked outside with the menu as though perusing it, and headed to the parking lot.

The red Viper was parked in a far corner of the lot in the shadow of a tree. A woman with a brown pixie cut sat in the driver's seat, her head bent.

Cammie pulled the papers out of her pocket and held them inside the menu she pretended to be reading.

She didn't walk straight to the Viper. Instead, she mean-dered toward another car parked near it, as though it were hers, preoccupied in her menu-reading. As she reached the car's passenger door, she swerved and headed straight to the open driver's window of the Viper. Closer, she saw what Laura was looking at. Cammie's smartphone.

She slapped shut the menu with the papers inside and tossed them in Laura's lap.

As Laura jumped back in her seat, emitting a curse that could clear a locker room, Cammie reached through the open window and snatched her smartphone.

"Laura McDonald," she barked, "you're served." She almost said *effing served,* but Marc wouldn't have approved.

Laura's forehead wrinkled. "Are you that private eye?"

"No, I'm your fairy godmother." Cammie started heading across the lot.

Behind her, a car door slammed.

"Get back here, you—"

If air could turn blue, their shared ether would have pulsed sapphire. Cammie picked up her pace, smiling politely at an elderly couple who'd stopped in their tracks and were star-ing, wide-eyed, at the epithet-shrieking woman hot on Cam-mie's tail.

"You can't serve me papers in a restaurant menu," Laura screamed, "you fu—"

Cammie could serve papers in a Spanx sandwich for all the courts cared, but she wasn't going to debate the issue with Miss Pissed-Off Pixie Head, who she hoped wasn't carrying a gun. Name-calling she could survive, but a bullet...

Passing Biggee's entrance, Cammie checked the reflection in its windows. Laura, fists raised high, was gaining on her. She wore a flouncy cropped top that could be covering a weapon stuck into the waistband of her pants, but if that were the case, she'd be reaching for it, which she wasn't.

Cammie began speed walking, but too late. A heavy punch to her back sent her teetering forward, fighting for her balance.

Catching herself, she darted to the side and spun to face Laura, who looked genuinely surprised.

For a fleeting instant, Cammie considered head butting her. A quick, vicious shot to put her out of commission. She'd used it once successfully, years ago, on a guy who didn't believe no meant no.

But Laura could be carrying Marc's baby. She was supposed to be five or six months along. No matter what craziness this nutzoid pulled, Cammie couldn't risk hurting that child.

"Take it easy," Cammie said coolly, showing her palms in a peacemaking gesture. "I'm only the messenger."

That reminder lasted all of two seconds.

Spitting a colorful two-word directive, Laura sprang forward, her hands clawed like a raptor descending on its prey.

Cammie jumped away and raised a defensive elbow, which caught Laura in the eye. With a screech, Laura staggered a few feet, holding her hands over her eye.

People were gathering outside the restaurant.

"Lady, you okay?" a guy yelled.

"That...that *dick* socked me in the eye," Laura wailed, pointing at Cammie.

In the skirmish, Laura's crop top had crept up almost indecently high. Between it and her low-slung jeans, Cammie got a good look at her flat, brown midriff. Not just flat, but concave with jutting hip bones.

"Somebody call the cops!" a woman yelled.

"I got a better idea," a shortish, fattish guy chimed in. Tucked into the front of his shirt was a ketchup-smeared napkin. "Let's throw some Jell-O on 'em and sell tickets." He and his buddy guffawed and slapped each other on the shoulders.

"The short-haired one started it," said a man in a white Stetson hat.

Easing in a calming breath, Cammie punched a few keys on

her smartphone and pulled up a photo of herself in front of the American flag, proudly holding her just-earned Nevada P.I. license. God, that photo seemed like a lifetime ago. Her license wasn't valid anymore and showing it might fall into the gray area. But Cammie decided to risk it. She wanted the crowd on her side. She held it up for people to see.

"I'm a private investigator working on behalf of attorney Marc Hamilton. This woman's name is Laura McDonald and she's been served a subpoena to appear in court for stealing thirty thousand dollars from Mr. Hamilton's law firm. You can call him at 303-555-7299 to confirm this."

Several people started punching numbers into their cell phones. My, how crimes had changed since Marlowe's days. Marc would be surprised at the influx of calls, but he'd also be keenly interested in first-person accounts of Laura's violent behavior, which could only have a positive effect in his case against her.

Cammie toyed with calling 9-1-1 herself and pressing third-degree-assault charges—another one would be such a lovely addition to Miss McDonald's rap sheet—but that would mean being stuck in San Clemente while cops interviewed her, and Cammie wanted to get to Vegas as soon as possible.

She snapped a few quick shots of the crowd and of Laura, whose blood had drained from her face, the resulting tan-over-pallor making her look a bit sickly.

The man in the white Stetson, pens clipped in the pocket of his utility-type cowboy shirt, stood next to Laura, his hand clamped like a vise on her shoulder. It was clear he intended for her to stay put whether she liked it or not, and from the bitter, beaten look on her face, she got the message.

Cammie stared at her. She should start the long drive back to Vegas, but there was a niggling question that only one person could answer.

"Why Marc?" she asked.

Laura laughed—a dark, disturbing sound—before fixing

unflinching eyes on Cammie. "I happened to be in Denver, and I read about his dad skimming a fortune off his clients' money. I thought, why not pull the same trick with Junior? When the theft was discovered, everybody would blame him. Like father, like son."

"You targeted him?"

"That's right. I expected a huge payoff, but sometimes you take what you can get. When I figured I couldn't get more than a lousy thirty thou, I moved on."

For a moment or two, all Cammie could do was look stupidly at her, her brain assimilating how a woman who had once seemed so silly, so Shopping Mall Queen, was capable of such diabolical actions.

But then, hadn't she once said that a Mall Queen was a lot more complex than people realized?

"You nearly destroyed a wonderful man's life," Cammie said quietly.

A look dawned on Laura's face. "God, how pathetic. You still carry a torch for him."

Cammie turned and started walking away.

"I could always tell you had a thing for him," Laura called out. "Even told him once and we had a good laugh about it."

Cammie focused on the swaying palm trees, the crush of the distant surf, the look in Marc's eyes when he said he'd be waiting for her.

"Because he never cared for you that way, honey," Laura yelled. "Never did, never will!"

The twist she gave to the word *honey* made it sound uglier than a dirty name.

After Cammie got into the Kia, she called Marc and got his voice mail. He was probably talking with one of the witnesses from the restaurant. He would be one busy guy fielding all the phone calls as he drove to Vegas.

"Hi, it's Cammie," she said. "Laura's been served. Yes, I gave your phone number to a group of strangers, most, if not all, of whom saw Laura McDonald go berserk after I served her. I'm heading back now, should be there by—" she checked the time "—2:00 p.m. Call me."

As she drove out of the lot, she passed Laura, who flipped her the bird.

"You're number one in my book, too, *honey*," Cammie murmured.

LAURA'S TAUNTS BUBBLED UP in Cammie's mind on the drive. Every time she pushed them down, reminding herself that Laura's ramblings were nothing more than the vengeful barbs of a criminal who'd been caught and would pay for her crimes.

After miles of road and several hours of thought, Cammie finally reached the conclusion that a corner of her heart hadn't caught up with current-day events. That the Cammie who had nursed an unrequited crush for years was still hanging around, a kind of ghost of Cammie Past, who was stuck there because she was afraid to embrace the future.

Really, if she ever got tired of being a P.I., she could be a shrink.

As she pulled out of a gas station in Barstow, California, Marc finally returned her call.

"Next time," he said, "why don't you just spray paint my private cell number on the side of a building?"

Next time. She liked that. "Because I don't do illegal things like deface private property."

He chuckled. "That's my girl."

My girl. She liked that even better. "But not indulging in gray activities is not just about you, you know. Little things like misdemeanor charges could put a serious crimp in getting my license back. Felony charges, forget it."

"Seriously," he said, "good job serving what's-her-name. How'd you find her at that burger place?"

"When I got to her house, my smartphone was missing. At the same time, she was backing her snazzy red Viper down the driveway—tried to follow her, lost her. Ended up at The Surfing Rooster, where a stoner short-order cook loaned me his smartphone. Checked my phone's geolocation through an iCloud connection, and learned it was at Biggee's Burgers."

"Good job, Mrs. Peel."

"Thank you, Mr. Steed."

"Witnesses have told me stories about her trying to start a cat fight."

"Yeah, Swagtastic knuckle rapped me from behind, and although I considered giving her a head butt, I refrained."

He half choked a laugh. "Head butt, really?"

"It was a passing thought," she mumbled, not wanting to explain what else had gone through her mind at that moment.

"Did she hurt you?" His tone had turned serious.

"No, Marc, I'm okay."

"Now we understand how she got that third-degree assault."

"Exactly what I thought." Maybe she should go ahead and tell him that Laura wasn't pregnant, but no, that would be an awkward conversation to have while they were driving in separate cars. Plus Cammie didn't want him to be alone when he heard the news. Either Laura lost the baby, or it had never existed. Regardless, Marc would grieve the loss.

"You're so quiet," he said.

"It's been a long day."

"Going to get even longer. I'm heading straight to Delilah's place to pick up Emily so I can chaperone her at her first political rally."

"Right. Eco-Glitter."

"Shame Amber can't join her. Seems she and Em have become bosom cell-phone pals, talking at all hours about environmental issues and social responsibility." He chuckled. "I should be getting into Vegas in an hour, tops. How about you?"

"I'm an hour behind you."

"Got to hand it to Em." The pride was evident in his tone. "She's walking the talk."

"Maybe she can use this experience to write a report at school or start some kind of student eco organization."

"I'll have to ask her about it when she's back…with her mom."

A pain sliced through Cammie as she realized how soon the three of them would be scattered hundreds of miles from each other.

"I'll miss her," she said.

"Me, too."

"I'll miss you, too."

"We'll have to talk about that."

She got his message as surely as if he'd waved a sign. What had transpired between them these past twenty-four hours was a building block to the next stage of their relationship.

"Yes," she agreed, "we'll have to talk about that."

Before they said their goodbyes, they made plans to get together later that night. Dinner, then spend the night together at her uncle's place.

After that, she found a radio station that played classic rock. She sang along with "Take It Easy," an old Eagles tune, feeling good and happy and, caution be damned, wallowing in being *in love*. Screw that "I'm not sure I love you anymore" speech she'd given on the beach.

The ghost of Cammie Past wasn't going to be hanging around much longer.

AN HOUR OUTSIDE VEGAS, Cammie's cell phone rang. Delilah's name displayed on the caller ID.

"Hey, Delilah," Cammie answered.

"Hello, dear," Delilah said, her voice barely audible.

"Let me turn down the radio. I can hardly hear you. Okay, what's up?"

"I'm keeping my voice low, dear, because I don't want Emily to overhear. Right now she's playing with Trazy in the back room."

"Is there a problem?"

"Yes." Cammie thought she heard a sniffling sound. "I feel bad tattling, but this is serious. I tried calling Marc several times, but he doesn't answer, and I don't feel comfortable leaving this message on his voice mail."

Cammie stared through the bug-splattered windshield at the stretch of Interstate 15 in front of her, trying to grasp what the older woman was talking about.

"Delilah, for God's sake, what is it? Did you find drugs? Is she drinking? Unprotected sex, *what?*"

"Worse!" Delilah, who cooed and kissed and blissfully knitted her way through life, cracked. "She's going to jail! My Lord almighty, our little Emily will be tossed like a piece of fresh meat into a holding cell with prostitutes, drug dealers and other political activists!" She released a weighty sob. "She's just learned how to use a cable needle, and now she'll be with junkies who stick real needles up their..."

While Delilah proceeded to describe in graphic detail something she'd seen in a prison documentary, Cammie put her phone on speaker and set it on her thigh.

Two words in particular had stood out.

"Political activists?" Cammie repeated, interrupting Delilah's description of a prison gang fight between the Aryan Brotherhood and La Nuestra.

"What, dear?"

"You said there'd be political activists in the jail—" A light went on. "This has something to do with the Eco-Glitter rally."

"Yes! That's what I've been trying to tell you. I overheard Emily talking on her cell phone with somebody named Dylan or Daven—"

"Daearen."

"Yes! That's it. At first they were talking about some kind of glitter show, which sounded lovely, and then I heard things about diminishing natural resources and sabotaging the political machine and—" she blew her nose loudly "—and then Cammie said she'd be *proud* to be arrested in order to bring attention to the rape of planet earth."

"Which she's planning on doing at today's rally."

"Yes!"

"Do you know where, exactly, this is occurring?"

"She mentioned a Green Planet gathering. Sounded as though they sold gecko glitter jewelry there."

"Eco glitter."

"What— *Oh!* I'm looking out the window and her father just picked her up. They're driving away! I'd hoped to talk to him before they left and now—"

"I'll be in Vegas in less than an hour," Cammie said, jamming her foot on the gas. "Emily wanted to see some band first, so she won't be arrested right away." Ah, the priorities of youth. "I'll head straight to the rally and find this Green Planet group."

"I'll go, too."

"No."

"But…I want to help."

Thoughts of cleavage and eco-radicalism were swirling with Aryan Brotherhood and La Nuestra gang warfare. "You can help by staying close to your phone. In cases like this," she said, fumbling for a good reason for Delilah to stay put, "it's critical that there's a go-to person available by phone at all times."

After a beat, Delilah said, "Yes, I'm happy to be that person. And one more thing."

Cammie waited. "Yes?"

"Did you know the world is ending in 2016?"

THIRTY-SEVEN MINUTES LATER, Cammie parked her car near the Lloyd George U.S. Courthouse in downtown Las Vegas, in front of which the Eco-Glitter rally was taking place. In the parking lot, a lone protestor—an uptight-looking woman with fire-engine-red hair and perfect makeup—carried a bright pink sign that read Everything's Fine, Keep Shopping.

The notorious Vegas winds had decided to lie low for a change, offering no respite from the afternoon sun. Cammie guessed temps were in the low eighties. Had to be broiling inside the dark police uniforms that were everywhere on foot, bike, even horseback. Cruisers were parked at both ends of Clark and Bridger Avenues on Las Vegas Boulevard, which had been blocked off for the event. Reporters and videographers were camped out at different areas at the rally, vultures waiting for their feedings.

Moving through the crowd, she caught scents of pineapple and apples from a Grow Local open-air booth. A guy in a G-string wandered through the crowd, playing "With a Little Help from My Friends" on a flute. A series of stalls labeled The Organic Free Trade People's Market advertised such items as lavender deodorant, recycled-textile jewelry and eco-friendly lingerie.

It was as if a corner of Woodstock had merged with Sin City.

It wasn't difficult to find the Green Planet activists. At least thirty of them, looking righteously solemn and wearing bright green armbands decorated with glittery emblems of the planet earth, had congregated in the middle of the courthouse steps.

A distant incantation drew Cammie's attention.

"Spare the earth. Spare the earth."

Five or six people, wearing Planet Earth armbands, marched solemnly in front of a small tractor rolling down a cleared area of Las Vegas Boulevard. Several waved American flags. A thirtysomething man with bushy black hair, apparently the leader, was yelling slogans into a bullhorn.

A line of cops in riot gear approached from the opposite end of Las Vegas Boulevard.

The media pushed through the crowds, vying with spectators for primo spots to witness the upcoming showdown.

"Cammie!"

Marc jogged toward her, his face lined with worry. Reaching her, he grabbed her shoulders and yelled over the growing buzz of the crowd.

"Em…I've lost her!"

Cammie scanned the courthouse steps, looking in vain for a flash of strawberry-blond hair.

"We were watching the band," he continued, "and next I knew, she was gone." Frantic, he scoured the crowd. "A mess is brewing and I want her out of here."

She glanced at the rolling tractor. The bushy-haired leader, walking alongside it, held up something. People started clapping, others yelling, fists raised high.

"What are they doing?" she said absently.

The leader bellowed into the bullhorn, "Death to the Machine! Death to the Machine!"

"Marc," Cammie said, tugging on his sleeve, "he's holding a Molotov cocktail!"

"Take off the gas cap!" the leader yelled into the bullhorn.

The tractor slowed as several Planet Green types began fiddling with the cap.

Marc looked anxiously through the crowd. "Damn fools, they're going to set fire to the tractor! Where's Emily?"

The line of riot-geared cops marched forward, one of them barking orders through a louder, badder bullhorn.

"Cease! Move away! Disperse! Now!"

Two cops in blue jackets with *Police* in bright yellow letters on their backs burst from the crowd and tackled the leader, forcing him to the ground. A third officer cuffed the leader's hands behind his back as he continued screaming orders, indicating his bullhorn that lay in the street.

A blonde in jeans and a Make Love, Not Trash T-shirt, wearing a Green Planet armband, darted into the street and picked up the bullhorn. It was Emily. The bullhorn looked huge in her hand. Cammie silently prayed that she would have the good sense to drop it and step away.

No such luck.

She saw Emily lift the bullhorn to her mouth. It was like watching a train wreck in slo-mo. Smart, pretty, well-meaning Emily was about to take a giant step in the wrong direction.

"Brute force can't subdue the earth," she said through the microphone.

People roared and raised their fists.

"Emily!" Marc pushed and shoved his way through the crowd.

"We stand with Mother Earth," Emily yelled. "Witness this brutality! Raise the voices of the people!"

"Emily!" Marc shouted, pushing past a reporter.

Cammie, jogging behind him, saw one of the cops in a blue jacket running toward Emily like a bull elephant about to trample Bambi.

She raised a defiant fist. "Deny the ruling-class pigs their brutal moment in the sun—"

The cop snatched her bullhorn, yelling, "You're interfering with a felony investigation and you will be arrested—"

"Stop!" Marc yelled. "She has a right to free speech."

A burly guy holding a video camera blocked Cammie.

"She doesn't have a right to help people blow up tractors, buddy," the cop yelled at Marc, pointing a finger for emphasis. "If you don't move away immediately, I'll charge you with obstruction of jus—"

Which was the last thing Marc needed. Not now, when his career, his father's freedom, was at stake.

Cammie jabbed her elbow into the fat guy. With a curse, he jumped aside, and Cammie ran as fast as she could across the asphalt, watching Marc argue with the officer, who was waving over reinforcements, directing them to Emily, who stood nearby, looking terrified and frightened.

Cammie knew what she had to do, and she had to act fast.

Stumbling to a stop between Emily and the cop, heaving breaths, she pressed both hands, palms down, on the chest of his uniform.

"Turn the brutality…away from the child," she said, keeping her hands on the officer's chest. "You won't…get past me… to this child."

She was vaguely aware of Marc yelling, Emily crying out, while one undercover cop grabbed Cammie's hands, and another shoved her to the ground. Her cheek against the hot, gritty street, she felt the zip-tie handcuffs tighten around her wrists. Overwhelmed with the stench of asphalt and oil, she did her best to remain calm despite people screaming, cops barking orders, even a reporter who got down on her hands and knees and shoved an iPhone in the vicinity of Cammie's face.

In a surreal moment of inconsequential thoughts, Cammie realized she and the reporter used the same recorder app.

The thought burst as cops hoisted her to a standing position and led her away, one on each side.

She glanced at Marc, who looked worried and furious, his arm around a distraught Emily, who kept mouthing *I'm sorry* to Cammie.

A few minutes later, the cops leaned her against a patrol car and began patting her down. The hot metal stung her hands. Her hair hung in her eyes. Another fugly day in paradise.

"I don't usually ask this of men who have their hands on my thighs," she said in her best casual voice, "but besides my inadvertently touching you, Officer, is something wrong?"

He snorted the word *inadvertently* under his breath. "You're being charged with obstruction of justice, assault on a police officer, disobeying an official order and, just because you really pissed me off, lady, conspiracy to commit arson."

The last one treaded into felony territory.

"Hey," she said lightly, "I'll plead to interference with a police officer and obstruction if you'll forget about the conspiracy to commit arson."

"What do you think this is," he barked, "a poker game?"

As he read the Miranda rights, she realized that's what she'd end up doing, dealing poker again, because she'd just lost her ability to ever be licensed as a P.I.

CHAPTER FIFTEEN

"THE CLARK COUNTY Detention Center is *not* the Waldorf Astoria."

As Cammie sat in the crowded jail facility with the other new female inmates, all of them waiting for their cell assignments at the Clark County Detention Center, she thought about the judge's infamous warning several years ago to heiress Paris Hilton. That judge had been lenient with the heiress, who had been charged with drug possession and lying to a Las Vegas police officer, by giving her a suspended sentence. Supposedly by explaining that the jail cells weren't a five-star hotel helped clarify just how bad incarceration could be for a pampered trust-fund baby.

With three misdemeanor charges, and one felony, Cammie doubted any judge would be as lenient with her.

A woman sat next to her. Her narrow, white face seemed to lack flesh, like a skull topped with a reddish-brown wig.

"Saw you on the news," she said in a barely audible monotone.

No hello or how ya doing? One of those people who cut the chatter and got down to what they wanted to say. Probably shaved a good five, ten minutes a year off boring conversations.

"Saw it, too." Four times at least. Clark County had not one, but two television sets in this holding area. Soap operas played on one, a local news station on the other. After repeatedly seeing footage of her hands on the police officer, telling him to turn his brutality away from the child, followed by the lovely shot of her face pressed into the asphalt, it was hard to tell which TV was airing the soaps and which the news.

"What'd they get you for?"

"Obstruction. Assault. Disobeying an official order. Conspiracy to commit arson." She'd had three hours to think about every single one of those charges, could probably rattle them off in her sleep.

The woman made a harrumph sound while her gaze darted around the room. "You musta pissed off them laws."

Cammie knew from the girls at Dignity House that *them laws* meant the police. "I believe I did, yes."

"Me, soliciting."

One measly charge? Cammie almost felt jealous.

After sitting in silence for several minutes, the woman droned, "Got a lawyer?"

"Maybe." Marc wasn't licensed as an attorney in Nevada, but he could give her friendly advice, although after today, she wasn't real sure how friendly their terms would be. Although her intention at the rally had been to protect Emily, Cammie being charged with a string of misdemeanors, and that one nasty felony meant her credibility as an upcoming witness was potentially tainted.

"I got a good one. Give you his number if you'd like."

"That's okay. I have a backup if mine doesn't work out."

The woman slid her a look. "Backup?"

"Local defense attorney…" Frankie's lawyer pal who got her out of the GPS mess, which he did for nothing because he owed a favor to her uncle. She doubted the lawyer would be a no-charge again, though, which meant she'd be paying off lawyers' fees for the next millennium.

"He's helped you out?"

"Pleaded down a felony to a misdemeanor."

She gave an approving nod. "What for?"

"Federal wiretapping charge." Cammie gave her new pal a can-you-believe-it look. "For attaching a GPS. I mean, really, if you want to split straws, placing any type of apparatus on a vehicle, be it on the side, the hood or underneath, can be deemed in plain view, and if an object is in plain view, it's legally there."

The woman arched an eyebrow. "You been giving it a lot of thought."

"Yeah."

"You're smart."

Considering where they both were sitting, Cammie didn't have a response to that.

"What's a GPS?"

Over on the soap-opera TV, a middle-aged actress with a facelift so tight it was a miracle she could speak her lines, pointed a gun at a man. The dozen or so women watching it looked unfazed.

"It's a device that uses satellite signals to pinpoint people's locations," Cammie answered.

The woman seemed to give it some thought. "Can one of them devices be dropped in someone's pocket?"

"Yes."

"I could use me one of those."

A corrections officer, wearing a sneer like Frau Farbissina in the Austin Powers movies, stepped into the room. Cammie half expected her to yell, "Bring in the Fembots!"

Instead, she called out, "Camilla Copello?"

Cammie raised her hand. "Here."

"Come with me," the officer said. "Your bail's been posted."

TWENTY MINUTES LATER, Cammie, dressed again in her sneakers, pants and T-shirt, entered the lobby of the detention center. Marc and Emily rose from their chairs.

Emily ran across the room and hugged her tight. "Cammie," the girl said, her voice breaking, "you were awesome."

Cammie wrapped her arms around the girl, not sure how to respond. She looked at Marc over Emily's head. He stood there, his arms crossed, the same look of fury on his face that she remembered when the cops had led her away.

"Let's go," he snapped, heading for the doors.

The three of them walked down Lewis Avenue in silence, Marc in the lead, moving as though he had a rod up his spine. Emily held Cammie's hand, occasionally squeezing it and giving her meaningful looks, trying to signal that everything would be okay.

Incoming clouds were breaking up the heat of the day. The temperatures had dropped from a disagreeable static heat to a breezy chill while she'd been in the jail. The palm trees swayed with the currents, which carried the faint smell of exhaust fumes and the metallic scent of impending rain. When they reached the parking lot, Marc turned abruptly.

"Phil's parked one row over," he said to Cammie, retrieving the car key from his pocket. "Delilah and Frankie helped me return your rental and get Phil here. Your purse is locked in the trunk."

She cringed inside, thinking how worried her uncle and Delilah must be after witnessing her arrest on TV. Delilah would be beside herself imaging what might have happened to Cammie in the jail.

"Thanks," she said, accepting the key. "They're probably anxious about me, so I'll go home and—"

"No." The single word was strained with ill temper. "We have a few things to discuss. Emily—" he handed her another key "—you know where the Prius is parked. Lock the doors after you get in and wait for me."

"No," she said, leaving no doubt she'd gotten her father's obstinate gene. "I want to talk to her, too."

"Emily." His voice held a warning.

"Daddy, I'm not some child you can order around. This might be my last chance to tell her in person…how much she means to me."

A pained look shuttled across his face, but he didn't put up an argument.

Emily turned to Cammie. "I'm grateful for what you did," she said in a low voice, "although I'm sorry that there will be problems because of it." She darted a look at Marc, back to Cammie.

"I'd do it again in a heartbeat," Cammie said.

The girl's eyes filled with emotion. Stepping forward, she took Cammie's hands in hers. "'There is no greatness,'" she said in a quivering voice, "'where there is not simplicity, goodness and truth.'"

"Tolstoy?"

Emily nodded.

"Do you memorize his quotes whenever you have a spare minute?"

A laugh bubbled out the girl's mouth. "I looked that one up earlier. I wanted something that, you know, was special for you."

"I'm afraid I'm not always truthful." She glanced at Marc, who was pacing, his head bent. "I promised your father something, and I broke my word."

Emily grew serious. "I don't know what you promised him, but I do know you acted unselfishly to protect me. Plus you drew attention to the cause."

"I have to be truthful here, Emily...I didn't do it for any cause. But you're right in that I'm a pretty simple person. When I care for someone, I care with all my heart."

Winds gusted past, ruffling their hair.

"Emily," Marc called out, "time's up. I need to talk to Cammie. *Alone.*"

Emily released her hands and started walking away, backward, not taking her eyes from Cammie. "We never got to see a true-crime show."

Cammie smiled. "We'll watch one virtually. The way you did with your pals the other night."

"Promise?"

Cammie started to speak, but the thought of never seeing Emily again lodged like a rock in her throat. *Promise,* she mouthed, making a crisscross over her heart.

Emily stopped. "I wish that you were my mother," she said fervently.

It was the last thing Cammie expected to hear. Fighting a well of emotion, she watched Emily jog across the lot. A moment later, a car door slammed.

Marc walked up to Cammie, stopping right in front of her. He looked at her, his eyes glistening with rage.

Undaunted, she stared back, wanting to see past the anger, wanting to catch a glimmer of understanding or compassion.

"Marc," she whispered, "I'm sorry."

"I had the situation under control," he said tightly, ignoring her apology. "You didn't need to barge in there and create a situation that none of us—you, me, my father, Emily—will ever recover from."

The world suddenly felt too light. The sun filtered eerily through the gathering clouds, which glowed like polished gunmetal. Across the lot, a woman and her child, holding hands, leaned forward against the gusty wind as they walked.

"I—" Her voice came out strangled, thin. "I was protecting Emily...and you—"

"Emily and *me?*" He barked a laugh. "I had my rights to speak up on behalf of my daughter, who also, by the way, was exercising her right to free speech. Granted, it was a heated moment, but a manageable one. Then you decided to go all... *Philip Marlowe* and insert yourself into the middle of things."

"That's ridic—"

"You didn't just wade into this gray area, Cammie, you stomped. And it's not as though you didn't know the consequences. You *knew,* damn it, and you did it anyway. You placed your hands on a police officer, *knowing* you'd be charged with obstruction of justice *at the very least.*" His lips clamped in a thin line and he squeezed shut his eyes, as though fighting to maintain control over his volatile emotions.

She'd never seen him like this. On edge, ready to explode.

"Marc, please hear me out. If you'd been arrested—"

"And how would that have happened? I was *talking* to the officer, not *assaulting* him—"

"I wasn't assaulting—"

"You know the law as well as I do," he snapped. "Even laying a *finger* on an officer will get you arrested, and in a volatile situation, it easily results in an assault charge. Anyway, to hell with your excuses. Face it, you have a thing for breaking the law. Makes you no better than a common criminal—"

"Stop it!" She turned away, pressing her hands over her ears.

He grabbed her hands and held them midair as he glared into her face. "Stop what? The *truth?* The reason you were working at the Shamrock Palace was because your investigator's license was *suspended* after you broke the law. But this time, Cammie, *my* license will be suspended."

They stood like a tableau, their bodies tense, their muscles coiled.

A red Mitsubishi Evo cruised into the lot. The fiftysomething driver nodded her coiffed head to the blasting strains of Lou Reed's "A Perfect Day." As the car rolled past, Cammie caught the license plate. CUINCRT.

If she wasn't so pissed, she might have laughed.

Turning her attention to Marc, she said with as much calm as she could muster, "Let go of me."

"Gladly," he responded, dropping her hands with a dramatic flourish.

She crossed her arms and glowered at him. "Look, Laura McDonald has been served. When is that deposition?"

"Five days."

"Attorney Disciplinary Agency will be there, no D.A., right?"

"Yes, it's set up for the ADA to hear and see how deeply Laura was involved in this crime."

"Well, she must show up for that deposition or be in contempt of court, and I don't think she's real keen on having a warrant for her arrest issued, so she'll be there."

He leaned forward, his jaw muscles dancing. "But my main witness, *you,* can't provide testimony at the depo, which sabotages my ability to exonerate myself. As we talked about before, I *need* your testimony about your investigative efforts that proved Laura was actively hiding after her theft. But with your *multiple* pending charges, and possibility of conviction on each, the ADA will view you as some kind of fringe protester nutcase, which damages *my* credibility. This kicks open the door for the agency to proceed with suspending my law license. No license, no ability to represent my father, whose parole hearing, as you know, is June 6. A month and a half away."

She felt as though her world was caving in, making it difficult to breathe, to think. "Can't he find another lawyer to represent him?"

He gave her an incredulous look. "You worked in legal investigations long enough to know that frantic clients scrambling to hire new lawyers at the last minute is often the death knell to a case. Besides, my father doesn't have the money to hire anyone, and nobody will do it *pro bono* because they either don't want to be associated with him and they think he should rot in jail for his crime, or they just don't care." Marc's jaw twitched. "I was doing it because—" his voice cracked "—I'm his *son.*"

For several long, excruciating moments, Marc didn't talk. Couldn't talk. It felt as though the world had tilted at a sickening angle. Blood roared in his ears, mimicking the distant clamor of thunder.

"And I'm Emily's *father,*" he continued, unable to hold back the words, the pain, as they tumbled from his mouth, "but the only time she's said the word *Daddy* this trip…it was in anger."

Cammie stepped toward him, arms extended, and when they hugged, a silent, awkward embrace, the world almost shifted to normal. He closed his eyes as he smelled her scent, felt the silkiness of her hair as the wind blew strands against his cheek. The back of her T-shirt felt damp, and underneath it, her body felt firm.

He wanted to give in to the moment. To pretend nothing had happened.

"Marc, I—I love you."

More words hitting him like hammer blows. He pulled her closer, close enough to whisper into her ear, "The last time you said that, you took it away in your next breath."

He felt her stiffen slightly as he stepped away and dropped his hands.

They simply stared into each other's eyes, and he noticed how the sparkle in her green eyes had dimmed, and how the corners of her lips turned down. He wanted to see her smile and to tell her that everything would be all right. But he couldn't lie. His association with Cammie had to end. For himself, he knew the toll this would take in sleepless nights and waking memories, and he thought how time aged people more kindly than heartache.

But their relationship could never work. Not after today.

And yet he'd been so ready. As a kid, he'd often dreamed of his dad returning home and all of them being a family again. After his own divorce, then the debacle with Gwen-Laura, he'd been afraid of such dreams. But with the gradual understanding that his feelings for Cammie went back years, and after their night together at the beach, he'd realized how self-defeating it would be to let old fears stand in the way of happiness. He'd been ready to complete the circle, to be a family, with Cammie.

It hurt like hell to watch the dream die.

"I'm sorry, Cammie.…"

TIME SUSPENDED—it could have been seconds, possibly minutes—as Cammie listened to him explain that it was over. His words fell on her, slicing through her with a sorrowful grief, piercing something sacred and fragile deep inside.

When his words finally stopped, she gave her head a slow, disbelieving shake. "My," she whispered, "it must be wonderful to sit so high up there, knowing what's right and wrong, black-and-white."

"Says the woman who likes to slide into the gray."

She mentally flinched, but held herself still, impassive. His accusation hit a wall. She was tired of apologizing for being who she was—a risk taker, a woman who would rather take a chance and pay the consequences than cower in fear and uncertainty.

"Yes, I've waded into questionable areas," she said over the rising winds. "Sometimes taking those risks means I've solved cases, some high-profile cases that brought you acclaim and money, Marc."

"But at the time," he said quietly, his brow wrinkling, "I didn't know—"

"Really? Absolutely *no* idea how I might have possibly found evidence of, oh, where that woman was buying drugs in the Campbell case, or how the husband was siphoning money to his girlfriend in the Verdon case?"

He gave her a lengthy, perplexed look as though trying to see inside her brain. "You're saying you illegally discovered evidence in those cases?"

"No. In the Campbell case, I attached a GPS on a vehicle registered to our client. In Verdon, I did a trash hit and found ATM receipts. In both cases, there were no issues about how I found the evidence. In the wrong judge's court, however, my means *could've* been considered illegal. If that were true, *you* would've been viewed as complicit in my breaking the law."

"Hypothesizing how a judge might have ruled doesn't

change the fact, Cammie, that you have a bad habit of willfully bending the law. That's what stands between us."

"No, what stands between us is that I'm not *perfect*. That I'm willing to stumble and even fail, in search of the truth. I'd rather be in the gray, and be real, than be like you, afraid to not be *exactly* right or wrong. Hate to break it to you, Marc, but your father's in the gray and so's Emily. Actually, so's most of the world. That's why you sit in that house alone, a perfect man in his perfect world."

He impaled her with steely blue eyes. "I think we've said enough."

She was about to turn away when she stopped herself. Despite their angry words, she owed it to him to let him know that Laura wasn't pregnant. Timing of the news wasn't exactly opportune, but if she didn't tell him now, when would she get another chance? It was only fair he knew before the deposition, and not be hit by the obvious fact when Laura walked into the room.

"There's one more thing, Marc, and I'm telling you this as a friend…"

He made a stopping gesture, his mouth twisted as though he couldn't bear to utter a single word more.

"Laura—" thunder rumbled overhead "—isn't pregnant."

He stared at her, stone-faced, then turned and strode away.

His hard, implacable response stunned her. Maybe he hadn't heard? Or maybe he didn't want to believe her.

Rain started spitting from the sky as she watched his retreat, the sound of his footsteps fading until she heard nothing…as though he'd never been there.

Raindrops fell, splattering the concrete with fat gray blobs. She leaned into the gusty winds, feeling spent and fragile. But she had to be strong, had to keep moving forward with her life. If she let her thoughts wander to him, if she allowed the memories of what they'd shared to resurface, they'd tear her apart and destroy her faster than any earthly storm.

Cammie parked Phil in front of her uncle Frankie's house and killed the engine. Rain splattered on the roof of the car, washed down the windshield. Through the blur, she could see the house was ablaze with lights, both from inside as well as the yellow porch lights and exterior yard lights.

"The electric company must love you, Uncle Frankie," she murmured.

After a mad dash to the house, holding her purse over her head as though that might prevent the rain from drenching her, she walked inside, dragging fingers through her damp hair. Scents of tomato sauce and warm bread infused the air. Frank Sinatra was crooning "You Make Me Feel so Young," with backup vocals by Uncle Frankie, his voice drowning the other Frank's. Tossing her purse on the living room couch, she headed into the kitchen where her uncle and Delilah were dancing, cheek to cheek.

When Frankie saw Cammie, he stopped and called out, "My li'l *figlia!*"

Delilah, wearing a low-cut tiger-print number and an apron with the words *Kiss the Cook,* opened her arms, her gold bracelets sparkling. "Oh, my dear, we were so worried!"

Despite Cammie's warning to them that she was a walking water puddle, they embraced her in a group hug that reeked of Chanel No. 5, lemony-musky cologne and enough garlic to cure the ills of the world.

If only that were true.

After that, Delilah ordered her to put on dry, clean clothes. When Cammie returned, dressed in a favorite soft pair of jeans and her Nuggets sweatshirt, Frankie escorted her to the dining room table and poured her a hefty glass of Chianti while Delilah served a little plate of olives, cheese and nuts, "to whet your appetite, dear."

While Delilah stayed in the kitchen to monitor the boiling pasta and sauce, Frankie sat across from Cammie and poured himself another glass of wine.

"Marc told me you and Delilah took back the rental car and delivered Phil to the parking lot," she said, trying to sound together, maybe even normal. "Thanks for doing that."

He shrugged. "That's what family's for." He gave her a knowing look. "Marc, he wasn't so happy with what happened this afternoon."

"That's right." She took a sip of her wine.

"He didn't give no particulars, but—" Frankie shrugged dramatically "—it was obvious, y'know? I mean, who hasn't seen my niece, the revolutionary, getting arrested on the news?"

"Oh, sweetheart!" Delilah called out from the kitchen. "Your face against the asphalt like that!"

"But she looks okay now, kitty doll," Frankie yelled back, tilting his head to check out Cammie's cheeks. "Don't see no oil spots or scratches." He leaned back in his chair. "So, where was we? Yeah, Marc wasn't real happy—"

"We broke up." She figured it was easier to simply say it.

Her uncle blinked. "I never even knew you two's were together. Can I tell Del?"

"No need," Del called out. "I can hear fine from the kitchen."

Cammie had to smile despite her misery. "It's okay that Del knows. After all, we're family."

"I was worried sick about you being in that jail," Delilah added.

"I'm fine."

"Those gangs…I told you about that documentary I saw."

"There was no gang warfare in the Clark County Detention Center. Well, there might've been if anybody changed the soap-opera channel."

"Soap opera?"

"I love you, my bride-to-be, but soap operas can wait. Me and Camilla got to talk." He turned his attention to her. "So, let's take it from the top."

Cammie told him about the issue of "wading into the gray" that had come up repeatedly between her and Marc. How they'd found Gwen, whose real name was Laura, in San Clemente, and after some girl-drama craziness, Cammie served Laura papers for her appearance at a deposition in five days. She explained how Marc had been counting on Cammie's testimony at this deposition to persuade the Attorney Disciplinary Agency to not suspend his license, and how, if he lost it, he wouldn't be able to represent his father at a parole hearing in a few weeks.

After a big sip of wine, she wrapped up the story by saying she'd screwed everything up by willfully getting arrested at today's rally. Her actions were meant to protect Emily, and although Marc didn't want to accept it, to protect him, too.

Frankie's brow furrowed. "I don't get the screwed-up part."

"My testimony at the deposition, remember? I can't do that now, which means his license will be suspended, which means he can't represent his father—" She choked back a sob. "That sweet old man...will spend the rest of his life...in prison."

And then she cried. Just let the tears fall.

After a flurry of commotion that included another group hug, Delilah plunked a box of tissues next to Cammie's dinner plate. "When a lady's heart has been broken, she has the right to cry at dinner, dear."

Then Delilah set the food on the table while Uncle Frankie, who'd donned his horn-rim glasses although he wasn't reading anything, gave his "three cents."

"Y'know, that wading into the gray area stuff isn't somethin' new in your life, Camilla. You did that all the time as a kid with your mother, God rest her soul. You always wanted to protect her, and the good Lord knows, she needed protecting. I protected her, too, but you were the one who was on the front line, and she leaned on you, too." He put some salad on Cammie's plate. "Eat, it's good for you."

She did what was good for her.

As he served salad to himself and Del, he continued, "Risking your own well-being for another isn't somethin' new, either. I remember coming over when you were ten, maybe eleven, and you were trying to get your mother out of that old Ford Escort she used to drive, remember? It was running in the garage with the door closed. Lucky I dropped by—you didn't know that both of you could be overcome with carbon monoxide. I brought your mother inside, and called 9-1-1."

"I remember," Cammie said solemnly. "She was in the hospital for several days, and you and Reggie stayed with me." During that time, her uncle and aunt had done everything in their power to help Cammie recover from the traumatic episode, including the three of them attending several meetings with a school counselor. She remembered how scared she'd been for her mother's well-being, as well as angry at her actions. After that, she'd been more vigilant than ever about her mom's safety.

He turned thoughtful. "Y'know, Camilla, I'm gonna give you another perspective on living, and I'd like for you to hear me out. Maybe it's okay sometimes to live a black-and-white life, to know what's wrong, to do what's right. Look at Frankie and the pope." He gestured to their photos on the wall.

She and Delilah looked.

"Frankie, he pretty much always lived in the gray, y'know? But the pope!" He crossed himself. "He understood black-and-white, and he helped many of us live by it. After all, with black-and-white, you can trust your choices." He took a sip of wine, set down the glass. "And 'nother thing. I like how you take care of others—your mother would be proud—just make sure you take care of Cammie, too."

"Your uncle is a wise man," Delilah murmured.

"And one more thing." He looked intently at Cammie, his eyes big and shiny behind the thick lens. "You want I help Marc understand the situation? Because after your uncle Frankie talks to him, your world could again be a beautiful place full of lollipops and rainbows."

Cammie nearly choked on a bite of pasta. After swallowing, she said quietly, "I think Marc has enough on his plate without that conversation, but tell you what. I might ask you to give that speech to the car mechanic next time I take in Phil."

CHAPTER SIXTEEN

ON THURSDAY, AT 5:00 P.M., Marc was in the living room of the suite at the Aria, his suitcase open, looking around for any last items he needed to pack. In the corner, he spied a wad of black material. He walked over and held it up, reading the white block words on the front of the black T-shirt.

Chicks Dig Me, Fish Fear Me.

His jaw hardened even as his heart shrank. A black-and-white T-shirt—it was as though Cammie was getting in the last word.

Which she had.

That's why you sit in that house alone, a perfect man in his perfect world had haunted him ever since she'd said the words yesterday. Then she'd added something about Laura, but he hadn't wanted to hear more.

He couldn't think of the last time he'd turned his back on someone and walked away. Had never done it to a client, and there had certainly been some belligerent ones who deserved it. He'd never done it to his ex-wife, and they'd had some fights where he should have. Had never done it to Gwen-Laura, who he wished he'd walked away from the very first time their eyes met.

But he'd walked away from Cammie. And every second since then, that last grief-eroded look on her face continued to stab at his heart.

He tossed the T-shirt aside, slammed shut his suitcase and snapped the locks.

"Em," he yelled to the closed bedroom door, "finished packing?"

Of course, she didn't answer. She'd been sullen ever since the fiasco yesterday. Hadn't spoken to him the entire ride to the hotel after he'd bailed out Cammie, wouldn't even respond when he asked her if he could take her out for a gluten-free, vegetarian, green-as-they-come meal. After they'd arrived at the hotel, she'd continued stonewalling him all the way to their suite, where she marched into her room and banged shut the door.

He'd called room service for dinner, picking the most exotic, organic-sounding dish for her—a rice pasta with morel mushrooms and walnut pesto—which he'd left on a tray outside her room. Around midnight she'd opened her door long enough to take the tray inside, then made a great show of locking the door, loudly.

He'd stayed up late, watching mind-numbing TV shows whose plots and characters he couldn't recall, his thoughts vacillating between telling himself it had been worthwhile bringing Emily out for a visit to chiding himself for thinking he could pull off being a full-time dad. And when he wasn't thinking about that, he was thinking about Cammie, wondering why the hell she'd put herself on the line like that, even while knowing she was always one to take action and test limits.

But understanding the motivations behind her actions didn't erase the consequences. He had a hell of a problem coming up with the deposition.

In the morning, Emily had grudgingly told him she was going downstairs to buy a green tea and gluten-free muffin, and he'd asked to accompany her. But even walking together to the bakery didn't heal their rift, because the only thing she'd wanted to talk about was his making up with Cammie, and he'd refused to discuss the matter. Back at the hotel, she'd retreated to her room again.

The hours of the day crawled past in a slow, dull haze. He

hadn't grown closer to his daughter this trip. He'd only managed to alienate her further.

Now, finally, it was time to go. This vacation from hell was over. He glanced again at the closed door. "Em, we need to check out, grab a bite to eat and get to the airport."

Silence.

He headed to the door and knocked gently. "Emily?"

Silence.

He tried the handle. Not locked. He opened the door.

Her suitcase lay packed on the bed. He quickly scanned the rest of the room. Her brightly patterned eco-friendly purse, made of recycled candy-and-gum wrappers, was gone.

He walked back into the main room, looked around as though maybe she'd magically materialized in the few moments he'd stepped into her bedroom. He checked the bathroom off the entrance way.

No Emily.

He called her cell phone and got her voice recording.

For once he hoped she was ignoring him. He didn't want to think of other, darker, reasons why she might not be answering.

He went to the room phone and called the front desk. "Get me security."

Within seconds, he had Iona on the line.

"I remember your daughter well, Mr. Hamilton. There have been no recent reports of an underage person fitting her description in the gambling areas. How long has she been missing?"

The last time he'd talked to her had been around three-thirty when he'd knocked on her door, said he was going downstairs to pick up a fax in the hotel business center.

"About an hour and a half."

"That's not very long. Maybe she went shopping?"

"I doubt it." Not Emily's style to wreak revenge through a decadent capitalist shopping spree, but on the other hand, what better way to punish a bourgeoisie father?

"It's only been a short while," Iona said quietly. "Maybe she's gone to the food court to get a drink or to check out some of the stores on the strip."

After leaving his cell number with Iona, he wrote a note to Emily that she shouldn't have left the room without telling him where she was going, that he was looking for her, that she needed to call his cell ASAP and that he loved her.

AT FIVE O'CLOCK, CAMMIE WALKED inside the front door of Dignity House to start her stint as study monitor. The place was dark, cloaked in an eerie silence that made her nerves itch.

She flicked on a light switch.

"Surprise!"

The girls appeared magically, some scampering in from the hallway, others popping up from behind couches and chairs. They laughed and clapped and yelled her name.

Carolyn, one of the resident counselors, slowly unfolded herself from where she'd been hiding behind an armchair.

"Hi, Cammie," she said, brushing hair out of her face. "Instead of study hour tonight, the girls asked to spend some special time with you."

Cammie gazed at the green-and-yellow streamers looped around the room. "It's...not my birthday," she said in a bewildered voice.

"No, but after today, you will have fulfilled your community hours, and the girls thought they might not be seeing you again, so they asked to surprise you with this goodbye party."

She'd been so caught up in everything else in her life, she hadn't counted how many hours she had to go to fulfill her community service, something she'd done every single day when she'd first started volunteering.

"And we also saw you get arrested on TV," another girl said, "so we figured we'd better have the party now in case you end up in juvie."

"Fool," another girl chimed in, "Miss Copello's too old for juvie."

Carolyn made a settling motion. "This is a party, girls, so let's keep it light, okay?"

"Yeah," Takira said, throwing a hip-hop move, "let's just marinate, not agitate."

Amber, who had been sitting solemnly at the end of the couch, stood. "And let's appreciate the one who effectuates people like us," she said quietly, "because we may never see her again."

The girls grew silent, their eyes all turned on Cammie.

The looks on their faces unraveled her. Not so long ago, she'd been angry that, on top of having to pay fines, she also had to fulfill seventy-five hours of community service to regain her license. And yet, if she hadn't had this experience, she never would have met these girls and learned their stories. She'd had it tough growing up, but her survival was a fairy tale compared to what many of these girls had experienced. They'd taught her that, despite what life has dealt, a person can still laugh and dance.

She opened her arms wide. "Get your behinds over here, 'cause I'm big into group hugs these days."

The girls morphed into a thriving mass of bodies and giggles and tears in her arms, and she hugged them all, grabbing loose arms and hands, kissing wet cheeks.

Looking over the heads of the girls, she saw one girl off by herself, standing awkwardly, her arms wrapped around her middle.

"Amber," she said, "we're not complete unless you're with us."

Amber blinked as though surprised to be called out. "I'm... not..."

"We got a thinning ozone layer over here, Amber-D," said Takira. "We need your skinny booty to save our girl planet."

At first, Cammie didn't realize Amber was smiling. The

girl pulled back her lips, exposing bright shiny teeth, but otherwise her face didn't change expression. Then her eyes turned bright, like glass, and seemed to melt a little.

"For sheezy, Amber-D!" another girl called out. "Shake it over here!"

She walked stiff-legged to the group. Hands reached out and drew her in, and as they all held on to each other—laughing and joking and sniffling—Cammie realized that they might think this was a going-away party, but she wasn't going away. These girls were going to see her again because she was going to re-up as a volunteer. She wanted them to know that there were people who stayed with them not because they had to discharge a commitment or earn a paycheck, but that they remained because they chose to stay.

But her realization went deeper than that. Like a bright penny cast into deep waters, the understanding glinted and sparkled as it sifted through the depths of her consciousness. This wasn't about their needing her.

She needed them, too. Maybe more so.

Many minutes later, everyone congregated in the kitchen. Some girls were setting the table, others were filling pitchers with Kool-Aid and iced tea. Takira commandeered several girls who were retrieving foil-covered casserole dishes from the oven.

"We know you're Italian," she said to Cammie, "so we figured you'd like lasagna, and if you don't, tough. Hey," she called out to one of the girls across the room, "put some trivets on the table for these hot dishes."

"What the hell's a trivet?"

"Watch the language," warned Carolyn, carrying glasses to the table.

"What the H is a trivet?" the girl corrected.

"Those iron plates with little feet," said a familiar voice.

Emily, a strawberry-blond braid draped over her shoulder, stood in the doorway of the kitchen, smiling shyly. Wearing a pink-and-lavender dress with matching pink sandals, she looked nothing like the bullhorn toting, riot-inciting leader of the revolution from yesterday.

Takira raised a fist. "To our sistah!"

"Boo yeah!" yelled another, raising hers.

"You took the power!" Amber raised both fists.

After the whooping and clapping subsided, Emily looked at Cammie. "I wanted to see you, but I didn't mean to interrupt a party."

Cammie looked over Emily's shoulder, but didn't see Marc. When she looked back at Em, the girl shook her head slightly.

"It's our goodbye party for her," Takira explained, setting a serving spoon next to the lasagna.

Emily's eyes widened. "Are they sending you to jail?"

"No," Cammie said casually, not wanting to trigger discussions of jail and prison, which were too real for most of these girls, either for themselves or their family members. "I've completed my community service today, so the girls surprised me with this party. Now's as good a time as any to share that I'd like to continue volunteering at Dignity House, so maybe this can be a goodbye and welcome-back party?"

The girls hollered and laughed.

"Do we still get cake?" one of them asked.

"Hush, she don't know 'bout that," chided another.

"When you come back," Takira said, "you'll have to tell us some sleuth stories 'cause you'll have your bad P.I. license back."

Cammie and Emily exchanged a look.

"Em," Cammie said, "how about we step outside while the girls finish setting the table? I'd like to talk to you alone for a moment."

The skies were overcast, the air still. Occasionally a breeze limped past like a bedraggled relic from yesterday's storm.

Looking over her shoulder to ensure no one could overhear, Emily said quietly, "I thought you'd lost your chance to be a P.I. again."

"I have, but they don't need to know that. They want me to have my dream, and for today, I want them to be happy believing I'll get it. Now, let's talk about you. How did you get here?"

"Took a taxi. I'd talked to Amber earlier and knew you'd be here."

Cammie groaned.

"I had enough money on me, so what's the problem?"

"You're too young to be hopping into taxis in Vegas. They're not safe for young, innocent women. Promise me you'll never do that again."

"Maybe I'll never be in Vegas again."

"Then promise me you'll never do it again in *any* large city. If you need a ride, talk to whatever parent is around. If you're stuck somewhere and frightened, call 9-1-1. Now, aren't you supposed to be on a flight back to Denver tonight?"

Emily nodded. "Eight o'clock. There's plenty of time to get to the airport."

Cammie waited for the other shoe to drop.

Emily rolled her eyes. "Okay. He doesn't know I'm here."

"I guessed as much. Where does he think you are?"

"In my room at the hotel?"

"Emily," Cammie chided softly, putting her arm around the girl. "You have to let him know you're here. Has he called you?"

Emily hesitated, then nodded.

"How many times?"

"I don't know." She wrapped her arms around her waist and shifted from foot to foot. "I've had the ringer off."

Cammie hesitated, then decided to dive in. "I'm one to talk about being obstinate because I have a problem myself with being a little, oh, stubborn at times…"

The corners of Emily's lips twitched a smile.

"But since that gives me the right to call the kettle black, now isn't the time to be willful. Get out your phone and call him, tell him you're here, let him know you're okay. He's your father, and he's probably worried sick."

"He's going to be pis—"

"And rightfully so, but I have a feeling he'll also be over-joyed to know you're safe and with friends. Now call him."

"I'll text him. I don't want to hear a lecture."

"Okay, text him. And add that I'm happy to drive you to the airport. The girls would be disappointed if we didn't stay for dinner, so tell him we'll leave at six, and I'll have you to the airport by six-thirty. That's plenty of time for the flight."

Emily took a few moments to type the message. "It's sent." She looked at Cammie. "What did you mean by 'calling a kettle black'?"

"It's a saying that means because someone's done some-thing, they have no right to tell someone else it's wrong to do." Or something like that.

"Sheesh," Emily said, looking down at her cell. "He must have been watching his phone nonstop because he's already written me back." She read in silence for a moment. "He says that's fine."

"Okay. Do me a favor?"

"What?"

Cammie wasn't one of those people who found relief in confession, but lately she seemed to be changing that habit. "Yesterday, when you said you wished I were your mother, my heart soared." She looked around, giving herself a moment to settle a rise of emotion. Meeting Emily's gaze again, she con-tinued softly, "If you can find it in your heart, call him Dad. And say it with love, not anger."

Blue eyes fastened on Cammie. "It's hard to call someone Daddy when you rarely see them."

"Is that his fault?"

She seemed to mull it over, but her single-word answer still reeked of resentment. "No."

"He told me he's wanted to see you more, but you always seem to have other plans."

"Maybe."

"Emily."

"Okay, I've turned down trips to visit him because I don't like not knowing where I belong." She sucked in a shaky breath and released it in a torrent of words. "When my mom gets married again, where am I supposed to go? Like, does Bernard, or whatever his name is, even want me around? Her last husband didn't. I was younger then, so my mom could ship me off to my dad whenever it was convenient for her lifestyle. I'd just get to know him again, feel comfortable and stuff, and bam! She'd have problems in her marriage or she'd be lonely and she'd want me back. I'd start to feel like a real daughter to her, then she'd work things out with her husband and I'd be invisible again."

It took a moment for Cammie's mind to catch up. "But your dad was always there for you, right?"

"Yeah."

"So…why be angry at him?"

"Because…he let this happen."

Cammie mentally connected the dots, which created a picture in her mind that she'd known too well as a kid. "He left you with your mom and a life of constant upheaval."

Emily turned her head to the side, as though looking at the distant mountains, but Cammie caught her peering back from the corners of her eyes.

"In your case, he and your mom divorced, but he could have also abandoned you by one day walking out the door and never returning…or by dying. Whatever the reason, it was still the same result."

"Yeah," she said. "Something like that."

"You told me your mom doesn't always say nice things about your dad. That you feel in the middle. Here's something you can do when you're feeling stressed. Shut out whatever is going on that's bugging you and imagine something wonderful—your favorite sunset, a painting by a favorite artist, Tolstoy's face."

"But that's not me. When something bugs me, I can't just forget about it."

Cammie realized that she was giving her the kind of advice that worked for her, helped her bottle up her feelings and keep from exploding. But Emily was different. More honest with her feelings. Willing to march in an Eco-Glitter rally and pick up the bullhorn when it fell to the street. "You're right. You have to do what feels right to you."

Emily nodded.

Cammie continued, "You need to find a way to take control of your attitude, which sometimes is all we have."

"How?"

"You can always call me. I promise to answer."

"You're the best."

"And I'm not the only person who cares about you. Your dad wants nothing more than to love you. One day, you might discover your mom is just a person, too, with failings and strengths like everybody else, and you can forgive her."

Her breath caught in her chest as those last words left her lips. In her mind's eye, she saw her mother's face—long and narrow, a fragile look in her eyes—and realized she'd been there all along, whenever Cammie wanted to remember her. Always waiting for her in memories.

She'd balked at going to that place, those special remembrances, not because she hadn't forgiven her mom, but because she hadn't forgiven herself.

Ten minutes later, all the girls were sitting around the dining room table chowing down on lasagna, salad and hummus, the latter a dish Amber had insisted on making.

"Miss Copello," Takira said, "we'd like to hear about what happened yesterday." The girls grew quietly solemn, staring at Cammie with curious eyes, like kids at story hour.

"I'm pretty sure all of you saw it on the news," Cammie said knowingly.

Heads bobbed.

"You're our hero," one of the girls said.

"Well, I don't know about that," Cammie answered.

"The way you went up to that officer," Amber said, "and put your hands on his chest…"

The girls murmured words of praise.

"Awesome."

"Really sick."

"Boom ting."

It was starting to feel like a hip-hop revival meeting. But Cammie wanted to get something straight.

"Thank you for your support, but I've thought a lot about what happened, what I did, and in some ways, I'm still not sure if my actions were…appropriate."

"But you were so cool."

"It was for the cause."

"You did it to protect Emily."

Cammie looked around the table at the girls. "It's true, I did it for Emily. But I also did it for Marc. He's a lawyer, as you all know, and he has some critical cases coming up. He was arguing with a police officer about his daughter's right to free speech, but it was a volatile situation, and the police officers were getting itchy—I mean, c'mon, protestors were threatening to blow up a tractor!—and I thought any moment that police would arrest and charge Marc with obstruction of justice, impeding an investigation and maybe more."

"That's not fair!" Amber said, her eyes blazing.

"All I knew," Cammie said gently, "is that if he were arrested, news of his arrest and charges would have become known by the Attorney Disciplinary Agency because they're watching Marc so carefully—they check him out for problems every week or so—and they would've suspended him immediately. In that instant of understanding, I decided to take the legal bullet."

"See," Takira said, "you were a hero!"

"But my arrest had repercussions I hadn't taken into consideration, so I can't say what I did was correct."

"But Marc gets to remain a lawyer, right?" one of the girls asked.

Cammie nodded.

"Then you did the right thing, Miss Copello."

She took a moment to phrase her thoughts. "Girls, sometimes it might seem okay to take a bold action. You might even believe you're helping someone or standing up for what's right, but feeling impassioned isn't always a suitable reason for doing something. Especially when you're breaking the law. Take it from me, what I did yesterday has had serious consequences… without realizing it, what I did also hurt people I love."

A motion caught her eye. Emily, standing in the doorway, was waving Cammie over.

"I told Emily I'd drive her to the airport, so I need to leave, girls, but I'll be back. Let's call this our goodbye and hello-again party."

After bumping fists and hugging a few girls, Cammie joined Emily in the hallway. Together they walked into the living room area.

"He's picking me up," Emily said quietly.

Cammie looked out the window. Marc stood in the street, next to his parked car. He glanced at the window and she smiled, although she doubted he could see her clearly behind the glass.

"Go talk to him," Emily pleaded.

Cammie put her hands on the girl's shoulders. "Emily, you two need to get to the airport. It doesn't help either of us to cram in a last-minute conversation with the clock ticking."

The girl nodded. "When will I see you again?"

"We'll figure something out."

"Will you two ever be boyfriend and girlfriend again?"

"No, that's over, but I'll always be your Cammie, and you'll always be my Emily. That sounds pretty good to me." She looked into the girl's eyes. "Remember the favor I asked?"

"I'll keep my word, too."

They hugged and Emily left, walking slowly down the sidewalk to the car. Marc hugged her, then opened her door. Emily paused, looked back up to the window and drew a crisscross over her heart.

CHAPTER SEVENTEEN

As THEY DROVE AWAY from Dignity House, Marc debated with himself on what he should say to his daughter. She needed to know that running off without telling him wasn't okay, but she knew that. It was why she'd texted him. And he was so damn glad to see her that he couldn't bring himself to scold.

"I wish you'd told me ahead of time that you wanted to see Cammie, Amber—I mean Daearen—and others, but I'm not mad at you. I'm glad you're safe."

She cast him a sidelong look. "I should have told you. I'm sorry."

He stared at the road, more than a little surprised at the apology, but not wanting to overreact.

"Your suitcase is in the back," he said.

"Thanks."

"Hungry?"

"I ate with the girls at Dignity House. It was Cammie's going-away party. There was a cake, too, but I wouldn't have eaten any even if I'd stayed. Did you know refined sugar is sometimes filtered through bone char?"

"No, I didn't." She hadn't spoken that many words to him in the past twenty-four hours. "It was a going-away party?"

"Yeah, she's finished her community-service hours, but she told them she's coming back. Daearen said that Cammie coming back means the girl planet will thrive, but I didn't know what she was talking about."

Just like Cammie to not give up on people. Yesterday, she wasn't giving up on him, either, until he'd forced the issue. In the hours since, he'd had the uncomfortable realization that he dealt much better with people in a courtroom, where everyone was at arm's length, than with those in his personal life.

"They have satellite radio in this rental," he said. "Want to find a station you like?"

"Sure."

Emily selected a station playing a rapid-fire song with eerie guitar chugs. For once, he recognized the music.

"I love this band," she said, her head bobbing in time to the beat.

"Me, too. Green Day."

"This is one of my *favorite* songs. 'Boulevard of Broken Dreams.'"

They were talking. She was sharing a piece of her world. Maybe he wasn't such a bad part-time dad, after all.

"Green Day," he said. "I never really thought about it, but did they name themselves that because they're eco-activists?"

She gave him a funny look. "It stands for a day of smoking weed. You know? A green day. But they're also an eco-friendly rock band. Like, they're really big on alternative fuel sources."

The words *smoking weed* stuck in his head. He'd never had a talk about drugs with her, but now wasn't the best time. Better to enjoy rebuilding a rapport with his daughter—after all, they only had a few more days together before she returned to her mom.

He listened to the vaguely familiar lyrics about walking alone. It seemed to foretell his future. He was alone, walking alone. Living alone in his big, empty house.

"This is a political song," Emily continued, "about the alienation of the people by the government. And by the way, I don't smoke marijuana, in case you're curious."

For a moment, he was dumbfounded at the out-of-left-field admission, but glad nonetheless.

"But I suppose," she continued, moving slightly to the

music, "if I knew it were grown without chemicals, I might try it."

Gladness was really overrated.

"Well," he said, minding his words, "I can only request that you refrain from ingesting mind-altering pharmaceuticals, legal or otherwise, unless they've been prescribed by a physician. But if you were to experiment, please practice restraint and moderation."

"In other words, don't do drugs."

"Right."

"Daddy, are you okay?"

Daddy.

He had to grip the wheel and blink to keep the road in focus. Ever since his daughter had gotten into the car, he'd been on a roller coaster of emotions, definitely not his style.

And now she'd called him Daddy.

He shoved down the feelings that roiled up within him, half inclined to say, "Hey, Em, why were you holding back?" but he didn't want to put her on the defensive.

Instead, he took a quiet moment to calm down, hold the word *daddy* close. He wanted to remember the sound of her voice, the overhead slate clouds, even the pop-rock tune blasting in the car. So many times these past few years, he'd hated the world for dropping him from the family equation and putting a minus in the father column.

But at this instant, he was 100 percent Emily's father. No part-time about it.

"Daddy?" she repeated.

He cleared his throat. "I'm fine."

"Is it about Cammie?"

He didn't answer. Couldn't answer.

"Maybe you two could talk and work things out."

"Too much has happened. Let's leave it at that."

Even if they tried, he feared he'd grow to resent her for what she'd done, and she'd inevitably grow angry and bitter with him for his resentments. He'd seen it happen over and over in legal cases he'd represented. He'd lived it, too, in his former marriage.

She twisted a dial, turning down the volume.

"I want to tell you something," she said softly.

"I'm all ears."

"Over dinner, Cammie explained to us that part of the reason she forced her arrest was to protect your license. She said that if you'd been arrested, the Attorney Disciplinary Agency would've found out within days because they're watching you so carefully right now." She paused. "She did it for you, Dad. Will you think things over? Please? She took the legal bullet for you."

After a beat, he said, "I'll think things over, but let's give it a rest, okay?"

"Sorry, can't give it a rest yet. What will she do next?"

"She's creative and smart. She'll figure out something."

"But she lost her dream."

He listened to the muffled grind of tires against asphalt as they traveled a few feet, another mile. He thought about his life moving forward over time, the minutes becoming hours, then days, then years, and wondered when, if ever, he'd stop thinking about Cammie, curious if she'd ever found a satisfying career, wondering if she were happy…and sometimes, when his defenses were down, pondering what the two of them could have been.

Emily turned up the volume, and they drove in silence, listening to the "Boulevard of Broken Dreams."

FOUR DAYS LATER, Val and Cammie sat in Uncle Frankie's living room. It was the second time Val had visited since Cammie had left the Cave.

"If we're gonna be Sherlock and Watson, we have gotta start getting together and planning our detective venture."

Although Cammie had accepted she'd lost her shot at being

a P.I. again—a view that Val didn't share—she enjoyed coaching her friend on the skills, tools and techniques necessary to run an investigations business. Today they'd been reviewing different smartphone apps that came in handy in investigations, from the motion detector to the digital recorder.

"Snooper, the way I see it," Val said, lounging on the couch and fiddling with her smartphone, "you can be the office manager. Not officially a P.I., but you can do things like pull online court records, conduct criminal background checks, that sort of stuff." She fingered a broad green leaf of a plant on the end table behind her head. "This a rubber plant?"

"Think so."

"Needs some water."

Val headed to the kitchen, tossing her Havana straw hat with the paisley headband on the dining room table.

In her everyday life, Val Leroy didn't look anything like the Christina Aguilera celebrity dealer at the Shamrock Palace. The real Val had a thing for hats. And little black dresses. Today she swore a sleeveless number that showed off a small fleur-de-lis tattoo on her left shoulder—"For N'awlins and my favorite team, the Saints." She'd be devoid of color if it wasn't for her bobbed red hair and ruby-red lips.

"Noticin' my dress?" Val asked, walking back in with a measuring cup half-filled with water. "It's crepe de chine."

As far as Cammie was concerned, crepe de chine could be crêpe suzette. "It's nice. New?"

"I never buy new, girl. Bought this from The Attic, that cute little vintage shop downtown. Nanny always bought me *reach-me-down* clothes—ya know, secondhand clothes—and I detested them. I swore I'd always buy spanking-new duds, right off the rack, when I grew up. That day came and guess what? I hated how scratchy they felt against my skin." She carefully poured the water into the clay container. "Started going to vintage clothing stores and liking the softness of reach-me-downs again. Plus it's like slippin' into other people's lives, ya know?"

"A definite skill for a private investigator." Cammie thought for a moment. "Val, I have to be very careful about the type of work I'd do with you. Without a license, I can never appear to be working as a private investigator, *ever*."

Val blinked her mink-brown eyes. "Maybe we could get an office in a law firm, and they'd hire you as a part-time para-legal. They do a lot of things private-eye-like, right?"

Cammie nodded. "Exactly the kind of tasks you mentioned, actually."

"Well, there you have it." Val sashayed into the kitchen with the empty measuring cup.

Although it gave Cammie leg cramps just thinking of sit-ting behind a desk for hours, being a quasi P.I. was better than not being one at all.

"Plus you'll be mentoring me," Val continued as she re-turned. "Teaching me things like how to do surveillance. Of course, you can't just talk to me about it or make me read a book on the subject, I'll need hands-on experience. Which means I'll need you to sit with me while we're out there watch-ing people and taking pictures."

Cammie smiled. "I like the way you think."

Ding-dong.

Val looked at the front door. "You expectin' company?"

"No." Frankie and Delilah had left that morning on a week-long trip to San Francisco and the wine country. "Maybe it's a delivery."

"Or maybe it's lawyer boy."

Just the thought of seeing Marc again made Cammie's heart race. As much as she told herself that it was over between them, her body was having trouble understanding.

"Lawyer boy is in Denver," she said, heading to the front window, "prepping for his deposition tomorrow."

"That means you're going to be there, too. At the deposi-tion."

"Not now, not after what happened." She peeked between the slats in the blind.

She felt as though her racing heart screeched to a cold stop.

On the porch stood Laura McDonald.

Stepping away from the window, Cammie held her finger to her lips.

Val, her eyes wide, nodded that she understood to keep quiet.

As the doorbell rang again, Cammie tip-toed over to her friend.

"Gwen—that woman I told you about—is here," she whispered. "Go to my bedroom."

"You're gonna answer the door?" Val whispered fiercely, her eyes wide as coasters. "That girl's missing a few bulbs in her chandelier—"

"Hush. Nothing's going to happen on the porch."

"Don't let her inside."

"If something goes wrong, I'll yell *Tolstoy* and you grab that bat I keep next to my bed and get your behind out here."

"Who's Tolstoy?"

"Go," Cammie ordered in a hushed tone, tugging her smartphone from the pocket in her jeans. She pulled up the recorder app, checked the settings and turned it on.

She watched Val slip into the bedroom. Crossing to the door, Cammie stuck the phone in her jean pocket.

Easing in a calming breath, she opened the door.

Laura looked as though she'd had a Fortune 500 makeover. She wore a camel-hair jacket over a pristine white turtleneck, and tan slacks with creases so sharp, a person could get cut on them.

"Cammie," she said in a voice that matched the look. "I behaved badly the other day. Will you accept my apology?"

The air suddenly felt thin, as though Laura had sucked all the reality out of it.

Cammie eyed the red Viper in the driveway. No one was

in it. She scanned the area. Except for Mrs. Osborne checking her mailbox across the street, nobody else was in the vicinity.

She turned her attention back to Laura. "How'd you know I'm living in Vegas?"

"Researched your name on the internet, saw you had a P.I. business here in Vegas, but when I called the number it was disconnected. Then I remembered your uncle Frankie calling the law firm in Denver, and it was easy to find Frank Copello's address, but not his phone number."

"It's unlisted."

Laura nodded, her diamond-stud earrings twinkling in the light. "I thought I'd drop by, ask him how to reach you, but here you are." Her smile was a parody of warmth.

"So you drove all the way from San Clemente just to apologize?"

"Actually, I have clients in Vegas."

Clients? As in other people to rip off? "And a deposition in Denver tomorrow."

"Yes," she said, with an almost imperceptible twitch of an eyebrow, "I do. After my meeting, I'm driving there."

"Long drive to do alone."

She shrugged. "Eleven hours. I'll stop halfway and spend the night. I've done it many times."

Cammie wondered what those many times were about as her gaze dropped to the plush leather shoes, up to the black leather bag embellished with *Prada* in gold letters. Cammie wasn't a shopper, but even she knew that purse alone would cost at least a week of a P.I.'s salary.

"You're probably wondering what kind of business I'm in."

Cammie met her eyes. "Got me there."

A bank of clouds moved over the sun, casting the street in shadow. The gloom added to the sour premonition in Cammie's stomach.

"My business is another reason I wanted to talk to you. May I come in?"

"You carrying?"

"No."

"Although I'm just thrilled to pieces to see you again, we share a certain history. May I see inside your Prada?"

Laura started to open it herself, then changed her mind and handed it to Cammie. "I have nothing to hide."

I bet. She opened it, rifled through several tubes of makeup, a leather-covered checkbook, keys, a shiny gold iPhone case. Not a lived-in purse like Cammie's, whose layers of odds and ends were like an archeological dig of her life. In contrast, Laura's handbag was like a showcase. A little too perfect, a little too staged.

"Open your coat, please." Cammie handed back the bag.

She did, accompanied by a hurt, almost bewildered look in her eyes.

What an actress.

Cammie reached over and patted under Laura's arms, along her sides, down the small of her back. All she felt were expensive fabrics.

"Come in," Cammie said, stepping aside.

She followed Laura inside—she'd learned the hard way to never walk in front of this woman—and observed how she surveyed the room as she strolled inside.

"It's how I imagined it'd be decorated," Laura said, turning to her.

"Early Saint Christopher?"

She pulled back her lips, exposing pearly white teeth. "I was going to say comfortable, family-like." She blinked, obviously waiting for something.

"Care to sit down?" This new version of Gwen-Laura was eerily polite and businesslike, although Cammie had already put together that the woman was cagey-smart.

"Thank you," Laura murmured, selecting a seat at the end of the couch where Val had been sitting minutes earlier.

Cammie sat a few feet down from her, close enough for her recorder to capture their conversation.

"Let's skip to why I wanted to see you," Laura said.

"Let's."

"I know from my internet research that you got into some trouble recently. Seems you got caught attaching a GPS device to a vehicle."

Probably the same article Marc read, but Cammie didn't feel like chatting about it. She nodded, once.

"I checked the licensing commission website and saw that your Nevada P.I. license has since been suspended."

Cammie nodded again. Never again would she tag a Mall Queen type as being dumb.

"Where does that leave you, workwise?" Laura asked pleasantly. "Are you a full-time process server or do you have a job?"

"Let's just say I'm looking."

Laura leaned forward slightly. "Given your tenacity, skills and intelligence, we have a business proposition for you."

She smelled something that might be helpful to Marc. "Who's we?"

"My business partner and I."

"Business partner as in boyfriend?"

"Yes."

"Same boyfriend you had while engaged to Marc?"

She smiled.

"What's the business proposition?"

"We need someone like you full-time in Vegas to work with clients, handle wholesale distribution and accounts receivable."

"What's the business?"

"In a minute. Have you ever worked with bookkeeping software?"

"Like the kind you used at Marc's firm?"

"Not quite. It actually runs in the background."

"Is this background accounting software what you used to cook the books at Hamilton and Hamilton?"

That smile again. Laura reached over with both hands and gently ran her fingertips along Cammie's hips. Touching the smartphone in her pocket, she locked her gaze with Cammie's while reaching inside her pocket. She was so close, Cammie could smell her spicy perfume, count every laugh line around her peach-glossed lips, although she doubted laughing was how she got them.

"I like you, Cammie," she murmured huskily, pulling out the phone, her free hand lingering on Cammie's other hip, "but trying to use your smartphone a second time to catch me is a little, oh, redundant, don't you think?"

Laura leaned back and looked at the recorder image on the face of the phone.

"Have I ever told you," she said softly, "how much I admire your sneaky ways?" She tapped a red stop button. "Now let's erase this recording and turn off your phone so we can really talk."

After a few more taps, Laura set the phone behind her on the end table. Looking at Cammie, she didn't seem the least bit upset to have caught her in the act.

Without material evidence as to what Laura had up her designer sleeve, Cammie was left with one option—memorize key points in this conversation and put them into an affidavit. The document might not sway the ADA reps at tomorrow's deposition, but it was better than nothing.

"In our business," Val said in a level, cool tone, "you could make a lot of money. Forty to fifty K per month, depending on the volume of material you receive and advance to us."

"What kind of material?"

"First, a few rules. No skimming, no cheating and we'll bonus you."

"So which federal crime are we talking? Drugs? Hijacked products?"

"Absolutely nothing that dirty. We're talking cash, the life-blood of our nation. All we want you to do is move the cash. Darling, we're talking truckloads."

Darling? "And the cash comes from?"

"From people who owe us, and that's all you need to know."

A picture started taking shape in Cammie's mind. "I'd be your Las Vegas hub."

"Yes."

"I'd use that software that runs in the background of another, legitimate accounting program."

"Yes."

"Like what you used at Marc's law firm."

"Exactly." Laura laughed a little breathlessly. "And it was like taking candy from Mr. Puppy Love. I created shell accounts, then moved money from his legitimate trust accounts to the other accounts in the background. With this shadow system, we can easily move money from underneath the U.S. Treasury's nose to our personal checking accounts and nobody's the wiser."

"Forty to fifty K a month? What's the bonus?"

"Five percent of volume. By the way, our Phoenix hub is running five mil a year."

"Lucrative."

"How do you think we can afford that house in San Clemente? We have one twice that size in Puerto Vallarta."

"Marc was small fry—why screw him out of money?"

"I already gave you the short version. But here's the full story. Let's just say my business partner got into a little trouble with the feds. A separate issue, unrelated to our business, but still a problem. He turned snitch and we had to leave town for a while. We headed to Denver, I met Marc, thought he had a ton of bucks to go with those great abs, and a girl's gotta make a living. What can I say?"

In the distance, a freight train rumbled toward its destination. Cammie had heard it many times, knew it to be a mile or so away, but at the moment it felt as though it were roaring right through the living room.

Laura had brought that kind of full-on, crashing destruction into innocent people's lives. All because *a girl's gotta make a living.* Cammie clasped her hands together for fear if she didn't, they'd strangle that girl.

Laura checked her wristwatch. "Look, I have a client meeting I need to get to." She met Cammie's eyes. "Here's the last part of the deal. You're a no-show at that depo tomorrow. I can't afford to have you put my empire in jeopardy. Plus, my business partner and I are prepared to give you an additional bonus for complying with this request—enough to buy a new, very nice car to replace that junker outside."

"That'll work," Cammie said tightly.

"You're in?"

Cammie nodded, once.

"Good. On my way back from Denver, I'll drop by again with that bonus, and we'll finalize our arrangement."

Cammie walked Laura to the door. As she reached to open it, Laura stepped in closer, her face nearly touching Cammie's.

"Here's to a long, profitable friendship," she whispered. She touched her lips against Cammie's. "Bye, baby."

Cammie shut the door, locked it and wiped her mouth. Through the blinds, she watched the red Viper reverse out of the driveway and head down the street.

She walked into the center of the living room. "Tolstoy!"

Val ran out, a worried look on her face, a bat in one hand, Cammie's bedside lamp in the other.

"What?" Val yelled, looking frantically around. "Where is she?"

"Gone." Cammie shook her head. "The lamp, too?"

"I thought I might need extra ammunition." Val tossed the bat on the couch, set the lamp on the coffee table. "Why'd you yell Tolstoy?"

"She kissed me."

"Lesbian-like?"

"Lesbian-like."

"Tongue?"

"I'm not going to dignify that with an answer." Cammie picked up her smartphone and released a heavy sigh. "She found my phone, saw I was recording everything and erased it. If I write it all down now while I can remember chunks of it, I can put it into an affidavit for Marc's deposition tomorrow."

"No need." Val walked to the rubber plant, reached inside and pulled out her phone. "You know that handy motion detector program you showed me how to use? It's been running this entire time, recording audio and taking video of this room."

Cammie smiled as a warming relief spread through her body. "Val, have I told you lately that I love you?"

"No, but you can start now. And, by the way..."

"Yeah?"

"Call me Watson."

"Okay. And, Watson, by the way?"

"Yeah?"

"No tongue."

CHAPTER EIGHTEEN

SEVERAL HOURS LATER, Cammie set up her laptop on her uncle's TV tray. After Regina had died, Frankie stopped eating at their dining table and ate all his meals in front of the TV. Now that he was with Delilah, he ate at his table again, even when he was alone, and the TV tray sat in a corner of the dining room with a Hamm's Beer ashtray on it for guests.

She turned the laptop so its screen faced the couch where she and Laura had been sitting. Then she pulled up one of the dining room chairs in front of the computer and sat.

She glanced up at the cuckoo clock on the wall, an heirloom of her grandmother's that she remembered from a long-ago visit to Nonna's house when she'd been three or four. Cammie remembered sitting in front of the clock, anxiously waiting for the hand-carved woodchopper to chop wood, and the little cuckoo to twitter, which occurred when the large white-scrolled hand was straight up or down. The woodchopper and cuckoo no longer worked, but the clock still kept time. Right now, it was five minutes to three.

A few hours ago, within minutes of Laura's departure, Cammie had called Marc on his cell to discuss Laura's visit and the recordings she'd obtained, but he'd been heading into a jail for a client visit and couldn't talk. They hurriedly scheduled a meeting via Skype at three o'clock.

Most people used Skype to communicate with friends and family, but Cammie used it primarily for her investigative work. When out in the field, she'd sometimes communicate with her clients using Skype on her smartphone. Using the video call feature, she could walk through a scene and share real-time video footage with a client while discussing it at the same time. More often, she used Skype to conference in attorneys during witness interviews. When possible, she preferred to use her laptop because of the larger screen image and the ability to access other programs, both of which she'd be doing today with Marc.

She blew out a nervous breath, looked at the clock again. Three minutes to go. She got up and checked her reflection in a wall mirror, even while telling herself it was vain and silly to care about her appearance. He'd ended it, right? What did it matter how she looked?

Who was she kidding? It mattered.

This would be the last time they'd see each other for a while, maybe ever, and she wanted his last memory of her to be, well, memorable. In the good sense.

She wore the Snooze T-shirt because it brought back good memories, besides being her favorite T. Her hair fell in loose dark curls past her shoulders. She wasn't a master at applying eyeliner, so the dark lines on her lids wobbled a bit, but only someone close up with a magnifying glass would notice. She had to smile. As a kid she couldn't draw a straight line with a crayon, either. And coloring within the lines of a box? Forget it.

Delilah had left some foundation and blush after the makeup adventure the night they'd all dined at Piero's, so Cammie had brushed some pink onto her cheeks and dabbed her lips with a dark pink lipstick named Divine Wine. Unlike Delilah, Cammie wasn't heavy-handed with the tinting—she put on just enough to give her some zip.

Although, it'd taken some extra effort to look *zippy* after Laura's surprise visit. Cammie had dealt with her share of felonious scheming psycho-criminals over the years, but not with one who'd tried to bribe *and* kiss her.

As Val had said, "That girl's got a hitch in her git-a-long."

She looked at the clock. A minute to three.

Cammie's hand trembled, her heart pounded. Reactions that had nothing to do with Laura's visit and everything to do with seeing Marc again.

She returned to the chair. She powered on the computer, set up Skype and pressed the video call button.

He appeared in the center of her screen like an image in a crystal ball. The seconds slowed, then froze in place as she stared at his face. She eased in a breath, missing his scents.

He looked like a well-groomed actor in a TV commercial. His hair was stylishly cut—the way she remembered it when they worked together. He wore a tweed jacket, blue oxford button-down shirt and yellow tie. She'd visited his home office once to deliver a case file, and recognized the credenza in the background filled with books and photographs of his father and Emily.

Time caught up to the present as she glanced at the corner of her screen and saw her face—long and pale with odd pink splotches on her cheeks—in a small box. That same image would be enlarged on Marc's screen.

"Hi, Cammie. I just got in." Maybe it was the video quality, but those eyes had lost their luster, their electric blue subdued to the color of twilight.

"Hi." She smiled. What she'd hoped passed for a genuine-looking smile appeared anxious and wan in the small box. She made a mental note to not look at her image again—it was bad enough being apprehensive talking to him, worse if she watched herself being so. "I don't remember you dressing up so much for jail visits."

"It's a business fraud case, and these guys are accustomed to lawyers in suits, even on Sundays."

"Case going well?"

He loosened his tie. "There's a lot of money involved, and some important people on the other side. This isn't going to be an easy haul, for either myself or the accused." He gave a wry smile. "Mostly for the accused, of course, because when this is over, they'll be reeling, wondering what hit them."

Lawyers going to trial were like boxers before a big fight. Both postured and bragged, making a crushing defeat of the opponent sound like a given.

"Thanks for making the time for this call."

"You said you had evidence for tomorrow's deposition. Let's get to it."

His voice was controlled to the point of being cold. Determined to not let that unravel her, she asked politely, "Did you have a chance to check your email?"

"No. I'll bring it up now in my browser." She heard the clatter of the keyboard as he typed. His gaze shifted to another part of his screen. "There it is."

"Double-click on the attachment."

A pause. "Done."

"Did a media player open on your screen?"

"Yes."

"Good. Don't press the play button yet." She hesitated, wondering if she should repeat what she had told Marc that stormy day outside the jail—that Laura wasn't pregnant. No, timing felt wrong. She'd broach the topic again at the end of the call. "I suggest you have a legal pad and pen handy for taking notes, especially when she gets to the part where she describes the deceptive accounting practices she used at your law firm."

"Got them here on my desk. How'd you capture the video without her knowing?"

"Have to give credit to Val. Laura had wised up to me, frisked me for my smartphone. Meanwhile, Val had been quick-witted enough to plant her phone with the motion detector program running."

"Laura frisked you?"

"I frisked her, then she frisked me." That sounded weird. "You'll see what happened on the video. Before we begin, I want to tell you that from my perspective, Laura McDonald is a big-time, big-dollar, dangerous career criminal. After you see the footage, you'll probably want to burn CDs for the depo tomorrow."

"All right, I'll hit Play now."

"Just a moment—I have one more note before we begin." She paused, wondering how to phrase this delicately. "When we get to the end, I want to say that our lips never touched."

He gave her a look. "Whose lips?"

"Mine and Laura's."

"I thought you meant yours and Val's."

"Oh, no. She was in a back room during this recording."

"Does this kissing have something to do with the frisking?"

"I can't believe you asked that with a straight face."

"You're the one who brought it up."

"I did." *Wish I hadn't.* "Just wanted to clarify things." She tried to read the expression on his face, but it'd be easier interpreting the stone ones on Mount Rushmore.

"Was Laura aware that someone else was in the vicinity?" he asked.

"No."

He paused. "Anything else?"

"You don't see Laura at first, but you'll hear us talking on the porch. Audio's muffled, but discernable. I turned up the volume during that part so you can hear our exchange. Then you'll see her as she enters the room. Eventually she sits on the couch…" Cammie looked over her right shoulder at the couch while gesturing to it. "Can you see it?"

"Quite well."

"Want me to hold up the screen so you can get the layout of the room?"

"No. I remember it."

Except for his frisking-kissing question, their businesslike rapport was unnerving. It was as though they'd never touched, never kissed, never stolen pleasures with greedy abandon.

"Val's smartphone was in that rubber plant," Cammie continued. "She has a wide-angle lens on it—attachment is the size of a quarter—so you can easily see the area from the front door to the couch."

"I understand. Shall I hit Play?"

"Go ahead."

He cocked his head and listened intently to the segment where Laura and Cammie were off camera, pausing the video when Laura said she was driving to Denver after her meeting.

He glanced at his wristwatch. "She's likely on the road now."

Cammie nodded. "Now or soon."

"She said she'd made the drive many times from Vegas to Denver. When we were…together…she made several weekend road trips, by herself, to Utah. Claimed they were to some spa. Now I'm realizing she was probably heading to Vegas."

"Makes sense."

"Does she discuss those trips further in this video?"

"Not specifically."

"All right," he said, pressing a button, "let's resume watching."

She heard Laura's voice in the video. "It's how I imagined it'd be decorated."

He leaned closer, his expression tightening. Cammie felt like a voyeur, watching him watching her.

She'd already viewed this video at least five times. Although it was difficult to tell that Laura had a flat tummy underneath that jacket, it wasn't impossible. If he hadn't wanted to believe Cammie when she told him Laura wasn't pregnant, maybe he could see it for himself.

His eyebrows pressed together, a black canopy over his eyes. "Can you believe this?" He glanced at Cammie. "She researched your Nevada P.I. license—knew it'd been suspended."

Cammie watched his face while listening to herself on the video ask Laura if her business partner was the boyfriend she'd had while involved with Marc. Except for a slight twitch at the corner of his mouth, he kept his face still, wooden. An ache sliced through her. It was almost worse seeing his self-control than if he had let down his guard and shown his feelings.

She told herself she should look away, but she couldn't. She was riveted by his responses, as minute as they were, for reasons she couldn't justify or explain. Although, if she were to be brutally honest with herself, she was holding on to any shred of emotion, even if it wasn't for her, as a last connection to the man she'd loved.

"Interesting," Marc murmured. He flicked a glance at Cammie. "You still have the name of that computer forensics guru in Denver?"

"Richard Ross."

"Maybe he can find that background accounting program," Marc muttered, writing something down.

After a few more moments, Cammie heard Laura make the "Mr. Puppy Love" reference.

Marc snorted something unintelligible under his breath, followed a few seconds later with a low whistle after Laura mentioned the Phoenix hub taking in five mil.

When it came to the exit scene, and the kiss, Cammie held her breath. She hadn't seen that coming, hated that it had happened, but Marc again showed no reaction.

The video ended.

He met her gaze. They looked at each other for a prolonged stretch of time.

"The ADA's going to back down when they see this," he said.

Maybe it was the angle of the monitor, but the look in his eyes had softened. Staring into the deep well of his eyes, she read in them that he'd finally forgiven her.

If he'd looked that way three days ago, she'd have been elated. But at this moment, she felt something different... something she couldn't put her finger on.

"As Laura says in the video," Cammie noted, "she's going to be in Denver for that deposition tomorrow."

"I'd like you to be here, too."

"You heard me promise her that I wouldn't be. If she sees me in that room, she'll bolt."

He nodded. "Good point. Bolting from a deposition would only get her a contempt of court citation. That's chump change considering her million-dollar problems."

"You're not referring to the tape while questioning her, right?"

"Not referring to it, not showing it, not giving her any reason to split. Although the way I phrase my questions will make it obvious they're based on information from you."

"No way around that."

"No."

"But considering she doesn't know a video exists, she'll view it as my word against hers. That won't throw her off all that much."

"My take, too." He folded his arms and leaned forward, looking squarely into the screen. "This video has wire fraud, theft, money laundering all over it. I'll contact the Denver P.D. as soon as we end this call and ask for a theft detective to sit in at the deposition. The detective will be in a suit and look like any of the other lawyers in the room, so Laura won't know there's a cop present. He'll arrest her at the end of the depo."

Cammie blew out a breath of relief. "Good to hear. Because, as you know, she wanted to visit me on her way back from Denver."

"Was she bringing roses?" He offered a lopsided smile.

"Funny," she said dryly.

He turned serious again. "I'll make a copy of the video for the feds. That business-partner boyfriend is in their get-rich scheme as deep as she is, although I wouldn't be surprised if they're already investigating this happy couple."

"What happens if she clams up and claims the fifth amendment?"

"There is no right to silence in a civil case. My case is civil, and she can't clam up and claim the privilege."

"Not worried she'll show up with a lawyer?"

He laughed, the sound dark and gruff. "Doubt it. For sake of argument, let's say somebody posts her bail, she gets out of jail, then skips the country to this unknown place in Puerto Vallarta. Her lawyer would be obligated to tell the court that address—or anywhere else she might be hiding."

"Wonder how much time she'll get behind bars."

"With her criminal history? Probably ten calendars."

They stared into each other's eyes for a prolonged moment. Cammie felt as though the physical space between herself and the screen dissolved, as though Marc were right here in front of her. She could almost reach up and sweep that chestnut curl off his forehead....

"Great work, Cammie. Your initiative and ability to hang in during tough investigations always produces phenomenal, case-changing results. We've had our differences, but you didn't let them minimize your skills. You're a great investigator."

"Thanks," she whispered.

"I need to end this connection," Marc said, "and call the Denver P.D."

"Absolutely, it's just..." She hesitated. "Maybe we should discuss one last thing."

"Yes?"

"I mentioned this before, but...Laura isn't pregnant."

He blew out a lungful of air. "It's for the best. If she had been, I would have fought like hell for full custody, but I'd likely have lost. Would probably have ended up with shared custody. Even if a mother goes to prison, it doesn't terminate her rights. And Laura's not fit to be a mother."

He sounded strong, resolved, but she knew differently. He'd lost a piece of his heart, but he'd never admit it. To anyone other than himself, anyway.

She straightened, forced herself to smile. "Goodbye, and best of luck tomorr—"

"You know what, Cammie?" he said, the question tumbling out with such force, she was momentarily taken aback.

"What?"

"We're a great team."

"You're right. We were a great lawyer-investigator team. That will never change. Yeah, and…if you ever need to hire a P.I. in Vegas, give me a call. Goodbye and best of luck to you—"

"I meant more than that," he said, leaning closer to the screen. "There's still so much between us."

Somewhere in the back of her mind, she had the insight that people who stick to the lines don't mesh well with those who can't be contained by them. At the same time, another thought fought its way to semiconscious status. Maybe she could change gears, be a different kind of woman, a different type of P.I. More willing to walk the line, not take chances, follow the rules even if they didn't make sense.

No. Not her style.

"And maybe," she said softly, "there's been too much between us."

She thought about saying goodbye, but she'd already said it twice. Sometimes the best way to end things was simply to end them.

She hit the end button.

The screen went blank.

CHAPTER NINETEEN

FOUR WEEKS AND as many days later, Cammie drove home after wrapping up another study-monitor gig at Dignity House. The school year was coming to an end for most of the girls, so she'd been leaning on them to study harder for their final exams. Rather than fight it, the girls were hitting the books. Even Takira, who'd replaced her Dinki Mini enthusiasm with the goal to become a teacher.

Cammie's phone chirped. She put it on speaker and answered.

"Hi, Cammie. Eddie Huttner."

Eddie was her attorney, Uncle Frankie's pal, who was representing the arson-police-assault case against her. Although he handled her GPS case at no charge as a favor to Frankie, this time he was charging by the hour because this new case was more complex. As a courtesy, he'd reduced his fees by a third, which left her paying two-twenty an hour. She figured she'd have him paid off before the world ended in 2016.

"Hi, Eddie."

"I have bad news and good news. Let's get the bad out of the way first."

"Let's."

"I tried to talk the D.A. into reducing the felony arson charge to a misdemeanor burning garbage in public."

"But I had nothing to do with fire, Eddie. I didn't even have a match on me."

"That's not the point. A complicitor aids another to commit

a crime and you, Cammie, were an accomplice by interfering with the officer's ability to stop the real arson on the tractor."

"That's ridiculous."

"Yes, well, welcome to my side of law and order. Anyway, I told the D.A. that you're willing to not dispute the other three misdemeanors. As you and I have discussed, if the felony charge is reduced to a misdo, it doesn't matter if you get convicted on one or all four misdemeanors, you can still be relicensed as a P.I. But the good state of Nevada will not issue a license to a P.I. if that person has even one felony conviction, so it hurts us to walk into that hearing with that felony charge hanging over your head."

"But the D.A. refused to reduce it to a misdo."

"That's right."

"So what's the good news? Your cell-phone plan provides free calls this time of day?"

"Grumpy, are we?"

"And tired and hungry. But I apologize. You're trying to help me."

"Which brings us to the good news. This should cheer you up. I think we can get creative here and fashion a win-win situation."

"I'm listening."

"I'm going to call the D.A. again and propose the following—three misdemeanor guilty pleas and a *deferred* prosecution to the felony. The latter entails a hundred hours community service and you keep your nose clean for six months. After that, the felony charge is dismissed."

"Meaning it disappears?"

"As in poof, like magic."

Her grumpy mood went poof, too. "Which means that in six months, I can be relicensed?"

"It gets better. The hearing's in two weeks. If the D.A. accepts this deal, you would be immediately eligible to be relicensed."

"Eddie, you're the bomb."

"We just got rid of the arson, no more exploding devices, please."

They ended the call, and she drove on, feeling happier than she had in days, weeks. Didn't solve all her problems, but Eddie's idea offered hope.

She parked Phil and headed inside her uncle's house. Rich scents of fried meatballs and garlic hit her as soon as she opened the door. Maybe the Italians had written great love songs, even sung a lot of them, but their real romance took place in the kitchen.

She tossed her purse on the couch, toed off her Keds and headed into the kitchen. A handwritten note lay on the dining room table.

I'm at Del's tonight. Food's for you, so eat!

XO.

P.S. There's spumoni in the fridge.

She grabbed a plate and filled it with several meatballs, a wedge of fresh bread and marinated tomatoes. Grabbing a fork, she ambled out to the patio to watch the sunset and eat dinner.

Sitting in the lounge chair was like falling into a soft cloud—she was that tired. Occasional passing breezes brought scents of jasmine and roses. Over the brick wall, she looked toward the northwest sky, wondering what strange events people were imagining tonight along the Extraterrestrial Highway. Her uncle had once told her it was a long, boring stretch of road in the middle of nowhere. Part of her wished her life had been like that road these past few months—boring, no distractions, the end in sight. Even if the end was the same thread of asphalt on the horizon, at least you knew what to expect.

Her cell phone rang.

She set down her plate and tugged the device loose from her pocket. The caller ID displayed a phone number she didn't recognize, although the area code was familiar. Somewhere in Massachusetts or Rhode Island?

She answered. "Hello?"

"Cammie? It's Emily."

"Everything okay?"

"Yeah."

After a moment of odd silence, Cammie said, "Well, I'm glad to know that."

"Well, there's a little problem," Emily admitted.

"What is it?"

"It's my granddad's parole hearing."

"It's still on, right? June 6, next week as I recall."

"Yeah."

Cammie waited for what felt like a small eternity for Emily to say more. In the sky, the first star twinkled to life.

"My dad," the girl finally said, "is nervous."

"All good lawyers are nervous before a trial or hearing. I've never trusted an attorney who doesn't get a little nervous."

"This one's different, though. It's about saving Granddad."

And finally having the father-son relationship that had slipped past both of them. But Cammie would never say that to Emily, although the girl may have already figured it out.

"Your granddad has done the time, made his restitution, shown humility for his acts. No court would withhold his freedom at this point."

In the following silence, several billy owls started their ghostly warbling, their rising trills like probing questions.

"The D.A. is Berto Martinez," Emily said quietly.

Back when she'd worked at Hamilton & Hamilton, Cammie had investigated a dozen or more cases in which Marc went up against Berto in the courtroom. Although many prosecutors had their eye on an eventual private practice where they could make the bucks, Berto had his eye on a political career, which made him a dangerous animal. He liked to sniff out corruption and crime and make examples of people, the kind of examples that splashed in sensationalist headlines and hot breaking-news stories. In the office, she and Marc referred to him as "Berto the Bastard" for his conniving, self-serving ways.

And now Harlan would be the latest opportunity for Berto the Bastard to be a hero. She still followed Colorado news. Harlan's case was well-timed, as Berto's name was being bandied about as the next Denver district attorney, which was only a four-year term away from being a gubernatorial candidate.

"I see," Cammie said quietly.

"Daddy didn't tell me about Berto. My mom did."

Nice. Just want a child needed to hear—confusing, stressful things about a court case that decided whether or not her grandfather would be allowed his freedom.

"I need to ask you a favor. It's a big one, but it really, really means a lot to me."

"What is it, Emily?"

"I'm flying out to be with Daddy at the hearing. At first he didn't want me to come, but I begged him. Especially after my mother told me about Berto Martinez. I think I can help by testifying about my grandfather. Young girl on the stand talking about how her granddad helped her through the loss of her parents' marriage? I figured it'd be a compelling statement about his good character."

"You certainly understand the value of witness testimony. Did you want me to help you prepare?"

"No. I want you to be there."

For a moment, Cammie couldn't catch her breath. It felt as though someone had coiled ropes around her chest and pulled tight.

"I know you and Daddy aren't...together...but you and I are, right?"

"We are," Cammie said, finding her voice.

"I'll feel stronger on the stand if I look out in the audience and see you there."

It didn't matter what had transpired between her and Marc,

this was about being there for Emily, for the girl's chance to bring together part of her family.

"I'll be there."

After ending the call, Cammie finished her dinner. In the distance, somewhere beyond the Extraterrestrial Highway, lightning flashed, accompanied by the faraway grumble of thunder. A muffled, indistinct storm that was a world away from her overhead blue skies and wisps of clouds. She'd heard on the news the storm would never reach Vegas, instead travelling south to Arizona.

She carried her dishes inside, then headed to her bedroom and picked up the white stick she'd placed next to her bed last night. Maybe she hoped the answer had changed or maybe she needed to look at it again and verify that it was real.

The plus sign confirmed she was pregnant.

So much for 100 percent, foolproof protection. But what she hadn't expected was her heart not being foolproof. How many times had she said she didn't want a child, that she'd already done her time as a mother...and yet...

Outside, the billy owl warbled its question, but she didn't have the answer.

THE NEXT MORNING, Cammie drove to Delilah's for "a fitting brunch," as the older woman called it. They were doing a final fitting on the maid of honor's dress, followed by lunch.

Delilah, dressed in an orange-and-peach caftan with the requisite plunging neckline, opened the door and beamed.

"Hello, my darling maid of honor," she cooed, wrapping her arms and a cloud of Chanel No. 5 around Cammie. "June 10 is the big day!"

"Uncle Frankie told me. Congratulations."

"Thank you, darling."

The older woman's face was pink and freshly washed. Her champagne hair was pulled back in a knot at the nape of her neck.

"Sorry if I arrived too early."

"Well, I didn't get a chance to put my face on or do my hair," Delilah said, ushering Cammie inside, "but we're almost family, so it's okay for you to see the wizardess behind the curtain." She laughed, her nose twitching like a bunny's.

A little dog yipped and yapped at their feet.

"Sampson, why don't you go to your bed? I have company."

Making a snuffling sound, the little dog trotted off.

"He understood you," Cammie said, amazed.

"I think he knows the word *bed,* plus it's where he likes to hang most of the day. He's twelve years old—elderly by dogs' standards. He and Trazy get along famously. I'm not sure if he thinks he's a cat or she thinks she's a dog, or they're just raging liberals." She looped her arm through Cammie's and steered her through the living room. "So many things have happened recently that Frankie and I were uncomfortable picking a date until we knew for sure that you could be there."

"Things like the arrest."

"Well, that and other whatsits…"

Delilah was being considerate not stating those other whatsits, but Cammie knew one of them had to be her whirlwind romance with Marc that had sputtered to an inglorious ending.

Cammie expected to see exotic furnishings, complete with red walls, bearskin rugs and zebra wallpaper in Delilah's place, but instead found the opposite. The room was peaceful with its overstuffed beige furniture, laminated wood floors and paintings of seascapes. On a fireplace mantel were several photos of Frankie and Delilah, a young man in military uniform and a picture of a much younger Delilah and some guy, both of them smiling at the camera.

"My former husband, Walter, and I lived for years on the Oregon coast," she explained, seeing Cammie's interest in one of the paintings. "Most of these were painted by regional artists—their scenes were places we'd visited, so they had a special meaning." Delilah stopped and looked around the room. "Frankie never minded that I kept these paintings from my former marriage, but then I never minded the mementos of Regina, either. That's what happens when you get a second chance at love late in life—you understand that each of you brings a history." She clapped her hands, causing her gold bracelets to jingle. "But now that I'm going to be Mrs. Copello, it's time to start over. I've decided to give away many things, including most of these paintings. If you see one you like, let me know."

A few minutes later, they stood in Delilah's crafts room. Workbenches strewn with fabrics, and bookshelves stuffed with boxes, lined the walls. Swatches of cloths lay strewn over a chair. A wall-mounted spice cabinet held jars of glitter.

Trazy lay stretched in a window, asleep, warming in the sun.

"This is her room, and she loves that window."

"She looks fat and happy."

"Like her great-auntie Delilah."

"Now, Del, you're gorgeous and you know it." Cammie looked at a computer attached to a device she didn't recognize. "What's that?"

"A sewing machine."

"Duh."

"It's all right, dear, I wouldn't know a GPS device if you planted it on my rump." She gestured to the computer. "It reads a CD-ROM of patterns and translates them into thread."

Cammie blinked in surprise. "Cool."

"I might dress like the seventies, but I'm definitely a state-of-the-art kinda gal."

"You'd probably rule the world if you had a smartphone."

"I've been thinking of getting one of those. Now, let's look at your to-die-for dress." Delilah opened a closet. "Mr. Bergstrom is a bit proprietary with his gowns, but he gave me the go-ahead to make any last-minute adjustments." She pulled out the red dress that Cammie had tried on at the bridal salon what seemed a lifetime ago. "Isn't this just divine!"

With some help, Cammie slinked into the dress. At the salon, it had been spray-on tight. Today, it felt even tighter around her middle, to the point that breathing was a sketchy activity. She looked at herself in the full-length mirror, turning this way and that. The wedding was nine days away—her tummy wouldn't grow that much between now and then, right?

As Delilah fussed with a shoulder strap, Cammie looked at herself in the mirror, wondered if others saw the uncertainty in her green eyes. These past few days, her emotions had bounced from worry to fear to bursts of hey-maybe-I-can-do-this giddiness—bursts of feelings that had to be by-products of her thrashing hormones. But when the feelings subsided, her rational self accepted that motherhood wasn't in the cards. After she attended the parole hearing next week, then the wedding a few days after, she'd talk to her doctor about options for terminating the pregnancy.

"What is it, dear?"

Cammie shifted her gaze to Delilah's, who stared at her in the mirror.

"Nothing."

Delilah waited a beat. "I believe that about as much as the moon is made of Roquefort."

"Just having...thoughts."

Delilah nodded. "Care to share any of them?"

"No."

As Delilah continued arranging the strap, she asked casually, "Are you interested in living with us?"

"At Frankie's home?"

"Yes. You could keep your room. You have your own bathroom. We love having you around."

Actually, with other worries crowding her mind, she hadn't thought about where she'd be living. "What about Trazy?"

"We've discussed that. We could put a door in the hallway so that Trazy could romp between your bedroom, the bathroom and that little room that Frankie uses for odds 'n' ends. With that area closed off, his allergies would never know the cat's there."

"I'll, uh, think about it."

Delilah checked a seam along the side of the dress. "Or you could live here, rent free, until you get on your feet."

"That's awfully generous."

"We're family. I want to help you out, dear, while you figure out what you're doing next."

"If Eddie's idea pans out, I might be a P.I. again very soon."

"Eddie's a wonderful lawyer, isn't he?" Delilah commented, checking the stitching around the waist. "I suppose wherever you live," she said quietly, "depends on your career and the baby."

Cammie froze. "How—how'd you guess?"

Delilah met her gaze again in the mirror again. "I've done a lot of living, Cammie, and, well, some things started adding up."

"They're that obvious?" She winced. "Does Uncle Frankie know?"

"No, and I seriously doubt anyone else has noticed. I see you all the time, plus I recognize the symptoms. You're more tired than usual, last week you complained of nausea, and this dress fits you a little differently than it did when we were at the bridal salon."

Cammie welled up. "And I'm more emotional." She swiped at the corner of her eye.

"Maybe that's a good thing. Now let's take this dress off, eat some of the best homemade chicken soup you've ever tasted and talk about you."

Dressed in her jeans and T-shirt again, Cammie sat at Delilah's kitchen counter. A pot of soup bubbled on the stove. Delilah set a glass of cranberry juice and apple slices in front of Cammie.

"Back in Denver, I never ate this healthily." Cammie took a sip of the juice.

"Imagine if Emily lived here." Delilah ladled some soup into a bowl. "We'd all be vegetarians."

"Or vegans."

"I never understood what they eat or why."

"Don't ask me. I didn't know that object in the other room was a sewing machine."

Delilah laughed. "Darling Emily. She'll probably live to a riper old age than any of us will." She set a steaming bowl of soup in front of Cammie.

"Smells wonderful."

"Nothing like chicken soup to fix what ails you." Delilah brought over her bowl and sat opposite Cammie at the counter.

After a few minutes of eating, Delilah said, "What do you want to do?"

Cammie sighed. "I'm not ready to be a mother."

"Many women have thought that, at first."

"But most women didn't grow up being a parent to their own."

"That wasn't easy for you, Cammie, certainly. On the other hand, maybe it makes you a wiser, more compassionate parent because you've learned the value of children being children."

"So you think I should have the baby."

Delilah paused. "I'm not judging, or thinking, what you should do one way or the other. I'm here to be your sounding board so you don't feel like you're handling this all by yourself. I've been there, alone with grief and worries, and it's so much better to have someone to talk things over with." She took a sip of her juice, set down the glass. "Have you told Val?"

"No."

"You're heading out to Denver next week—planning on telling Marc?"

"No!" Cammie felt herself sag. "Didn't mean to be so emphatic, it's just that he's been through a lot lately. That woman he was engaged to, the whack-case I served the papers to, had told someone she was pregnant and Marc got his hopes up that…"

Delilah nodded thoughtfully, stirring her spoon in her soup. "He's a family man."

"Without a family. There's Emily, but he only sees her once or twice a year. Hopefully, his father will be paroled, but that's still a big if."

"Your uncle's a family man, too. He and Regina so wanted to have a child. I think you fill that slot for him."

Cammie smiled. "Did you and your husband have kids?"

"One. After we had Peter, we wanted more but it didn't turn out that way." An emotion flickered across Delilah's face. "I lost Peter in 1991 in the Gulf War. Twenty-two years old, an army sergeant. I'm a child of the sixties, so imagine my surprise that my son wanted to make the military his career! But it was his dream and, despite our trepidations, his father and I supported him. Peter…died shielding another soldier's body with his own during a raid."

"I'm so sorry, Delilah." Cammie reached across the table and held her hand.

"Me, too, dear. Before that, I thought I knew what grief was like. But I had no idea that losing a child would be an all-consuming impairment of my body, mind, spirit. Walter, my husband, wasn't one to talk about his feelings—what men are?—so I felt very alone with my craziness for months. Eventually, I learned to let go of the bitterness—it was difficult enough to handle the grief—but I still thought I'd never be the same again. Then one day I woke up and realized that I wanted to honor Peter with how I lived life, not how I was letting it beat me down. Now I wear clothes I enjoy, hang out with people I like, love wearing gold jewelry—" she shook her free wrist so the gold bracelets jingled softly "—and I don't judge people. Here's my one rule about life—there are no rules, except those of the heart."

Cammie blinked. "You're amazing."

"I prefer to think of myself as well marinated. I've absorbed life's lessons and I'm the better for it."

They resumed eating their lunch.

"I'm afraid to be a single mother," Cammie finally said, breaking the silence.

Delilah looked up and smiled. "You'd have Frankie and me."

"If Marc were to know, he'd insist on marrying me. I don't want to rush into that kind of bond because of an unplanned baby."

"He might want to live together instead."

Cammie picked up a slice of apple and bit into it, the fruit sweet and tangy as she chewed thoughtfully.

"He'd want to live in Denver," she said.

"Probably."

"But Val and I have talked about our agency being located in Las Vegas."

Delilah's brow compressed as she mulled that over. "Maybe you and Marc could have a bicoastal relationship without the coasts."

"I've always wondered if such long-distance relationships really work."

"I suppose if the two people are extraordinarily independent, they could."

Cammie ran her finger along the pattern in the granite countertop. "I've made an appointment with my doctor to discuss… other things." She looked at Delilah. "Would you go with me?"

"Absolutely, darling."

Cammie looked past the woman into the kitchen. Above the stove, a single light burned, its glow fading to nothing by the time it reached the cabinets, the floor.

"I'm scared. I don't want to do the wrong thing."

"Listen to your heart, dear. It's telling you the answer."

CHAPTER TWENTY

MARC SET DOWN HIS BRIEFCASE on the large oak table and sat next to his father. In contrast to Marc's upscale navy blue double-breasted jacket and pants, Harlan wore a prison-issued orange jumpsuit. They'd both waited for this day, June 6, to appear in the Denver District Courtroom. What happened over the next hour or so meant Marc's father would again enjoy freedom or remain incarcerated.

It meant they'd have a chance to be a family or not.

"Want a glass of water, Dad?"

His father nodded, the overhead lights gleaming off his shiny dome. "I tried a lot of cases here in my day," he murmured, surveying the ornately carved wood around the jury box, the marble floors, the brass light fixtures. "Did you know Raymond Burr filmed that old TV show *Ironside* here?"

"Yes, we used to talk about that, remember?" Marc picked up the plastic pitcher and poured water into a foam cup.

"I used to raise hell if my paralegal didn't bring my crystal glass to court, remember that?" Harlan said, lifting his shackled hands to accept the cup.

"I still have that glass." Marc noticed his father's hands were shaking as he drank. "It's in a bookcase at home."

His father finished drinking, struggled to set the cup on the table. "What good does it do there?"

"Saving it for the Smithsonian."

His father half choked a laugh. "I'm not that pompous guy anymore."

"Pompous, no. Brilliant lawyer in your day, yes."

COLLEEN COLLINS   277

"What about that former bookkeeper of yours—she still in jail?"

"Got arrested at the deposition, judge set bail at a half mil."

Harlan flexed his eyebrows. "Hefty."

"Judge viewed her as a flight risk. She'll probably be sitting in that cell for several more months until her trial." He glanced over at the prosecutor's table. "I'll be right back, Dad."

Marc crossed to the table opposite his, where Deputy D.A. Berto Martinez sat, scrolling through his smartphone. In the past few years, Marc noticed that Berto had grown fond of his sun lamp, which gave him a tan just a shade shy of orange. But on the Channel 7 news, where Berto liked to pontificate about the current state of justice, he looked perennially robust and healthy.

Some of those Channel 7 reporters were here today, sitting with other media types and tagalongs in the corners behind both attorney tables.

Marc halted before Berto. Standing over him, he had a bird's-eye view of a comb-over job that reminded him of strings on a guitar. He wondered if anyone had ever told Berto that a dab of cologne went a long way.

"Good morning, Counsel."

Berto looked up, feigned surprise. "Hello, Counselor. I see it's father-son day in Denver District Court." He glanced at his vintage wristwatch, a black-dial Ulysse Nardin that had probably set him back a grand. "I have a fund-raiser at eleven, so can we wrap this up by ten-thirty?"

"Never knew a judge to rule by a stopwatch, Berto. And, yes, it's father-son day because this is about my father, Harlan Hamilton, a rehabilitated man, a family man, a man who desperately needs medical care that he can't get in prison."

Berto snorted a laugh. "Save your pitch for the judge and keep it short."

"Funny, I remembered when you cared more about justice than your fifteen seconds of fame on late-night news."

Marc headed to his side and sat.

Harlan leaned over. "What was that about?" he asked under his breath.

"Just courthouse pleasantries, Dad."

Harlan turned to the deputy sheriff sitting behind him. "Can I talk to my granddaughter? She flew from back East to be here today."

"You'll have to keep it short, Mr. Hamilton, but feel free."

Harlan turned in his seat and admired Emily, who sat in the front row of the gallery. She was layered in blue—cobalt dress, denim jacket—which set off her eyes. Her shiny blond hair fell loosely around her face.

He puckered a kiss to her. "You're more beautiful in real life than in pictures, sweetheart."

She blew him back a kiss. "I love you, Granddad."

A man and a woman in casual business attire walked out of the judge's chambers and sat in chairs on either side of a large leather chair. A few moments later, the bailiff stood.

"All rise. The honorable Judge Jack Benning presiding."

A fortyish man with a defiant step crossed to the leather chair in a swirl of black robes. After sitting, he adjusted his wire-rim glasses and said into the microphone, "You may be seated."

He opened a file, quickly perused it, then said, "The petitioner's, Harlan Hamilton's, request for parole will now be heard. Seated with me are Richard Castro and Sharon Brown, who are parole-board members. They will also participate in considering Mr. Hamilton's petition today." He scanned the courtroom over the top of his glasses. "All parties keep in mind that today's proceedings are digitally recorded, so do not leave the microphone at the table or at the witness stand. Petitioner's counsel has the burden of proving to the court and the board that this petition should be granted. I will hear your opening statement first, the younger Mr. Hamilton. You may proceed."

Marc stood, his case binder in hand, and glanced at Emily,

who smiled and made a show of looking over her shoulder. He followed her line of vision and saw Cammie several rows back, dressed in a tailored charcoal pants suit with a soft green blouse. Her raven hair was pulled back in a sleek ponytail. Cammie had always called it her *L.A. Law* look and wore it whenever she went to court, whether as a spectator or witness.

He was surprised, yet relieved to see her. As his investigator, she'd always had his back. Maybe she came here on her own or maybe a young eco-activist implored her. Whatever the reason, he was glad.

He nodded in acknowledgement to Cammie and continued to the podium.

After opening his binder, he leaned toward the microphone. "If it pleases the court…"

The judge nodded.

He glanced at Berto Martinez. "…and counsel…"

Berto glanced at his watch then to Marc.

"…I will provide my opening statement."

He paused and looked directly at the judge. In the silence could be heard the shuffle of feet and a murmured conversation.

"Your Honor, this is a case about a man who has cultivated his inner goodness through hard experience. In the distant past, he was calloused and arrogant and dishonest. So much so, that he deprived—yes, stole—thousands of dollars from his own clients. But today he is a changed man. Similar to Paul on the road to Damascus, Harlan Hamilton has undergone a moral transformation in his journey from selfish to sharing. The evidence, your Honor, will establish beyond any doubt that Harlan Hamilton has been rehabilitated, shows remorse and has made full restitution to his victims. He also has community support, a place to live and a plan for counseling upon release." He turned to his father. "I call Mr. Harlan Hamilton to the stand."

With the deputy's help, Harlan stood and shuffled to the

stand, his leg shackles clattering on the floor. The deputy put his arm around the elderly man as he painstakingly navigated the single step to the witness box.

"Mr. Hamilton," said the judge, "do you, under the penalty of perjury, swear to tell the whole truth?"

"Yes, I do."

"For the record," Marc said from the podium, "please state your name."

"Harlan Charles Hamilton."

"Where do you currently reside?"

"Arrowhead Correctional Center in Canon City, Colorado."

"What is the length of your sentence?"

"Ten to twelve years."

"How far are you into that sentence?"

"Five years, eight months."

"What were you convicted of?"

"I pleaded guilty to five counts of felony theft in excess of ten thousand dollars per count."

"This was a plea bargain down from ten counts, and the total amount of how much?"

"One hundred thirty-six thousand."

"That's a very serious crime. How devastating was that to your victims?"

"I've thought about this every day for—" Harlan's voice broke "—five years and eight months. My actions were unconscionable, and caused tremendous devastation to innocent people."

"What have you done to make your victims whole?"

"Complete repayment to the victims was made within four years of my sentencing. I've also written letters of apology to each."

"Why did you steal?"

"I needed the money to cover financial losses in my investment and retirement accounts." Even from where Marc stood, he could see his father's chin quivering. "Horribly, horribly selfish of me."

Seeing his father's weakened health, shackled arms and legs, and emotional desolation was ripping him apart. Marc looked at his file notes as though reading them, buying a few moments to calm himself.

"Where did you get the money to repay the victims?" he finally asked.

"You loaned it to me. Thank you, son." Harlan looked at the judge. "Your Honor, I have only one son and he's also my lawyer today."

"I know, Mr. Hamilton. It's obvious your son faithfully stands by you."

Marc scratched the side of his face. "Mr. Hamilton, do you have family in the area who you plan to have around you, should you be released?"

"Yes. I have you. Some friends. I have my dearest granddaughter, who visits Denver. I have a long-standing friendship with a young woman seated in the gallery."

"For the record, what is her name and how do you know her?"

"Cammie Copello is a confidante who I came to know while I was in prison. We share aspects of our lives in common, and her compassion and strength of character are not found many places these days."

Marc flipped a page in the binder and briefly read something. "How is your health?"

"I have issues relating to kidney failure and high blood pressure. At Arrowhead—the prison I'm in—the state can't afford to treat me."

"Do you have the ability to pay for these treatments should you be released?"

"I'm by no means a wealthy man anymore, but my son has told me that I don't have to worry about my medical care. He'll take care of me."

"Do you have arrangements for ongoing psychological counseling upon your possible release?"

"Yes. The pastor of my church has put me in touch with a local social worker, Darcy King."

"What assurances can you give this board that you will not steal again?"

"I'm ashamed of my past actions, and am no longer that person. When I die, I want to be known as a person who once failed, but learned his lessons and died a trustworthy man."

Marc nodded to Berto. "I pass the witness to you."

Berto stepped briskly to the stand. "Mr. Hamilton," he said into the microphone, "the people gave you money, right?"

"Yes."

"And you promised to provide them legal work for value, but what you really did was lie to them, manipulate them and steal from them. Is that correct?"

"Yes."

"As a result of your theft you were disbarred."

"Yes."

"Up to your disbarment, your only career had been as a lawyer. Therefore, you have *no* career and *no* means of making money if you are released into society today. Seems to me, Harlan, you're destined to be a thief and to steal from innocent people again."

"My son will support me—"

"Oh!" Berto said with a dramatic double take at Marc. "The son who was recently under suspicion of theft himself from his own clients? Like father, like son?"

"He was exonerated—"

"Yes," Berto snapped, cutting him off, "nice of your son to help and give you all that money that he's come legitimately by—"

"Objection!" Marc surged to his feet. "This is irrelevant and pertains to a case that has been favorably resolved in my favor by the Attorney Disciplinary Agency."

"Sustained," said the judge. "Any further questions, Mr. Martinez?"

"Yes, Your Honor. Mr. Hamilton, you lied six years ago.... How do we know you're not lying today?"

Harlan straightened, held his head high. "Six years ago, I was a pride-filled, selfish man who only saw things my way. Today I am broken and humble, but I know that life is lived with compromise and sharing, and that it's better to speak the truth than to shape it to get what you want."

Berto looked up from checking his watch. "Versus what you did—bend the truth to get what you want. I pass the witness." He returned to his seat.

The judge spoke into the microphone. "Your next witness, Mr. Hamilton."

Marc returned to the podium. "I call Mr. Hamilton's granddaughter, Emily Hamilton."

With a last glance at Cammie, who smiled her encouragement, Emily crossed to the stand and took the oath.

"For the record, can you please repeat your name, and how you're related to Harlan Hamilton?"

"My name is Emily Corinne Hamilton. I'm Harlan Hamilton's granddaughter." She smiled at her granddad.

"Can you please describe how your grandfather's changed since getting into trouble and going to prison?"

"He's more considerate, selfless, and when he talks to me, he really listens. Change is hard, you know. As Tolstoy said, 'Everyone thinks of changing the world, but no one thinks of changing himself.'"

"Thank you, Emily, but Tolstoy isn't testifying today, so let's limit your testimony to your own observations and thoughts, all right? Please give an example of how he really listens."

"When you and Mom—I mean, when my parents— divorced, he was the only one in my family who wasn't in the battle. I could call him at any time of the day or night, and he'd listen to me. Sometimes I'd call him in the wee hours and he never got mad. I had a lot of trouble sleeping then."

An old, familiar ache rocked Marc's insides as he remembered yet again what his daughter had gone through because of his own mistakes.

"Thank you, Emily," he said quietly before sitting down.

"Your witness," the judge said to Berto.

Berto snatched his smartphone and crossed to the podium. "Good people who really take care of other people don't get sent to prison, right?"

"Nelson Mandela went to prison," answered Emily.

"Speaking of political activists…" He tapped buttons on his smartphone. "Your blog posts on the internet show you to be quite the little radical. Let me see here…this is a quote from April. 'We must remember that the more days we spend in jail, the more change we can effect.' Did you write that?"

"Yes, but—"

"Here's another one," he interrupted. "'The property rights of the ruling class are meaningless and must be sacrificed to the will of the people.' You write that, too?"

"This isn't fair."

He drilled her with a hard, level look. "Please answer the question yes or no, Miss Hamilton."

"Yes."

"Your grandfather took the property of others to accommodate his whims. Like father, like son, like granddaughter." He shifted his attention to the judge. "The witness can step down now."

Reading Emily's startled look, Marc indicated with a quiet nod that she needed to comply with the D.A.'s request and exit the witness box.

While walking past his seat, Emily flashed him a this-is-so-wrong look. He agreed, but kept his face immobile, stoic, because his next task was the toughest yet.

"Your next witness, Mr. Hamilton?" the judge asked.

"By agreement of the parties," he said, "I'm moving to admit petitioner's exhibit A, the statement from Dr. Christenson, prison physician at the Arrowhead Correctional Center at Canon City, Colorado." He eased in a calming breath before reading from the statement. "'Harlan Hamilton is a seventy-four-year-old Caucasian male who appeared at this facility numerous times over the past four years with symptoms consistent with advanced renal failure. The prison hospital, at some great expense, has conducted tests that confirm Mr. Hamilton is in the—'" Marc felt as though his throat was filled with marbles, but forced himself to continue "'—end states of renal failure. Without further treatment, which unfortunately is not available to inmates at this facility, his life expectancy is eight to twelve months.'"

"That's unfair!" cried Emily from her seat in the gallery. "Nobody told me!"

Marc glanced behind him. Emily had taken a seat next to Cammie, who had her arms around the girl and was quietly talking to her.

"One more outburst, Miss Hamilton," the judge said gently, "and the bailiff will escort you to the hallway." He looked at Marc. "Any further witnesses?"

Marc glanced again at Cammie and Emily, both of whom looked stricken. It wasn't fair that they'd learned of his father's prognosis in such a public setting, but he hadn't received the physician's statement until minutes before the hearing.

As his gaze locked with Cammie's, it was as though the brightness in the room dimmed, the way the world fell into shade when clouds blocked the sun. Around them, shapes blurred, lost their contrast. Only the two of them were clear and defined—call it sixth sense, but he knew she knew what he was about to ask.

Her expression told him her answer. No.

Holding her gaze, he subtly made the gesture—*trust*—that she'd shown him that night that seemed so long ago, yet had only been a few months. The gesture the little girl had made to her deaf mother.

Trust me, Cammie. I need you, my family needs you.

CAMMIE RECOGNIZED the hand sign. Trust.

She knew Marc wanted her on the stand to testify about Harlan's character. Her first instinct had been not to do it. She hadn't prepared her testimony, wasn't ready to be cross-examined by Berto the Bastard. Call her weak, but she also didn't know if she could set aside her own unresolved issues to help anyone else, even a deserving man like Harlan.

But Marc was asking her to trust him. To take the risk, to believe that, under his guidance, she wouldn't fail Harlan...or Emily...or even Marc.

Her heart pumping spastically, she stood, crossed to the witness box and took a seat. After taking the oath and stating her name for the record, she mentally psyched herself for Marc's questions.

"Miss Copello, how many years have you worked as a private investigator?"

"Ten."

"You've also written articles on the profession for *Professional Investigator Magazine* and have taught courses on private investigations at state private-investigator conferences, correct?"

"Yes."

"Do you recognize the man seated to my left?"

"Yes."

"Who is he?"

"Harlan Hamilton."

"Have you had the opportunity to work on Mr. Hamilton's behalf through my office over the past few years?"

"Yes."

"Precisely, what did you do?"

"I met with him personally at the Arrowhead Correctional

Center. I interviewed him to help develop his request for release, which included identifying victims so that I could transport restitution to them."

"And by restitution, you mean checks to make victims whole from his theft."

"Yes. To pay back money he stole from them when they had been his legal clients."

"In your meetings with Harlan Hamilton, did you have conversations about his remorse over his crimes?"

"Yes."

"Can you tell us about those conversations?"

"Harlan often said he regretted his thefts. He said he thought about the pain and inconvenience he'd caused innocent people every single day. Once he cried. In fact, he was ashamed and humbled by what he had done not only to his victims, but to others close to him."

After a beat, Marc asked, "To whom are you referring?"

"In the many hours I spent talking with him, it became very clear to me that he wanted to live the rest of his life working on behalf of others, not on behalf of himself. Harlan also yearned to be a father, and to have a relationship with his granddaughter. He was quite aware of the fact that time was slipping through his fingers, and he didn't want to wait any more."

"Do you think," Marc asked with a slight hitch in his voice, "that he can be a valuable member of society again?"

"Absolutely. He can bring his background to the local legal aid society—"

"Objection, Your Honor!" Berto stood and held up his smartphone like it was some kind of sword of justice. "I've just looked up Miss Copello's history on the internet, and she has *three* misdemeanors pending in Nevada, one for assaulting a peace officer, as well as a pending *felony* for complicity in an act of arson. She's simply not a credible witness and no weight should be given to her testimony."

"Your Honor," Marc quickly countered, "may I respond?"
The judge, his brow wrinkled, nodded brusquely.

"Mr. Berto Martinez, as a deputy district attorney, represents the people of Colorado. Not the perfect people, but *all* people. In fact, in this very courtroom are some of those people, such as the court clerk who had her driver's license suspended a year ago, representatives of the sheriff's office who have been struggling with gender bias for years. Even my esteemed colleague, Mr. Martinez, was once disciplined for misrepresentations to a witness. Each one of these officers of the court have had second chances to correct their lives. Likewise, Cammie has failed, but she is working to correct her life. This also pertains to my client, my father Harlan Hamilton, in that—"

"Objection, Your Honor," Berto interrupted. "This is about Miss Copello's lack of credibility, reliability and trustworthiness—not about whether or not the petitioner, Mr. Harlan Hamilton, is eligible for parole."

Judge Benning adjusted his glasses. "Mr. Martinez, your objection is overruled. First, I will hear Miss Copello's testimony because her criminal history does not affect her truth-telling ability. Second, this *does* apply to Mr. Harlan Hamilton's eligibility because this board is interested in why it should give him a second chance. Please continue, Mr. Hamilton."

Marc bent his head, feeling the burden, the heavy weight, of what he should say next. Like in a relay, his words were the last to perform in this race. He needed to pull Emily's and Cammie's testimonies over the line to win his father's freedom.

Looking up, he said calmly, clearly, "He should be given a second chance because life isn't about failure. If it was, everything would be black-and-white. But there's a middle ground, a gray area, which is where second chances live, those corrective measures people take to change not only themselves, but others—family, friends, associates, even strangers—for the better. Second chances are fueled by good deeds and amends, both of which Miss Copello has attested to. Everyone deserves a second chance. Maybe especially…my father."

The judge turned his attention to the prosecution. "Mr. Martinez, would you like to cross-examine the witness?"

"I believe I have sufficiently refuted her testimony," he said, obviously agitated, "and I have nothing further."

Judge Benning addressed the courtroom. "The board members and I will now confer and announce our decision in a few minutes."

Marc sat next to his father and placed his hand on his arm.

Harlan turned red-rimmed eyes to Marc. "Whatever happens, son, I love you."

Marc squeezed his arm. "I love you, too."

"That Emily…she's a spitfire."

Marc had to smile. "She'll be a dynamite lawyer one day."

"You think?"

"I *know*. But don't tell her I said so."

Harlan gave a slow smile. "I'd like to be there when she walks down the aisle."

"You'll be there."

"I'm not so sure."

"I'm going to take good care of you. You're going to beat that prognosis."

"I also want to be at your wedding." He leaned closer and whispered, "That girl loves you, you know."

Marc didn't know how to respond, so he didn't.

"Tell her you love her," Harlan continued. "I've made a lot of mistakes in my life.… If I'd been smarter, wiser, I wouldn't have treated love like it was grass greener on the other side. Don't let that one get away, son. Chase her, track her down, crawl on all fours if you have to, but let her know how you feel. Nothing else matters in this crazy world."

There was a scuffling of feet and murmurings as the judge and officers reentered the courtroom. They resumed their seats at the bench. Judge Benning leaned forward to the microphone.

"The board members and I have heard sufficient evidence to persuade us that Harlan Hamilton should be released immediately—as of this moment, in fact—from the Colorado Department of Corrections."

"All right, Granddaddy!" Emily yelled.

"We are impressed not only with your progress, Mr. Hamilton," the judge continued, "but also with the caring people who encircle you. And now, for the first time in five years, eight months, you may hug your granddaughter."

As whoops and clapping filled the courtroom, Marc wrapped his arms around his father.

"Now you're stuck with your old man," Harlan joked, a tear spilling down his cheek.

Marc brushed it away. "Lucky me."

Reporters descending on the table, thrusting forward digital recorders. Behind them, videographers took footage. With a loud squeal, Emily ran up as the deputy removed the handcuffs.

Harlan wrapped his trembling arms around his granddaughter.

Marc looked around the room for Cammie. She stood in the aisle, beaming at him. *Wait for me,* he mouthed.

"Emily," Marc said, turning back to his daughter, "stay with your granddad. I'll be right back."

"Stay with him?" She laughed through her tears, embracing the old man. "I'm never letting him go!"

Marc looked at Cammie, but she was gone. He slipped past reporters and hurriedly walked down the aisle to the doors. Stepping into the hallway outside the courtroom, he saw her far down the corridor, walking away.

"Cammie!" He jogged after her.

She halted, turned.

He reached her and stopped. "Hey," he said, catching his breath, "why did you leave?"

"This is yours and Emily's time—"

"He's close to you, too, you know."

She looked over his shoulder. "The vultures followed you."

He glanced behind him, saw an eager-looking reporter, her cameraman in tow, making a beeline in their direction.

"Then let me say what needs to be said." He put his arms on Cammie's shoulders. "I'm sorry I was so full of myself, for saying things that—"

"Shh." She put her finger on his lips. "We both said things."

"When I talked about second chances in there, I meant us, too." He searched her eyes. "Do we have one?"

She hugged her stomach and looked up at him, her green eyes glistening with a look he couldn't decipher.

"Cammie?"

"I...don't know," she whispered.

He plowed his hand through his hair, fighting the urge to grab her, demand a better answer. This wasn't the way it was supposed to have played out. Today was a day of answers and celebration, but here they were like two people stuck in a past they couldn't move beyond.

A sick feeling knotted his insides. But maybe it wasn't too late. Maybe if she knew...

"I love you, Cammie," he whispered.

"Mr. Hamilton," said a reporter, sticking a digital recorder between him and Cammie. "Did you think your father, Harlan Hamilton, would be released today?"

A beefy guy with a camera and the distinct odor of beer stumbled, caught himself. "Shit, sorry," he muttered.

"One of the witnesses," the reporter continued, "said your father planned to volunteer with the Denver legal community—is that true?"

The cameraman moved, providing Marc a view of the hallway and Cammie walking away.

CHAPTER TWENTY-ONE

DELILAH, DRESSED IN A cream-colored, cleavage-popping caftan, sat on a settee before an ornate gold-framed mirror. Looking at her reflection, she gently placed a gardenia behind one ear.

"What do you think, dear? Too much?"

Cammie and Delilah were in the bridal dressing chamber at the Las Vegas Elvis Chapel. On the outside of the door were the words *For Elvis's Ladies* scrolled around a picture of The King in a white jumpsuit and cape, bowing on one knee, looking like a Prince Charming who had naughty on his mind. The inside of the room was decorated with posters from Elvis's most popular movie, *Viva Las Vegas,* that showed him and Ann-Margret dancing, kissing, singing and more kissing. Over the speakers, Elvis crooned the heart-wrenching "Wonder of You."

"Considering where we are," Cammie said, "it's a little difficult to say anything's *too much,* but I think the gardenia is perfect. Especially as you decided to not wear a veil today."

Standing behind Delilah, Cammie checked out her reflection in the mirror. She wasn't "showing," but the sexy red dress was so tight around her middle, it was difficult to breathe normally.

Delilah closed her eyes and took a sniff. "The gardenia is so fragrant. When Frankie kisses me after we're pronounced husband and wife, he'll smell its sweetness." Her heavily mascaraed eyes popped open. "Does it clash with my perfume?"

Cammie leaned in closer. "No, the flower's scent is so light, it's a lovely mix of fragrances."

Because of the popularity of June weddings, especially those taking place on weekends, the only time available for Delilah and Frankie's Sunday wedding was at 9:00 a.m. Twenty minutes from now. Delilah didn't care—"Let's make it a wedding-and-brunch!"—and Frankie liked a morning wedding, so they could enjoy a leisurely drive to their honeymoon spot, the historic Hotel del Coronado in San Diego.

Delilah met Cammie's eyes in the mirror. "Can't believe I'm so nervous!"

"It's your big day."

As Delilah held up her hand, several gold bracelets jingled softly. "Look, I'm shaking!"

"No one will notice. Maybe the Elvis minister will sing 'All Shook Up' to get your nerves to settle."

Delilah laughed, her nose doing the bunny-twitching thing. "We asked him to sing 'I Can't Help Falling in Love with You,' for our first dance."

"There's a dance?"

"A one-song dance after we're pronounced husband and wife. It's part of the Burning Love package. We also get a video of the wedding, that lovely rose bouquet…and other things that I forget." She clasped her hands together. "I'm so nervous, I just blanked on my great-aunt's name!"

"Care for a little more comfort in your coffee?"

"You were a dear to bring the Frangelico, but no, thank you. Another dose of comfort and that poor Elvis will have to carry me down the aisle." Delilah admired her platinum manicured nails. "I don't mind Elvis escorting me, but I wish…"

Cammie thought of Peter. "Wouldn't that have been nice."

"He would have looked gallant in his dress blues."

"Walking proudly down the aisle with you on his arm."

"If wishes were horses…" Delilah took a sip of her coffee.

"I have no doubt he's watching from above."

"Or over the webcam," Delilah said lightly, setting down her cup.

"The wedding's being broadcast live?"

"Part of the Burning package."

"Burning Love."

"Right. They give you a web address.... Where is that..." Delilah looked around the dressing table. "Here it is." She handed a piece of paper to Cammie. "It's printed there. Plug that URL into a browser at nine o'clock, and voilà, it's the Delilah and Frankie nuptials."

"I'll send it to Val so she can watch—she's at work today, but she can sneak a peek on her phone."

Cammie retrieved her smartphone and tapped some keys. While putting the phone back into her purse, it rang.

"That Val's fast!" Delilah said with a laugh.

"No, it's not Val," Cammie murmured. "It's Marc. He's trying to connect with me on Skype."

"What's that?"

"A phone-video connection."

"Answer it, darling. He's been calling you nonstop since you left Denver a few days ago, and you never answer."

"But the wedding starts in fifteen minutes."

"Then tell him you have to make it brief and you can talk more later. Put the poor man out of his misery—he's trying so hard to resolve things with you." Delilah opened a compact and dabbed some sparkling powder on her cleavage.

Cammie walked to a corner of the room and pressed a button on her phone. Marc's face appeared on the screen. Same clean-cut look he'd had in court a few days ago, although she caught shadows under his eyes.

For a moment, he stared at her as though paralyzed. "Cammie," he murmured.

Seeing him, hearing his voice—she swore she could feel her pulse thrum in her temples, her wrists, the back of her knees.

"Hi," she whispered.

"I'm glad you answered because I didn't want to surprise you."

"Surprise me?"

There was some jostling of the image, then Uncle Frankie's face appeared.

"Can you see me, Camilla? I can see you."

"What...?"

"You look lovely, my *figlia*. Don't point this thing at my bride-to-be because I don't want to see her before we say our vows."

Cammie looked at the closed door to the bridal dressing chamber, back to Frankie's face. "Where are you?"

"In the other changing room—I think they call it the Elvis Grooming Room or somethin'. This place, what a kick! Del and I wanted a good time filled with laughter and that's exactly what we're getting."

"Marc is *here?*" she rasped.

"Yes, but let me explain..."

Cammie looked at Delilah, who was fussing with her hair, then turned her attention to Frankie, who was explaining that Marc had called yesterday, that the guy had been frustrated because Cammie wouldn't answer his calls, and that in the course of their conversation Frankie "just happened to mention" that he and Del were getting married this morning and if Marc "just happened to be" in Vegas, he could join the festivities.

Cammie lowered the phone. "Did you hear any of that?" she said to Delilah.

Delilah was spritzing hair spray on her frothy hair. "What, dear?"

"Did you know Marc's *here?*"

Delilah set down the hair spray can. "Here—as in this chapel?"

"Yes."

"Oh!" Delilah clapped her hands. "He's chasing you, my darling!"

"So you didn't know?"

"No! But I do know this—if you keep running, at some point that man's going to give up."

"But...I haven't made any decisions yet!"

"And you think this is about using your brain?" Delilah stood, a vision of chiffon, cleavage and champagne hair. She crossed to Cammie and ushered her to the door. "You need to listen to your heart. Now, go talk to that man, and while you're at it, ask if he'll walk me down the aisle."

Reluctantly, Cammie exited the room and looked across the foyer at the door marked Elvis's Grooms and Best Men under a picture of Elvis in a black leather jacket.

The door opened and Marc stepped out.

The breath rushed out of her lungs. From the ever-present speakers, Elvis started singing the song "I Want You, I Need You, I Love You." The schmaltzy, agonizing delivery almost made her laugh, but the lyrics—a lover questioning, then expressing eternal devotion—went straight to her heart.

Their stares locked and held. The distance between them blurred and for a surreal moment, she was again locked in his arms, heard his heated murmurings in her ear, tasted the salty sweat on his skin.

I want you, I need you, I love you.

As though awakening from a dream, the world sharpened, came back into focus. He wore the same navy blue double-breasted jacket as the other day, which set off those startlingly blue eyes. A curl of his chestnut hair hung like a question mark over his brow.

He stared at her with such intensity, for a moment she wasn't sure if he was glad or mad to see her.

"Cammie," he finally said, closing the space between them.

He stopped short, close enough that she could smell that apple cologne and see the shadows under his eyes. He looked troubled, off-center, just like the first time he'd arrived unannounced in Vegas.

"Is everything okay?" she asked.

"Sure," he murmured, his eyes searching hers.

"Harlan?"

"Dad's great, considering. He's seeing a doctor next week."

"Emily?"

"She's staying with us this summer, and maybe next school year, too. Her mother isn't happy with the idea, but you know Emily once she's made up her mind."

Cammie smiled. "Watch out world."

He scratched the stubble on his chin. "Didn't get a chance to shave. Caught a red-eye flight, which got grounded in Arizona due to a storm, then finagled a connecting flight that landed less than an hour ago. I tipped a cabbie to break the speed limit to get me here on time."

"You? Breaking rules?"

He smiled, the look in his eyes softening. "Weren't you listening in court when I talked about the value of that gray middle ground?" He turned somber. "Cammie, I've been thinking about you. Us. I think we should—"

An Elvis lookalike strolled up to them, swiveled his hip and struck a classic Elvis pose—half-lunge with one hand pointing into the air. Despite the midnight-black dye job and costume-rental gold jacket, for a crazy instant, he actually looked like the real deal.

He straightened and flashed a half-cocked Elvis grin. "Hey, you two lovebirds, it's almost time."

He even sounded like Elvis.

"We're not Delilah and Frankie," Cammie explained. "I'm the maid of honor and he'll be walking the bride down the aisle."

"Thought she wanted me," faux Elvis said, flipping the lapels of his jacket.

Wow, this is really going to be a Viva Las Vegas *experience,* Cammie thought. But the silliness was exactly what she needed. Lately everything had felt too heavy, and it was a welcome change to be lighthearted and playful, which was obviously what Delilah and Frankie had in mind when they'd picked this place.

"I'd be honored to walk her down the aisle," Marc said.

"After the ceremony, the newlyweds will have their first dance," Elvis said. "I'll sing. After a few moments, you're welcome to join in. The dance, not the singing." He winked. "Okay, let's get this show on the road because the wedding is starting in—" he lunged into another Elvis pose and pointed at a wall clock "—five minutes."

As he swaggered away, Marc smiled. "Wish Harlan could see this. He's a big Elvis fan."

"Yeah, but was Elvis this schmaltzy?"

"Sure he was. Haven't you ever seen videos of him entertaining? He was like Dean Martin, always cracking up and schmoozing with the audience."

Cammie handed him the piece of paper. "There's the web address—send it to Harlan and Emily and tell them they can watch the wedding. I should go check in with Delilah, tell her it's almost time."

"I'll be here, waiting to walk her down the aisle."

Moments later, Cammie stood in front of Delilah, adjusting the gardenia.

"You're a beautiful bride."

Delilah smiled. "Thank you. How'd your talk with Marc go?"

"He's going to walk you down the aisle."

"The man flies all the way out to Vegas to see you, and the two of you talk about me? Darling, I need to give you some man lessons."

There was a knocking at the door, followed by the Elvis minister singing the refrain from one of the real Elvis's hits, "Until It's Time for You to Go."

Delilah's eyes sparkled. "I love this chapel!"

"Yes, it's almost like being at Graceland," Cammie muttered. She lifted a white-rose bouquet off a table and handed it to the bride. "Here we go."

The older woman sniffed as she hooked her arm through Cammie's. "Today's the most wonderful day of my life."

They stepped into the foyer. Marc stood there, handsome in his blue suit. He extended a hand to Delilah.

"And he's in dress blues," she murmured, taking his hand.

Elvis started warbling "It's Now or Never."

"I believe that's your cue, dear," Delilah said to Cammie.

She began walking down the green-carpeted aisle to a small stage with white Ionic columns. An elderly woman and a young girl—Delilah's relatives—sat on one of the benches in the audience, the two of them sniffling and smiling. Frankie, wearing a tan suit, blue shirt and a champagne-colored tie, stood to one side of the stage, rocking slightly on the balls of his feet, a habit Cammie knew meant he was anxious or happy. Today, probably both.

Elvis, his gold jacket shining under the lights, stood in the center of the stage. It wasn't until she got closer that she realized he was actually singing. The guy was good—could probably work as a celebrity-dealer at the Cave if times got tough in the chapel business.

Elvis pointed to where Cammie should stand.

Marc escorted Delilah down the aisle, and she took her place opposite Frankie. Marc stood behind him.

After the music faded, Elvis the minister took a dramatic pause.

"Ladies and gentlemen," he said, looking at the video camera pointed at the stage, "we are live from Las Vegas with Delilah and Frank, who are sharing the greatest day of their lives as they become husband and wife. Please hold hands, Delilah and Frank."

Delilah handed her bouquet to Cammie, then took Frankie's hands in hers.

"Today we come together as Delilah and Frank make promises of holy matrimony to each other, to promise to love and respect each other as they travel together for the rest of their days."

Cammie's eyes met Marc's, and she imagined loving and respecting him for the rest of their days. They'd already been together for years as friends, and recently as lovers. It wasn't such a stretch to envision their spending more years, all the way to the end of their days, together.

"Frank, please put the ring on Delilah's hand," Elvis said.

Frank fumbled in his jacket and pulled out a ring, which he slid onto her finger.

"Please repeat after me," said Elvis. "I, Frank, give you this ring as a symbol of my love…"

Cammie's vision blurred as she watched Frankie, then Delilah, offer rings to the other.

"Now, Frank, please repeat after me," continued Elvis. "I, Frank, give you my solemn vow to be your faithful partner…"

She looked at Marc.

"…in good times and in bad…"

They'd certainly weathered their share of those.

"…to support your goals…"

He was always there for her career, and she in turn had fought for his.

"…to cherish you for as long as we both shall live."

Marc mouthed *I do*.

Her heart lurched in her chest, followed by a knowledge that was surer than words written on granite. Her heart had spoken, and she'd finally listened.

She quietly made the "trust" hand sign to Marc. A slow smile filled his face.

"You may now kiss the bride," said Elvis.

As Frankie and Delilah kissed, Elvis began singing "I Can't Help Falling in Love."

Delilah and Frankie began their first dance as husband and wife. After a moment, Elvis gestured for Cammie and Marc to join in.

His arms closed around her, crushing her against him. She buried her face in his jacket, breathing in his familiar masculine scents. They moved, swaying in sync to the music, as though they'd danced this dance a dozen, a hundred times.

She lifted her head and looked into his eyes. "I love you."

"I love you more."

"I'll go with that," she teased. "I'm curious, is Harlan staying in the room that was formerly the guest bedroom?"

"Right." He kissed her forehead.

"And Emily, of course, is in her room."

"Correct."

"And we'd share your room."

"It'll be *our* room," he said huskily, brushing his lips against her cheek.

"And Trazy, of course, will have the run of the house."

"Absolutely." After a beat, he asked, "Why are you asking about the rooms?"

"Because…" Her breath caught as he nuzzled her ear. "I have a yen to be an interior decorator."

He paused. "Instead of a private investigator?"

"I only want to decorate one room. Since the other bedrooms are taken, maybe I can do the den."

"Sure."

They danced in silence for a few moments while Elvis crooned how some things are meant to be.

"How do you want to decorate it?" he finally asked.

"I know blue's for boys and pink's for girls, but I say why follow the rules? Let's brave the middle ground and do it up in yellow."

He froze, then pulled back his head and studied her face. "How…"

"Nothing's perfect, what can I say?"

"You're… We're—"

Cammie nodded, her eyes wet with happiness.

He emitted a strangled cry of joy as he hugged her close, and she melted into his embrace, and they danced, two people who couldn't help falling in love.

* * * * *

COMING NEXT MONTH FROM

HARLEQUIN

super romance

Available April 2, 2013

#1842 TALK OF THE TOWN • *In Shady Grove*
by Beth Andrews

Neil Pettit and Maddie Montesano share a history and a daughter. But that's it. Their relationship has been, well, *tense* for years. That wasn't a problem when Neil lived out of state. But now that he's in town, sparks are flying and everyone's talking about where they'll end up!

#1843 RIGHT FROM THE START by Jeanie London

A divorce mediator, Kenzie James has seen it all when it comes to commitment. And she can tell Will Russell is *not* a good bet. So why does she look forward to their encounters at work? Luckily she knows better than to fall for this single dad...or does she?

#1844 THE FIRST MOVE by Jennifer Lohmann

Seeing Renia Milek again is a clear sign to Miles Brislenn. Back in high school he might not have had the courage to approach her, but this chance meeting...? He's not letting it pass him by. The attraction is clearly mutual, until Renia's past threatens to come between them.

#1845 A BETTER FATHER by Kris Fletcher

Sam Catalano needs to prove he's a good father to his young son. And to do that he needs stability, which is why he's bought the summer camp he used to attend. But buying it puts him in conflict with Libby Kovak—his old flame and the rightful owner.

#1846 YOU ARE INVITED... • *A Valley Ridge Wedding*
by Holly Jacobs

The best man? Mattie Keith—maid of honor—thinks Finn Wallace is anything but. She's the legal guardian for his nieces and nephew, but he's suing for custody! They've vowed not to let their conflict spoil their friends' wedding, but when temperatures and attraction rise, promises may be broken....

#1847 THE SUMMER PLACE by Pamela Hearon

When it comes to fun and games, Rick Warren and Summer Delaney are definitely on opposite sides. Summer has a lot at stake in making this camp program work and proving she's right. Too bad the working rivalry is sparking a big attraction!

YOU CAN FIND MORE INFORMATION ON UPCOMING HARLEQUIN® TITLES, FREE EXCERPTS AND MORE AT WWW.HARLEQUIN.COM.

HSRCNM0313

REQUEST YOUR FREE BOOKS!
2 FREE NOVELS PLUS 2 FREE GIFTS!

HARLEQUIN

super romance

Exciting, emotional, unexpected!

HSR13